An Inspector Calls

THE GRAPHIC NOVEL
J. B. Priestley

ORIGINAL TEXT VERSION

Script Adaptation: Jason Cobley
Linework: Will Volley
Coloring: Alejandro Sanchez
Lettering: Jim Campbell
Design & Layout: Jo Wheeler,
Jenny Placentino & Carl Andrews
Associate Editor: Joe Sutliff Sanders
Editor in Chief: Clive Bryant

An Inspector Calls: The Graphic Novel
Original Text Version
J. B. Priestley

First US edition

Published by: Classical Comics Ltd
with the permission of The Estate of J. B. Priestley
for which the publisher extends their sincere thanks.

Play first published by William Heinemann Ltd 1947.

All rights whatsoever in this play are strictly reserved and applications for performances,
etc., should be made in advance by professional companies to United Agents,
12-26 Lexington Street, London WIF OLE and by amateur companies to
Samuel French Ltd, 52 Fitzroy Street, London WIT 5JR.

Acknowledgments: Every effort has been made to trace copyright holders of
material reproduced in this book. Any rights not acknowledged here will be
acknowledged in subsequent editions if notice is given to Classical Comics Ltd.

All enquiries should be addressed to:
Classical Comics Ltd
PO Box 7280
Litchborough
Towcester
NN12 9AR
United Kingdom

info@classicalcomics.com
www.classicalcomics.com

ISBN: 978-1-907127-23-6

Printed in the USA

This book is printed by CG Book Printers using environmentally safe inks, on paper from
responsible sources. This material can be disposed of by recycling, incineration for energy
recovery, composting and biodegradation.

Contents

An Inspector Calls

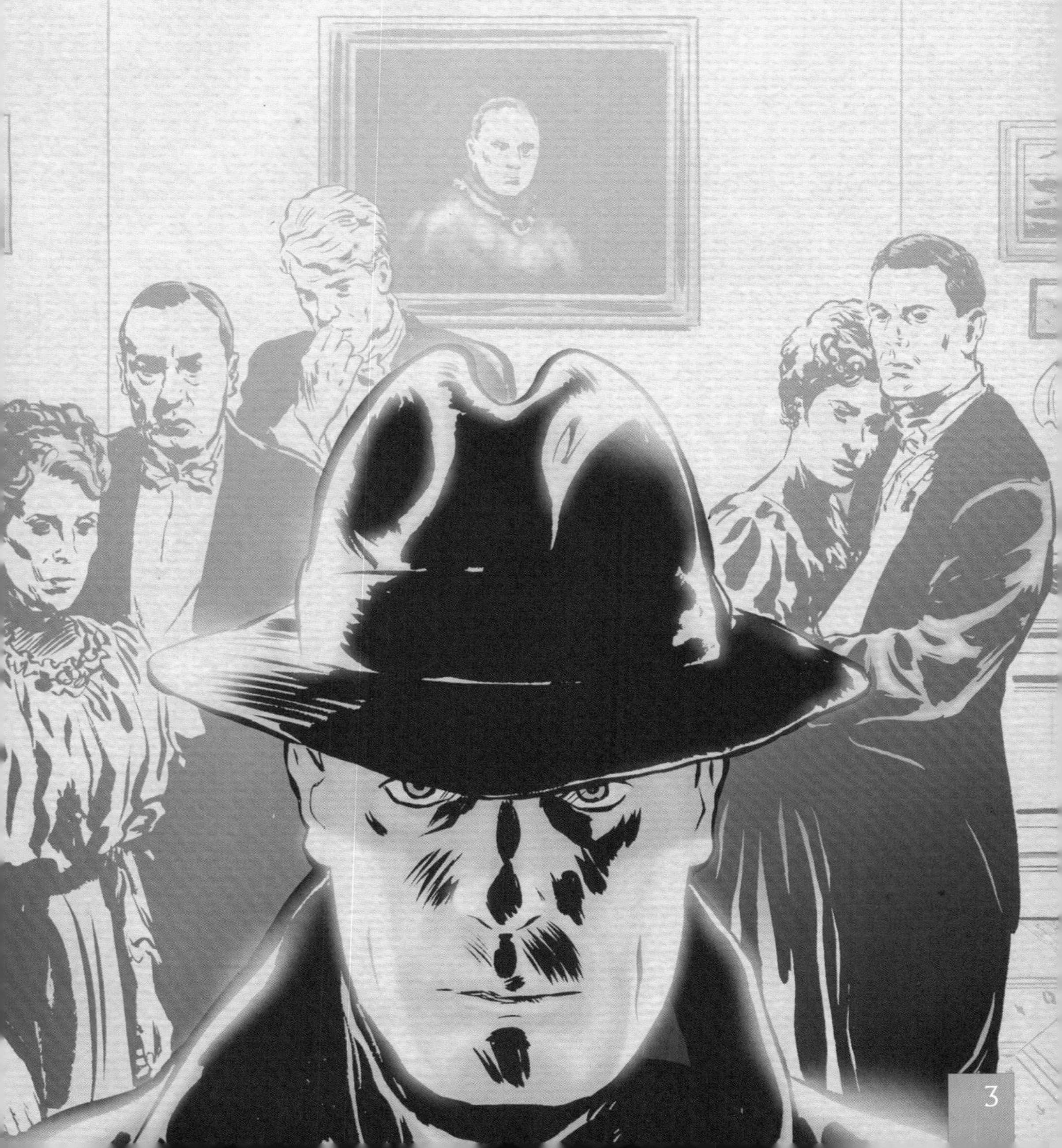

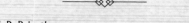

Dramatis Personæ

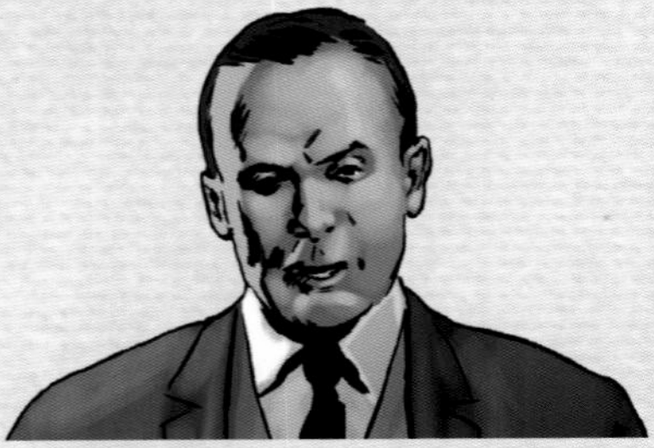

Inspector Goole

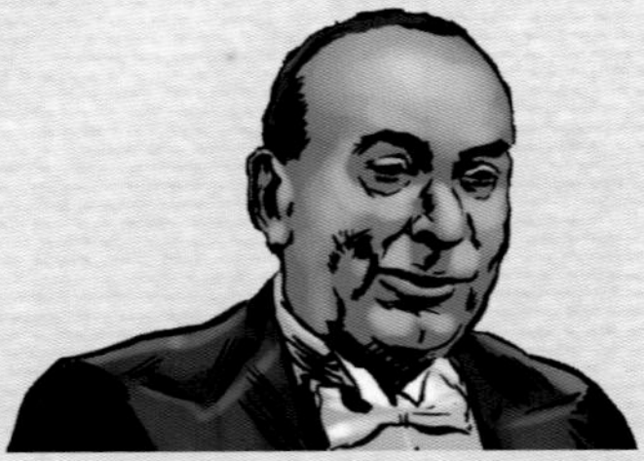

Arthur Birling
A wealthy industrialist

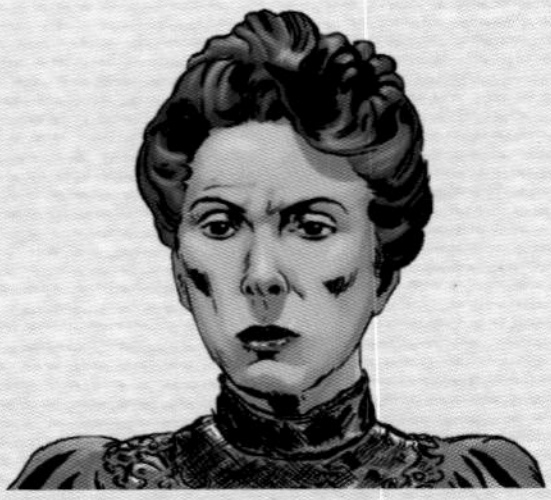

Sybil Birling
Arthur Birling's wife

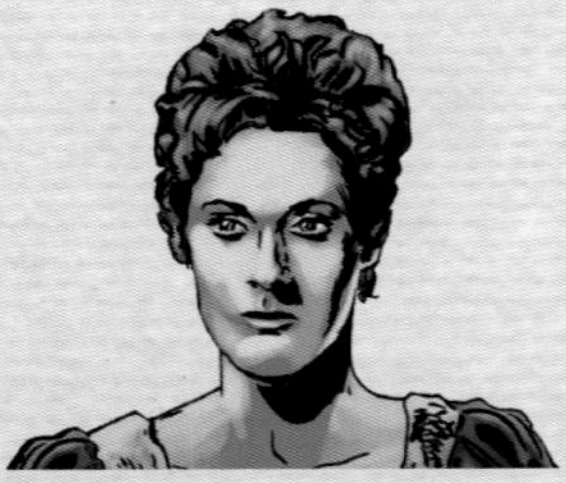

Sheila Birling
Arthur & Sybil's daughter

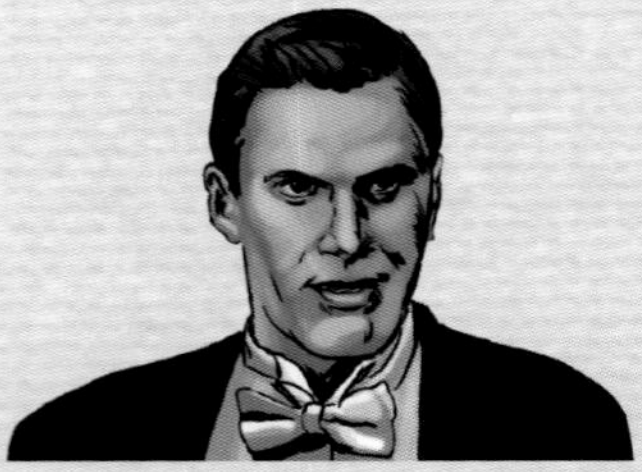

Gerald Croft
Sheila's fiancé

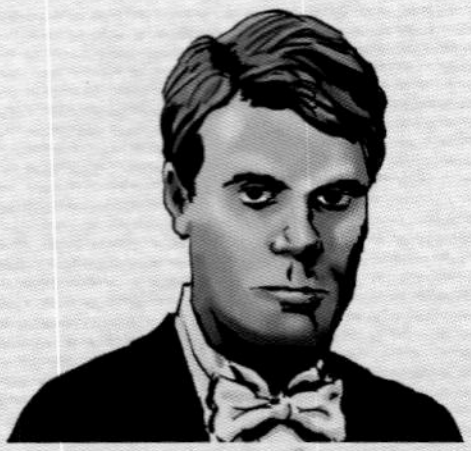

Eric Birling
Arthur & Sybil's son

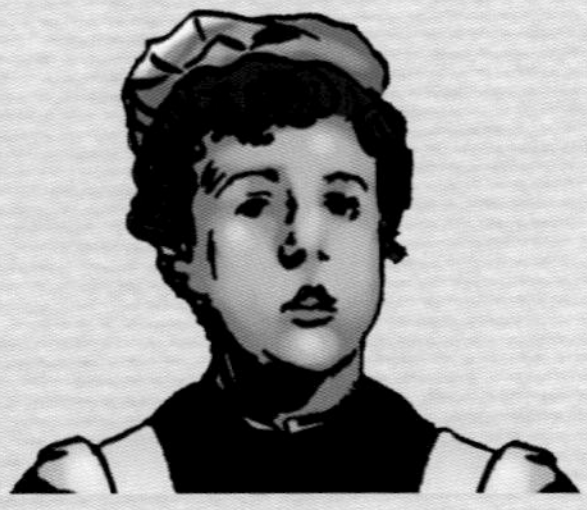

Edna
The Birlings' parlor-maid

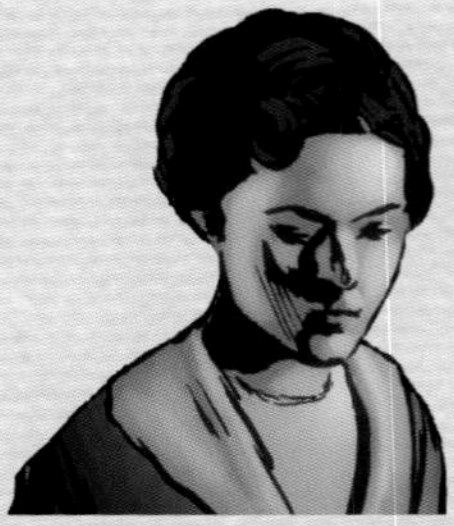

Eva Smith / Daisy Renton

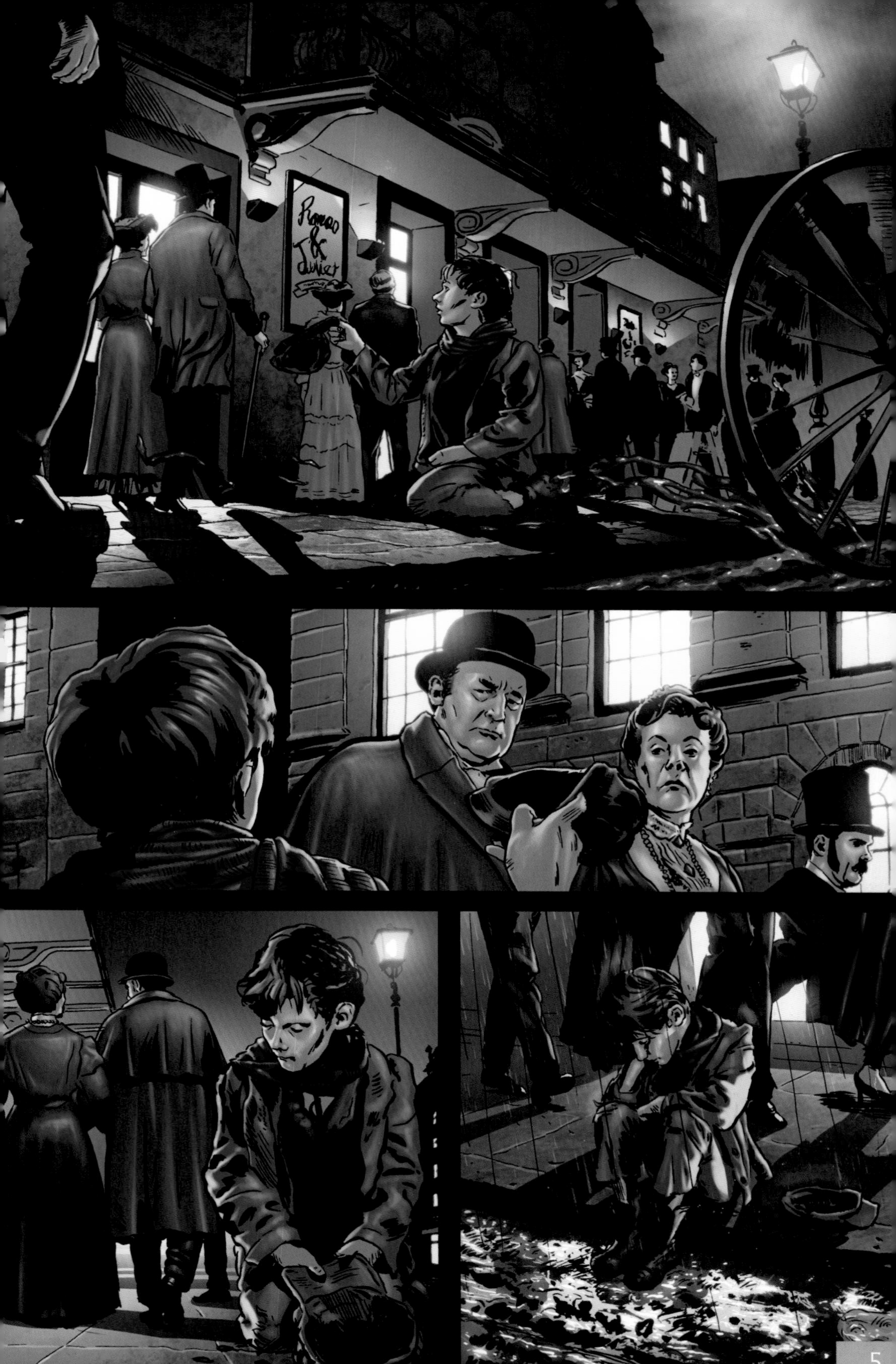
Romeo & Juliet

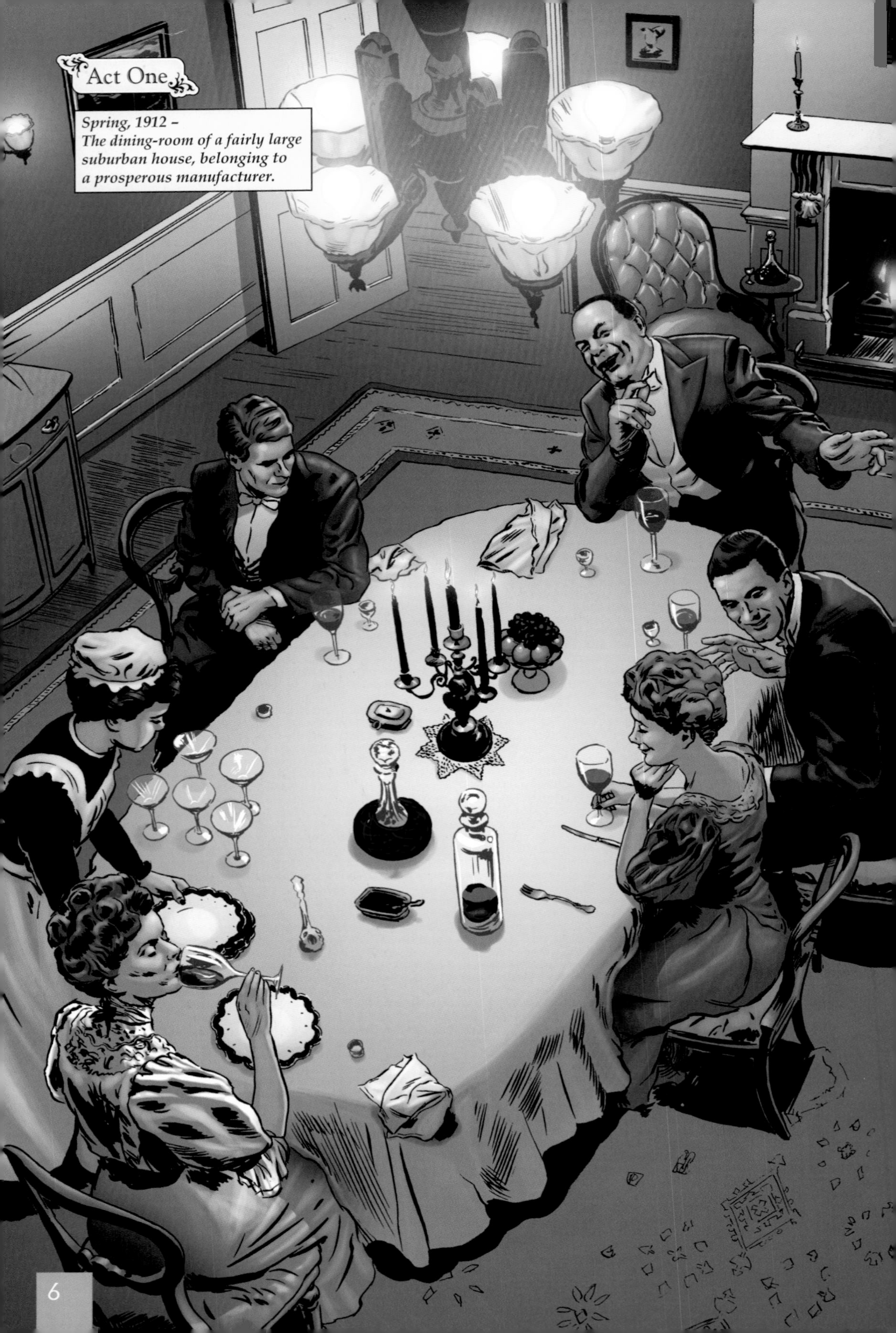
Act One
Spring, 1912 –
The dining-room of a fairly large suburban house, belonging to a prosperous manufacturer.

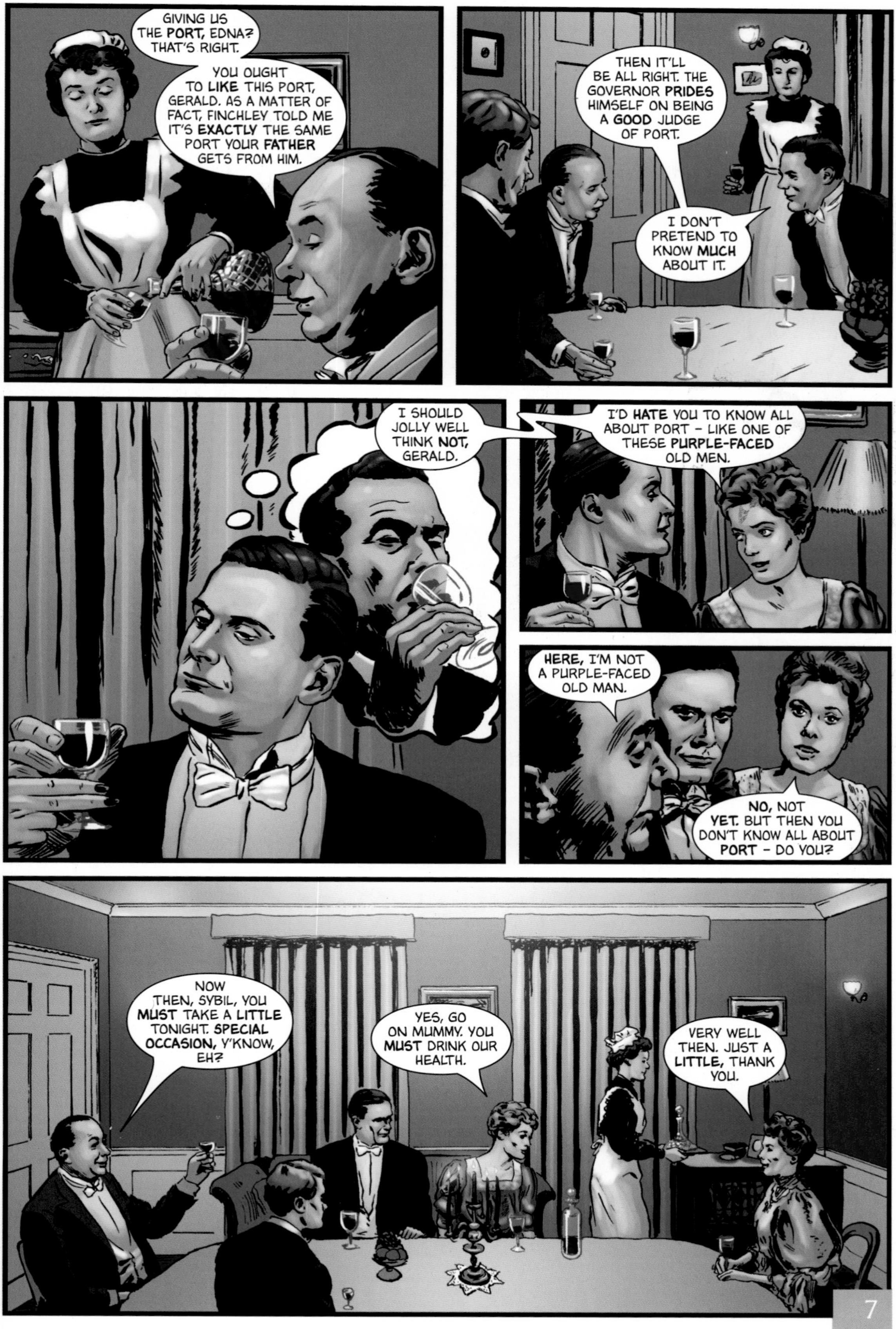

GIVING US THE PORT, EDNA? THAT'S RIGHT.
YOU OUGHT TO LIKE THIS PORT, GERALD. AS A MATTER OF FACT, FINCHLEY TOLD ME IT'S EXACTLY THE SAME PORT YOUR FATHER GETS FROM HIM.
THEN IT'LL BE ALL RIGHT. THE GOVERNOR PRIDES HIMSELF ON BEING A GOOD JUDGE OF PORT.
I DON'T PRETEND TO KNOW MUCH ABOUT IT.
I SHOULD JOLLY WELL THINK NOT, GERALD.
I'D HATE YOU TO KNOW ALL ABOUT PORT – LIKE ONE OF THESE PURPLE-FACED OLD MEN.
HERE, I'M NOT A PURPLE-FACED OLD MAN.
NO, NOT YET. BUT THEN YOU DON'T KNOW ALL ABOUT PORT – DO YOU?
NOW THEN, SYBIL, YOU MUST TAKE A LITTLE TONIGHT. SPECIAL OCCASION, Y'KNOW, EH?
YES, GO ON MUMMY. YOU MUST DRINK OUR HEALTH.
VERY WELL THEN. JUST A LITTLE, THANK YOU.

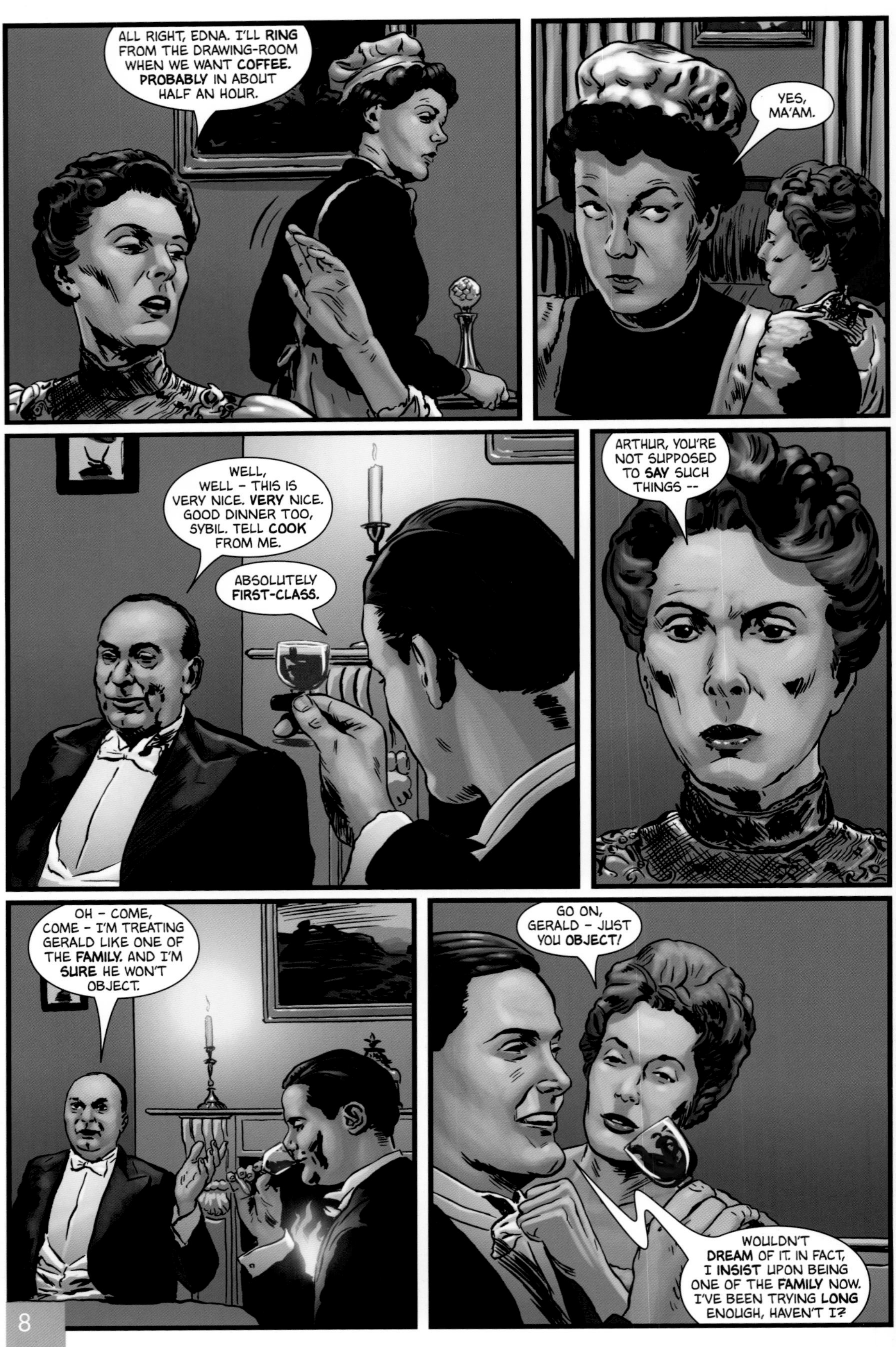
ALL RIGHT, EDNA. I'LL RING FROM THE DRAWING-ROOM WHEN WE WANT COFFEE. PROBABLY IN ABOUT HALF AN HOUR.
YES, MA'AM.
WELL, WELL – THIS IS VERY NICE. VERY NICE. GOOD DINNER TOO, SYBIL. TELL COOK FROM ME.
ABSOLUTELY FIRST-CLASS.
ARTHUR, YOU'RE NOT SUPPOSED TO SAY SUCH THINGS --
OH – COME, COME – I'M TREATING GERALD LIKE ONE OF THE FAMILY. AND I'M SURE HE WON'T OBJECT.
GO ON, GERALD – JUST YOU OBJECT!
WOULDN'T DREAM OF IT. IN FACT, I INSIST UPON BEING ONE OF THE FAMILY NOW. I'VE BEEN TRYING LONG ENOUGH, HAVEN'T I?

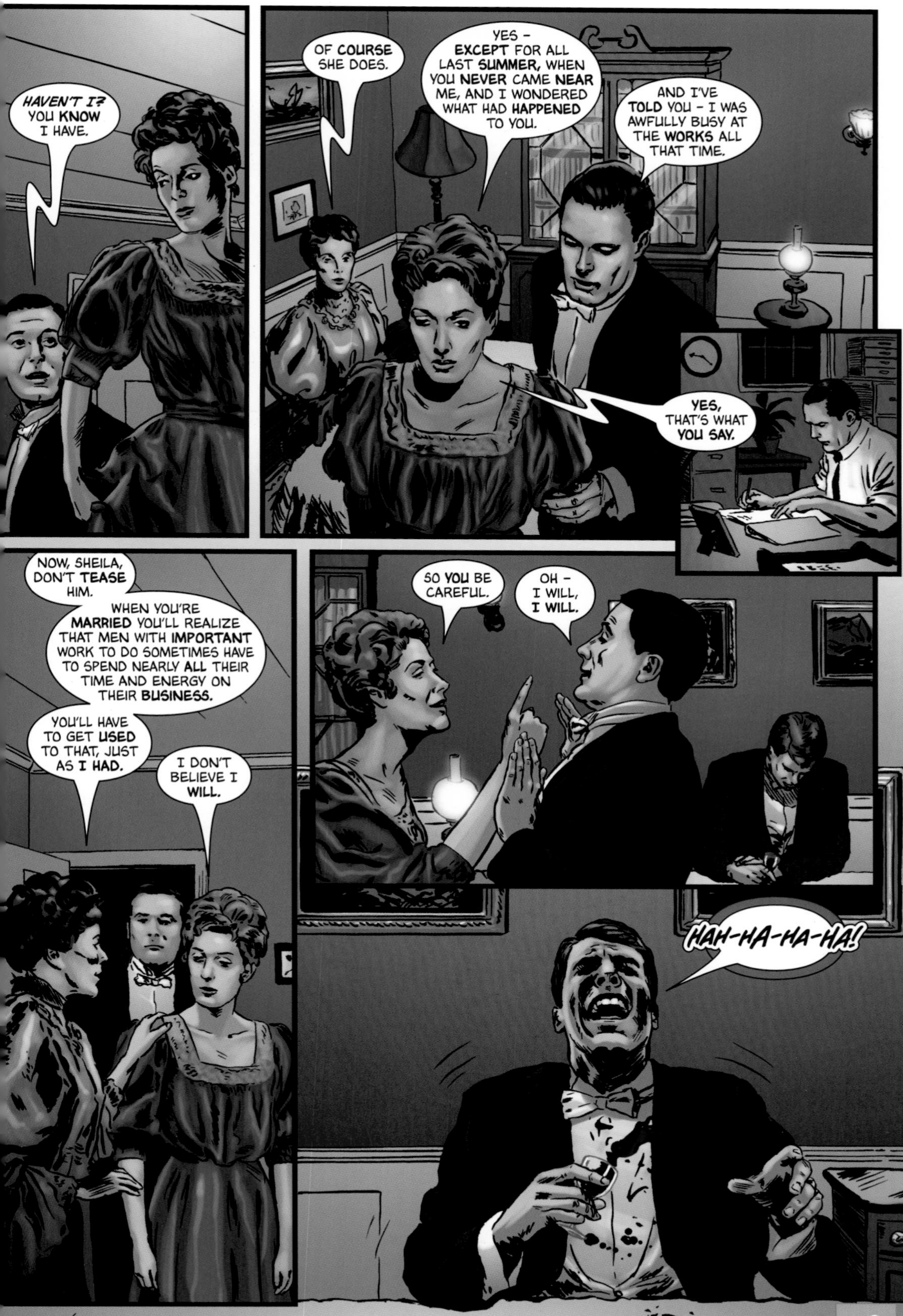
HAVEN'T I? YOU KNOW I HAVE.
OF COURSE SHE DOES.
YES – EXCEPT FOR ALL LAST SUMMER, WHEN YOU NEVER CAME NEAR ME, AND I WONDERED WHAT HAD HAPPENED TO YOU.
AND I'VE TOLD YOU – I WAS AWFULLY BUSY AT THE WORKS ALL THAT TIME.
YES, THAT'S WHAT YOU SAY.
NOW, SHEILA, DON'T TEASE HIM.
WHEN YOU'RE MARRIED YOU'LL REALIZE THAT MEN WITH IMPORTANT WORK TO DO SOMETIMES HAVE TO SPEND NEARLY ALL THEIR TIME AND ENERGY ON THEIR BUSINESS.
YOU'LL HAVE TO GET USED TO THAT, JUST AS I HAD.
I DON'T BELIEVE I WILL.
SO YOU BE CAREFUL.
OH – I WILL, I WILL.
HAH-HA-HA-HA!

NOW – WHAT'S THE JOKE?

I DON'T **KNOW** – REALLY. SUDDENLY I FELT I JUST **HAD** TO LAUGH.

YOU'RE **SQUIFFY**.

I'M **NOT**.

WHAT AN EXPRESSION, SHEILA! REALLY, THE **THINGS** YOU GIRLS PICK UP THESE DAYS!

IF YOU THINK THAT'S THE **BEST** SHE CAN DO –

DON'T BE AN **ASS**, ERIC.

NOW **STOP** IT, YOU TWO.

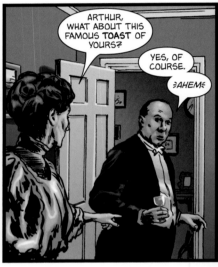

ARTHUR, WHAT ABOUT THIS FAMOUS **TOAST** OF YOURS?

YES, OF COURSE.

≶AHEM≶

WELL, GERALD, I KNOW YOU **AGREED** THAT WE SHOULD **ONLY** HAVE THIS QUIET LITTLE **FAMILY** PARTY. IT'S A **PITY** SIR **GEORGE** AND – ER – LADY **CROFT** CAN'T BE WITH US, BUT THEY'RE **ABROAD** AND SO IT CAN'T BE HELPED.

AS I TOLD YOU, THEY SENT ME A **VERY** NICE CABLE – COULDN'T BE **NICER**. I'M **NOT** SORRY THAT WE'RE CELEBRATING QUIETLY LIKE THIS –

MUCH NICER REALLY.

I AGREE.

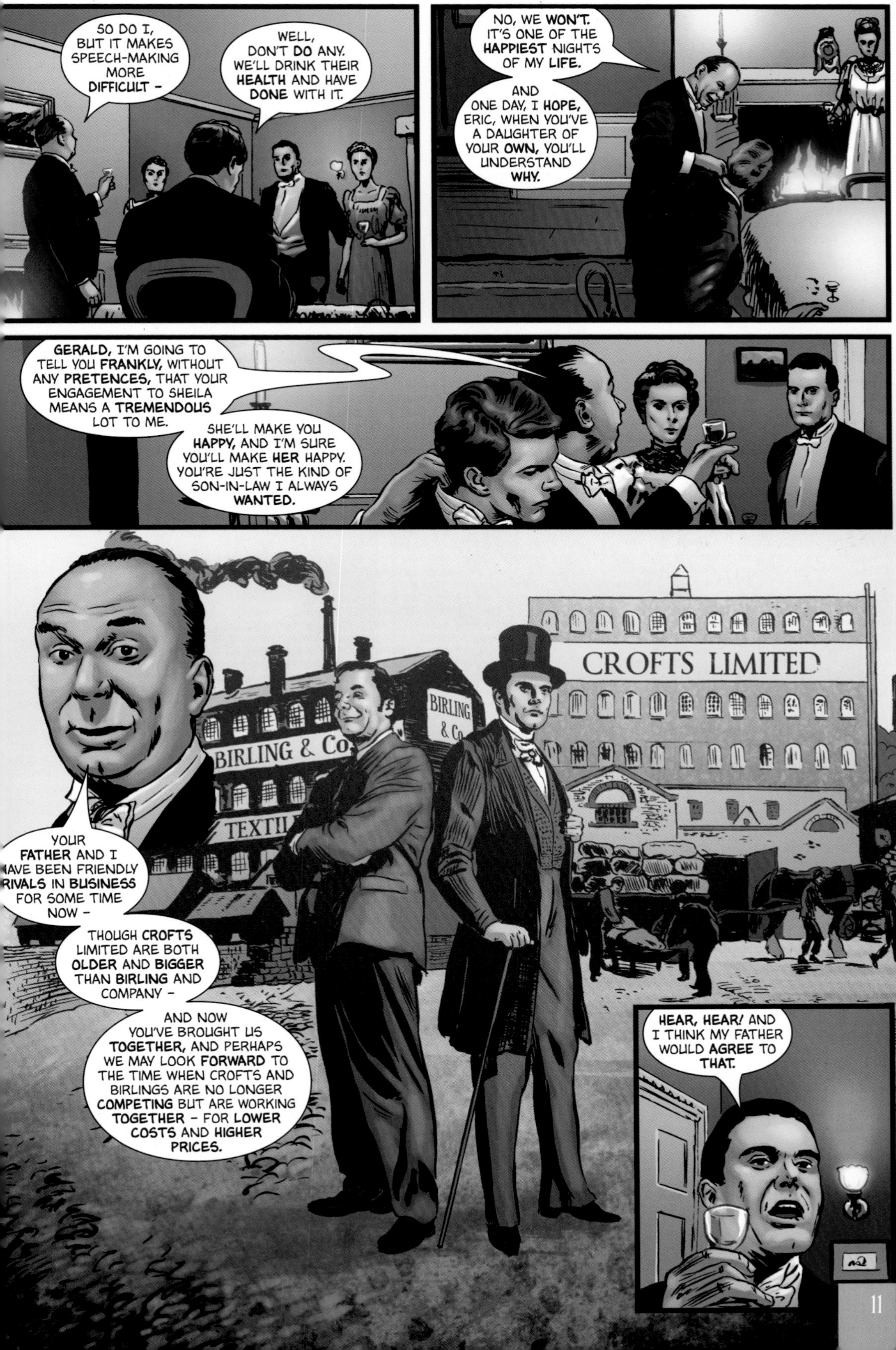

SO DO I, BUT IT MAKES SPEECH-MAKING MORE DIFFICULT –
WELL, DON'T DO ANY. WE'LL DRINK THEIR HEALTH AND HAVE DONE WITH IT.
NO, WE WON'T. IT'S ONE OF THE HAPPIEST NIGHTS OF MY LIFE.
AND ONE DAY, I HOPE, ERIC, WHEN YOU'VE A DAUGHTER OF YOUR OWN, YOU'LL UNDERSTAND WHY.
GERALD, I'M GOING TO TELL YOU FRANKLY, WITHOUT ANY PRETENCES, THAT YOUR ENGAGEMENT TO SHEILA MEANS A TREMENDOUS LOT TO ME.
SHE'LL MAKE YOU HAPPY, AND I'M SURE YOU'LL MAKE HER HAPPY. YOU'RE JUST THE KIND OF SON-IN-LAW I ALWAYS WANTED.
CROFTS LIMITED
BIRLING & Co
BIRLING & Co
YOUR FATHER AND I HAVE BEEN FRIENDLY RIVALS IN BUSINESS FOR SOME TIME NOW –
THOUGH CROFTS LIMITED ARE BOTH OLDER AND BIGGER THAN BIRLING AND COMPANY –
AND NOW YOU'VE BROUGHT US TOGETHER, AND PERHAPS WE MAY LOOK FORWARD TO THE TIME WHEN CROFTS AND BIRLINGS ARE NO LONGER COMPETING BUT ARE WORKING TOGETHER – FOR LOWER COSTS AND HIGHER PRICES.
HEAR, HEAR! AND I THINK MY FATHER WOULD AGREE TO THAT.

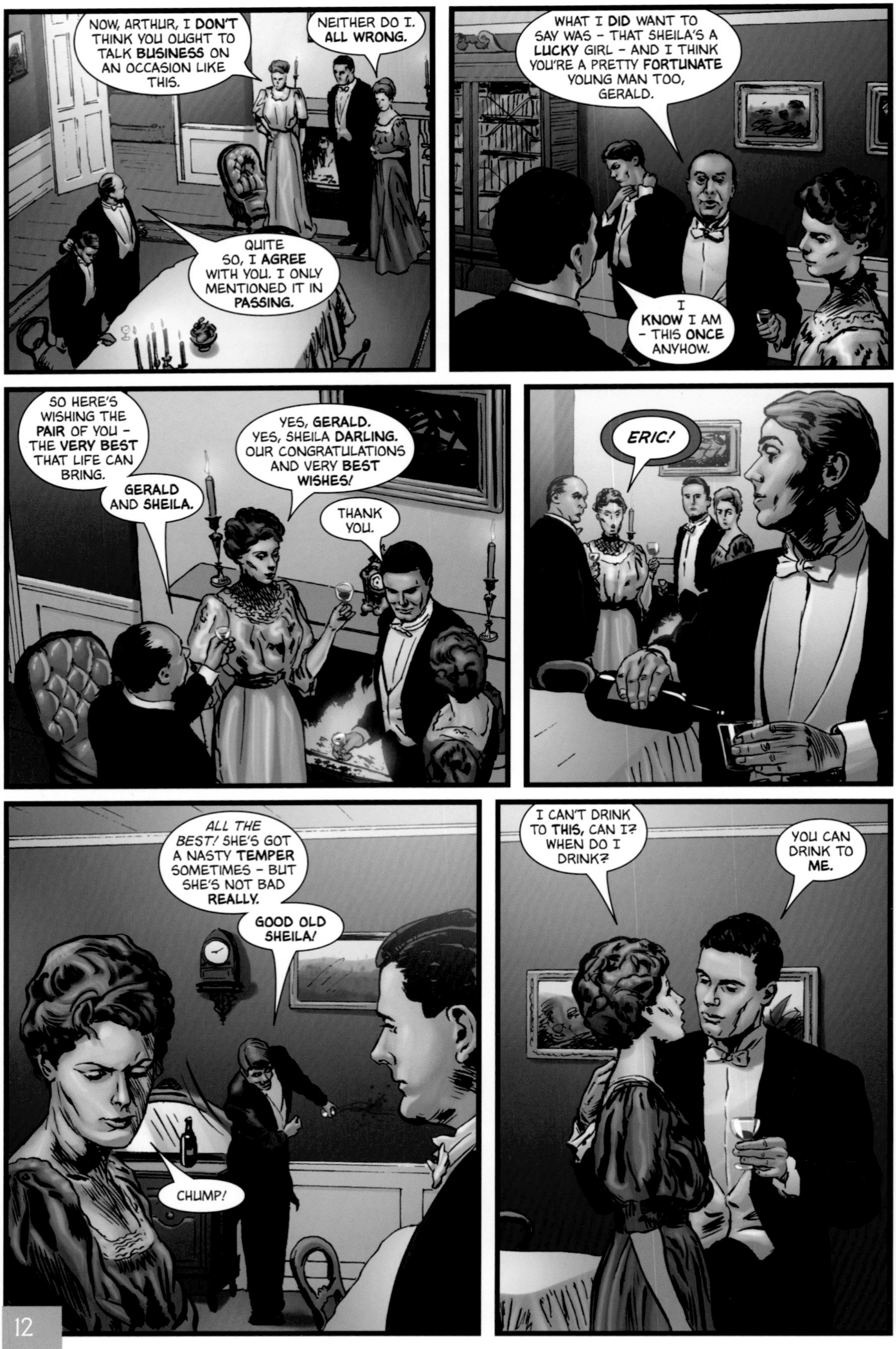
NOW, ARTHUR, I DON'T THINK YOU OUGHT TO TALK BUSINESS ON AN OCCASION LIKE THIS.
NEITHER DO I. ALL WRONG.
QUITE SO, I AGREE WITH YOU. I ONLY MENTIONED IT IN PASSING.
WHAT I DID WANT TO SAY WAS – THAT SHEILA'S A LUCKY GIRL – AND I THINK YOU'RE A PRETTY FORTUNATE YOUNG MAN TOO, GERALD.
I KNOW I AM – THIS ONCE ANYHOW.
SO HERE'S WISHING THE PAIR OF YOU – THE VERY BEST THAT LIFE CAN BRING.
GERALD AND SHEILA.
YES, GERALD. YES, SHEILA DARLING. OUR CONGRATULATIONS AND VERY BEST WISHES!
THANK YOU.
ERIC!
ALL THE BEST! SHE'S GOT A NASTY TEMPER SOMETIMES – BUT SHE'S NOT BAD REALLY.
GOOD OLD SHEILA!
CHUMP!
I CAN'T DRINK TO THIS, CAN I? WHEN DO I DRINK?
YOU CAN DRINK TO ME.

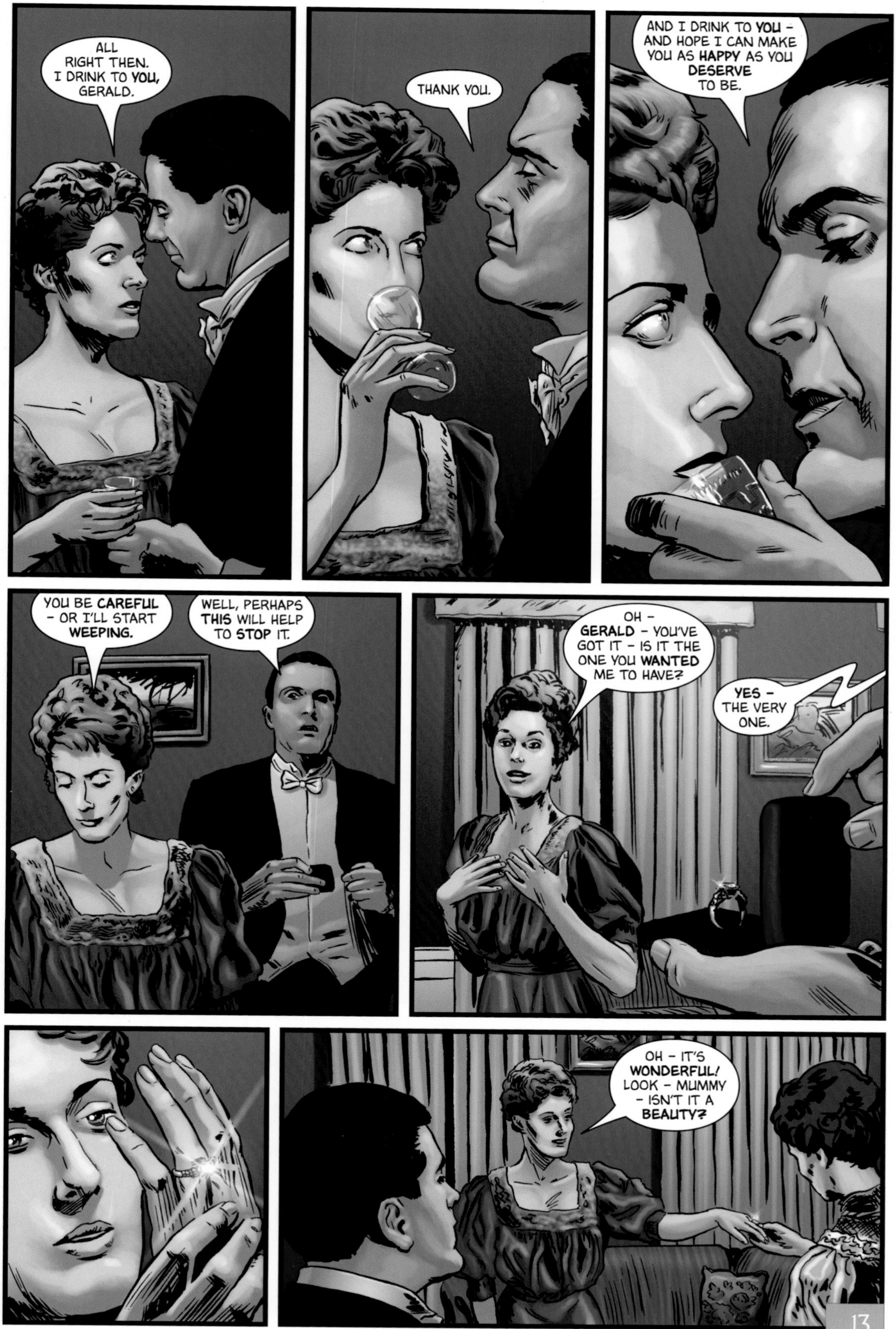
ALL RIGHT THEN. I DRINK TO YOU, GERALD.
THANK YOU.
AND I DRINK TO YOU - AND HOPE I CAN MAKE YOU AS HAPPY AS YOU DESERVE TO BE.
YOU BE CAREFUL - OR I'LL START WEEPING.
WELL, PERHAPS THIS WILL HELP TO STOP IT.
OH - GERALD - YOU'VE GOT IT - IS IT THE ONE YOU WANTED ME TO HAVE?
YES - THE VERY ONE.
OH - IT'S WONDERFUL! LOOK - MUMMY - ISN'T IT A BEAUTY?

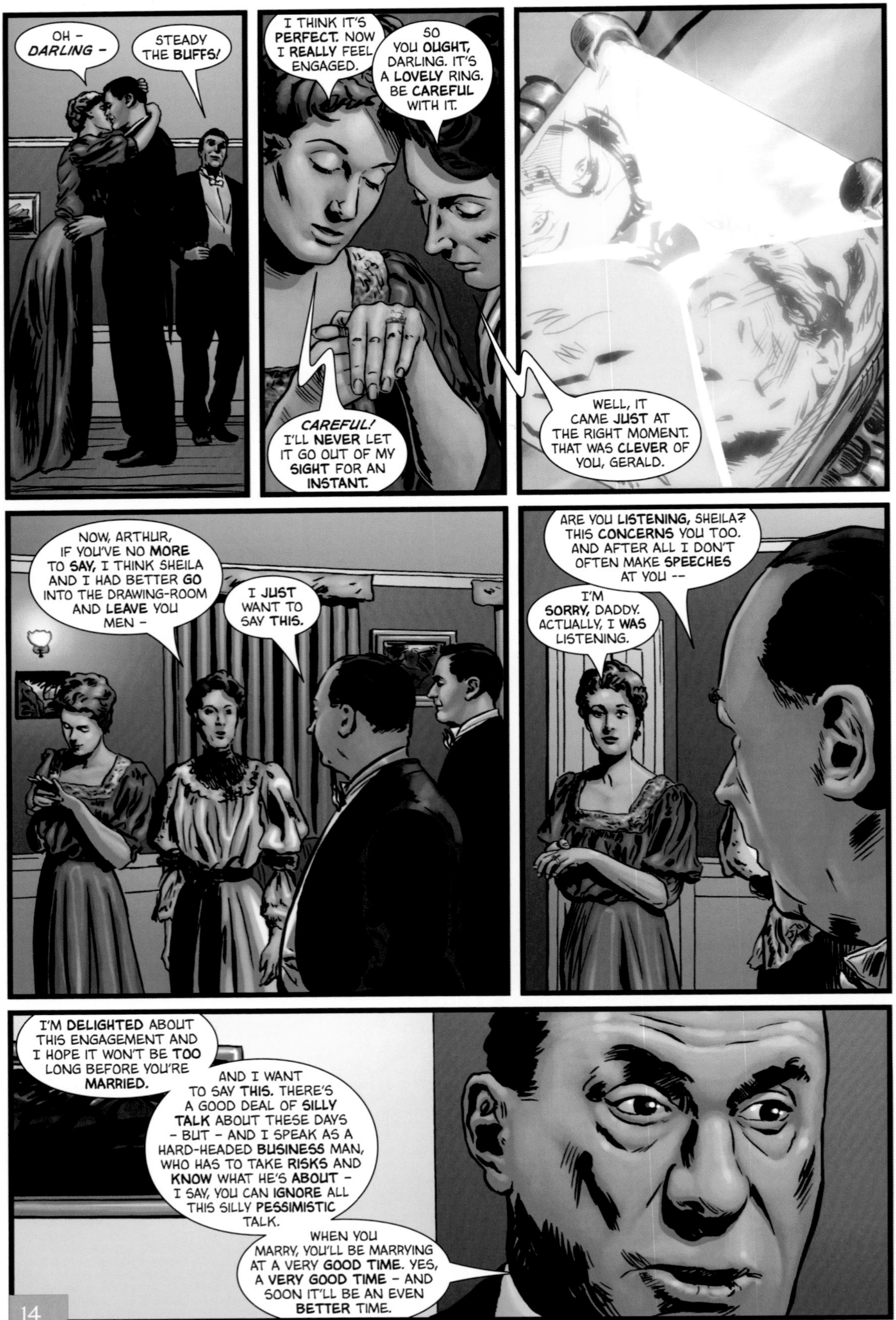

OH – DARLING –
STEADY THE BUFFS!
I THINK IT'S PERFECT. NOW I REALLY FEEL ENGAGED.
SO YOU OUGHT, DARLING. IT'S A LOVELY RING. BE CAREFUL WITH IT.
CAREFUL! I'LL NEVER LET IT GO OUT OF MY SIGHT FOR AN INSTANT.
WELL, IT CAME JUST AT THE RIGHT MOMENT. THAT WAS CLEVER OF YOU, GERALD.
NOW, ARTHUR, IF YOU'VE NO MORE TO SAY, I THINK SHEILA AND I HAD BETTER GO INTO THE DRAWING-ROOM AND LEAVE YOU MEN –
I JUST WANT TO SAY THIS.
ARE YOU LISTENING, SHEILA? THIS CONCERNS YOU TOO. AND AFTER ALL I DON'T OFTEN MAKE SPEECHES AT YOU --
I'M SORRY, DADDY. ACTUALLY, I WAS LISTENING.
I'M DELIGHTED ABOUT THIS ENGAGEMENT AND I HOPE IT WON'T BE TOO LONG BEFORE YOU'RE MARRIED.
AND I WANT TO SAY THIS. THERE'S A GOOD DEAL OF SILLY TALK ABOUT THESE DAYS – BUT – AND I SPEAK AS A HARD-HEADED BUSINESS MAN, WHO HAS TO TAKE RISKS AND KNOW WHAT HE'S ABOUT – I SAY, YOU CAN IGNORE ALL THIS SILLY PESSIMISTIC TALK.
WHEN YOU MARRY, YOU'LL BE MARRYING AT A VERY GOOD TIME. YES, A VERY GOOD TIME – AND SOON IT'LL BE AN EVEN BETTER TIME.

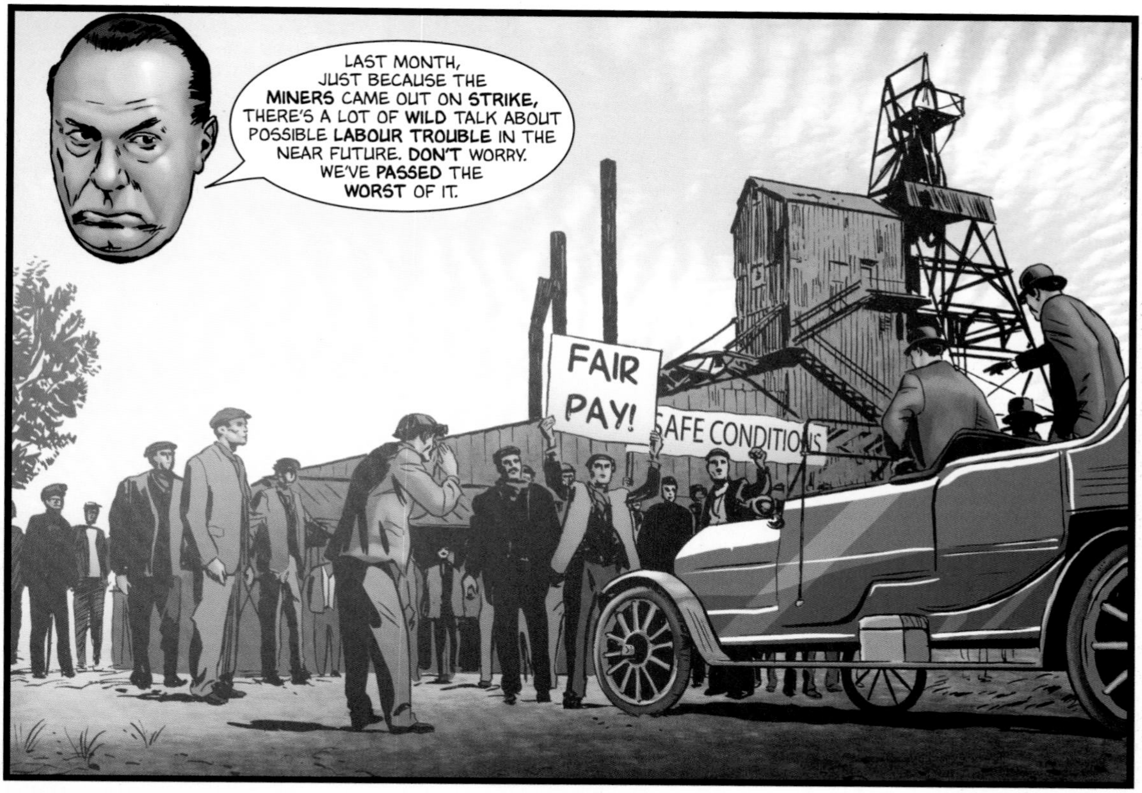
LAST MONTH, JUST BECAUSE THE MINERS CAME OUT ON STRIKE, THERE'S A LOT OF WILD TALK ABOUT POSSIBLE LABOUR TROUBLE IN THE NEAR FUTURE. DON'T WORRY. WE'VE PASSED THE WORST OF IT.
FAIR PAY!
SAFE CONDITIONS

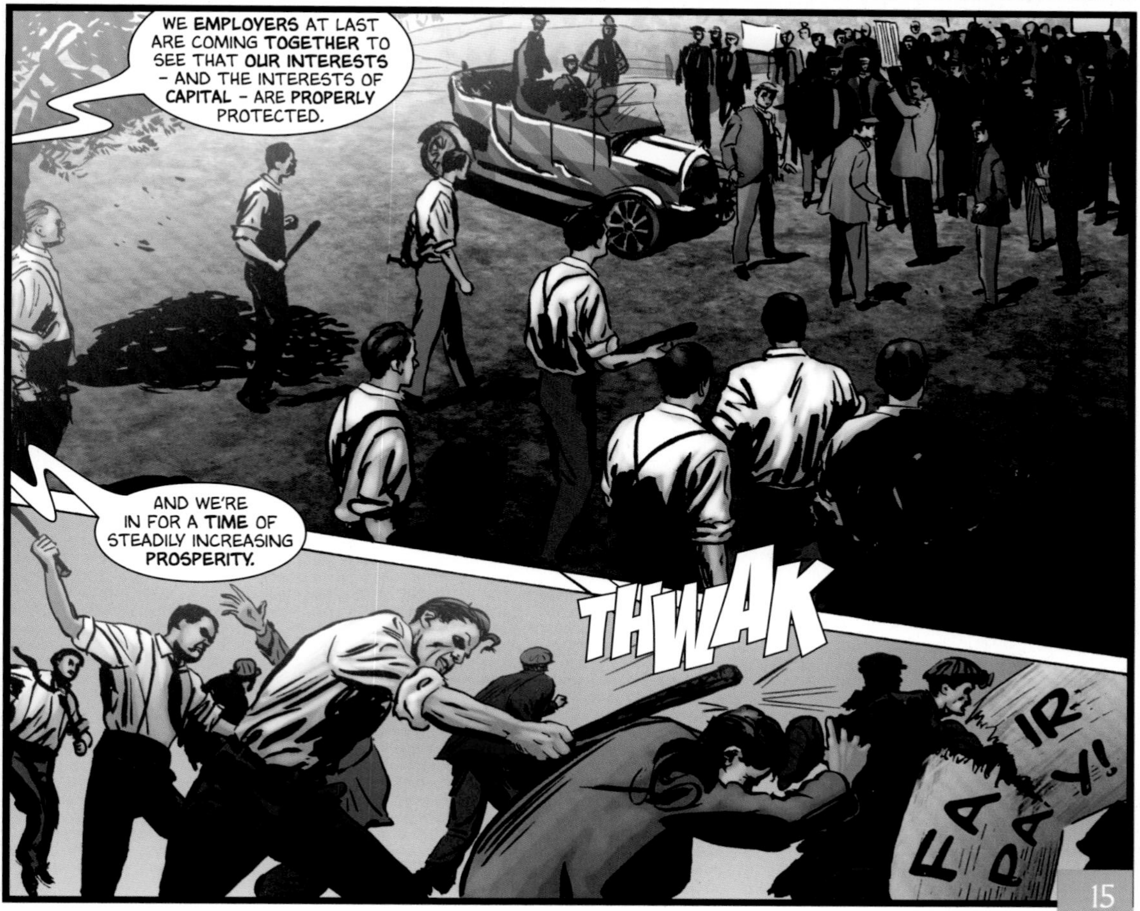
WE EMPLOYERS AT LAST ARE COMING TOGETHER TO SEE THAT OUR INTERESTS – AND THE INTERESTS OF CAPITAL – ARE PROPERLY PROTECTED.
AND WE'RE IN FOR A TIME OF STEADILY INCREASING PROSPERITY.
THWAK
FA IR PAY!

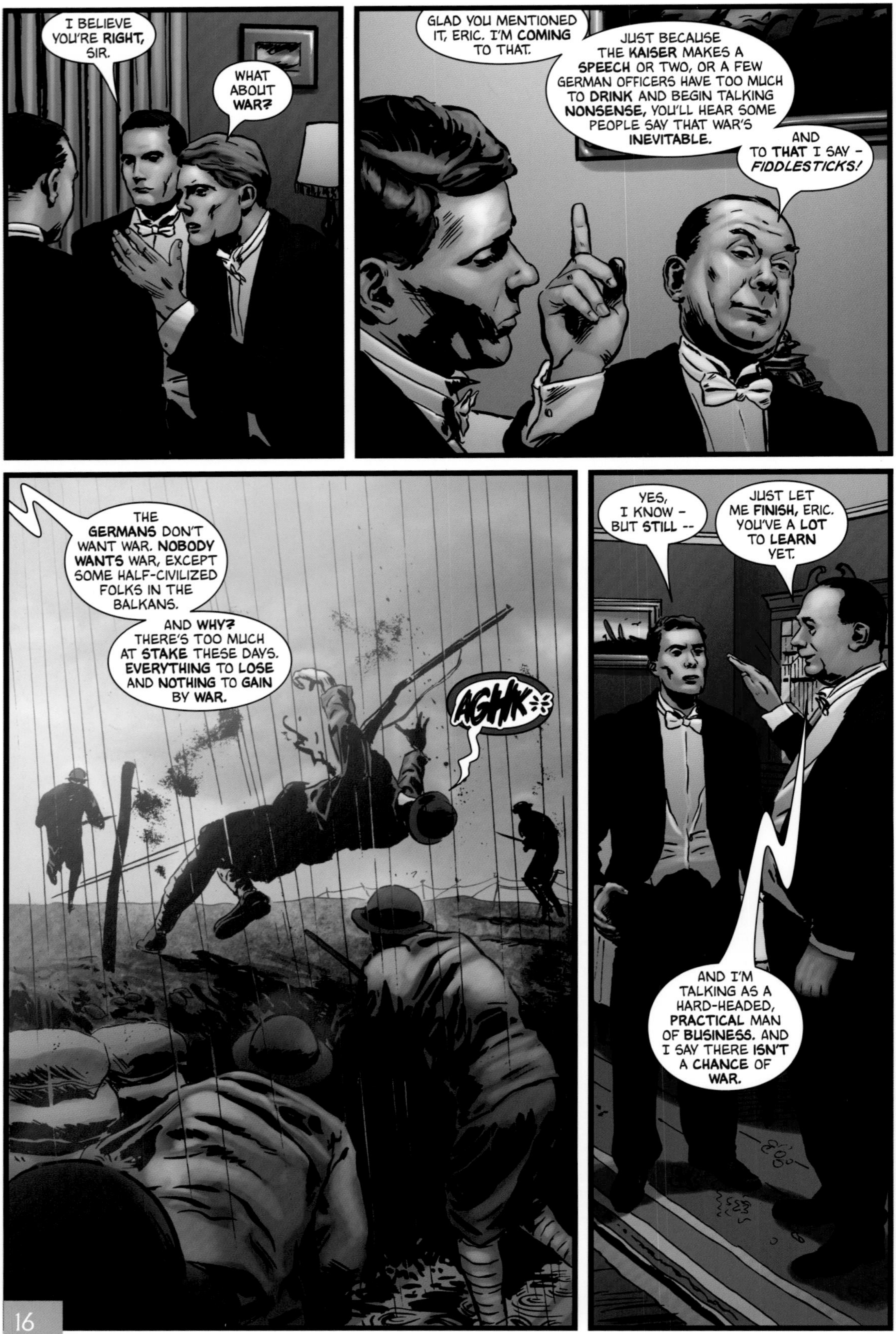
I BELIEVE YOU'RE RIGHT, SIR.
WHAT ABOUT WAR?
GLAD YOU MENTIONED IT, ERIC. I'M COMING TO THAT.
JUST BECAUSE THE KAISER MAKES A SPEECH OR TWO, OR A FEW GERMAN OFFICERS HAVE TOO MUCH TO DRINK AND BEGIN TALKING NONSENSE, YOU'LL HEAR SOME PEOPLE SAY THAT WAR'S INEVITABLE.
AND TO THAT I SAY - FIDDLESTICKS!
THE GERMANS DON'T WANT WAR. NOBODY WANTS WAR, EXCEPT SOME HALF-CIVILIZED FOLKS IN THE BALKANS.
AND WHY? THERE'S TOO MUCH AT STAKE THESE DAYS. EVERYTHING TO LOSE AND NOTHING TO GAIN BY WAR.
AGHK
YES, I KNOW - BUT STILL --
JUST LET ME FINISH, ERIC. YOU'VE A LOT TO LEARN YET.
AND I'M TALKING AS A HARD-HEADED, PRACTICAL MAN OF BUSINESS. AND I SAY THERE ISN'T A CHANCE OF WAR.

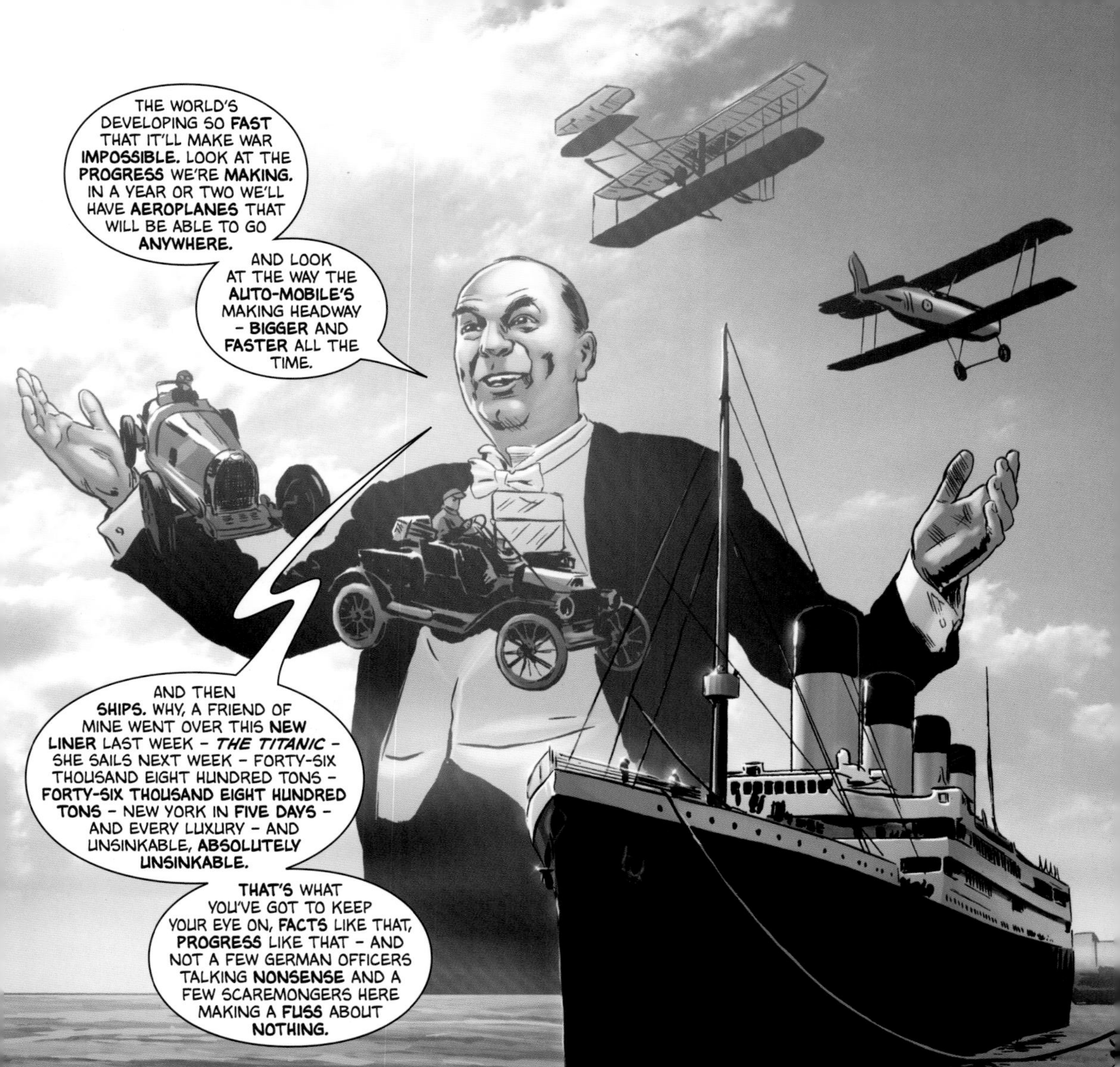
THE WORLD'S DEVELOPING SO FAST THAT IT'LL MAKE WAR IMPOSSIBLE. LOOK AT THE PROGRESS WE'RE MAKING. IN A YEAR OR TWO WE'LL HAVE AEROPLANES THAT WILL BE ABLE TO GO ANYWHERE.
AND LOOK AT THE WAY THE AUTO-MOBILE'S MAKING HEADWAY – BIGGER AND FASTER ALL THE TIME.
AND THEN SHIPS. WHY, A FRIEND OF MINE WENT OVER THIS NEW LINER LAST WEEK – THE TITANIC – SHE SAILS NEXT WEEK – FORTY-SIX THOUSAND EIGHT HUNDRED TONS – FORTY-SIX THOUSAND EIGHT HUNDRED TONS – NEW YORK IN FIVE DAYS – AND EVERY LUXURY – AND UNSINKABLE, ABSOLUTELY UNSINKABLE.
THAT'S WHAT YOU'VE GOT TO KEEP YOUR EYE ON, FACTS LIKE THAT, PROGRESS LIKE THAT – AND NOT A FEW GERMAN OFFICERS TALKING NONSENSE AND A FEW SCAREMONGERS HERE MAKING A FUSS ABOUT NOTHING.

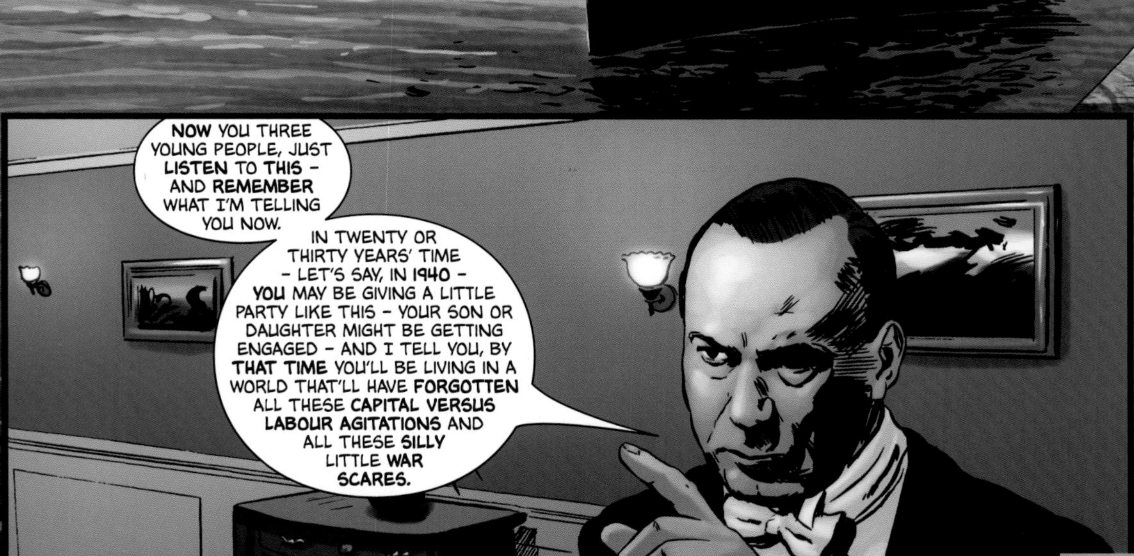
NOW YOU THREE YOUNG PEOPLE, JUST LISTEN TO THIS – AND REMEMBER WHAT I'M TELLING YOU NOW.
IN TWENTY OR THIRTY YEARS' TIME – LET'S SAY, IN 1940 – YOU MAY BE GIVING A LITTLE PARTY LIKE THIS – YOUR SON OR DAUGHTER MIGHT BE GETTING ENGAGED – AND I TELL YOU, BY THAT TIME YOU'LL BE LIVING IN A WORLD THAT'LL HAVE FORGOTTEN ALL THESE CAPITAL VERSUS LABOUR AGITATIONS AND ALL THESE SILLY LITTLE WAR SCARES.

THERE'LL BE PEACE AND PROSPERITY AND RAPID **PROGRESS** EVERYWHERE –

EXCEPT OF COURSE IN **RUSSIA**, WHICH WILL **ALWAYS** BE **BEHINDHAND** NATURALLY.

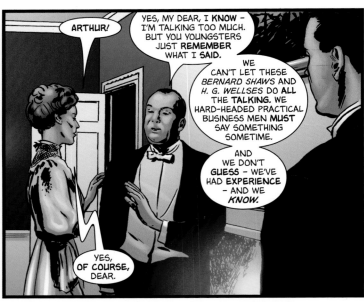

ARTHUR!

YES, MY DEAR, I **KNOW** – I'M TALKING TOO MUCH. BUT YOU YOUNGSTERS JUST **REMEMBER** WHAT I SAID.

WE CAN'T LET THESE *BERNARD SHAWS* AND *H. G. WELLSES* DO **ALL** THE **TALKING**. WE HARD-HEADED PRACTICAL BUSINESS MEN **MUST** SAY SOMETHING SOMETIME.

AND WE DON'T **GUESS** – WE'VE HAD **EXPERIENCE** – AND WE *KNOW.*

YES, OF COURSE, DEAR.

WELL – DON'T KEEP GERALD IN HERE **TOO** LONG.

ERIC – I WANT YOU A MINUTE.

CIGAR?

NO, **THANKS.** CAN'T REALLY ENJOY THEM.

AH, YOU DON'T KNOW WHAT YOU'RE **MISSING.** I LIKE A GOOD CIGAR.

HELP YOURSELF.

THANK YOU.

THANKS. BY THE WAY, THERE'S **SOMETHING** I'D LIKE TO MENTION –

– IN **STRICT** CONFIDENCE – WHILE WE'RE BY **OURSELVES**.

I HAVE AN IDEA THAT YOUR **MOTHER** – LADY CROFT – WHILE SHE DOESN'T OBJECT TO MY GIRL – FEELS YOU MIGHT HAVE DONE **BETTER** FOR YOURSELF SOCIALLY –

OH, **NO** –

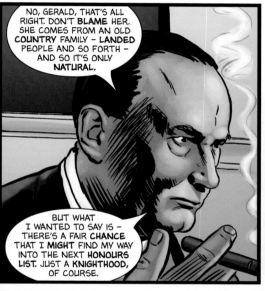

NO, GERALD, THAT'S ALL RIGHT. DON'T **BLAME** HER. SHE COMES FROM AN OLD **COUNTRY** FAMILY – **LANDED** PEOPLE AND SO FORTH – AND SO IT'S ONLY **NATURAL**.

BUT WHAT I WANTED TO SAY IS – THERE'S A FAIR **CHANCE** THAT I **MIGHT** FIND MY WAY INTO THE NEXT **HONOURS** LIST. JUST A KNIGHTHOOD, OF COURSE.

OH – **I SAY** – CONGRATULATIONS!

THANKS. BUT IT'S A BIT TOO **EARLY** FOR THAT. SO DON'T SAY **ANYTHING**. BUT I'VE HAD A **HINT** OR TWO.

YOU SEE, I WAS **LORD MAYOR** HERE TWO YEARS AGO WHEN **ROYALTY** VISITED US. AND I'VE ALWAYS BEEN REGARDED AS A SOUND USEFUL **PARTY** MAN.

SO – WELL – I GATHER THERE'S A VERY **GOOD CHANCE** OF A KNIGHTHOOD – SO LONG AS WE **BEHAVE** OURSELVES, DON'T GET INTO THE POLICE COURT OR START A **SCANDAL** – EH?

HA-HA-HA!

HA-HA-HA! YOU **SEEM** TO BE A **NICE** WELL-BEHAVED FAMILY –

WE **THINK** WE ARE –

tink

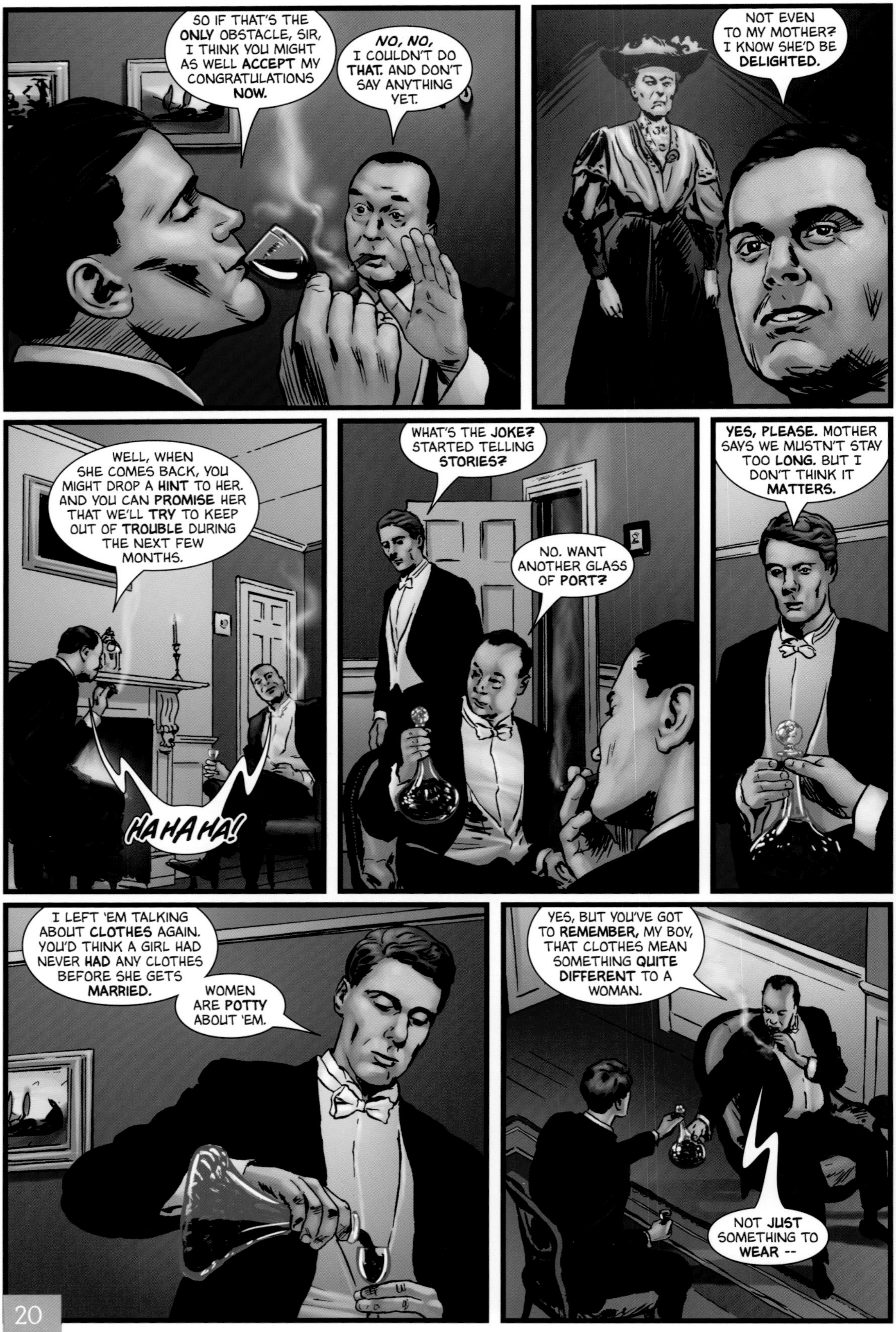

SO IF THAT'S THE ONLY OBSTACLE, SIR, I THINK YOU MIGHT AS WELL ACCEPT MY CONGRATULATIONS NOW.
NO, NO, I COULDN'T DO THAT. AND DON'T SAY ANYTHING YET.
NOT EVEN TO MY MOTHER? I KNOW SHE'D BE DELIGHTED.
WELL, WHEN SHE COMES BACK, YOU MIGHT DROP A HINT TO HER. AND YOU CAN PROMISE HER THAT WE'LL TRY TO KEEP OUT OF TROUBLE DURING THE NEXT FEW MONTHS.
HAHAHA!
WHAT'S THE JOKE? STARTED TELLING STORIES?
NO. WANT ANOTHER GLASS OF PORT?
YES, PLEASE. MOTHER SAYS WE MUSTN'T STAY TOO LONG. BUT I DON'T THINK IT MATTERS.
I LEFT 'EM TALKING ABOUT CLOTHES AGAIN. YOU'D THINK A GIRL HAD NEVER HAD ANY CLOTHES BEFORE SHE GETS MARRIED.
WOMEN ARE POTTY ABOUT 'EM.
YES, BUT YOU'VE GOT TO REMEMBER, MY BOY, THAT CLOTHES MEAN SOMETHING QUITE DIFFERENT TO A WOMAN.
NOT JUST SOMETHING TO WEAR --

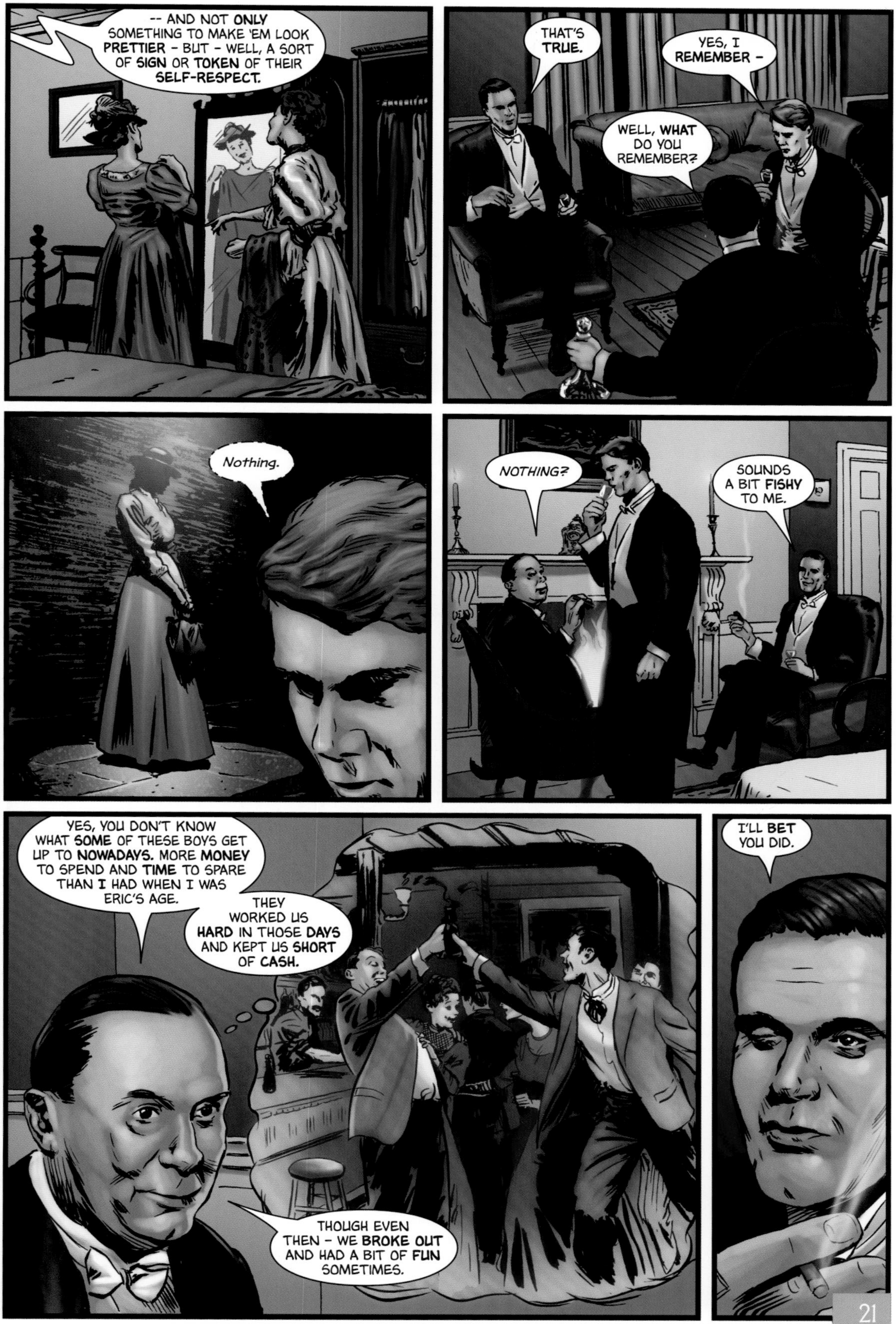
-- AND NOT ONLY SOMETHING TO MAKE 'EM LOOK PRETTIER - BUT - WELL, A SORT OF SIGN OR TOKEN OF THEIR SELF-RESPECT.
THAT'S TRUE.
YES, I REMEMBER -
WELL, WHAT DO YOU REMEMBER?
Nothing.
NOTHING?
SOUNDS A BIT FISHY TO ME.
YES, YOU DON'T KNOW WHAT SOME OF THESE BOYS GET UP TO NOWADAYS. MORE MONEY TO SPEND AND TIME TO SPARE THAN I HAD WHEN I WAS ERIC'S AGE.
THEY WORKED US HARD IN THOSE DAYS AND KEPT US SHORT OF CASH.
THOUGH EVEN THEN - WE BROKE OUT AND HAD A BIT OF FUN SOMETIMES.
I'LL BET YOU DID.

BUT **THIS** IS THE POINT. I DON'T WANT TO **LECTURE** YOU TWO YOUNG FELLOWS **AGAIN.**

BUT WHAT SO MANY OF YOU **DON'T** SEEM TO UNDERSTAND NOW, WHEN THINGS ARE SO MUCH **EASIER,** IS THAT A **MAN** HAS TO MAKE HIS **OWN** WAY --

-- HAS TO **LOOK** AFTER **HIMSELF** - AND HIS **FAMILY** TOO, OF COURSE, WHEN HE HAS ONE --

AND SO LONG AS HE DOES THAT HE **WON'T** COME TO MUCH **HARM.**

BUT THE WAY SOME OF THESE **CRANKS** TALK AND WRITE NOW, YOU'D THINK **EVERYBODY** HAS TO LOOK AFTER **EVERYBODY ELSE** --

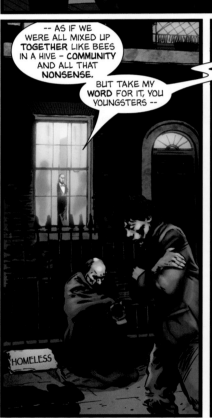

-- AS IF WE WERE ALL MIXED UP **TOGETHER** LIKE BEES IN A HIVE - **COMMUNITY** AND ALL THAT **NONSENSE.**

BUT TAKE MY **WORD** FOR IT, YOU YOUNGSTERS --

HOMELESS

-- AND I'VE LEARNT IN THE GOOD HARD SCHOOL OF **EXPERIENCE** --

-- THAT A MAN HAS TO **MIND** HIS **OWN** BUSINESS AND **LOOK** AFTER HIMSELF AND HIS **OWN** --

-- AND --

DING-A-LING-A-LING

DING-A-LING-A-LING

SOMEBODY AT THE **FRONT** DOOR.

EDNA'LL ANSWER IT.

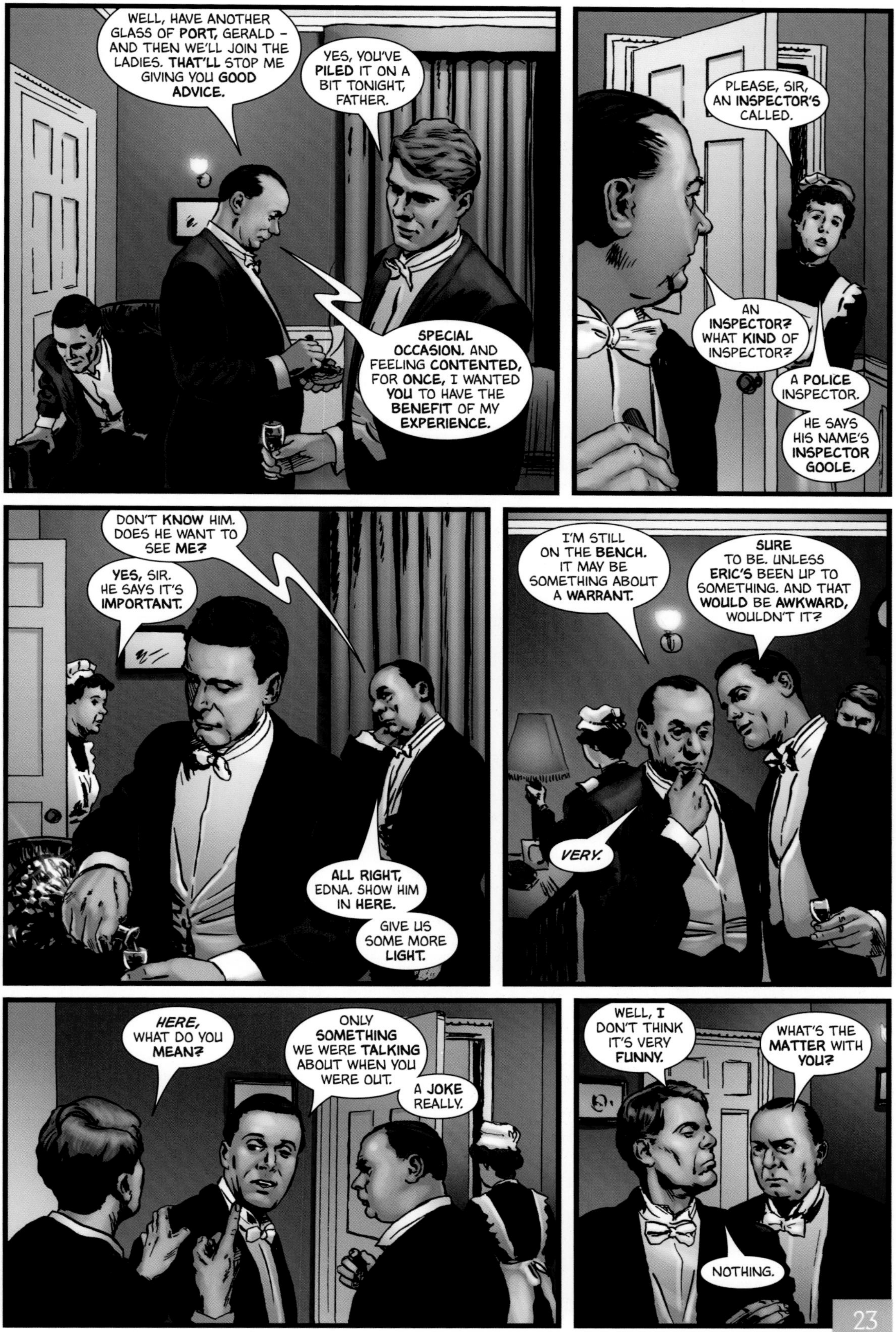
WELL, HAVE ANOTHER GLASS OF PORT, GERALD – AND THEN WE'LL JOIN THE LADIES. THAT'LL STOP ME GIVING YOU GOOD ADVICE.
YES, YOU'VE PILED IT ON A BIT TONIGHT, FATHER.
SPECIAL OCCASION. AND FEELING CONTENTED, FOR ONCE, I WANTED YOU TO HAVE THE BENEFIT OF MY EXPERIENCE.
PLEASE, SIR, AN INSPECTOR'S CALLED.
AN INSPECTOR? WHAT KIND OF INSPECTOR?
A POLICE INSPECTOR.
HE SAYS HIS NAME'S INSPECTOR GOOLE.
DON'T KNOW HIM. DOES HE WANT TO SEE ME?
YES, SIR. HE SAYS IT'S IMPORTANT.
ALL RIGHT, EDNA. SHOW HIM IN HERE.
GIVE US SOME MORE LIGHT.
I'M STILL ON THE BENCH. IT MAY BE SOMETHING ABOUT A WARRANT.
SURE TO BE. UNLESS ERIC'S BEEN UP TO SOMETHING. AND THAT WOULD BE AWKWARD, WOULDN'T IT?
VERY.
HERE, WHAT DO YOU MEAN?
ONLY SOMETHING WE WERE TALKING ABOUT WHEN YOU WERE OUT.
A JOKE REALLY.
WELL, I DON'T THINK IT'S VERY FUNNY.
WHAT'S THE MATTER WITH YOU?
NOTHING.

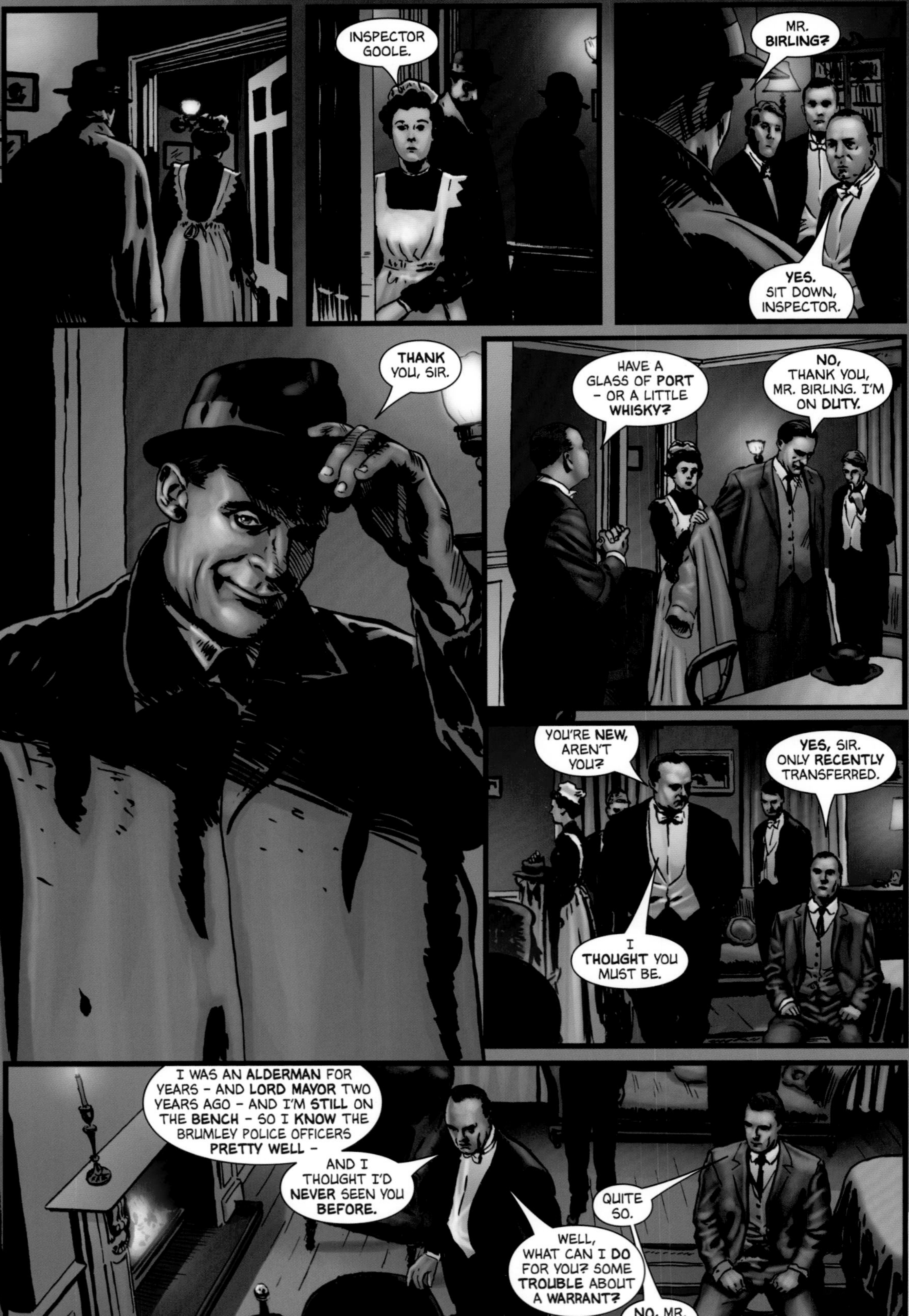

INSPECTOR GOOLE.
MR. BIRLING?
YES. SIT DOWN, INSPECTOR.
THANK YOU, SIR.
HAVE A GLASS OF PORT - OR A LITTLE WHISKY?
NO, THANK YOU, MR. BIRLING. I'M ON DUTY.
YOU'RE NEW, AREN'T YOU?
YES, SIR. ONLY RECENTLY TRANSFERRED.
I THOUGHT YOU MUST BE.
I WAS AN ALDERMAN FOR YEARS - AND LORD MAYOR TWO YEARS AGO - AND I'M STILL ON THE BENCH - SO I KNOW THE BRUMLEY POLICE OFFICERS PRETTY WELL -
AND I THOUGHT I'D NEVER SEEN YOU BEFORE.
QUITE SO.
WELL, WHAT CAN I DO FOR YOU? SOME TROUBLE ABOUT A WARRANT?
NO, MR. BIRLING.

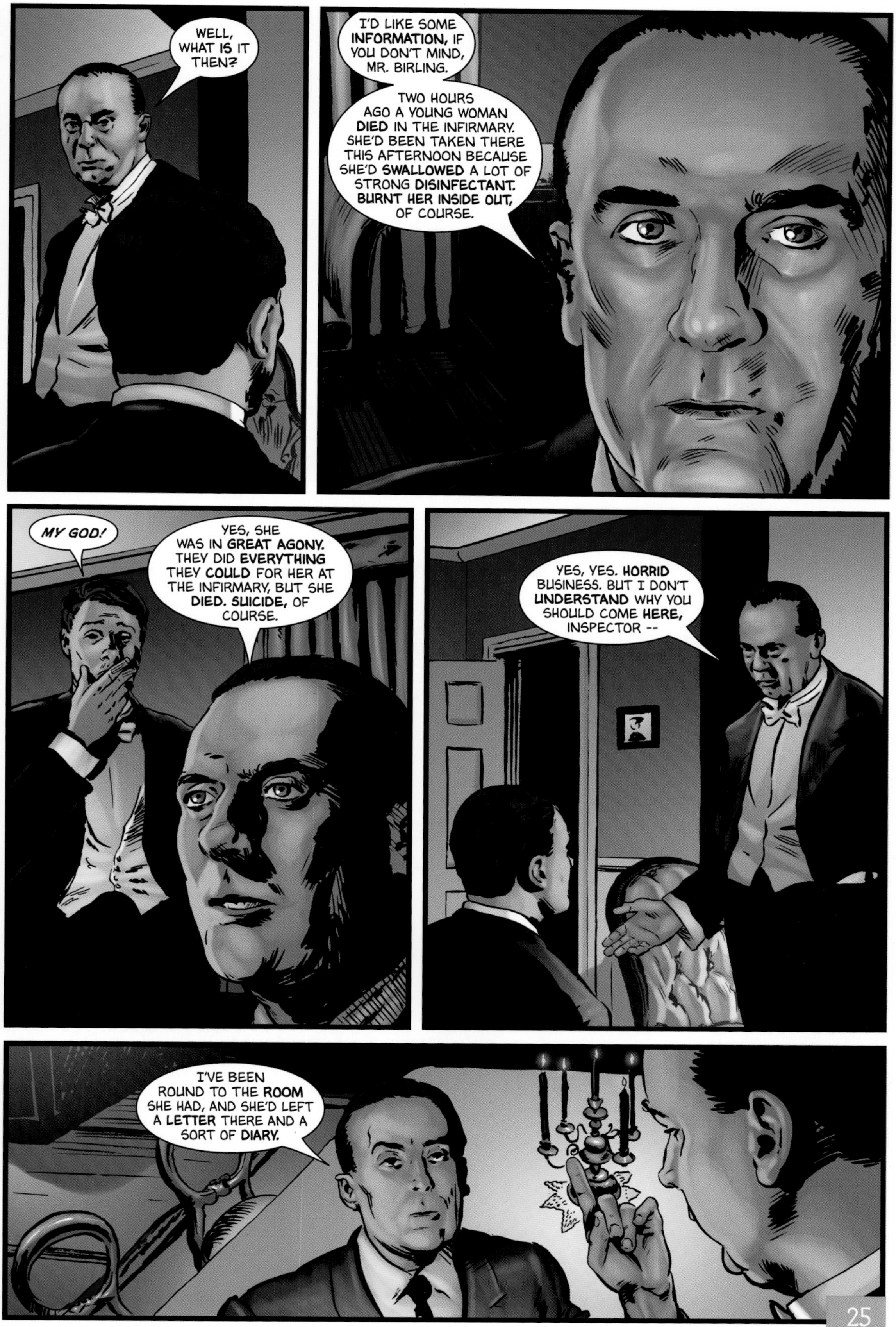
WELL, WHAT IS IT THEN?
I'D LIKE SOME INFORMATION, IF YOU DON'T MIND, MR. BIRLING.
TWO HOURS AGO A YOUNG WOMAN DIED IN THE INFIRMARY. SHE'D BEEN TAKEN THERE THIS AFTERNOON BECAUSE SHE'D SWALLOWED A LOT OF STRONG DISINFECTANT. BURNT HER INSIDE OUT, OF COURSE.
MY GOD!
YES, SHE WAS IN GREAT AGONY. THEY DID EVERYTHING THEY COULD FOR HER AT THE INFIRMARY, BUT SHE DIED. SUICIDE, OF COURSE.
YES, YES. HORRID BUSINESS. BUT I DON'T UNDERSTAND WHY YOU SHOULD COME HERE, INSPECTOR --
I'VE BEEN ROUND TO THE ROOM SHE HAD, AND SHE'D LEFT A LETTER THERE AND A SORT OF DIARY.

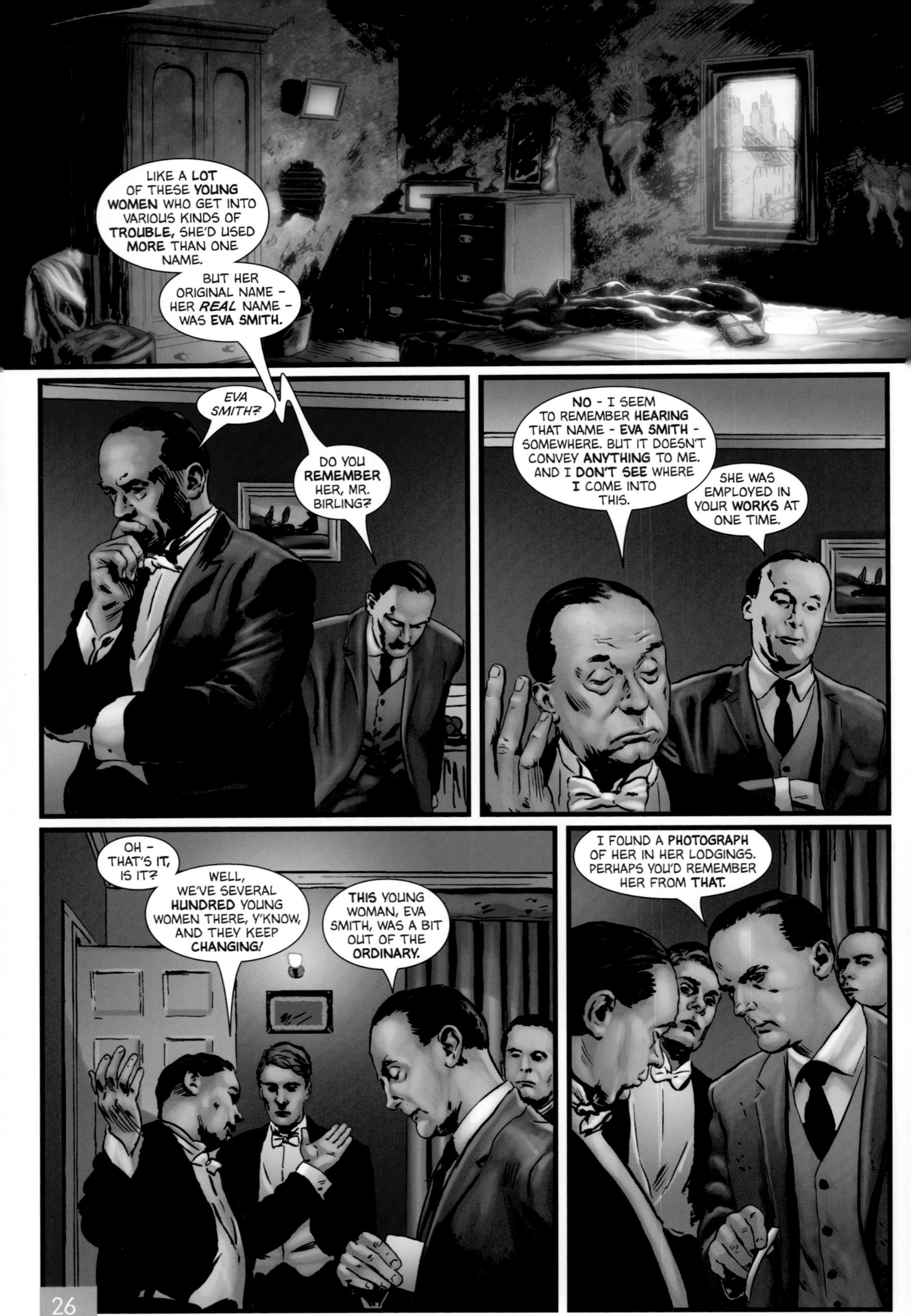
LIKE A LOT OF THESE YOUNG WOMEN WHO GET INTO VARIOUS KINDS OF TROUBLE, SHE'D USED MORE THAN ONE NAME.
BUT HER ORIGINAL NAME - HER REAL NAME - WAS EVA SMITH.
EVA SMITH?
DO YOU REMEMBER HER, MR. BIRLING?
NO - I SEEM TO REMEMBER HEARING THAT NAME - EVA SMITH - SOMEWHERE. BUT IT DOESN'T CONVEY ANYTHING TO ME. AND I DON'T SEE WHERE I COME INTO THIS.
SHE WAS EMPLOYED IN YOUR WORKS AT ONE TIME.
OH - THAT'S IT, IS IT?
WELL, WE'VE SEVERAL HUNDRED YOUNG WOMEN THERE, Y'KNOW, AND THEY KEEP CHANGING!
THIS YOUNG WOMAN, EVA SMITH, WAS A BIT OUT OF THE ORDINARY.
I FOUND A PHOTOGRAPH OF HER IN HER LODGINGS. PERHAPS YOU'D REMEMBER HER FROM THAT.

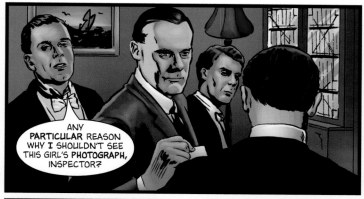

ANY PARTICULAR REASON WHY I SHOULDN'T SEE THIS GIRL'S PHOTOGRAPH, INSPECTOR?

THERE MIGHT BE.

AND THE SAME APPLIES TO ME, I SUPPOSE?

YES.

NEITHER CAN I.

I CAN'T IMAGINE WHAT IT COULD BE.

AND I MUST SAY, I AGREE WITH THEM, INSPECTOR.

IT'S THE WAY I LIKE TO GO TO WORK.

ONE PERSON AND ONE LINE OF INQUIRY AT A TIME.

OTHERWISE, THERE'S A MUDDLE.

I SEE. SENSIBLE REALLY.

27

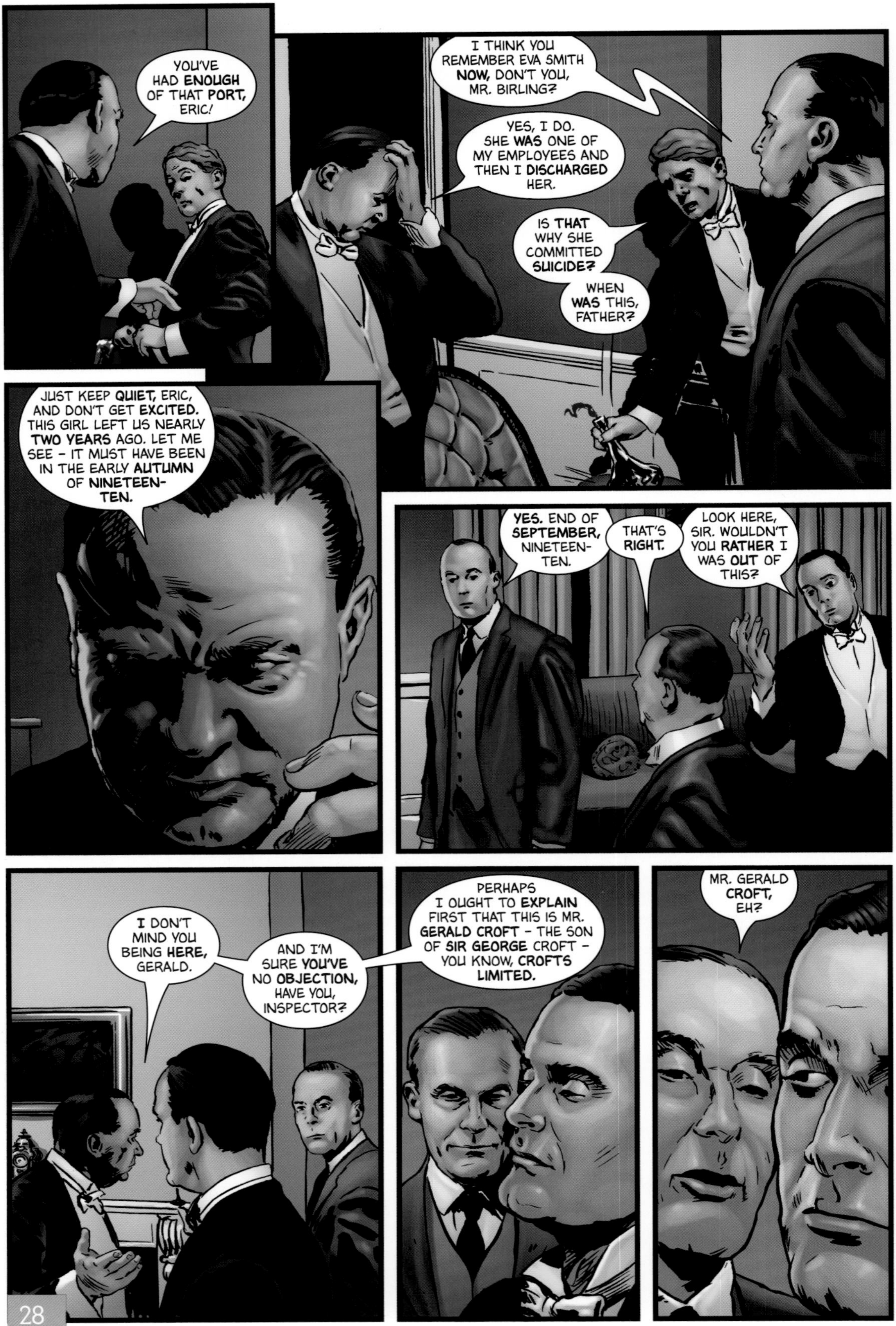
YOU'VE HAD ENOUGH OF THAT PORT, ERIC!
I THINK YOU REMEMBER EVA SMITH NOW, DON'T YOU, MR. BIRLING?
YES, I DO. SHE WAS ONE OF MY EMPLOYEES AND THEN I DISCHARGED HER.
IS THAT WHY SHE COMMITTED SUICIDE?
WHEN WAS THIS, FATHER?
JUST KEEP QUIET, ERIC, AND DON'T GET EXCITED. THIS GIRL LEFT US NEARLY TWO YEARS AGO. LET ME SEE – IT MUST HAVE BEEN IN THE EARLY AUTUMN OF NINETEEN-TEN.
YES. END OF SEPTEMBER, NINETEEN-TEN.
THAT'S RIGHT.
LOOK HERE, SIR. WOULDN'T YOU RATHER I WAS OUT OF THIS?
I DON'T MIND YOU BEING HERE, GERALD.
AND I'M SURE YOU'VE NO OBJECTION, HAVE YOU, INSPECTOR?
PERHAPS I OUGHT TO EXPLAIN FIRST THAT THIS IS MR. GERALD CROFT – THE SON OF SIR GEORGE CROFT – YOU KNOW, CROFTS LIMITED.
MR. GERALD CROFT, EH?

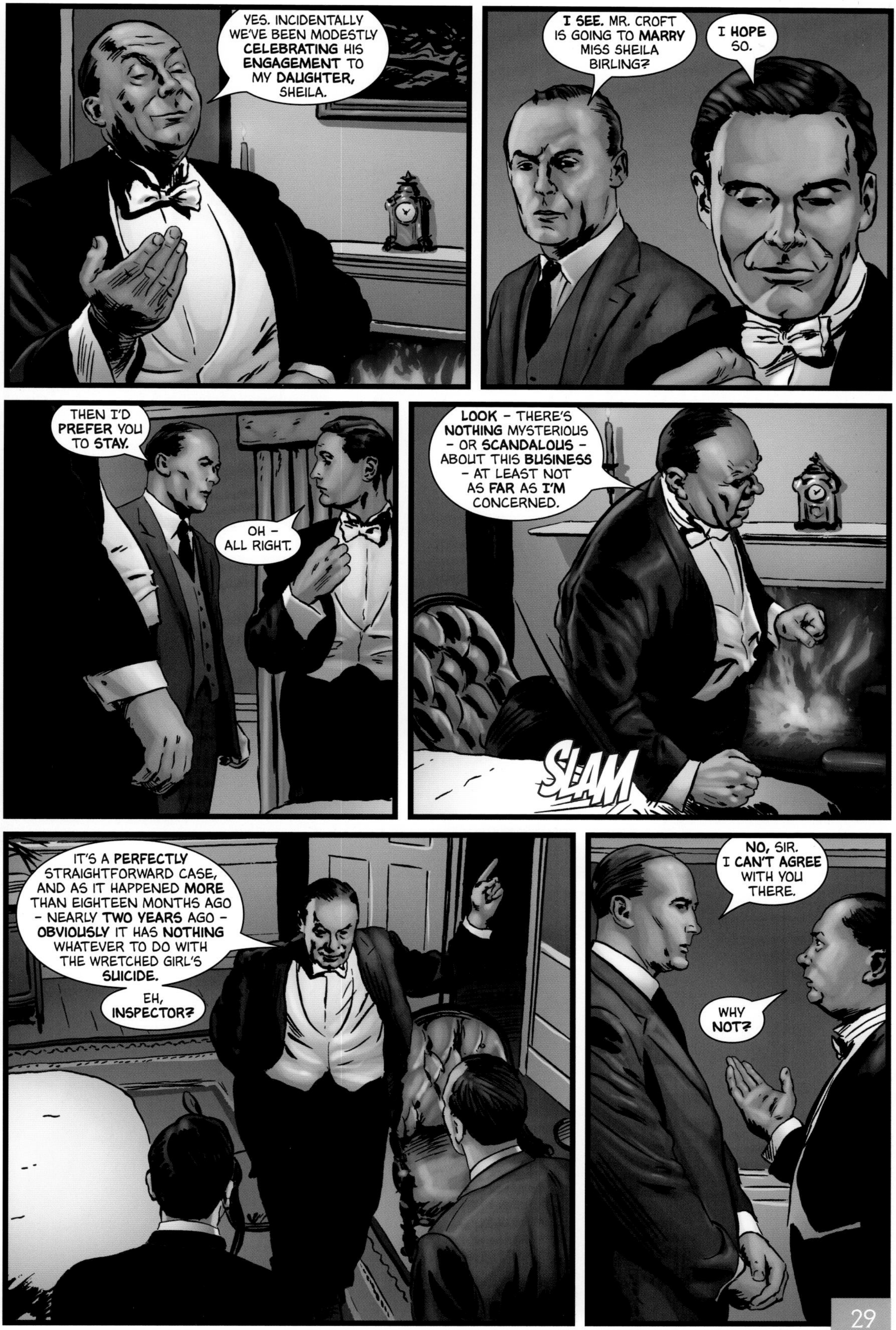
YES. INCIDENTALLY WE'VE BEEN MODESTLY CELEBRATING HIS ENGAGEMENT TO MY DAUGHTER, SHEILA.
I SEE. MR. CROFT IS GOING TO MARRY MISS SHEILA BIRLING?
I HOPE SO.
THEN I'D PREFER YOU TO STAY.
OH – ALL RIGHT.
LOOK – THERE'S NOTHING MYSTERIOUS – OR SCANDALOUS – ABOUT THIS BUSINESS – AT LEAST NOT AS FAR AS I'M CONCERNED.
SLAM
IT'S A PERFECTLY STRAIGHTFORWARD CASE, AND AS IT HAPPENED MORE THAN EIGHTEEN MONTHS AGO – NEARLY TWO YEARS AGO – OBVIOUSLY IT HAS NOTHING WHATEVER TO DO WITH THE WRETCHED GIRL'S SUICIDE.
EH, INSPECTOR?
NO, SIR. I CAN'T AGREE WITH YOU THERE.
WHY NOT?

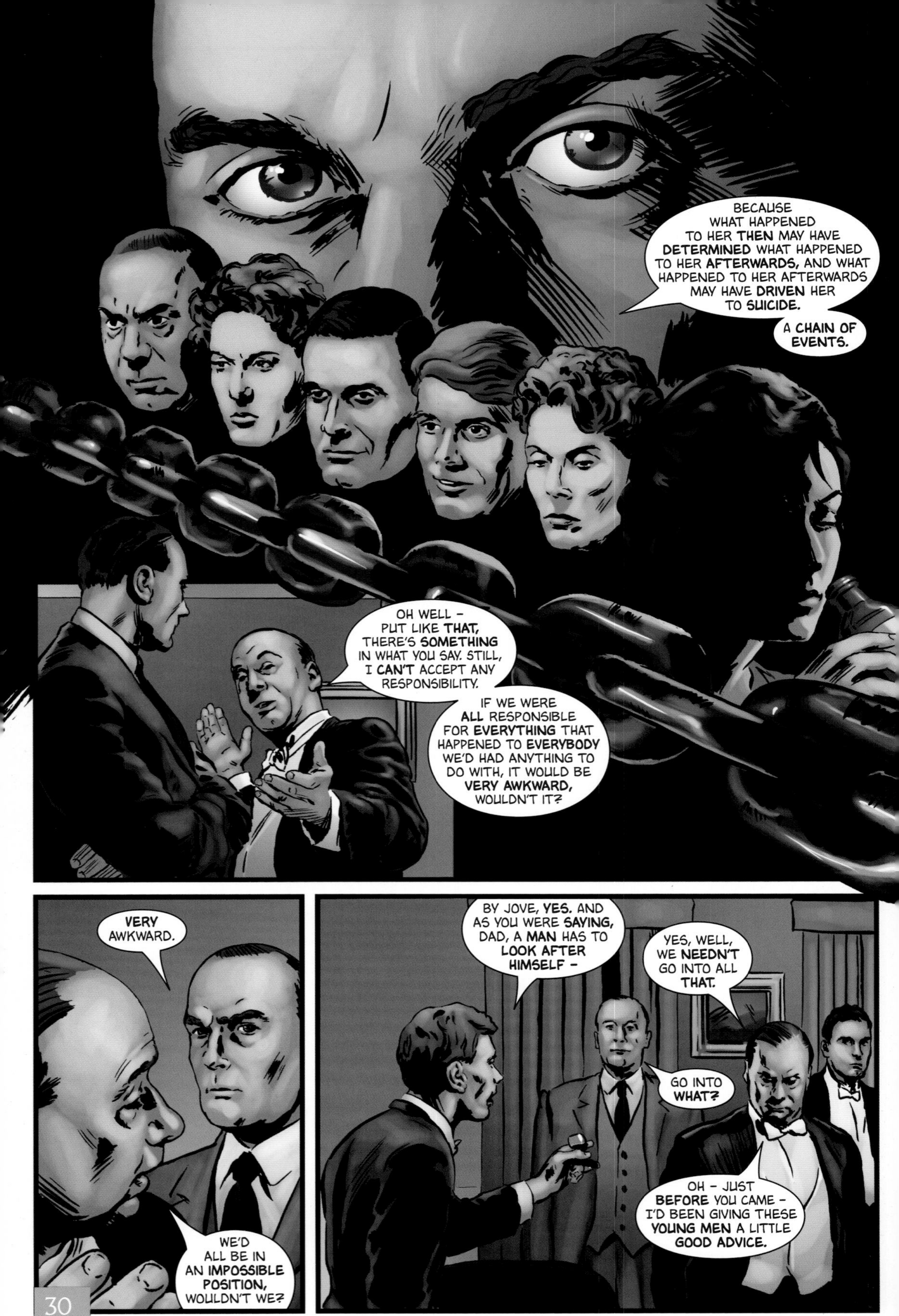
BECAUSE WHAT HAPPENED TO HER THEN MAY HAVE DETERMINED WHAT HAPPENED TO HER AFTERWARDS, AND WHAT HAPPENED TO HER AFTERWARDS MAY HAVE DRIVEN HER TO SUICIDE.
A CHAIN OF EVENTS.
OH WELL – PUT LIKE THAT, THERE'S SOMETHING IN WHAT YOU SAY. STILL, I CAN'T ACCEPT ANY RESPONSIBILITY.
IF WE WERE ALL RESPONSIBLE FOR EVERYTHING THAT HAPPENED TO EVERYBODY WE'D HAD ANYTHING TO DO WITH, IT WOULD BE VERY AWKWARD, WOULDN'T IT?
VERY AWKWARD.
WE'D ALL BE IN AN IMPOSSIBLE POSITION, WOULDN'T WE?
BY JOVE, YES. AND AS YOU WERE SAYING, DAD, A MAN HAS TO LOOK AFTER HIMSELF –
YES, WELL, WE NEEDN'T GO INTO ALL THAT.
GO INTO WHAT?
OH – JUST BEFORE YOU CAME – I'D BEEN GIVING THESE YOUNG MEN A LITTLE GOOD ADVICE.

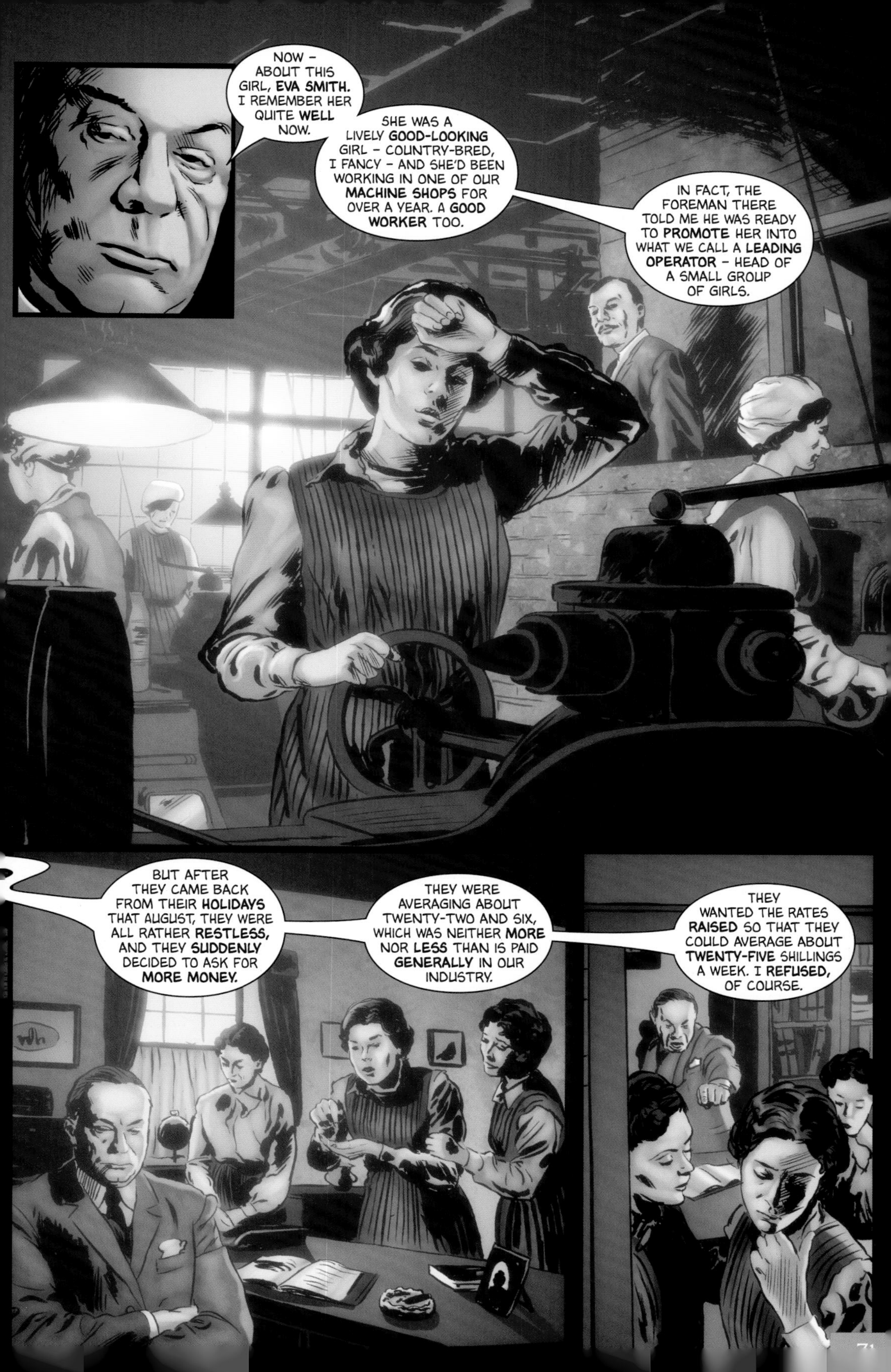
NOW – ABOUT THIS GIRL, EVA SMITH. I REMEMBER HER QUITE WELL NOW.
SHE WAS A LIVELY GOOD-LOOKING GIRL – COUNTRY-BRED, I FANCY – AND SHE'D BEEN WORKING IN ONE OF OUR MACHINE SHOPS FOR OVER A YEAR. A GOOD WORKER TOO.
IN FACT, THE FOREMAN THERE TOLD ME HE WAS READY TO PROMOTE HER INTO WHAT WE CALL A LEADING OPERATOR – HEAD OF A SMALL GROUP OF GIRLS.
BUT AFTER THEY CAME BACK FROM THEIR HOLIDAYS THAT AUGUST, THEY WERE ALL RATHER RESTLESS, AND THEY SUDDENLY DECIDED TO ASK FOR MORE MONEY.
THEY WERE AVERAGING ABOUT TWENTY-TWO AND SIX, WHICH WAS NEITHER MORE NOR LESS THAN IS PAID GENERALLY IN OUR INDUSTRY.
THEY WANTED THE RATES RAISED SO THAT THEY COULD AVERAGE ABOUT TWENTY-FIVE SHILLINGS A WEEK. I REFUSED, OF COURSE.

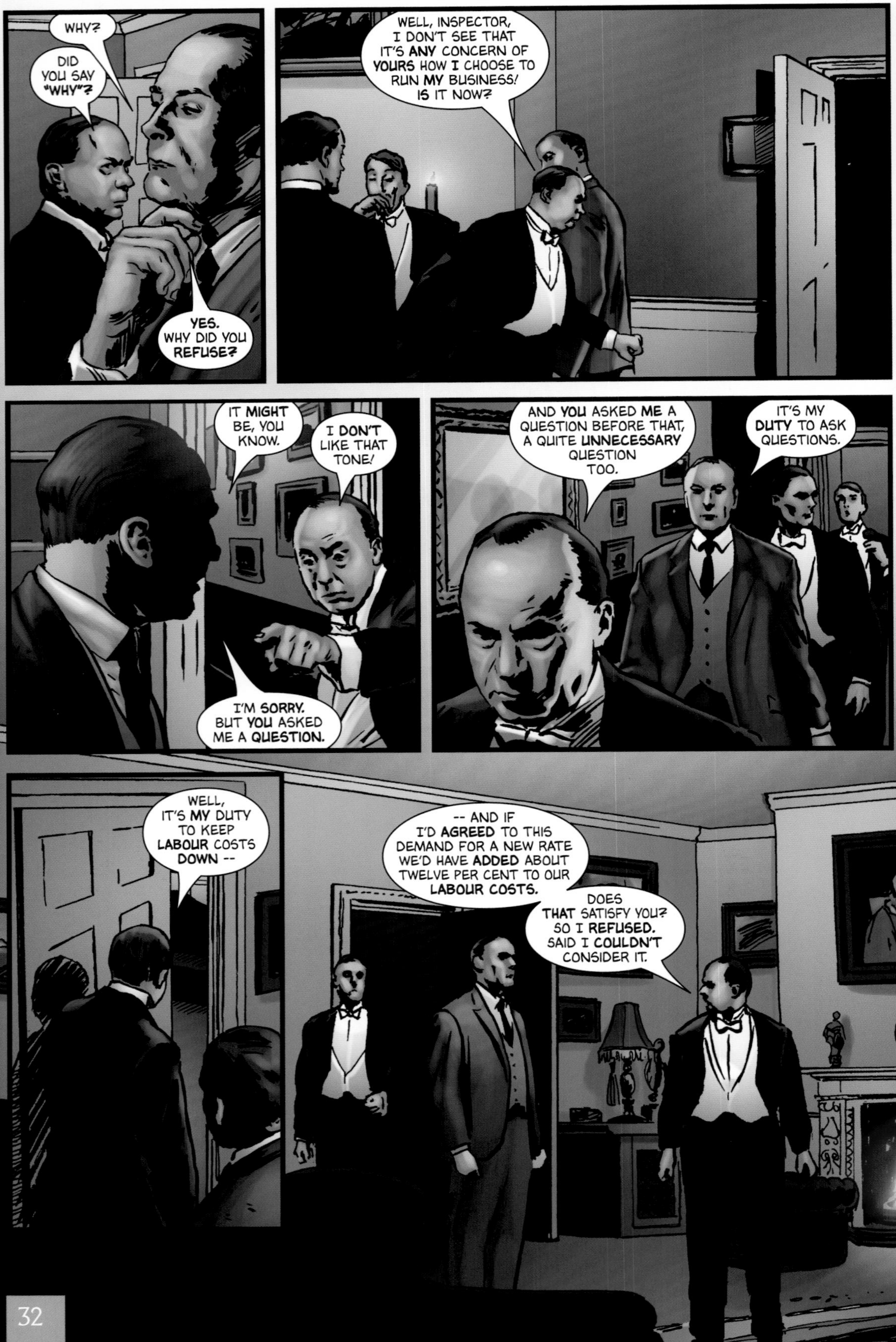
WHY?
DID YOU SAY "WHY"?
YES. WHY DID YOU REFUSE?
WELL, INSPECTOR, I DON'T SEE THAT IT'S ANY CONCERN OF YOURS HOW I CHOOSE TO RUN MY BUSINESS! IS IT NOW?
IT MIGHT BE, YOU KNOW.
I DON'T LIKE THAT TONE!
I'M SORRY. BUT YOU ASKED ME A QUESTION.
AND YOU ASKED ME A QUESTION BEFORE THAT, A QUITE UNNECESSARY QUESTION TOO.
IT'S MY DUTY TO ASK QUESTIONS.
WELL, IT'S MY DUTY TO KEEP LABOUR COSTS DOWN --
-- AND IF I'D AGREED TO THIS DEMAND FOR A NEW RATE WE'D HAVE ADDED ABOUT TWELVE PER CENT TO OUR LABOUR COSTS.
DOES THAT SATISFY YOU? SO I REFUSED. SAID I COULDN'T CONSIDER IT.

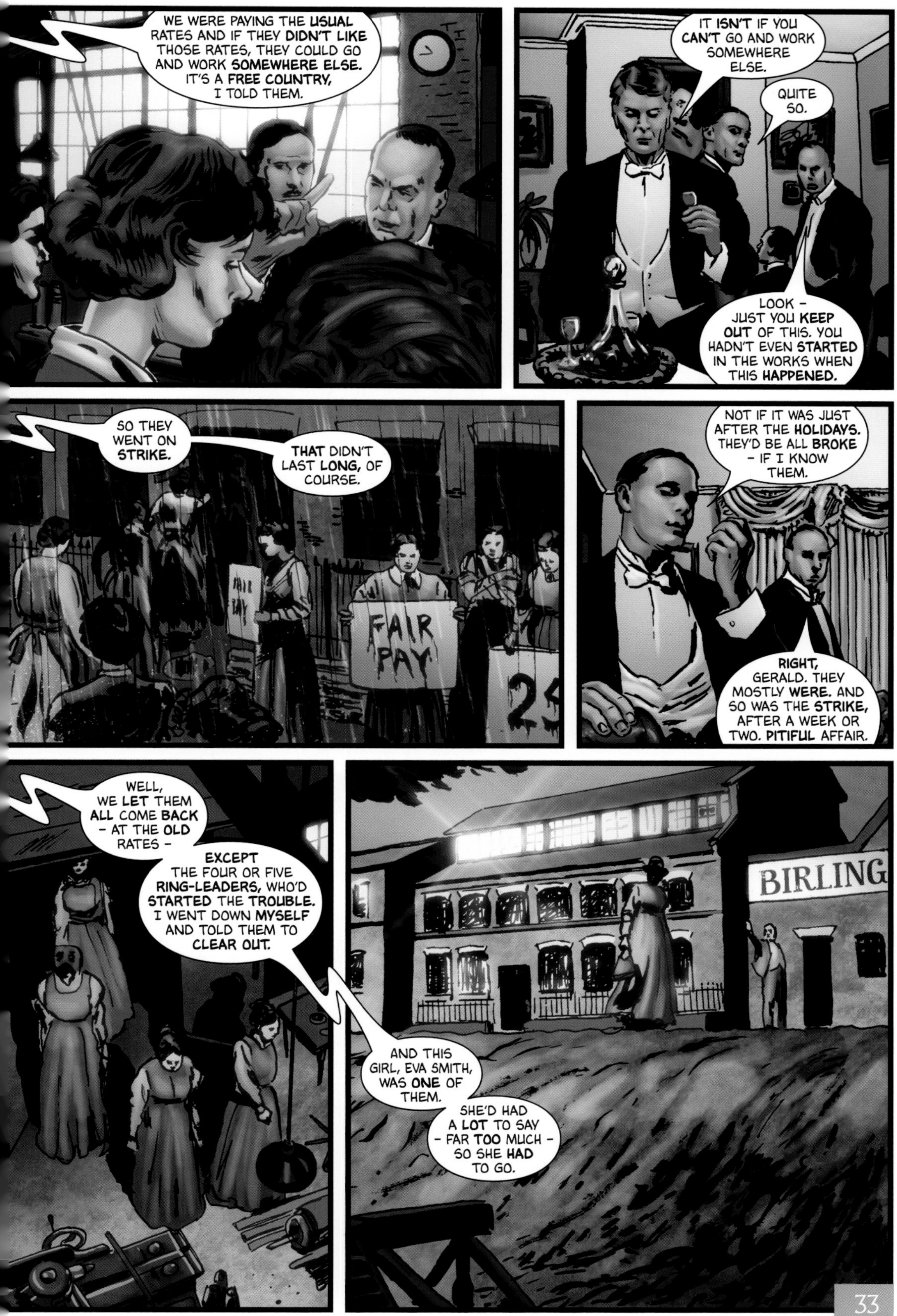
WE WERE PAYING THE USUAL RATES AND IF THEY DIDN'T LIKE THOSE RATES, THEY COULD GO AND WORK SOMEWHERE ELSE. IT'S A FREE COUNTRY, I TOLD THEM.
IT ISN'T IF YOU CAN'T GO AND WORK SOMEWHERE ELSE.
QUITE SO.
LOOK - JUST YOU KEEP OUT OF THIS. YOU HADN'T EVEN STARTED IN THE WORKS WHEN THIS HAPPENED.
SO THEY WENT ON STRIKE.
THAT DIDN'T LAST LONG, OF COURSE.
FAIR PAY
NOT IF IT WAS JUST AFTER THE HOLIDAYS. THEY'D BE ALL BROKE - IF I KNOW THEM.
RIGHT, GERALD. THEY MOSTLY WERE. AND SO WAS THE STRIKE, AFTER A WEEK OR TWO. PITIFUL AFFAIR.
WELL, WE LET THEM ALL COME BACK - AT THE OLD RATES -
EXCEPT THE FOUR OR FIVE RING-LEADERS, WHO'D STARTED THE TROUBLE. I WENT DOWN MYSELF AND TOLD THEM TO CLEAR OUT.
BIRLING
AND THIS GIRL, EVA SMITH, WAS ONE OF THEM.
SHE'D HAD A LOT TO SAY - FAR TOO MUCH - SO SHE HAD TO GO.

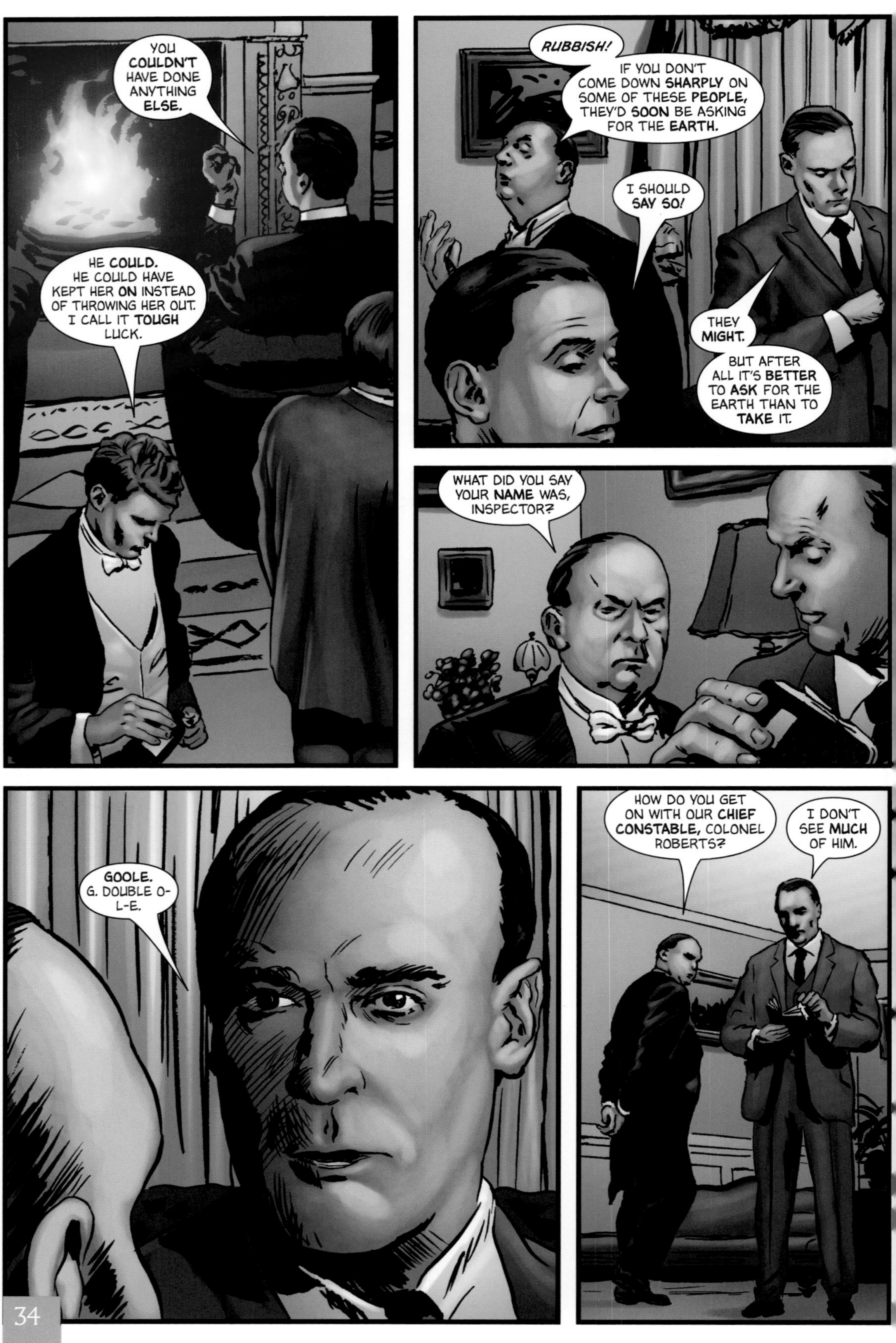
YOU COULDN'T HAVE DONE ANYTHING ELSE.
HE COULD. HE COULD HAVE KEPT HER ON INSTEAD OF THROWING HER OUT. I CALL IT TOUGH LUCK.
RUBBISH!
IF YOU DON'T COME DOWN SHARPLY ON SOME OF THESE PEOPLE, THEY'D SOON BE ASKING FOR THE EARTH.
I SHOULD SAY SO!
THEY MIGHT.
BUT AFTER ALL IT'S BETTER TO ASK FOR THE EARTH THAN TO TAKE IT.
WHAT DID YOU SAY YOUR NAME WAS, INSPECTOR?
GOOLE. G. DOUBLE O-L-E.
HOW DO YOU GET ON WITH OUR CHIEF CONSTABLE, COLONEL ROBERTS?
I DON'T SEE MUCH OF HIM.

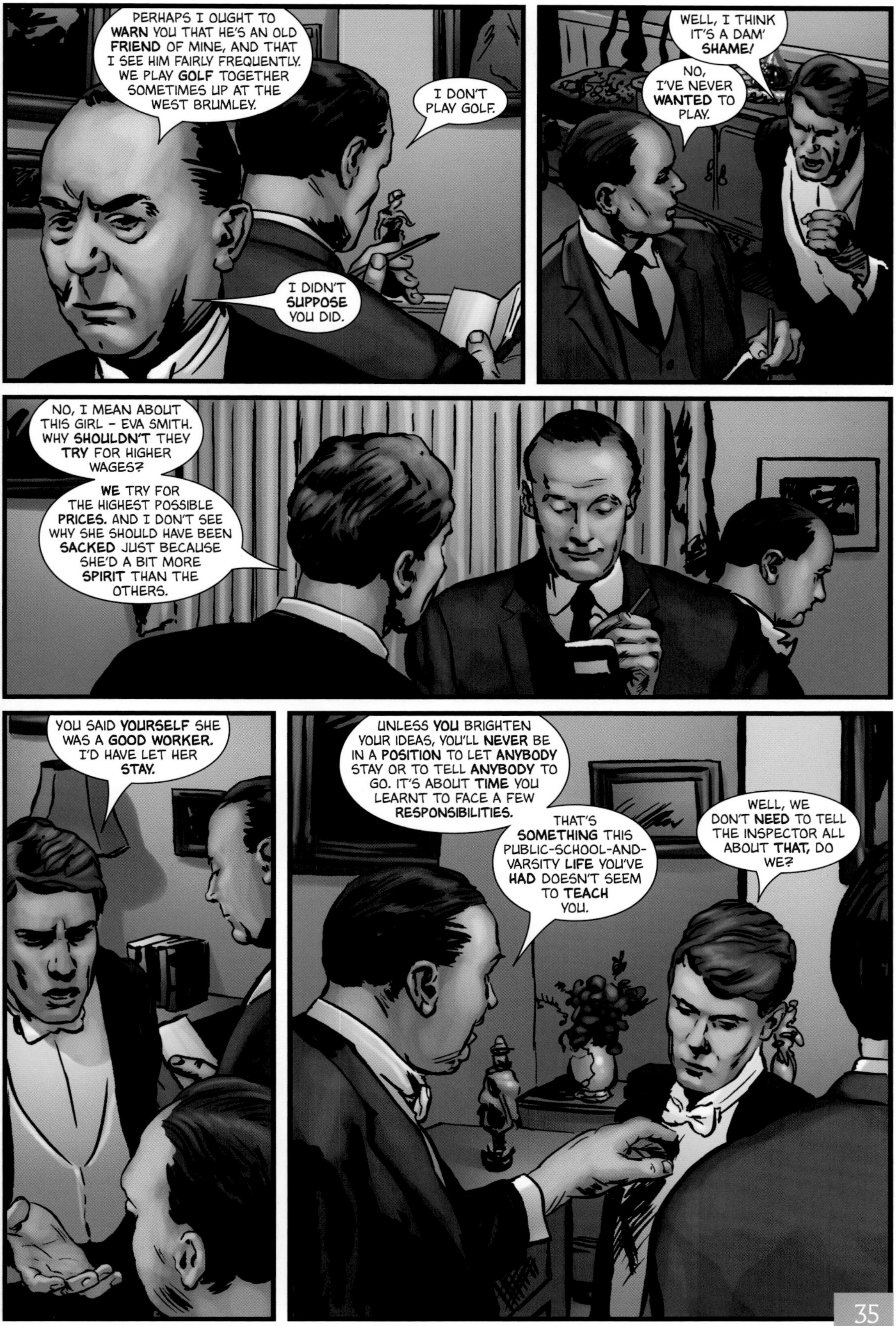
PERHAPS I OUGHT TO WARN YOU THAT HE'S AN OLD FRIEND OF MINE, AND THAT I SEE HIM FAIRLY FREQUENTLY. WE PLAY GOLF TOGETHER SOMETIMES UP AT THE WEST BRUMLEY.
I DON'T PLAY GOLF.
I DIDN'T SUPPOSE YOU DID.
WELL, I THINK IT'S A DAM' SHAME!
NO, I'VE NEVER WANTED TO PLAY.
NO, I MEAN ABOUT THIS GIRL – EVA SMITH. WHY SHOULDN'T THEY TRY FOR HIGHER WAGES?
WE TRY FOR THE HIGHEST POSSIBLE PRICES. AND I DON'T SEE WHY SHE SHOULD HAVE BEEN SACKED JUST BECAUSE SHE'D A BIT MORE SPIRIT THAN THE OTHERS.
YOU SAID YOURSELF SHE WAS A GOOD WORKER. I'D HAVE LET HER STAY.
UNLESS YOU BRIGHTEN YOUR IDEAS, YOU'LL NEVER BE IN A POSITION TO LET ANYBODY STAY OR TO TELL ANYBODY TO GO. IT'S ABOUT TIME YOU LEARNT TO FACE A FEW RESPONSIBILITIES.
THAT'S SOMETHING THIS PUBLIC-SCHOOL-AND-VARSITY LIFE YOU'VE HAD DOESN'T SEEM TO TEACH YOU.
WELL, WE DON'T NEED TO TELL THE INSPECTOR ALL ABOUT THAT, DO WE?

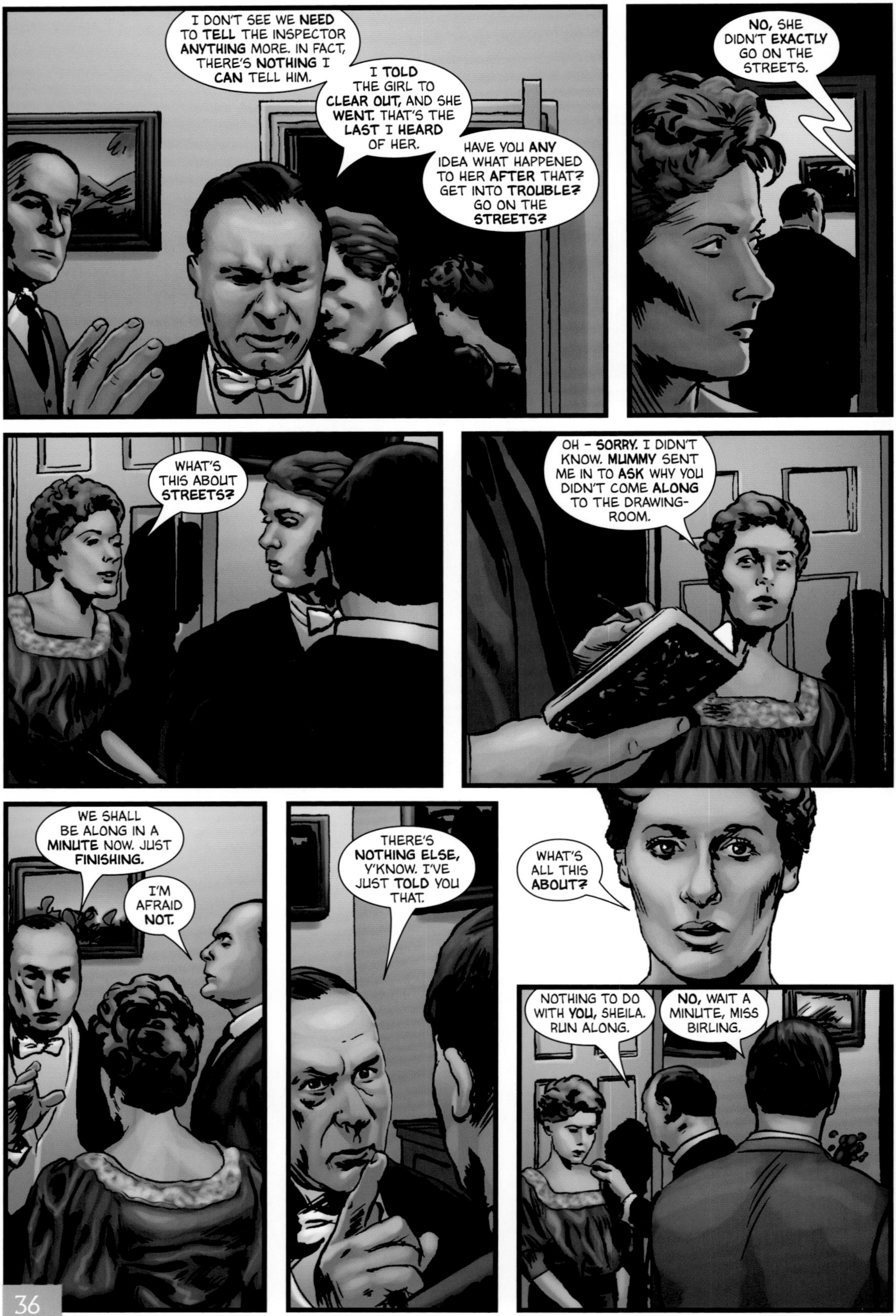

I DON'T SEE WE NEED TO TELL THE INSPECTOR ANYTHING MORE. IN FACT, THERE'S NOTHING I CAN TELL HIM.
I TOLD THE GIRL TO CLEAR OUT, AND SHE WENT. THAT'S THE LAST I HEARD OF HER.
HAVE YOU ANY IDEA WHAT HAPPENED TO HER AFTER THAT? GET INTO TROUBLE? GO ON THE STREETS?
NO, SHE DIDN'T EXACTLY GO ON THE STREETS.
WHAT'S THIS ABOUT STREETS?
OH – SORRY. I DIDN'T KNOW. MUMMY SENT ME IN TO ASK WHY YOU DIDN'T COME ALONG TO THE DRAWING-ROOM.
WE SHALL BE ALONG IN A MINUTE NOW. JUST FINISHING.
I'M AFRAID NOT.
THERE'S NOTHING ELSE, Y'KNOW. I'VE JUST TOLD YOU THAT.
WHAT'S ALL THIS ABOUT?
NOTHING TO DO WITH YOU, SHEILA. RUN ALONG.
NO, WAIT A MINUTE, MISS BIRLING.

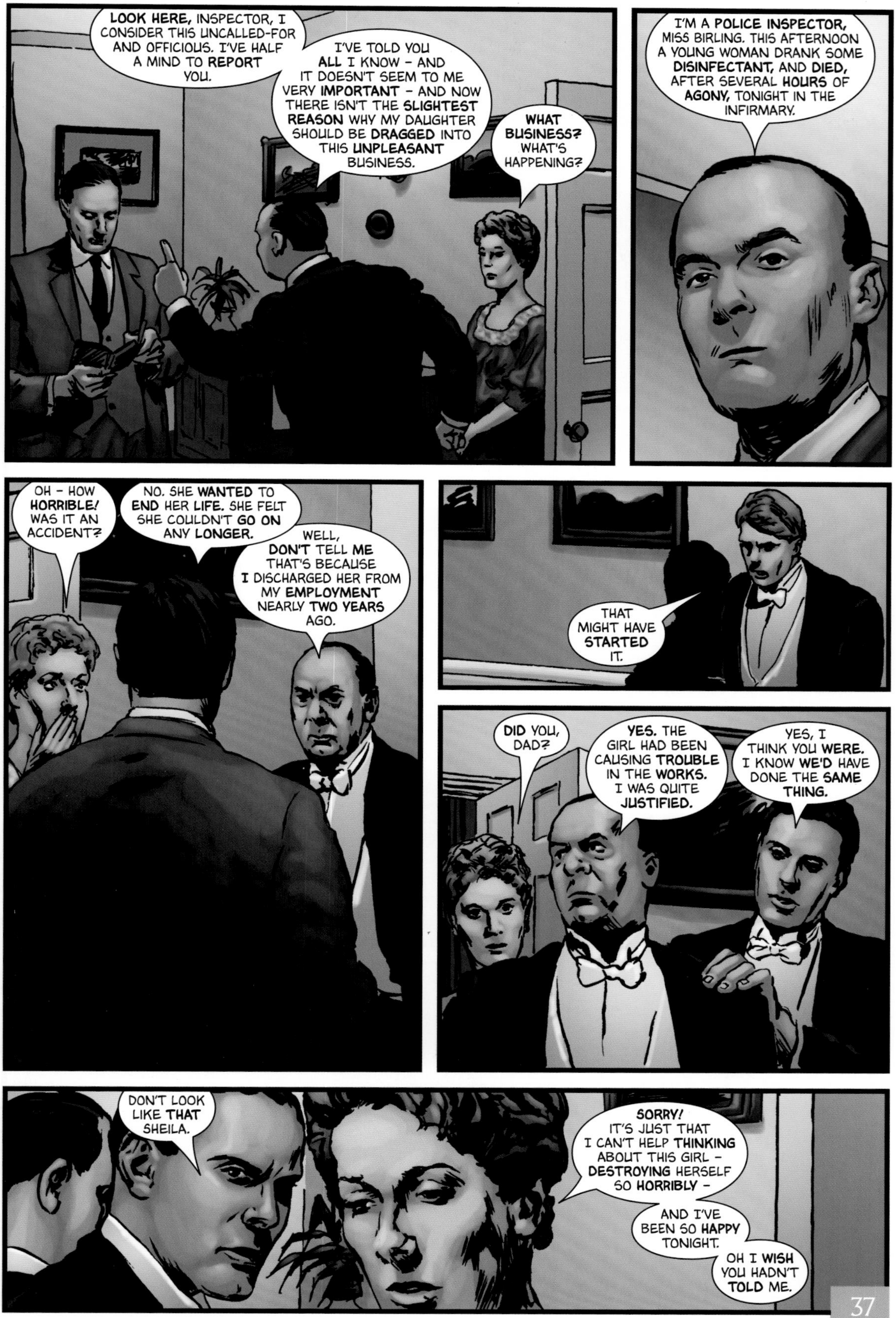
LOOK HERE, INSPECTOR, I CONSIDER THIS UNCALLED-FOR AND OFFICIOUS. I'VE HALF A MIND TO REPORT YOU.
I'VE TOLD YOU ALL I KNOW – AND IT DOESN'T SEEM TO ME VERY IMPORTANT – AND NOW THERE ISN'T THE SLIGHTEST REASON WHY MY DAUGHTER SHOULD BE DRAGGED INTO THIS UNPLEASANT BUSINESS.
WHAT BUSINESS? WHAT'S HAPPENING?
I'M A POLICE INSPECTOR, MISS BIRLING. THIS AFTERNOON A YOUNG WOMAN DRANK SOME DISINFECTANT, AND DIED, AFTER SEVERAL HOURS OF AGONY, TONIGHT IN THE INFIRMARY.
OH – HOW HORRIBLE! WAS IT AN ACCIDENT?
NO. SHE WANTED TO END HER LIFE. SHE FELT SHE COULDN'T GO ON ANY LONGER.
WELL, DON'T TELL ME THAT'S BECAUSE I DISCHARGED HER FROM MY EMPLOYMENT NEARLY TWO YEARS AGO.
THAT MIGHT HAVE STARTED IT.
DID YOU, DAD?
YES. THE GIRL HAD BEEN CAUSING TROUBLE IN THE WORKS. I WAS QUITE JUSTIFIED.
YES, I THINK YOU WERE. I KNOW WE'D HAVE DONE THE SAME THING.
DON'T LOOK LIKE THAT SHEILA.
SORRY! IT'S JUST THAT I CAN'T HELP THINKING ABOUT THIS GIRL – DESTROYING HERSELF SO HORRIBLY –
AND I'VE BEEN SO HAPPY TONIGHT.
OH I WISH YOU HADN'T TOLD ME.

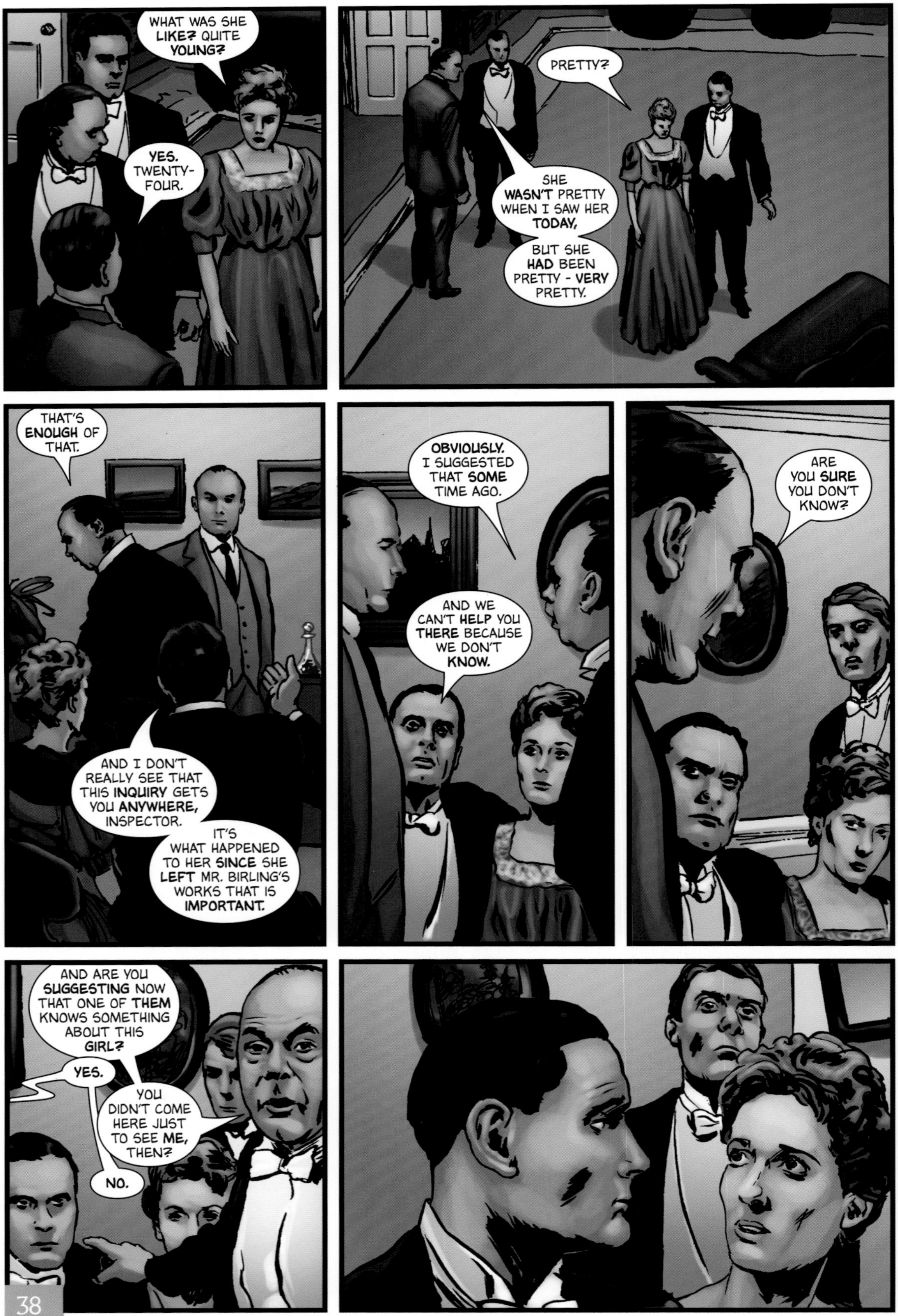
WHAT WAS SHE LIKE? QUITE YOUNG?
YES. TWENTY-FOUR.
PRETTY?
SHE WASN'T PRETTY WHEN I SAW HER TODAY,
BUT SHE HAD BEEN PRETTY - VERY PRETTY.
THAT'S ENOUGH OF THAT.
AND I DON'T REALLY SEE THAT THIS INQUIRY GETS YOU ANYWHERE, INSPECTOR.
IT'S WHAT HAPPENED TO HER SINCE SHE LEFT MR. BIRLING'S WORKS THAT IS IMPORTANT.
OBVIOUSLY. I SUGGESTED THAT SOME TIME AGO.
AND WE CAN'T HELP YOU THERE BECAUSE WE DON'T KNOW.
ARE YOU SURE YOU DON'T KNOW?
AND ARE YOU SUGGESTING NOW THAT ONE OF THEM KNOWS SOMETHING ABOUT THIS GIRL?
YES.
YOU DIDN'T COME HERE JUST TO SEE ME, THEN?
NO.

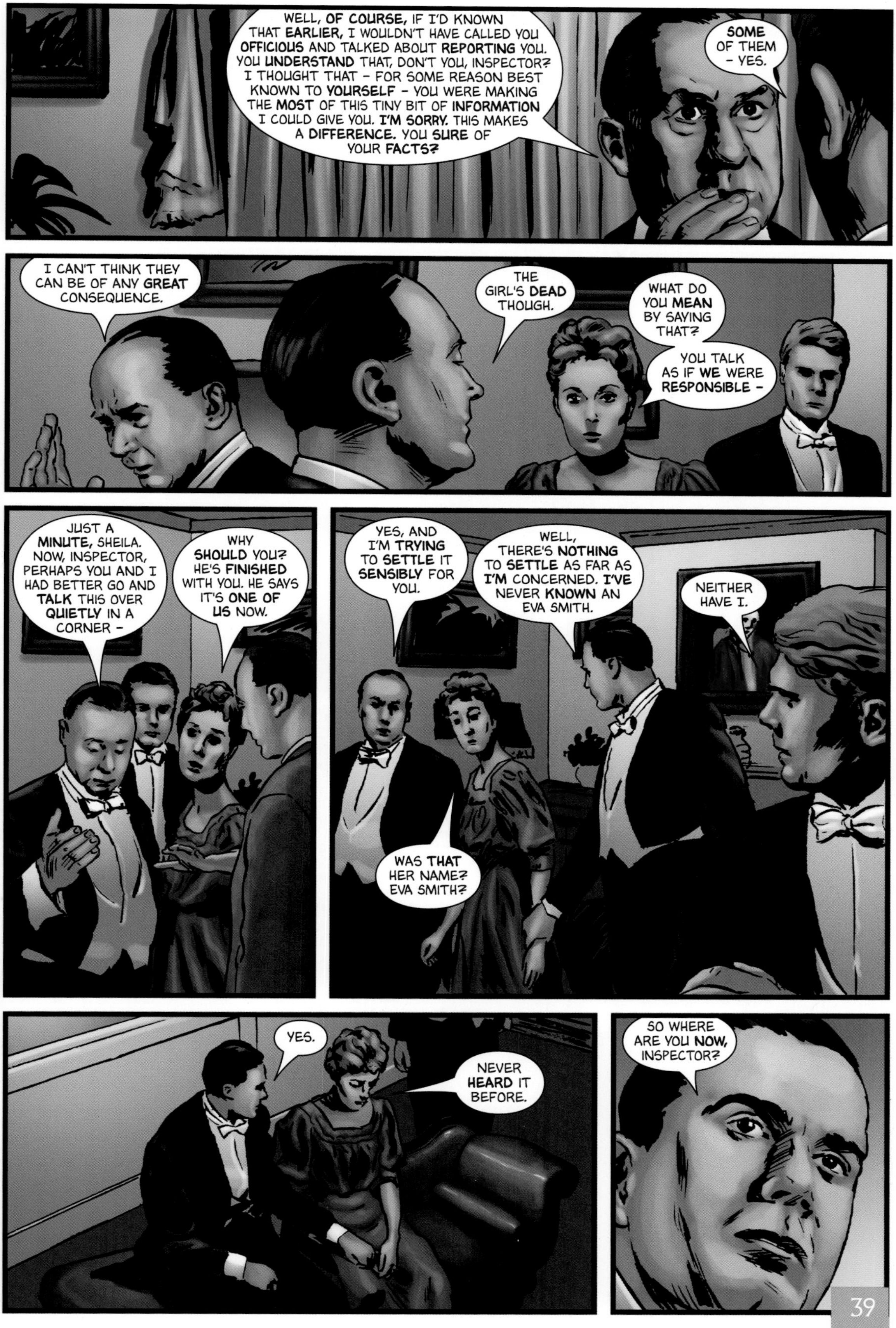
WELL, OF COURSE, IF I'D KNOWN THAT EARLIER, I WOULDN'T HAVE CALLED YOU OFFICIOUS AND TALKED ABOUT REPORTING YOU. YOU UNDERSTAND THAT, DON'T YOU, INSPECTOR? I THOUGHT THAT – FOR SOME REASON BEST KNOWN TO YOURSELF – YOU WERE MAKING THE MOST OF THIS TINY BIT OF INFORMATION I COULD GIVE YOU. I'M SORRY. THIS MAKES A DIFFERENCE. YOU SURE OF YOUR FACTS?
SOME OF THEM – YES.
I CAN'T THINK THEY CAN BE OF ANY GREAT CONSEQUENCE.
THE GIRL'S DEAD THOUGH.
WHAT DO YOU MEAN BY SAYING THAT?
YOU TALK AS IF WE WERE RESPONSIBLE –
JUST A MINUTE, SHEILA. NOW, INSPECTOR, PERHAPS YOU AND I HAD BETTER GO AND TALK THIS OVER QUIETLY IN A CORNER –
WHY SHOULD YOU? HE'S FINISHED WITH YOU. HE SAYS IT'S ONE OF US NOW.
YES, AND I'M TRYING TO SETTLE IT SENSIBLY FOR YOU.
WELL, THERE'S NOTHING TO SETTLE AS FAR AS I'M CONCERNED. I'VE NEVER KNOWN AN EVA SMITH.
NEITHER HAVE I.
WAS THAT HER NAME? EVA SMITH?
YES.
NEVER HEARD IT BEFORE.
SO WHERE ARE YOU NOW, INSPECTOR?

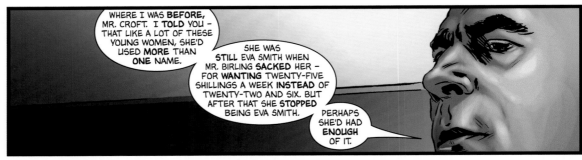

WHERE I WAS **BEFORE**, MR. CROFT. I **TOLD** YOU – THAT LIKE A LOT OF THESE YOUNG WOMEN, SHE'D USED **MORE** THAN ONE NAME.

SHE WAS **STILL** EVA SMITH WHEN MR. BIRLING **SACKED** HER – FOR **WANTING** TWENTY-FIVE SHILLINGS A WEEK **INSTEAD** OF TWENTY-TWO AND SIX. BUT AFTER THAT SHE **STOPPED** BEING EVA SMITH.

PERHAPS SHE'D HAD **ENOUGH** OF IT.

CAN'T **BLAME** HER.

I THINK IT WAS A **MEAN** THING TO DO. PERHAPS THAT SPOILT **EVERYTHING** FOR HER.

RUBBISH!

DO YOU KNOW WHAT **HAPPENED** TO THIS GIRL **AFTER** SHE LEFT MY WORKS?

YES. SHE WAS **OUT** OF WORK FOR THE NEXT **TWO** MONTHS.

BOTH HER **PARENTS** WERE **DEAD**, SO THAT SHE'D NO **HOME** TO GO **BACK** TO. AND SHE HADN'T BEEN ABLE TO **SAVE** MUCH OUT OF WHAT BIRLING AND COMPANY HAD **PAID** HER.

SO THAT AFTER TWO MONTHS, WITH NO **WORK**, NO **MONEY** COMING IN, AND LIVING IN **LODGINGS**, WITH NO RELATIVES TO **HELP** HER, FEW FRIENDS, **LONELY**, HALF-STARVED, SHE WAS FEELING **DESPERATE**.

I SHOULD **THINK** SO. IT'S A ROTTEN **SHAME**.

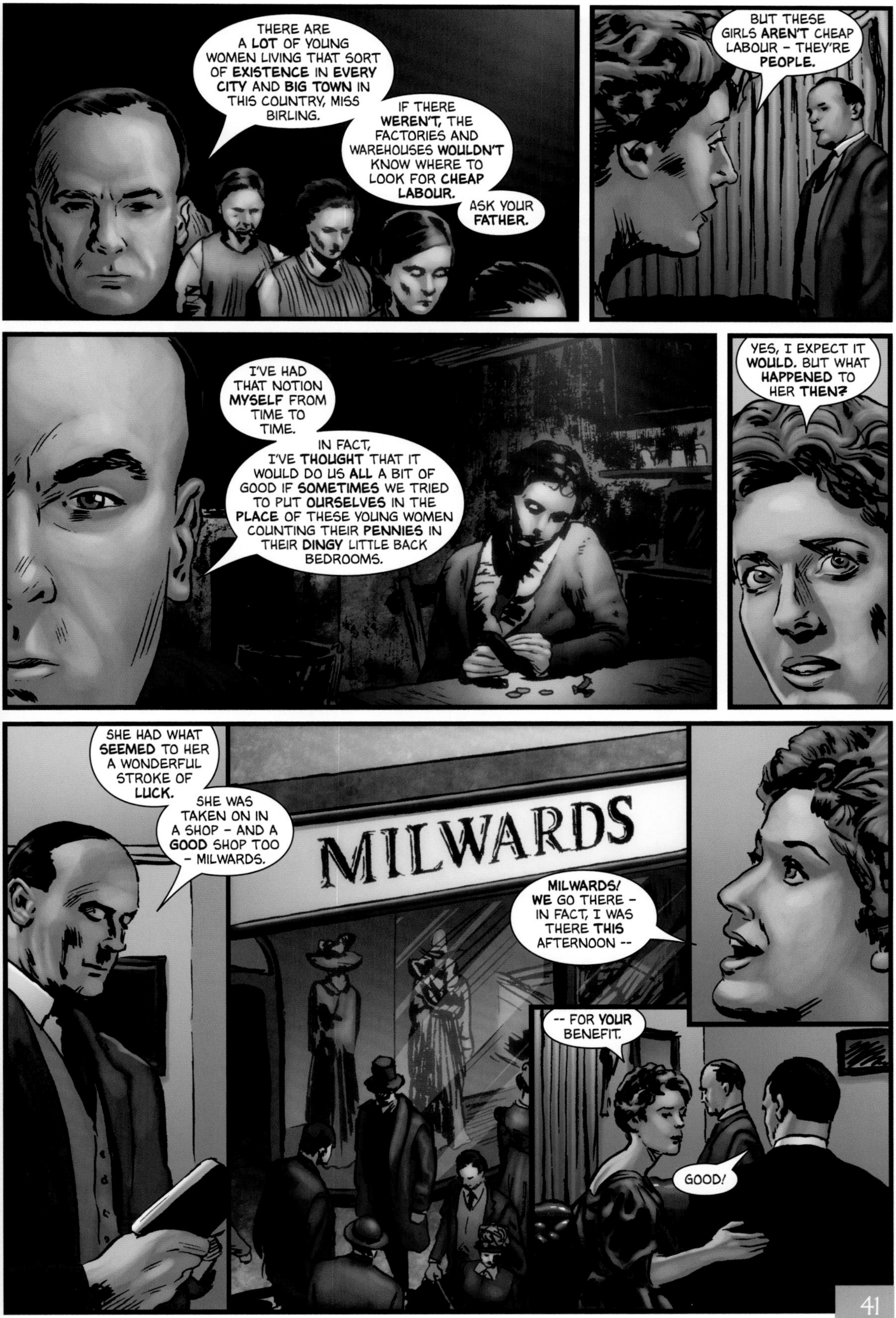
THERE ARE A LOT OF YOUNG WOMEN LIVING THAT SORT OF EXISTENCE IN EVERY CITY AND BIG TOWN IN THIS COUNTRY, MISS BIRLING.
IF THERE WEREN'T, THE FACTORIES AND WAREHOUSES WOULDN'T KNOW WHERE TO LOOK FOR CHEAP LABOUR.
ASK YOUR FATHER.
BUT THESE GIRLS AREN'T CHEAP LABOUR – THEY'RE PEOPLE.
I'VE HAD THAT NOTION MYSELF FROM TIME TO TIME.
IN FACT, I'VE THOUGHT THAT IT WOULD DO US ALL A BIT OF GOOD IF SOMETIMES WE TRIED TO PUT OURSELVES IN THE PLACE OF THESE YOUNG WOMEN COUNTING THEIR PENNIES IN THEIR DINGY LITTLE BACK BEDROOMS.
YES, I EXPECT IT WOULD. BUT WHAT HAPPENED TO HER THEN?
SHE HAD WHAT SEEMED TO HER A WONDERFUL STROKE OF LUCK.
SHE WAS TAKEN ON IN A SHOP – AND A GOOD SHOP TOO – MILWARDS.
MILWARDS
MILWARDS! WE GO THERE – IN FACT, I WAS THERE THIS AFTERNOON --
-- FOR YOUR BENEFIT.
GOOD!

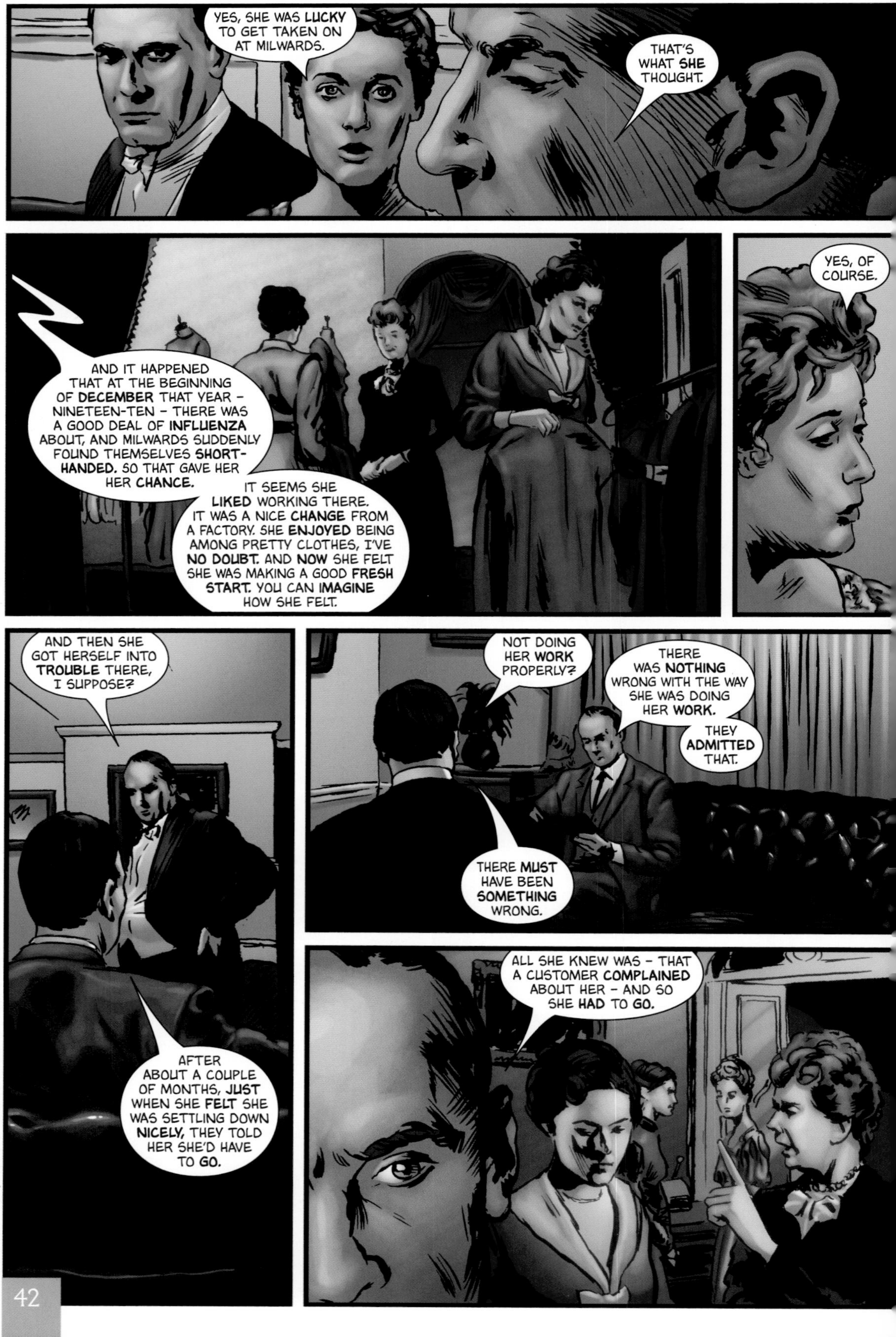
YES, SHE WAS LUCKY TO GET TAKEN ON AT MILWARDS.
THAT'S WHAT SHE THOUGHT.
AND IT HAPPENED THAT AT THE BEGINNING OF DECEMBER THAT YEAR – NINETEEN-TEN – THERE WAS A GOOD DEAL OF INFLUENZA ABOUT, AND MILWARDS SUDDENLY FOUND THEMSELVES SHORT-HANDED. SO THAT GAVE HER HER CHANCE.
IT SEEMS SHE LIKED WORKING THERE. IT WAS A NICE CHANGE FROM A FACTORY. SHE ENJOYED BEING AMONG PRETTY CLOTHES, I'VE NO DOUBT. AND NOW SHE FELT SHE WAS MAKING A GOOD FRESH START. YOU CAN IMAGINE HOW SHE FELT.
YES, OF COURSE.
AND THEN SHE GOT HERSELF INTO TROUBLE THERE, I SUPPOSE?
AFTER ABOUT A COUPLE OF MONTHS, JUST WHEN SHE FELT SHE WAS SETTLING DOWN NICELY, THEY TOLD HER SHE'D HAVE TO GO.
NOT DOING HER WORK PROPERLY?
THERE WAS NOTHING WRONG WITH THE WAY SHE WAS DOING HER WORK.
THEY ADMITTED THAT.
THERE MUST HAVE BEEN SOMETHING WRONG.
ALL SHE KNEW WAS – THAT A CUSTOMER COMPLAINED ABOUT HER – AND SO SHE HAD TO GO.

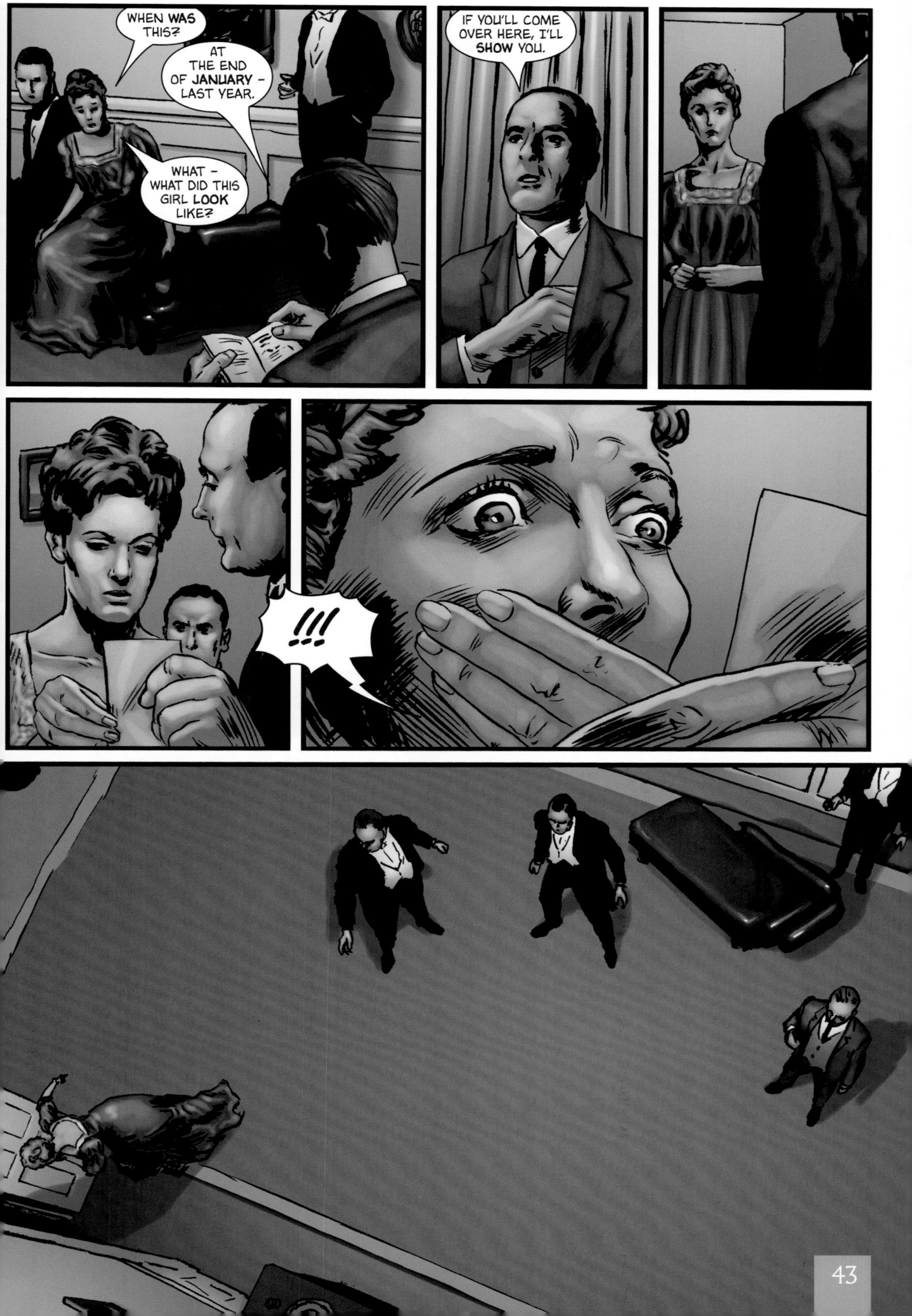
WHEN WAS THIS?
AT THE END OF JANUARY - LAST YEAR.
WHAT - WHAT DID THIS GIRL LOOK LIKE?
IF YOU'LL COME OVER HERE, I'LL SHOW YOU.
!!!

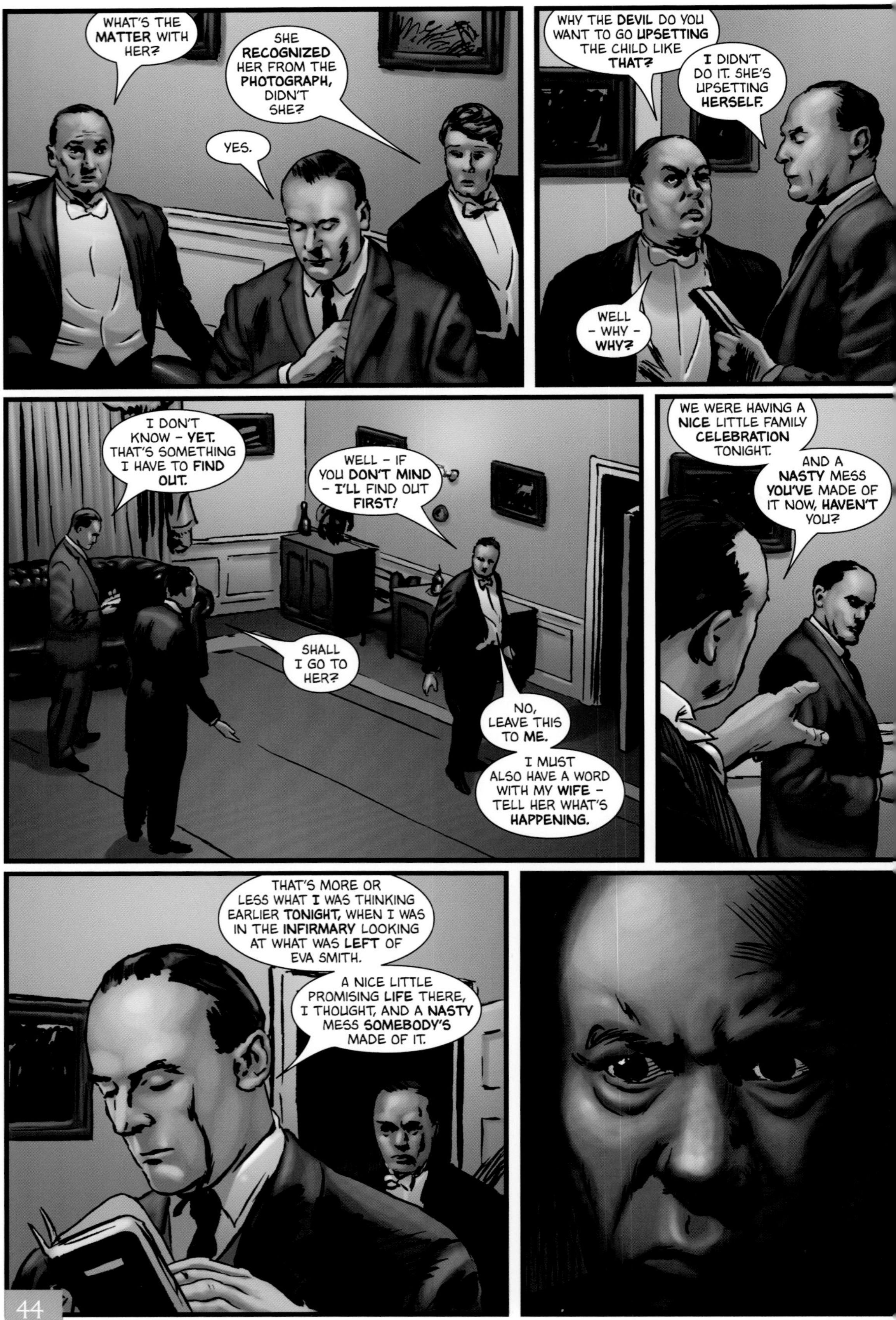
WHAT'S THE MATTER WITH HER?
SHE RECOGNIZED HER FROM THE PHOTOGRAPH, DIDN'T SHE?
YES.
WHY THE DEVIL DO YOU WANT TO GO UPSETTING THE CHILD LIKE THAT?
I DIDN'T DO IT. SHE'S UPSETTING HERSELF.
WELL - WHY - WHY?
I DON'T KNOW - YET. THAT'S SOMETHING I HAVE TO FIND OUT.
WELL - IF YOU DON'T MIND - I'LL FIND OUT FIRST!
SHALL I GO TO HER?
NO, LEAVE THIS TO ME.
I MUST ALSO HAVE A WORD WITH MY WIFE - TELL HER WHAT'S HAPPENING.
WE WERE HAVING A NICE LITTLE FAMILY CELEBRATION TONIGHT.
AND A NASTY MESS YOU'VE MADE OF IT NOW, HAVEN'T YOU?
THAT'S MORE OR LESS WHAT I WAS THINKING EARLIER TONIGHT, WHEN I WAS IN THE INFIRMARY LOOKING AT WHAT WAS LEFT OF EVA SMITH.
A NICE LITTLE PROMISING LIFE THERE, I THOUGHT, AND A NASTY MESS SOMEBODY'S MADE OF IT.

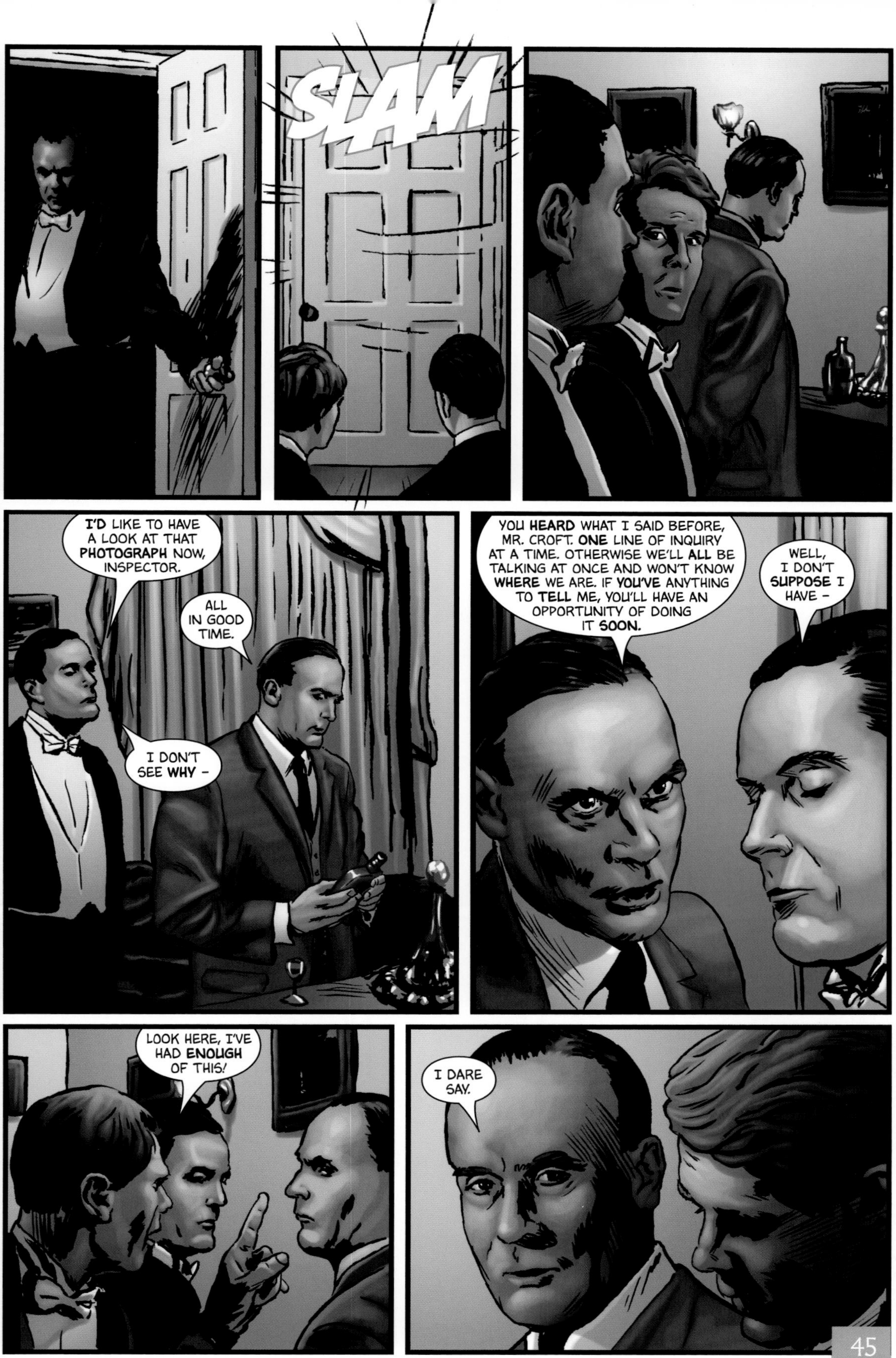
SLAM
I'D LIKE TO HAVE A LOOK AT THAT PHOTOGRAPH NOW, INSPECTOR.
ALL IN GOOD TIME.
I DON'T SEE WHY –
YOU HEARD WHAT I SAID BEFORE, MR. CROFT. ONE LINE OF INQUIRY AT A TIME. OTHERWISE WE'LL ALL BE TALKING AT ONCE AND WON'T KNOW WHERE WE ARE. IF YOU'VE ANYTHING TO TELL ME, YOU'LL HAVE AN OPPORTUNITY OF DOING IT SOON.
WELL, I DON'T SUPPOSE I HAVE –
LOOK HERE, I'VE HAD ENOUGH OF THIS!
I DARE SAY.

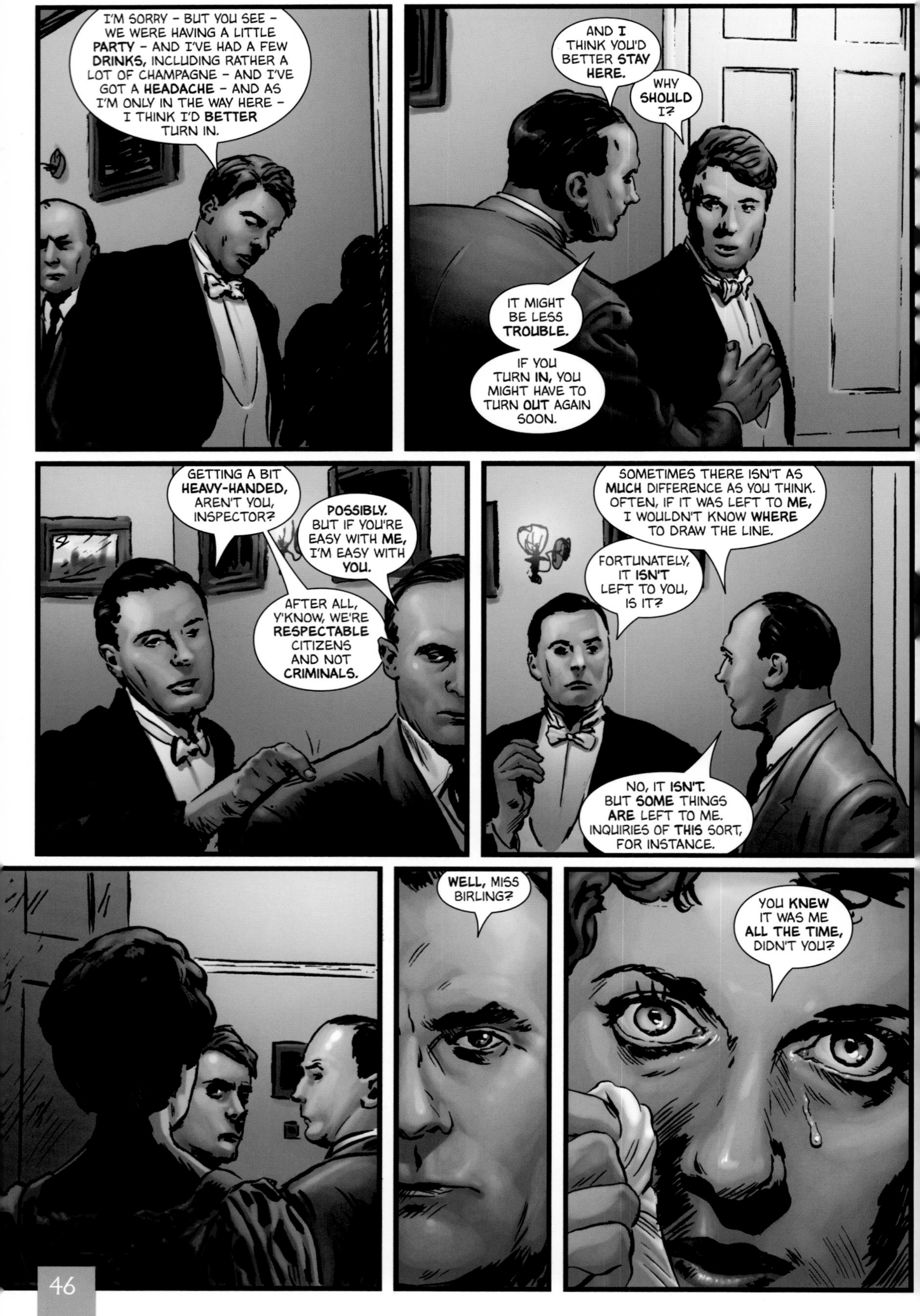
I'M SORRY – BUT YOU SEE – WE WERE HAVING A LITTLE PARTY – AND I'VE HAD A FEW DRINKS, INCLUDING RATHER A LOT OF CHAMPAGNE – AND I'VE GOT A HEADACHE – AND AS I'M ONLY IN THE WAY HERE – I THINK I'D BETTER TURN IN.
AND I THINK YOU'D BETTER STAY HERE.
WHY SHOULD I?
IT MIGHT BE LESS TROUBLE.
IF YOU TURN IN, YOU MIGHT HAVE TO TURN OUT AGAIN SOON.
GETTING A BIT HEAVY-HANDED, AREN'T YOU, INSPECTOR?
POSSIBLY. BUT IF YOU'RE EASY WITH ME, I'M EASY WITH YOU.
AFTER ALL, Y'KNOW, WE'RE RESPECTABLE CITIZENS AND NOT CRIMINALS.
SOMETIMES THERE ISN'T AS MUCH DIFFERENCE AS YOU THINK. OFTEN, IF IT WAS LEFT TO ME, I WOULDN'T KNOW WHERE TO DRAW THE LINE.
FORTUNATELY, IT ISN'T LEFT TO YOU, IS IT?
NO, IT ISN'T. BUT SOME THINGS ARE LEFT TO ME. INQUIRIES OF THIS SORT, FOR INSTANCE.
WELL, MISS BIRLING?
YOU KNEW IT WAS ME ALL THE TIME, DIDN'T YOU?

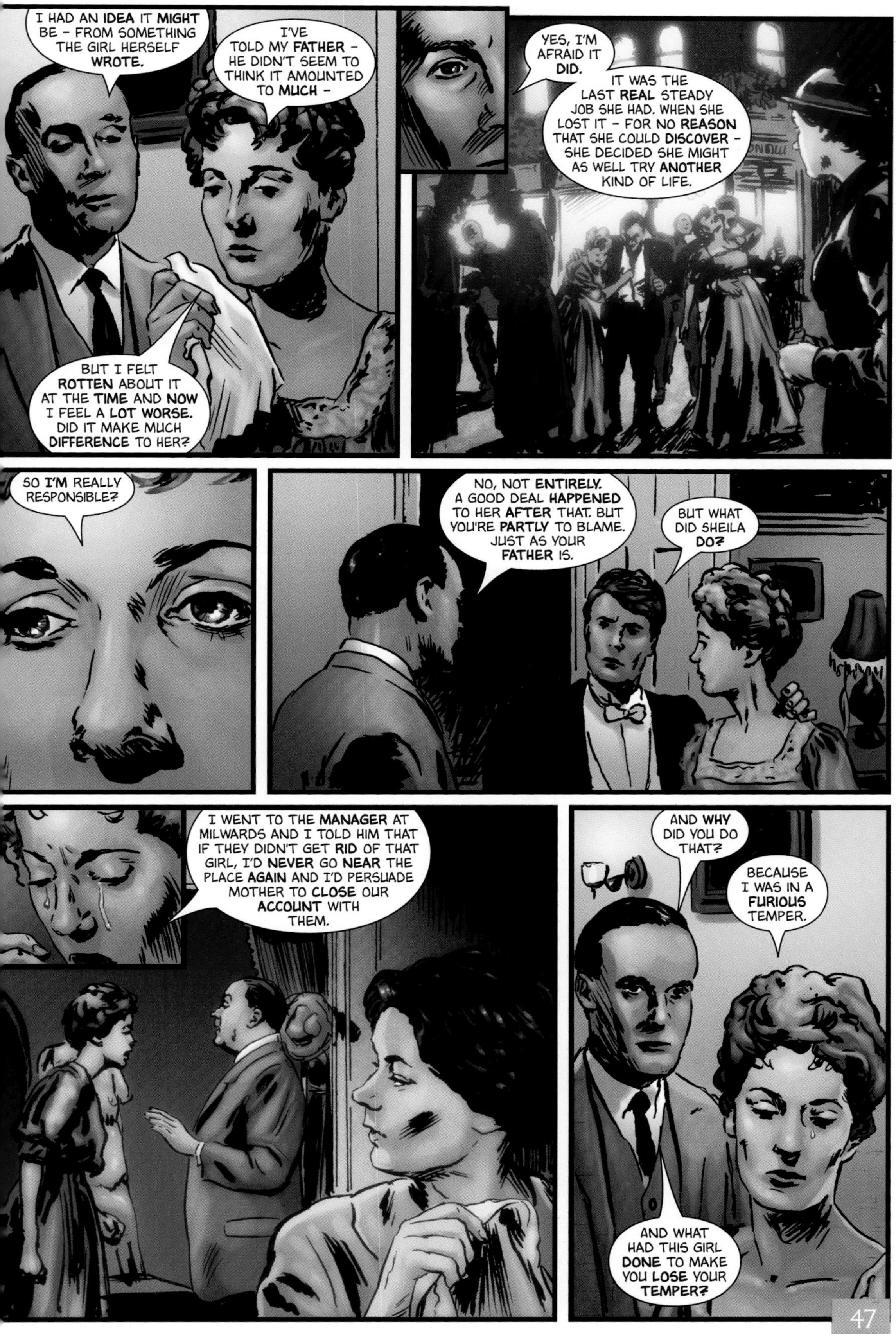
I HAD AN IDEA IT MIGHT BE – FROM SOMETHING THE GIRL HERSELF WROTE.
I'VE TOLD MY FATHER – HE DIDN'T SEEM TO THINK IT AMOUNTED TO MUCH –
BUT I FELT ROTTEN ABOUT IT AT THE TIME AND NOW I FEEL A LOT WORSE. DID IT MAKE MUCH DIFFERENCE TO HER?
YES, I'M AFRAID IT DID.
IT WAS THE LAST REAL STEADY JOB SHE HAD. WHEN SHE LOST IT – FOR NO REASON THAT SHE COULD DISCOVER – SHE DECIDED SHE MIGHT AS WELL TRY ANOTHER KIND OF LIFE.
SO I'M REALLY RESPONSIBLE?
NO, NOT ENTIRELY. A GOOD DEAL HAPPENED TO HER AFTER THAT. BUT YOU'RE PARTLY TO BLAME. JUST AS YOUR FATHER IS.
BUT WHAT DID SHEILA DO?
I WENT TO THE MANAGER AT MILWARDS AND I TOLD HIM THAT IF THEY DIDN'T GET RID OF THAT GIRL, I'D NEVER GO NEAR THE PLACE AGAIN AND I'D PERSUADE MOTHER TO CLOSE OUR ACCOUNT WITH THEM.
AND WHY DID YOU DO THAT?
BECAUSE I WAS IN A FURIOUS TEMPER.
AND WHAT HAD THIS GIRL DONE TO MAKE YOU LOSE YOUR TEMPER?

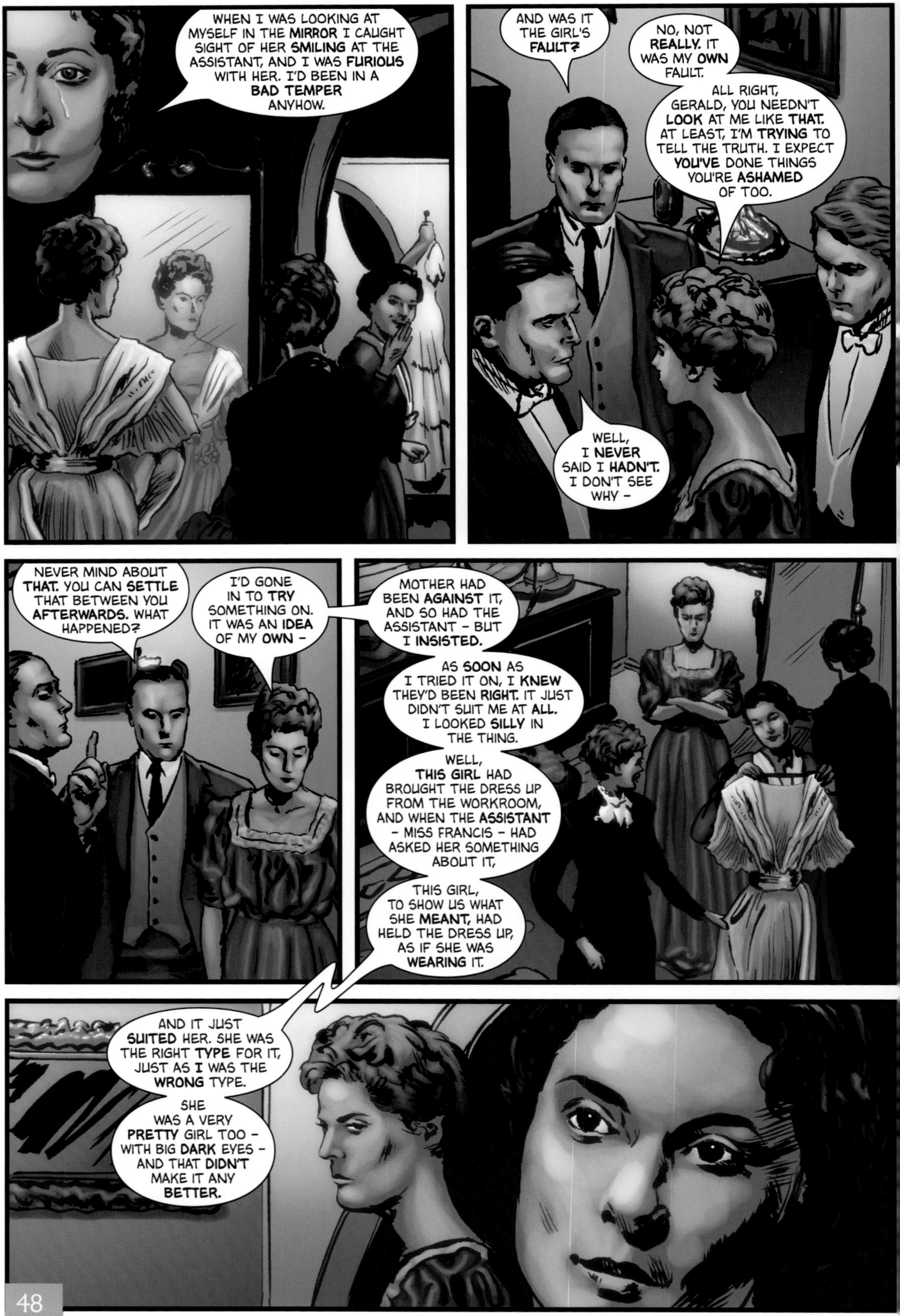
WHEN I WAS LOOKING AT MYSELF IN THE MIRROR I CAUGHT SIGHT OF HER SMILING AT THE ASSISTANT, AND I WAS FURIOUS WITH HER. I'D BEEN IN A BAD TEMPER ANYHOW.
AND WAS IT THE GIRL'S FAULT?
NO, NOT REALLY. IT WAS MY OWN FAULT.
ALL RIGHT, GERALD, YOU NEEDN'T LOOK AT ME LIKE THAT. AT LEAST, I'M TRYING TO TELL THE TRUTH. I EXPECT YOU'VE DONE THINGS YOU'RE ASHAMED OF TOO.
WELL, I NEVER SAID I HADN'T. I DON'T SEE WHY –
NEVER MIND ABOUT THAT. YOU CAN SETTLE THAT BETWEEN YOU AFTERWARDS. WHAT HAPPENED?
I'D GONE IN TO TRY SOMETHING ON. IT WAS AN IDEA OF MY OWN –
MOTHER HAD BEEN AGAINST IT, AND SO HAD THE ASSISTANT – BUT I INSISTED.
AS SOON AS I TRIED IT ON, I KNEW THEY'D BEEN RIGHT. IT JUST DIDN'T SUIT ME AT ALL. I LOOKED SILLY IN THE THING.
WELL, THIS GIRL HAD BROUGHT THE DRESS UP FROM THE WORKROOM, AND WHEN THE ASSISTANT – MISS FRANCIS – HAD ASKED HER SOMETHING ABOUT IT,
THIS GIRL, TO SHOW US WHAT SHE MEANT, HAD HELD THE DRESS UP, AS IF SHE WAS WEARING IT.
AND IT JUST SUITED HER. SHE WAS THE RIGHT TYPE FOR IT, JUST AS I WAS THE WRONG TYPE.
SHE WAS A VERY PRETTY GIRL TOO – WITH BIG DARK EYES – AND THAT DIDN'T MAKE IT ANY BETTER.

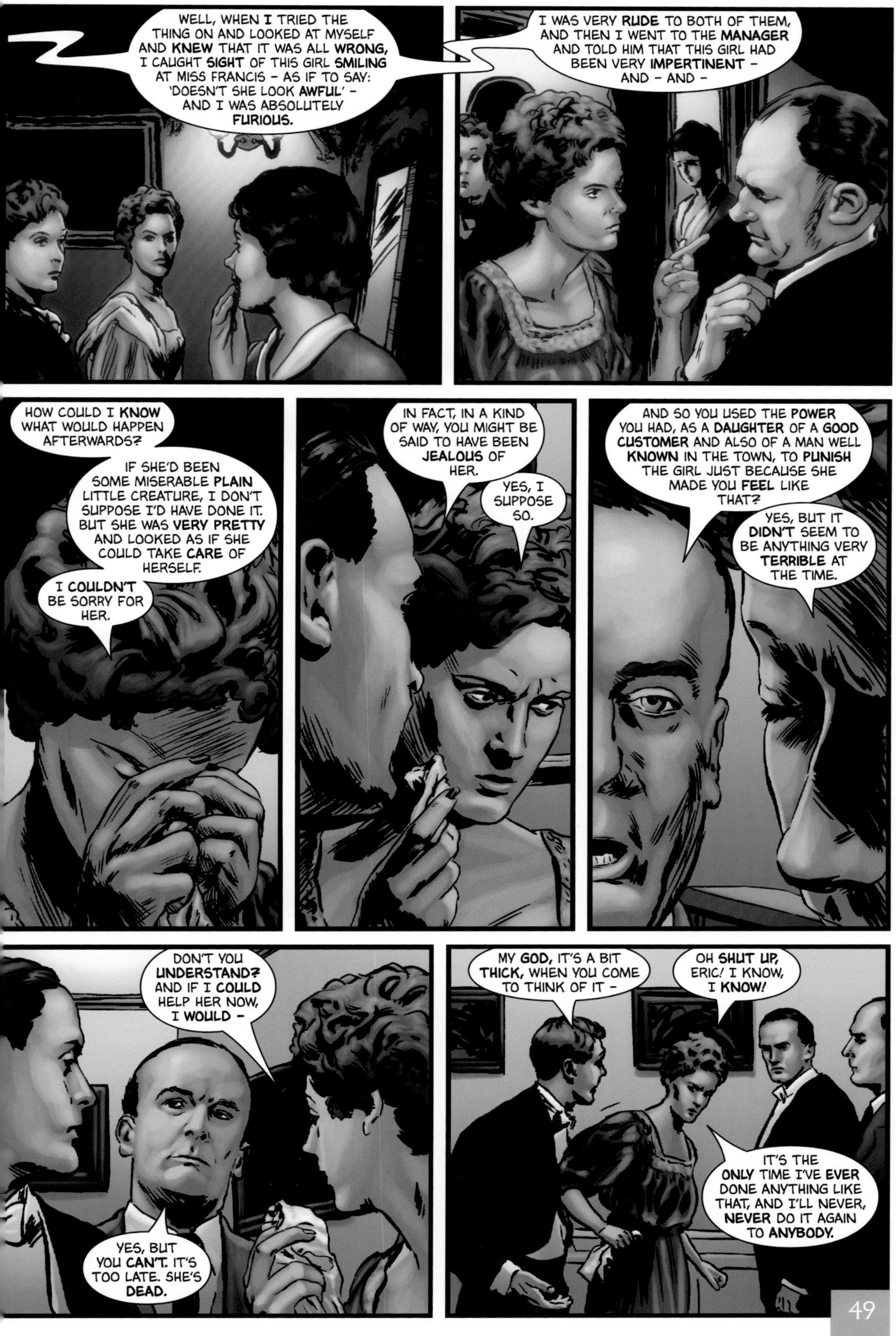
WELL, WHEN I TRIED THE THING ON AND LOOKED AT MYSELF AND KNEW THAT IT WAS ALL WRONG, I CAUGHT SIGHT OF THIS GIRL SMILING AT MISS FRANCIS – AS IF TO SAY: 'DOESN'T SHE LOOK AWFUL' – AND I WAS ABSOLUTELY FURIOUS.
I WAS VERY RUDE TO BOTH OF THEM, AND THEN I WENT TO THE MANAGER AND TOLD HIM THAT THIS GIRL HAD BEEN VERY IMPERTINENT – AND – AND –
HOW COULD I KNOW WHAT WOULD HAPPEN AFTERWARDS?
IF SHE'D BEEN SOME MISERABLE PLAIN LITTLE CREATURE, I DON'T SUPPOSE I'D HAVE DONE IT. BUT SHE WAS VERY PRETTY AND LOOKED AS IF SHE COULD TAKE CARE OF HERSELF.
I COULDN'T BE SORRY FOR HER.
IN FACT, IN A KIND OF WAY, YOU MIGHT BE SAID TO HAVE BEEN JEALOUS OF HER.
YES, I SUPPOSE SO.
AND SO YOU USED THE POWER YOU HAD, AS A DAUGHTER OF A GOOD CUSTOMER AND ALSO OF A MAN WELL KNOWN IN THE TOWN, TO PUNISH THE GIRL JUST BECAUSE SHE MADE YOU FEEL LIKE THAT?
YES, BUT IT DIDN'T SEEM TO BE ANYTHING VERY TERRIBLE AT THE TIME.
DON'T YOU UNDERSTAND? AND IF I COULD HELP HER NOW, I WOULD –
YES, BUT YOU CAN'T. IT'S TOO LATE. SHE'S DEAD.
MY GOD, IT'S A BIT THICK, WHEN YOU COME TO THINK OF IT –
OH SHUT UP, ERIC! I KNOW, I KNOW!
IT'S THE ONLY TIME I'VE EVER DONE ANYTHING LIKE THAT, AND I'LL NEVER, NEVER DO IT AGAIN TO ANYBODY.

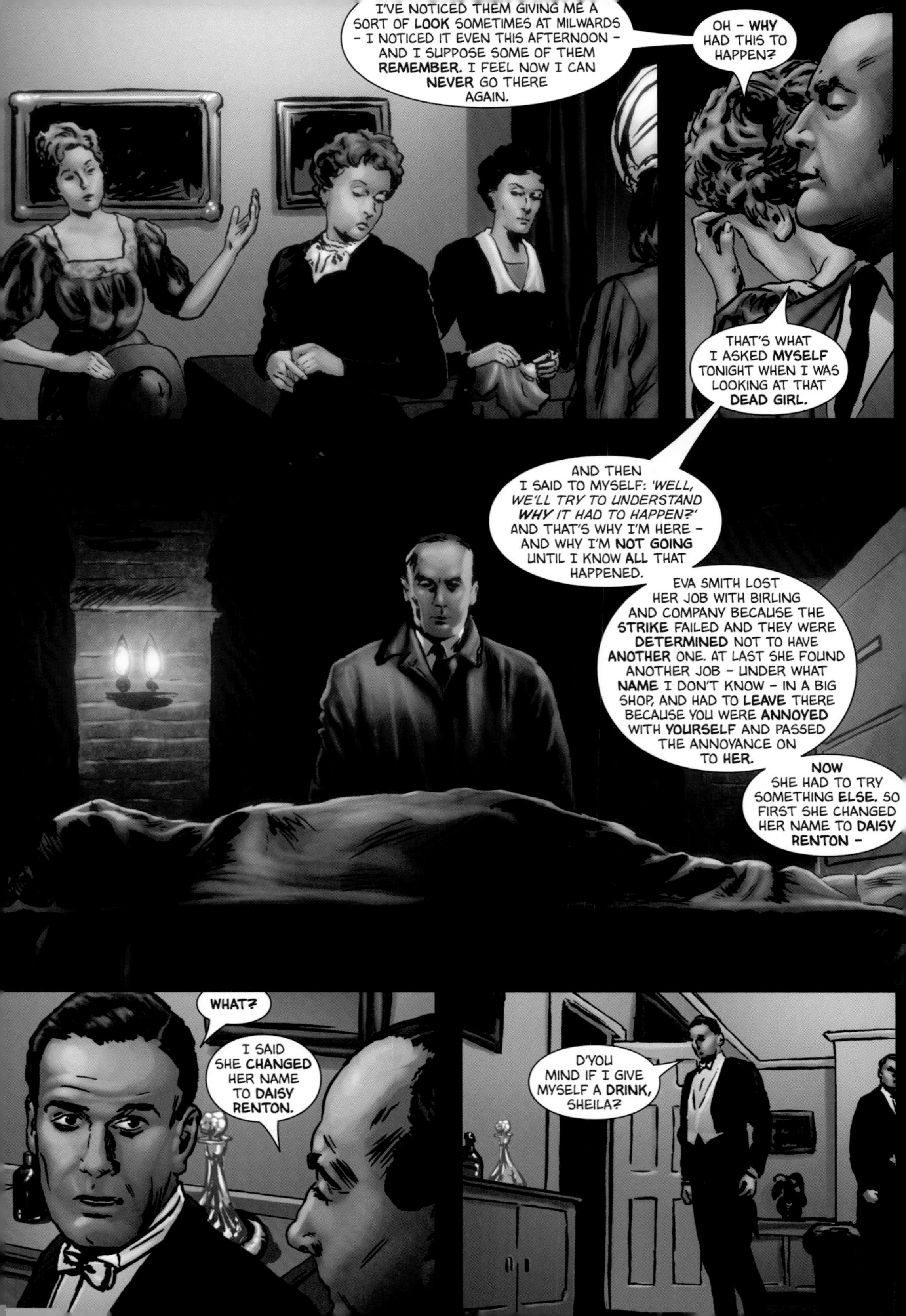
I'VE NOTICED THEM GIVING ME A SORT OF LOOK SOMETIMES AT MILWARDS – I NOTICED IT EVEN THIS AFTERNOON – AND I SUPPOSE SOME OF THEM REMEMBER. I FEEL NOW I CAN NEVER GO THERE AGAIN.
OH – WHY HAD THIS TO HAPPEN?
THAT'S WHAT I ASKED MYSELF TONIGHT WHEN I WAS LOOKING AT THAT DEAD GIRL.
AND THEN I SAID TO MYSELF: 'WELL, WE'LL TRY TO UNDERSTAND WHY IT HAD TO HAPPEN?' AND THAT'S WHY I'M HERE – AND WHY I'M NOT GOING UNTIL I KNOW ALL THAT HAPPENED.
EVA SMITH LOST HER JOB WITH BIRLING AND COMPANY BECAUSE THE STRIKE FAILED AND THEY WERE DETERMINED NOT TO HAVE ANOTHER ONE. AT LAST SHE FOUND ANOTHER JOB – UNDER WHAT NAME I DON'T KNOW – IN A BIG SHOP, AND HAD TO LEAVE THERE BECAUSE YOU WERE ANNOYED WITH YOURSELF AND PASSED THE ANNOYANCE ON TO HER.
NOW SHE HAD TO TRY SOMETHING ELSE. SO FIRST SHE CHANGED HER NAME TO DAISY RENTON –
WHAT?
I SAID SHE CHANGED HER NAME TO DAISY RENTON.
D'YOU MIND IF I GIVE MYSELF A DRINK, SHEILA?

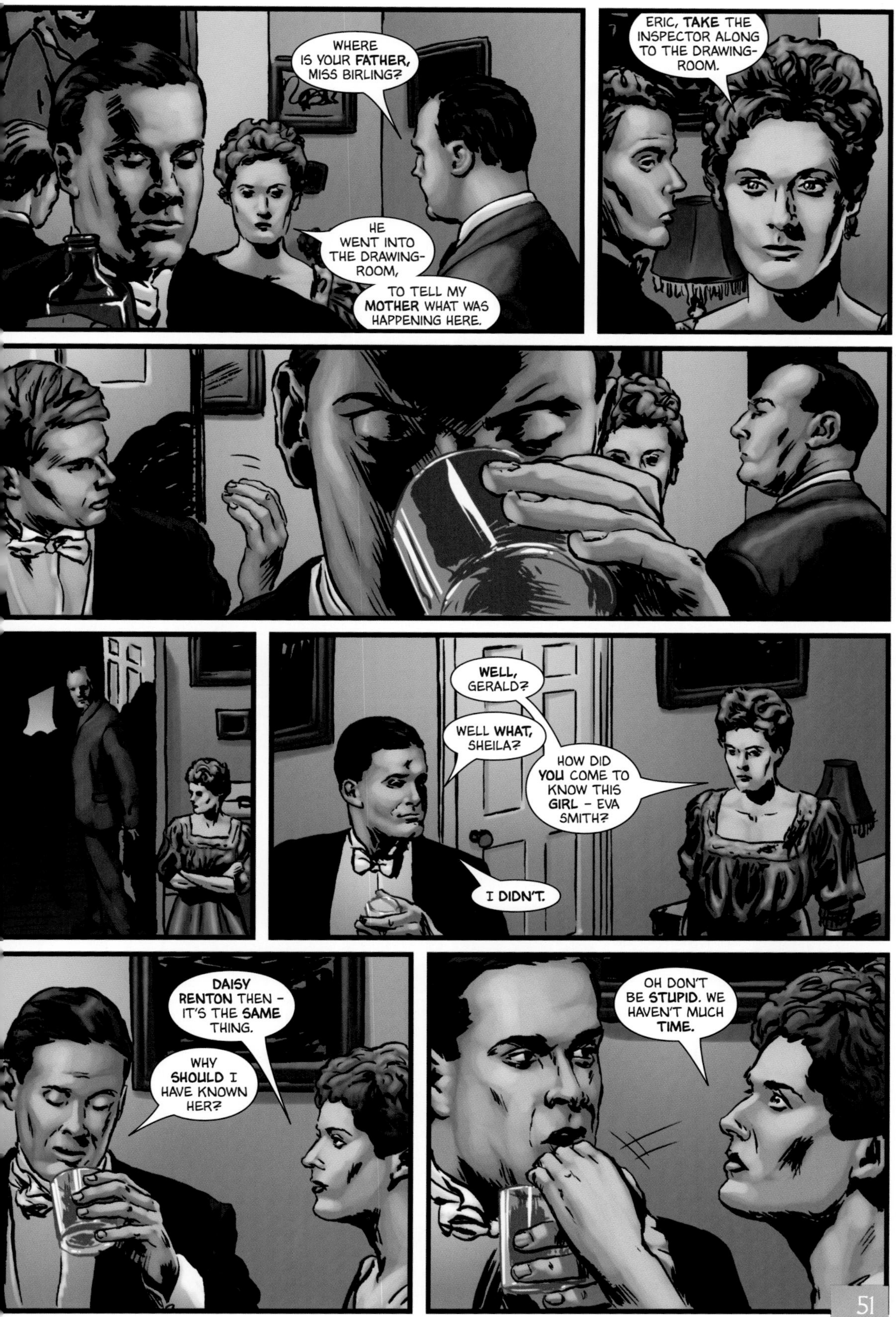
WHERE IS YOUR FATHER, MISS BIRLING?
HE WENT INTO THE DRAWING-ROOM,
TO TELL MY MOTHER WHAT WAS HAPPENING HERE.
ERIC, TAKE THE INSPECTOR ALONG TO THE DRAWING-ROOM.
WELL, GERALD?
WELL WHAT, SHEILA?
HOW DID YOU COME TO KNOW THIS GIRL – EVA SMITH?
I DIDN'T.
DAISY RENTON THEN – IT'S THE SAME THING.
WHY SHOULD I HAVE KNOWN HER?
OH DON'T BE STUPID. WE HAVEN'T MUCH TIME.

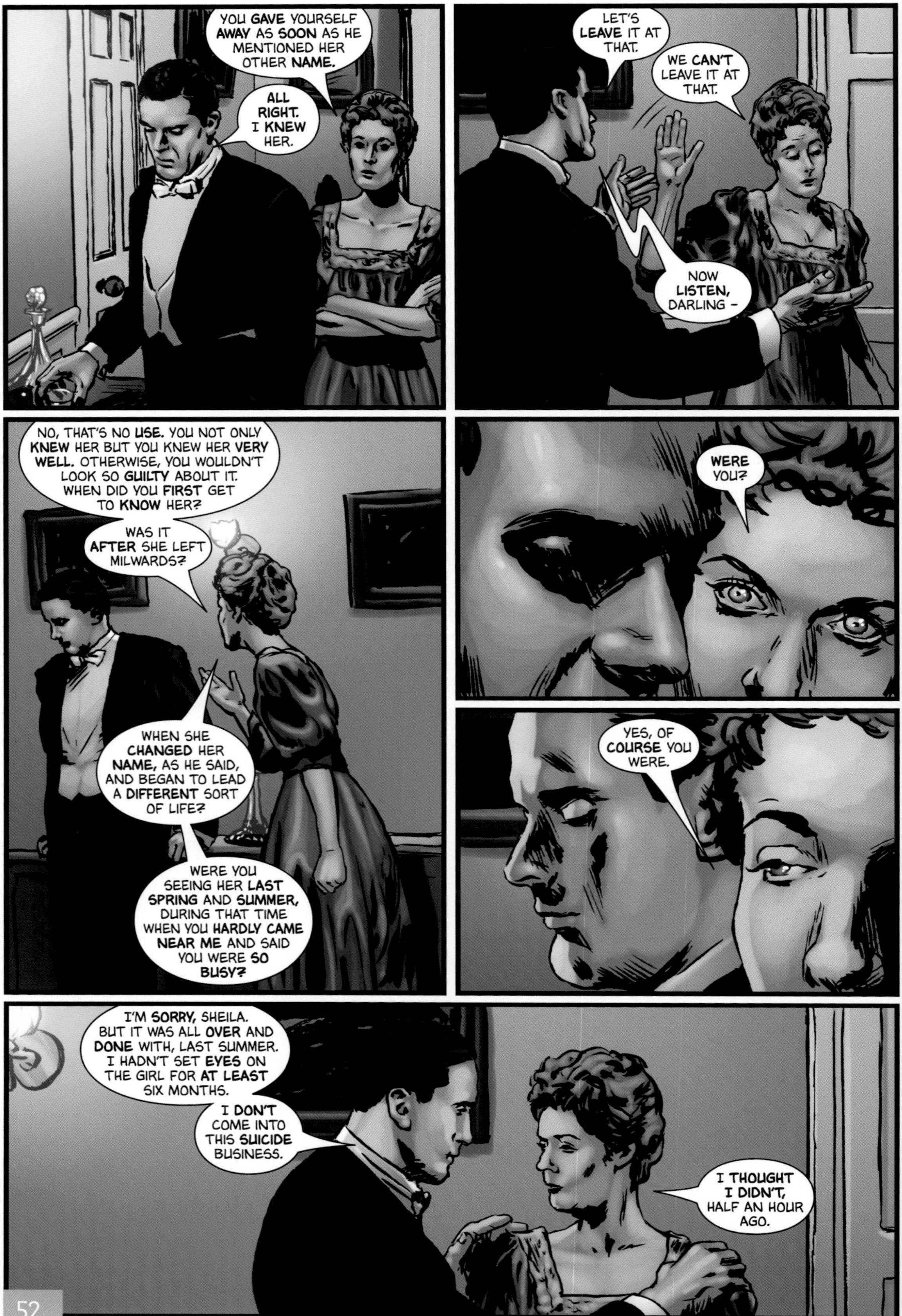
YOU GAVE YOURSELF AWAY AS SOON AS HE MENTIONED HER OTHER NAME.
ALL RIGHT. I KNEW HER.
LET'S LEAVE IT AT THAT.
WE CAN'T LEAVE IT AT THAT.
NOW LISTEN, DARLING –
NO, THAT'S NO USE. YOU NOT ONLY KNEW HER BUT YOU KNEW HER VERY WELL. OTHERWISE, YOU WOULDN'T LOOK SO GUILTY ABOUT IT. WHEN DID YOU FIRST GET TO KNOW HER?
WAS IT AFTER SHE LEFT MILWARDS?
WHEN SHE CHANGED HER NAME, AS HE SAID, AND BEGAN TO LEAD A DIFFERENT SORT OF LIFE?
WERE YOU SEEING HER LAST SPRING AND SUMMER, DURING THAT TIME WHEN YOU HARDLY CAME NEAR ME AND SAID YOU WERE SO BUSY?
WERE YOU?
YES, OF COURSE YOU WERE.
I'M SORRY, SHEILA. BUT IT WAS ALL OVER AND DONE WITH, LAST SUMMER. I HADN'T SET EYES ON THE GIRL FOR AT LEAST SIX MONTHS.
I DON'T COME INTO THIS SUICIDE BUSINESS.
I THOUGHT I DIDN'T, HALF AN HOUR AGO.

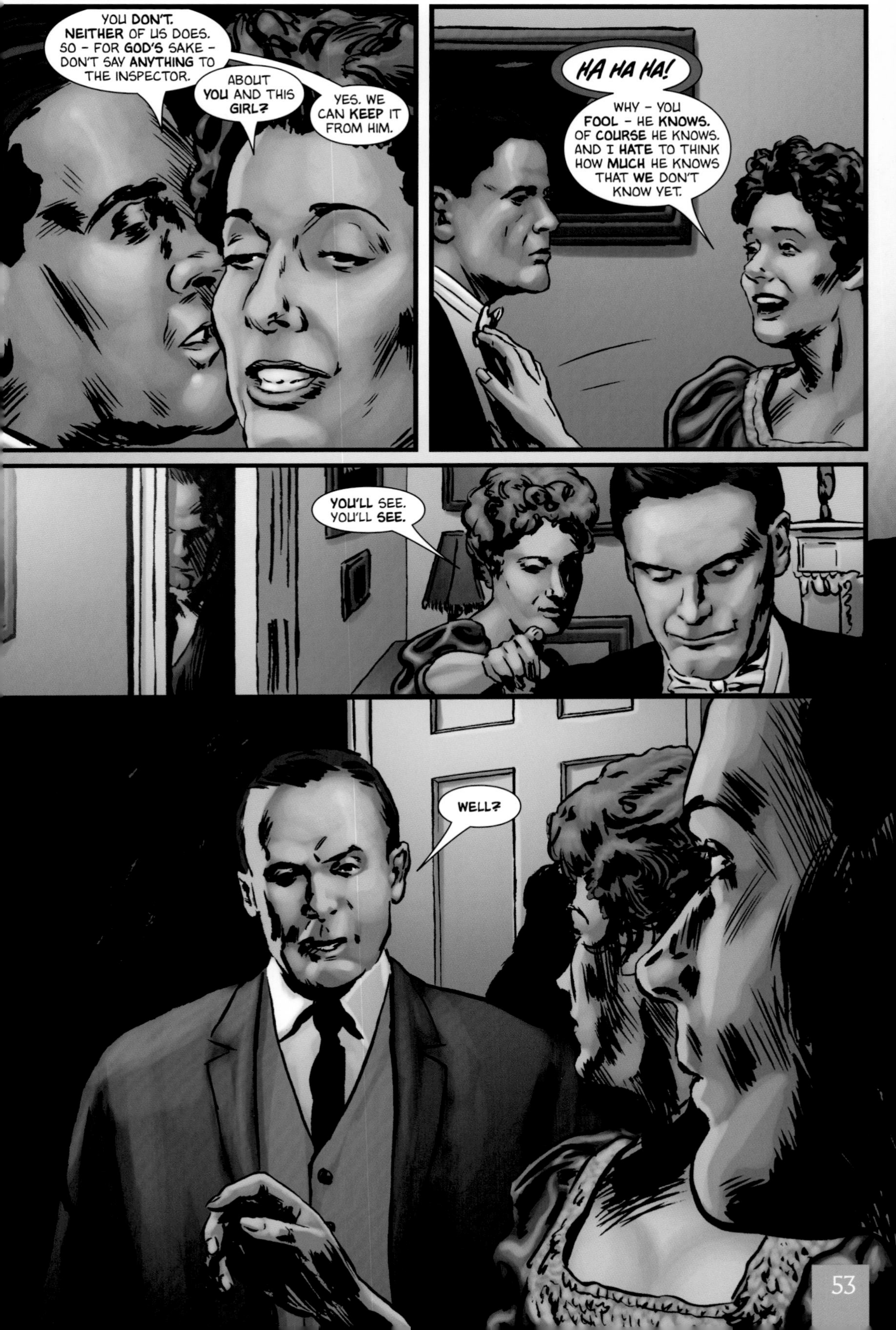
YOU DON'T. NEITHER OF US DOES. SO – FOR GOD'S SAKE – DON'T SAY ANYTHING TO THE INSPECTOR.
ABOUT YOU AND THIS GIRL?
YES. WE CAN KEEP IT FROM HIM.
HA HA HA!
WHY – YOU FOOL – HE KNOWS. OF COURSE HE KNOWS. AND I HATE TO THINK HOW MUCH HE KNOWS THAT WE DON'T KNOW YET.
YOU'LL SEE. YOU'LL SEE.
WELL?

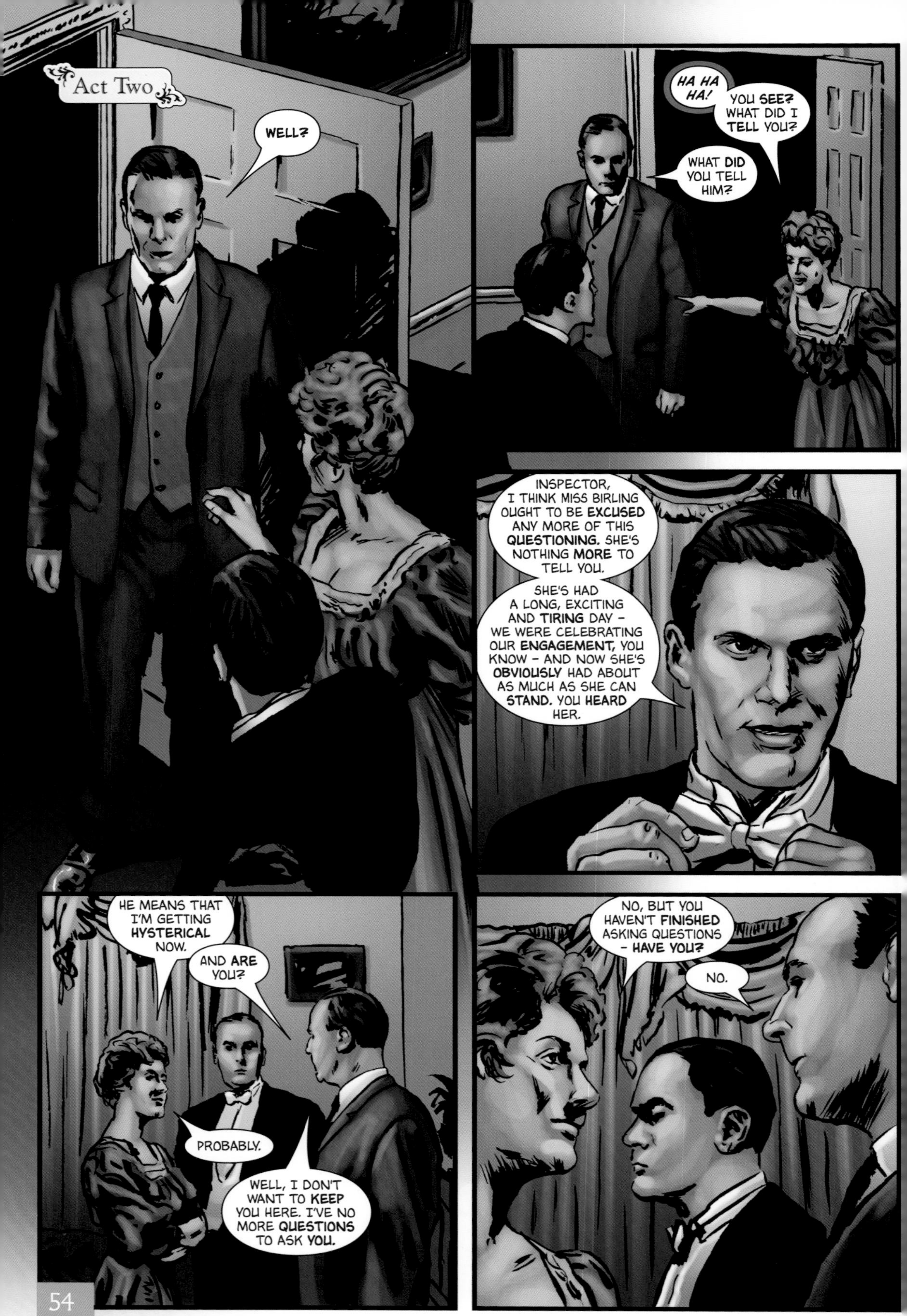
Act Two
WELL?
HA HA HA!
YOU SEE? WHAT DID I TELL YOU?
WHAT DID YOU TELL HIM?
INSPECTOR, I THINK MISS BIRLING OUGHT TO BE EXCUSED ANY MORE OF THIS QUESTIONING. SHE'S NOTHING MORE TO TELL YOU.
SHE'S HAD A LONG, EXCITING AND TIRING DAY – WE WERE CELEBRATING OUR ENGAGEMENT, YOU KNOW – AND NOW SHE'S OBVIOUSLY HAD ABOUT AS MUCH AS SHE CAN STAND. YOU HEARD HER.
HE MEANS THAT I'M GETTING HYSTERICAL NOW.
AND ARE YOU?
PROBABLY.
WELL, I DON'T WANT TO KEEP YOU HERE. I'VE NO MORE QUESTIONS TO ASK YOU.
NO, BUT YOU HAVEN'T FINISHED ASKING QUESTIONS – HAVE YOU?
NO.

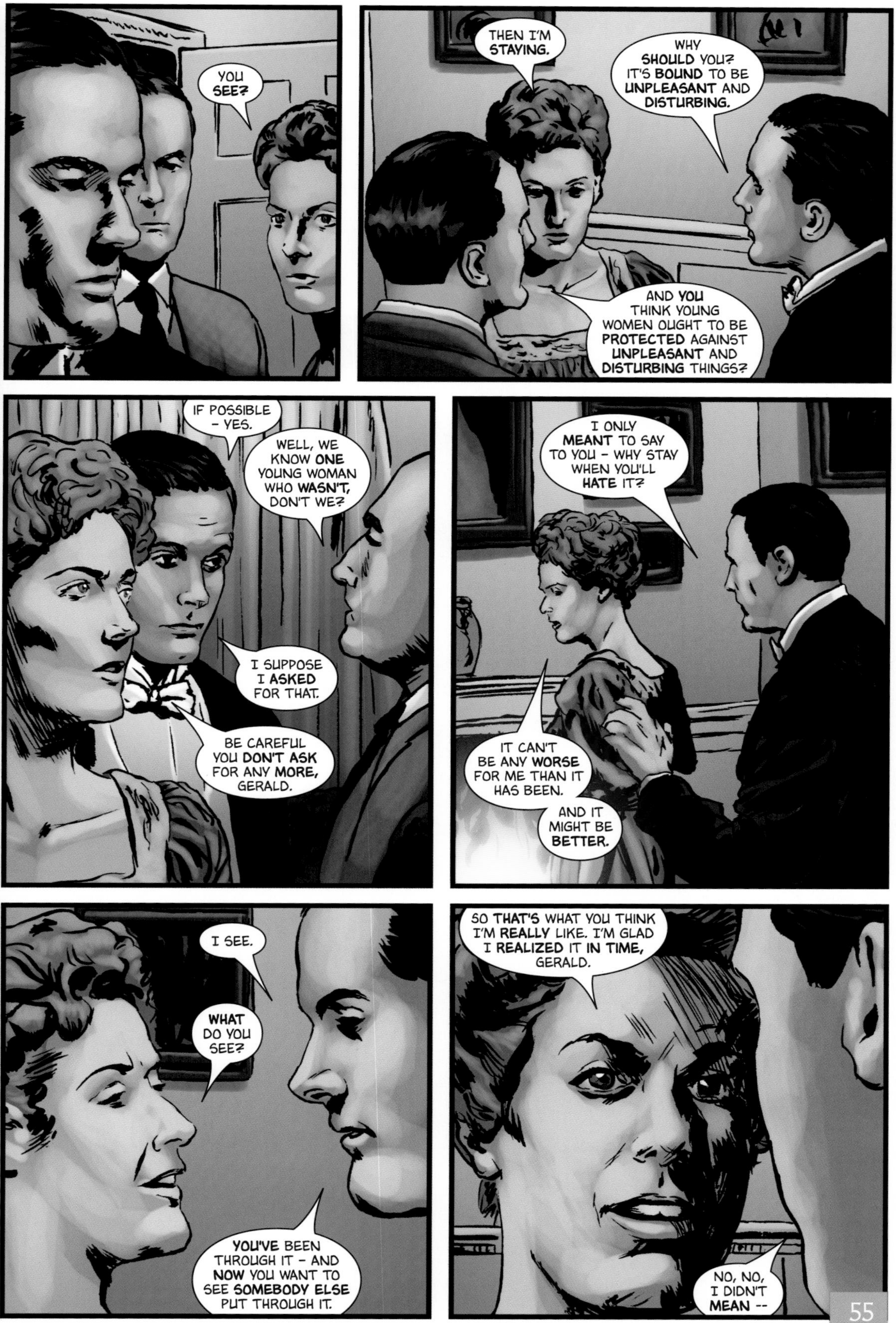
YOU SEE?
THEN I'M STAYING.
WHY SHOULD YOU? IT'S BOUND TO BE UNPLEASANT AND DISTURBING.
AND YOU THINK YOUNG WOMEN OUGHT TO BE PROTECTED AGAINST UNPLEASANT AND DISTURBING THINGS?
IF POSSIBLE – YES.
WELL, WE KNOW ONE YOUNG WOMAN WHO WASN'T, DON'T WE?
I SUPPOSE I ASKED FOR THAT.
BE CAREFUL YOU DON'T ASK FOR ANY MORE, GERALD.
I ONLY MEANT TO SAY TO YOU – WHY STAY WHEN YOU'LL HATE IT?
IT CAN'T BE ANY WORSE FOR ME THAN IT HAS BEEN.
AND IT MIGHT BE BETTER.
I SEE.
WHAT DO YOU SEE?
YOU'VE BEEN THROUGH IT – AND NOW YOU WANT TO SEE SOMEBODY ELSE PUT THROUGH IT.
SO THAT'S WHAT YOU THINK I'M REALLY LIKE. I'M GLAD I REALIZED IT IN TIME, GERALD.
NO, NO, I DIDN'T MEAN --

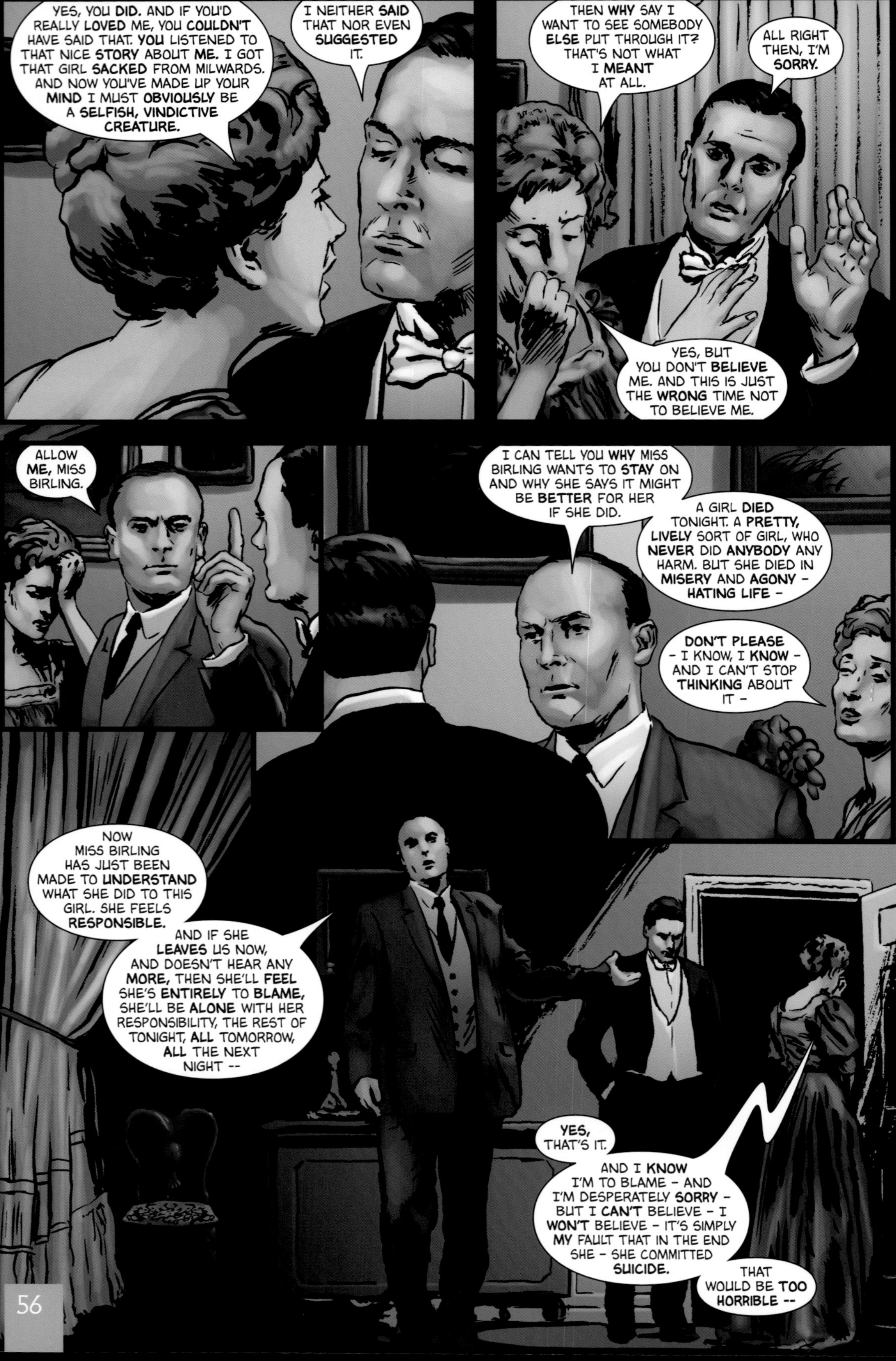
YES, YOU DID. AND IF YOU'D REALLY LOVED ME, YOU COULDN'T HAVE SAID THAT. YOU LISTENED TO THAT NICE STORY ABOUT ME. I GOT THAT GIRL SACKED FROM MILWARDS. AND NOW YOU'VE MADE UP YOUR MIND I MUST OBVIOUSLY BE A SELFISH, VINDICTIVE CREATURE.
I NEITHER SAID THAT NOR EVEN SUGGESTED IT.
THEN WHY SAY I WANT TO SEE SOMEBODY ELSE PUT THROUGH IT? THAT'S NOT WHAT I MEANT AT ALL.
ALL RIGHT THEN, I'M SORRY.
YES, BUT YOU DON'T BELIEVE ME. AND THIS IS JUST THE WRONG TIME NOT TO BELIEVE ME.
ALLOW ME, MISS BIRLING.
I CAN TELL YOU WHY MISS BIRLING WANTS TO STAY ON AND WHY SHE SAYS IT MIGHT BE BETTER FOR HER IF SHE DID.
A GIRL DIED TONIGHT. A PRETTY, LIVELY SORT OF GIRL, WHO NEVER DID ANYBODY ANY HARM. BUT SHE DIED IN MISERY AND AGONY – HATING LIFE –
DON'T PLEASE – I KNOW, I KNOW – AND I CAN'T STOP THINKING ABOUT IT –
NOW MISS BIRLING HAS JUST BEEN MADE TO UNDERSTAND WHAT SHE DID TO THIS GIRL. SHE FEELS RESPONSIBLE.
AND IF SHE LEAVES US NOW, AND DOESN'T HEAR ANY MORE, THEN SHE'LL FEEL SHE'S ENTIRELY TO BLAME, SHE'LL BE ALONE WITH HER RESPONSIBILITY, THE REST OF TONIGHT, ALL TOMORROW, ALL THE NEXT NIGHT --
YES, THAT'S IT.
AND I KNOW I'M TO BLAME – AND I'M DESPERATELY SORRY – BUT I CAN'T BELIEVE – I WON'T BELIEVE – IT'S SIMPLY MY FAULT THAT IN THE END SHE – SHE COMMITTED SUICIDE.
THAT WOULD BE TOO HORRIBLE --

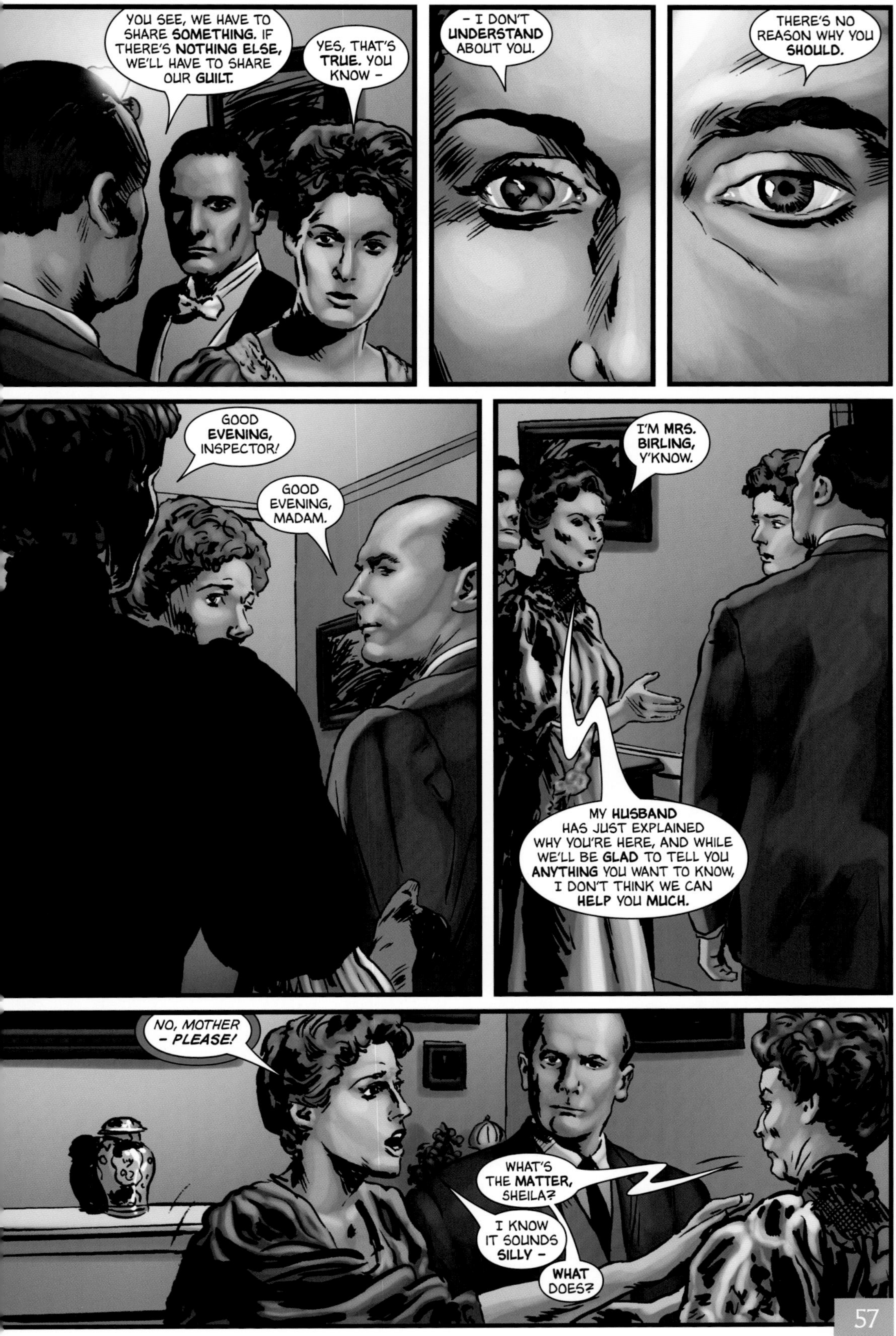
YOU SEE, WE HAVE TO SHARE **SOMETHING.** IF THERE'S **NOTHING ELSE,** WE'LL HAVE TO SHARE OUR **GUILT.**
YES, THAT'S **TRUE.** YOU KNOW –
– I DON'T **UNDERSTAND** ABOUT YOU.
THERE'S NO REASON WHY YOU **SHOULD.**
GOOD **EVENING,** INSPECTOR!
GOOD EVENING, MADAM.
I'M **MRS. BIRLING,** Y'KNOW.
MY **HUSBAND** HAS JUST EXPLAINED WHY YOU'RE HERE, AND WHILE WE'LL BE **GLAD** TO TELL YOU **ANYTHING** YOU WANT TO KNOW, I DON'T THINK WE CAN **HELP** YOU **MUCH.**
NO, MOTHER – ***PLEASE!***
WHAT'S THE **MATTER,** SHEILA?
I KNOW IT SOUNDS **SILLY** –
WHAT DOES?

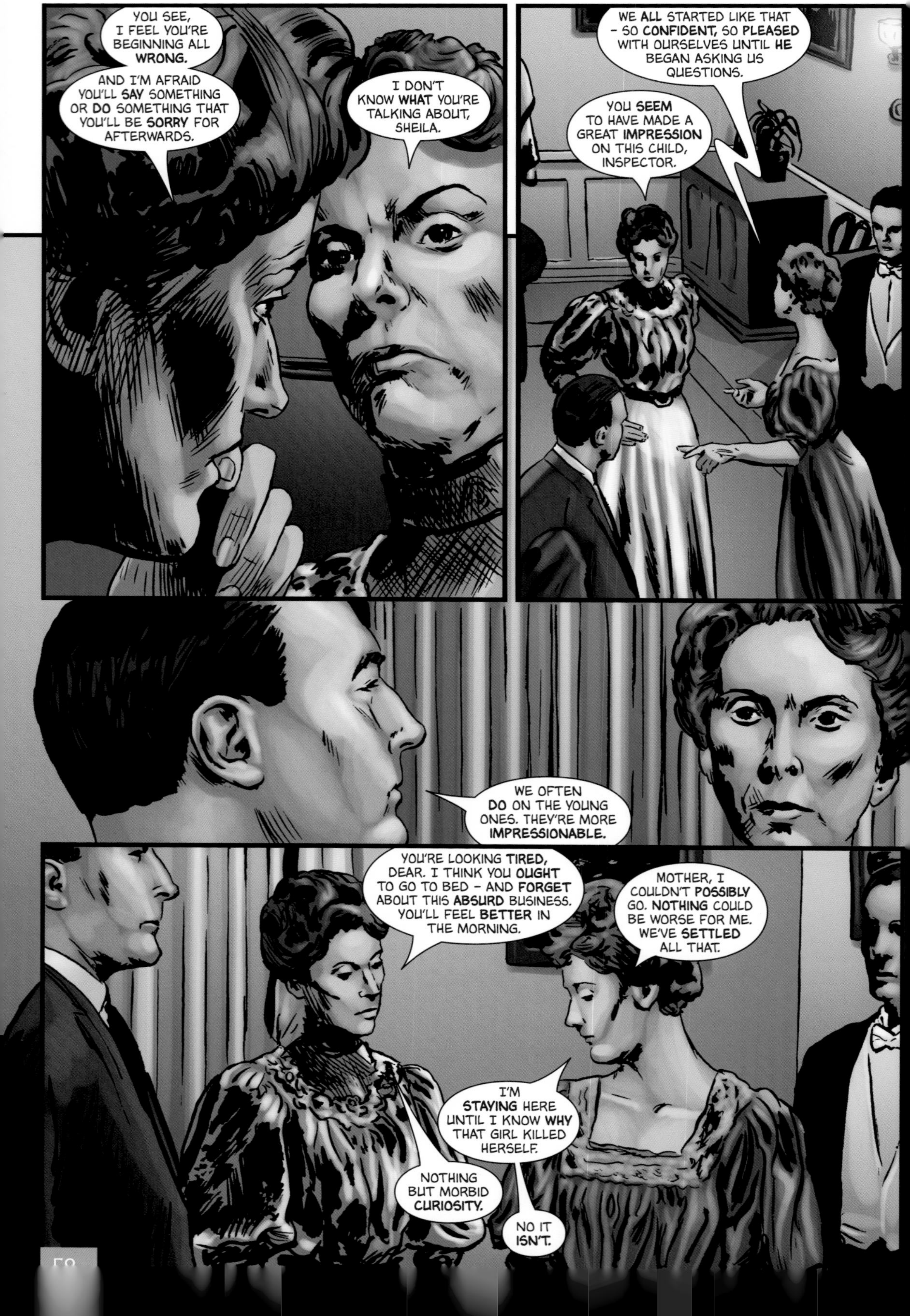

YOU SEE, I FEEL YOU'RE BEGINNING ALL WRONG.
AND I'M AFRAID YOU'LL SAY SOMETHING OR DO SOMETHING THAT YOU'LL BE SORRY FOR AFTERWARDS.
I DON'T KNOW WHAT YOU'RE TALKING ABOUT, SHEILA.
WE ALL STARTED LIKE THAT - SO CONFIDENT, SO PLEASED WITH OURSELVES UNTIL HE BEGAN ASKING US QUESTIONS.
YOU SEEM TO HAVE MADE A GREAT IMPRESSION ON THIS CHILD, INSPECTOR.
WE OFTEN DO ON THE YOUNG ONES. THEY'RE MORE IMPRESSIONABLE.
YOU'RE LOOKING TIRED, DEAR. I THINK YOU OUGHT TO GO TO BED - AND FORGET ABOUT THIS ABSURD BUSINESS. YOU'LL FEEL BETTER IN THE MORNING.
MOTHER, I COULDN'T POSSIBLY GO. NOTHING COULD BE WORSE FOR ME. WE'VE SETTLED ALL THAT.
I'M STAYING HERE UNTIL I KNOW WHY THAT GIRL KILLED HERSELF.
NOTHING BUT MORBID CURIOSITY.
NO IT ISN'T.

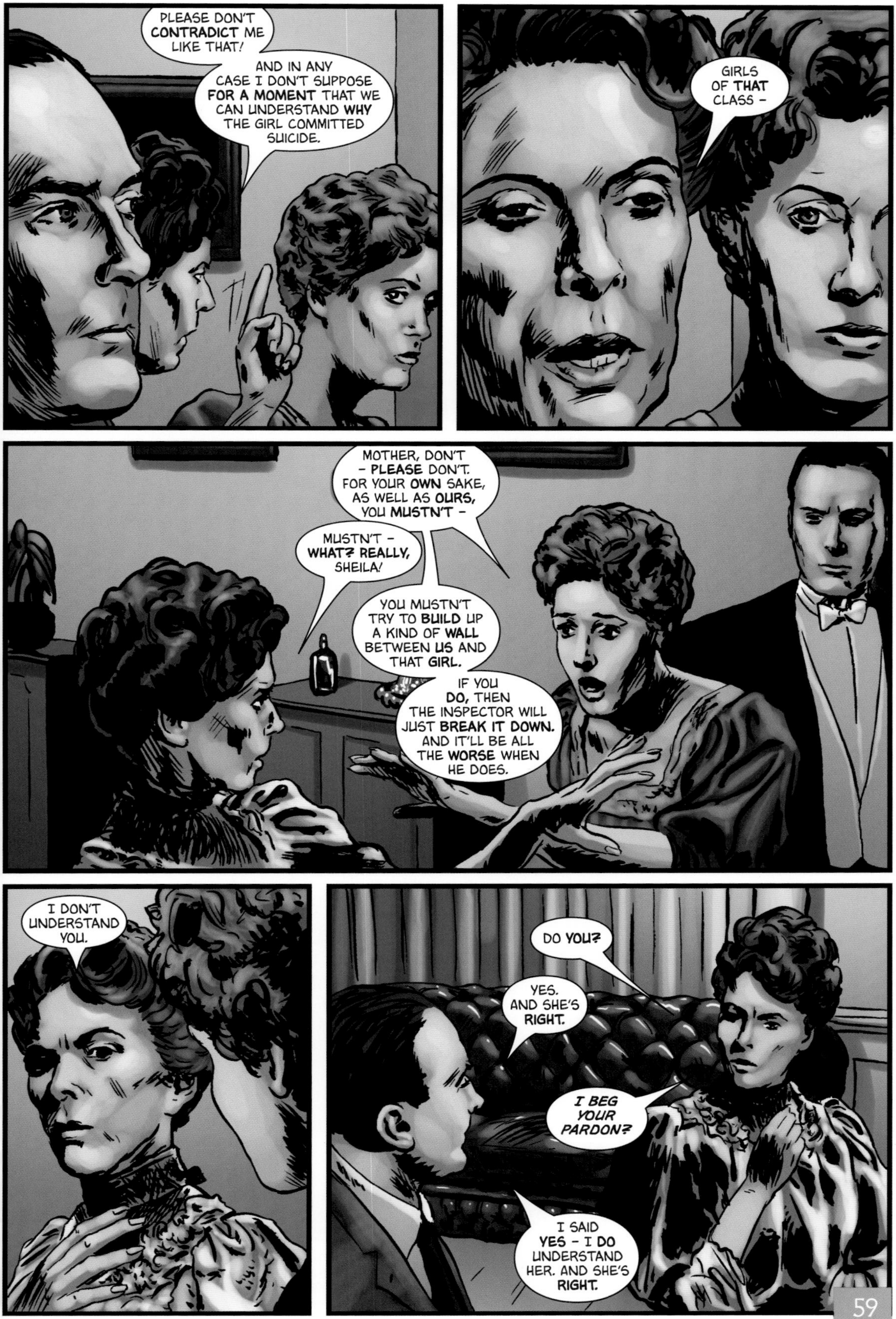
PLEASE DON'T CONTRADICT ME LIKE THAT!
AND IN ANY CASE I DON'T SUPPOSE FOR A MOMENT THAT WE CAN UNDERSTAND WHY THE GIRL COMMITTED SUICIDE.
GIRLS OF THAT CLASS –
MOTHER, DON'T – PLEASE DON'T. FOR YOUR OWN SAKE, AS WELL AS OURS, YOU MUSTN'T –
MUSTN'T – WHAT? REALLY, SHEILA!
YOU MUSTN'T TRY TO BUILD UP A KIND OF WALL BETWEEN US AND THAT GIRL.
IF YOU DO, THEN THE INSPECTOR WILL JUST BREAK IT DOWN. AND IT'LL BE ALL THE WORSE WHEN HE DOES.
I DON'T UNDERSTAND YOU.
DO YOU?
YES. AND SHE'S RIGHT.
I BEG YOUR PARDON?
I SAID YES – I DO UNDERSTAND HER. AND SHE'S RIGHT.

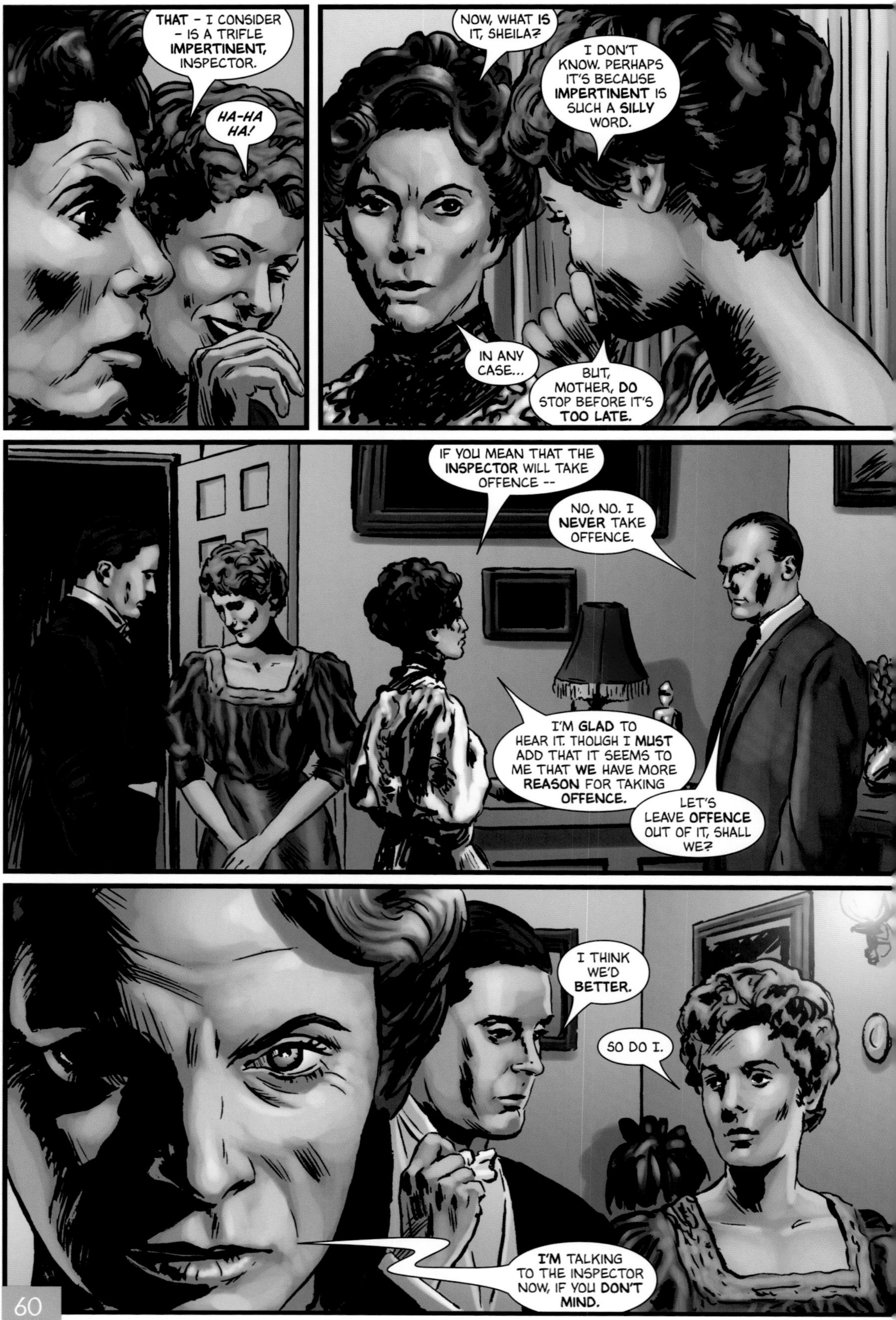
THAT - I CONSIDER - IS A TRIFLE IMPERTINENT, INSPECTOR.
HA-HA HA!
NOW, WHAT IS IT, SHEILA?
I DON'T KNOW. PERHAPS IT'S BECAUSE IMPERTINENT IS SUCH A SILLY WORD.
IN ANY CASE...
BUT, MOTHER, DO STOP BEFORE IT'S TOO LATE.
IF YOU MEAN THAT THE INSPECTOR WILL TAKE OFFENCE --
NO, NO. I NEVER TAKE OFFENCE.
I'M GLAD TO HEAR IT. THOUGH I MUST ADD THAT IT SEEMS TO ME THAT WE HAVE MORE REASON FOR TAKING OFFENCE.
LET'S LEAVE OFFENCE OUT OF IT, SHALL WE?
I THINK WE'D BETTER.
SO DO I.
I'M TALKING TO THE INSPECTOR NOW, IF YOU DON'T MIND.

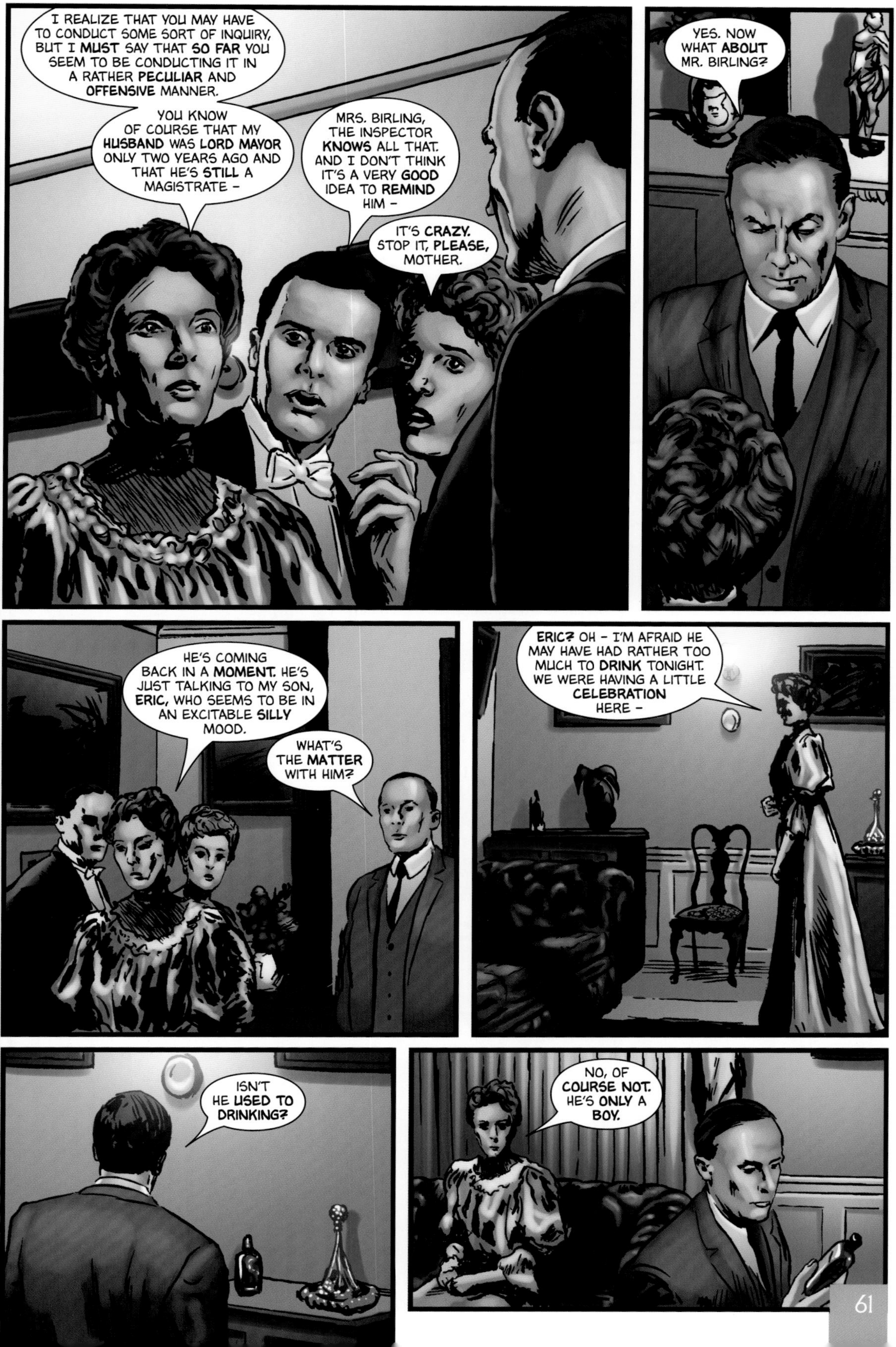
I REALIZE THAT YOU MAY HAVE TO CONDUCT SOME SORT OF INQUIRY, BUT I MUST SAY THAT SO FAR YOU SEEM TO BE CONDUCTING IT IN A RATHER PECULIAR AND OFFENSIVE MANNER.
YOU KNOW OF COURSE THAT MY HUSBAND WAS LORD MAYOR ONLY TWO YEARS AGO AND THAT HE'S STILL A MAGISTRATE –
MRS. BIRLING, THE INSPECTOR KNOWS ALL THAT. AND I DON'T THINK IT'S A VERY GOOD IDEA TO REMIND HIM –
IT'S CRAZY. STOP IT, PLEASE, MOTHER.
YES. NOW WHAT ABOUT MR. BIRLING?
HE'S COMING BACK IN A MOMENT. HE'S JUST TALKING TO MY SON, ERIC, WHO SEEMS TO BE IN AN EXCITABLE SILLY MOOD.
WHAT'S THE MATTER WITH HIM?
ERIC? OH – I'M AFRAID HE MAY HAVE HAD RATHER TOO MUCH TO DRINK TONIGHT. WE WERE HAVING A LITTLE CELEBRATION HERE –
ISN'T HE USED TO DRINKING?
NO, OF COURSE NOT. HE'S ONLY A BOY.

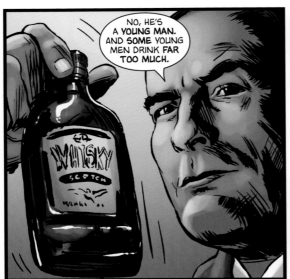

NO, HE'S A YOUNG MAN. AND SOME YOUNG MEN DRINK FAR TOO MUCH.

WHISKY
SCOTCH

AND ERIC'S ONE OF THEM.

SHEILA!

I DON'T WANT TO GET POOR ERIC INTO TROUBLE. HE'S PROBABLY IN ENOUGH TROUBLE ALREADY. BUT WE REALLY MUST STOP THESE SILLY PRETENCES.

THIS ISN'T THE TIME TO PRETEND THAT ERIC ISN'T USED TO DRINK. HE'S BEEN STEADILY DRINKING TOO MUCH FOR THE LAST TWO YEARS.

IT ISN'T TRUE.

YOU KNOW HIM, GERALD – AND YOU'RE A MAN – YOU MUST KNOW IT ISN'T TRUE.

WELL, MR. CROFT?

I'M AFRAID IT IS, Y'KNOW. ACTUALLY I'VE NEVER SEEN MUCH OF HIM OUTSIDE THIS HOUSE – BUT– WELL, I HAVE GATHERED THAT HE DOES DRINK PRETTY HARD.

AND THIS IS THE TIME YOU CHOOSE TO TELL ME!

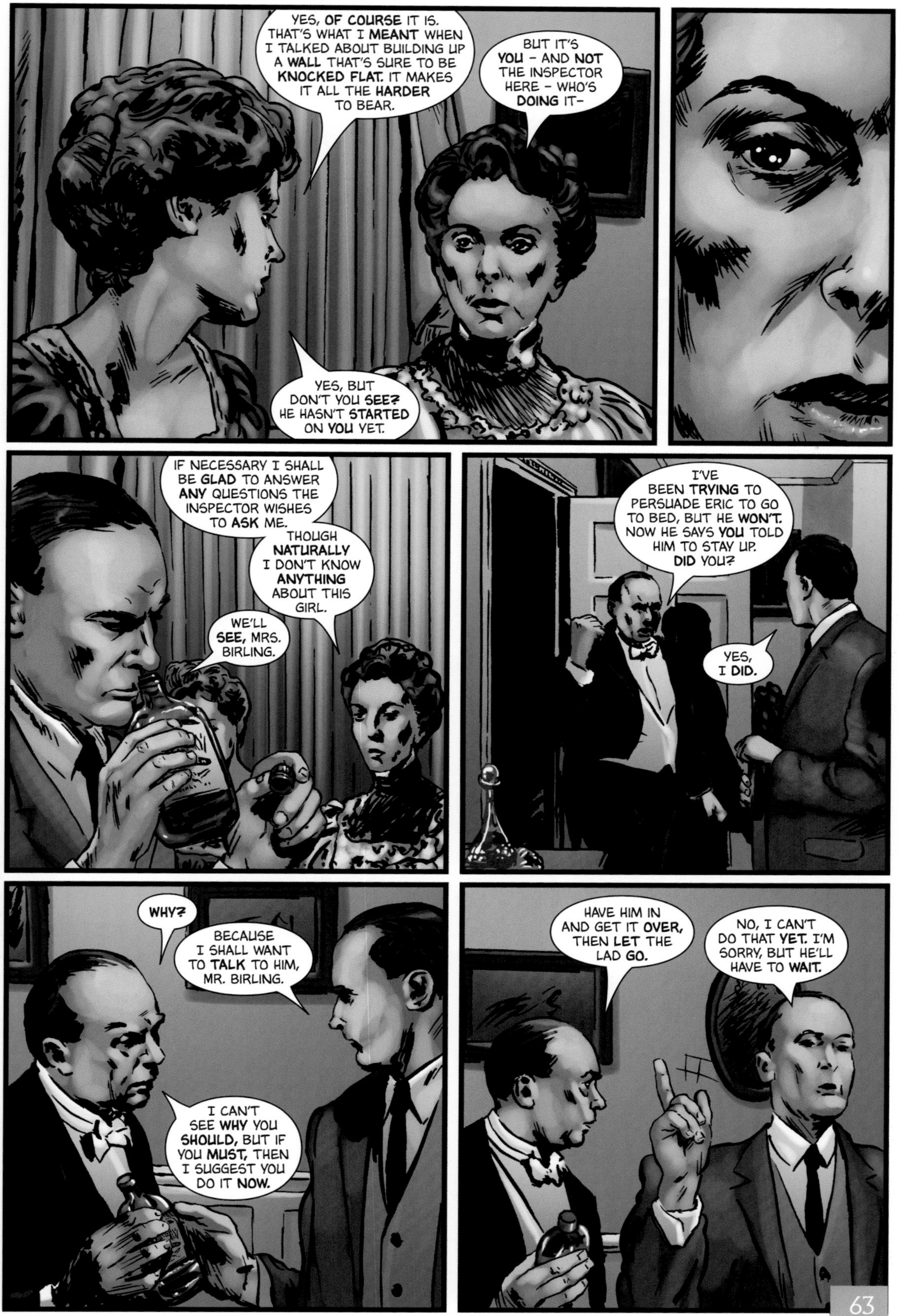
YES, OF COURSE IT IS. THAT'S WHAT I MEANT WHEN I TALKED ABOUT BUILDING UP A WALL THAT'S SURE TO BE KNOCKED FLAT. IT MAKES IT ALL THE HARDER TO BEAR.
BUT IT'S YOU – AND NOT THE INSPECTOR HERE – WHO'S DOING IT–
YES, BUT DON'T YOU SEE? HE HASN'T STARTED ON YOU YET.
IF NECESSARY I SHALL BE GLAD TO ANSWER ANY QUESTIONS THE INSPECTOR WISHES TO ASK ME.
THOUGH NATURALLY I DON'T KNOW ANYTHING ABOUT THIS GIRL.
WE'LL SEE, MRS. BIRLING.
I'VE BEEN TRYING TO PERSUADE ERIC TO GO TO BED, BUT HE WON'T. NOW HE SAYS YOU TOLD HIM TO STAY UP. DID YOU?
YES, I DID.
WHY?
BECAUSE I SHALL WANT TO TALK TO HIM, MR. BIRLING.
I CAN'T SEE WHY YOU SHOULD, BUT IF YOU MUST, THEN I SUGGEST YOU DO IT NOW.
HAVE HIM IN AND GET IT OVER, THEN LET THE LAD GO.
NO, I CAN'T DO THAT YET. I'M SORRY, BUT HE'LL HAVE TO WAIT.

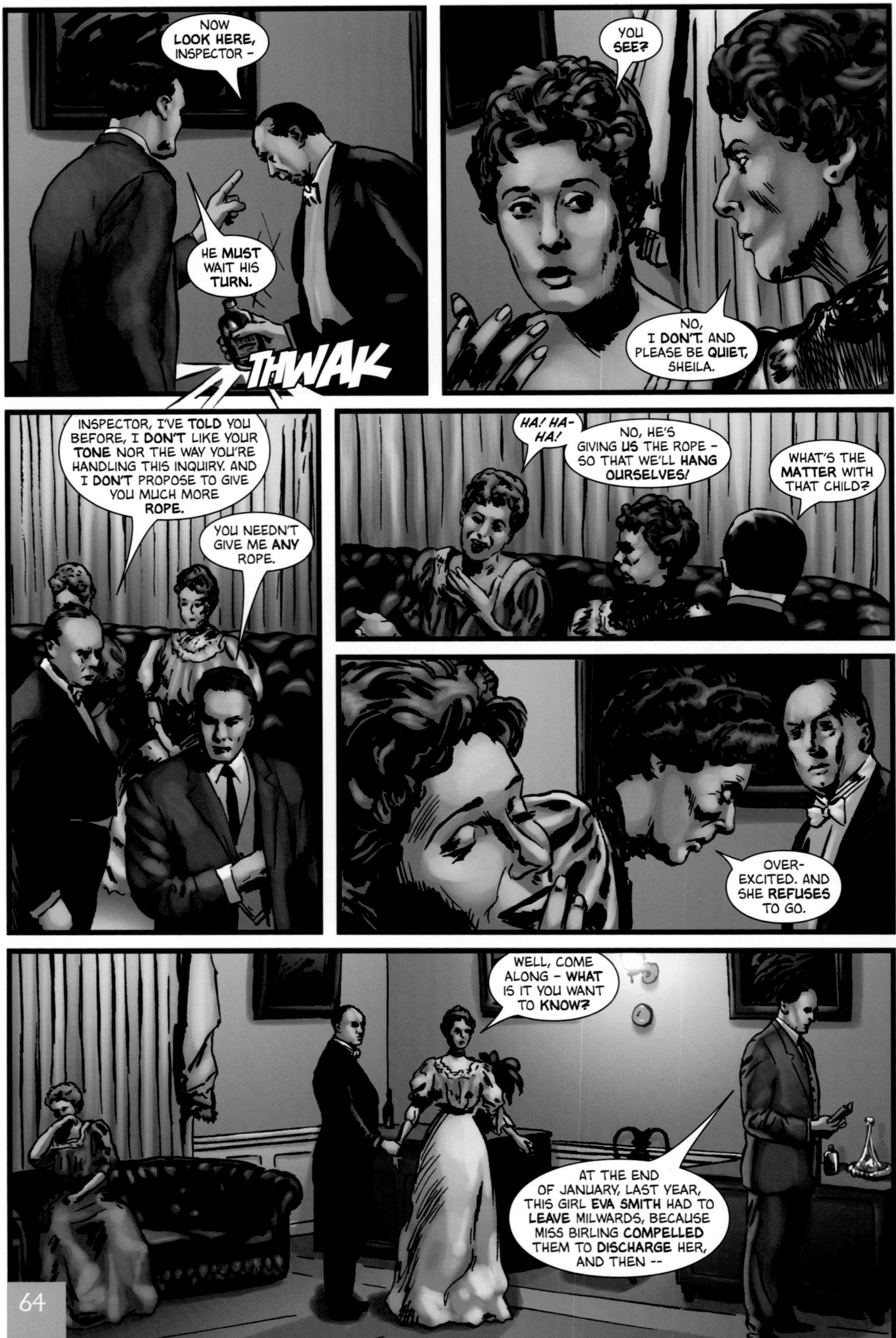
NOW LOOK HERE, INSPECTOR -
HE MUST WAIT HIS TURN.
THWAK
YOU SEE?
NO, I DON'T. AND PLEASE BE QUIET, SHEILA.
INSPECTOR, I'VE TOLD YOU BEFORE, I DON'T LIKE YOUR TONE NOR THE WAY YOU'RE HANDLING THIS INQUIRY. AND I DON'T PROPOSE TO GIVE YOU MUCH MORE ROPE.
YOU NEEDN'T GIVE ME ANY ROPE.
HA! HA-HA!
NO, HE'S GIVING US THE ROPE - SO THAT WE'LL HANG OURSELVES!
WHAT'S THE MATTER WITH THAT CHILD?
OVER-EXCITED. AND SHE REFUSES TO GO.
WELL, COME ALONG - WHAT IS IT YOU WANT TO KNOW?
AT THE END OF JANUARY, LAST YEAR, THIS GIRL EVA SMITH HAD TO LEAVE MILWARDS, BECAUSE MISS BIRLING COMPELLED THEM TO DISCHARGE HER, AND THEN --

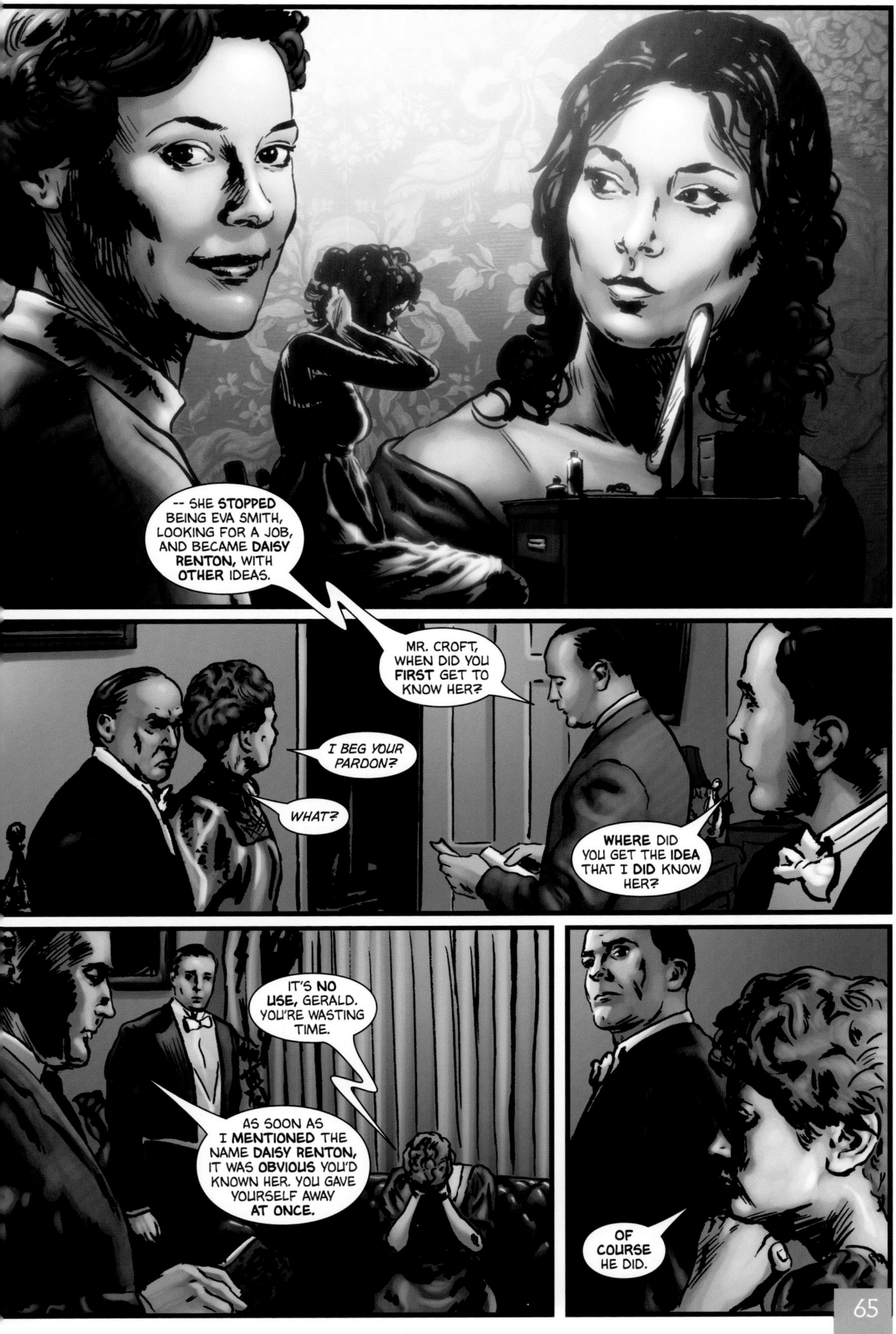
-- SHE STOPPED BEING EVA SMITH, LOOKING FOR A JOB, AND BECAME DAISY RENTON, WITH OTHER IDEAS.
MR. CROFT, WHEN DID YOU FIRST GET TO KNOW HER?
I BEG YOUR PARDON?
WHAT?
WHERE DID YOU GET THE IDEA THAT I DID KNOW HER?
IT'S NO USE, GERALD. YOU'RE WASTING TIME.
AS SOON AS I MENTIONED THE NAME DAISY RENTON, IT WAS OBVIOUS YOU'D KNOWN HER. YOU GAVE YOURSELF AWAY AT ONCE.
OF COURSE HE DID.

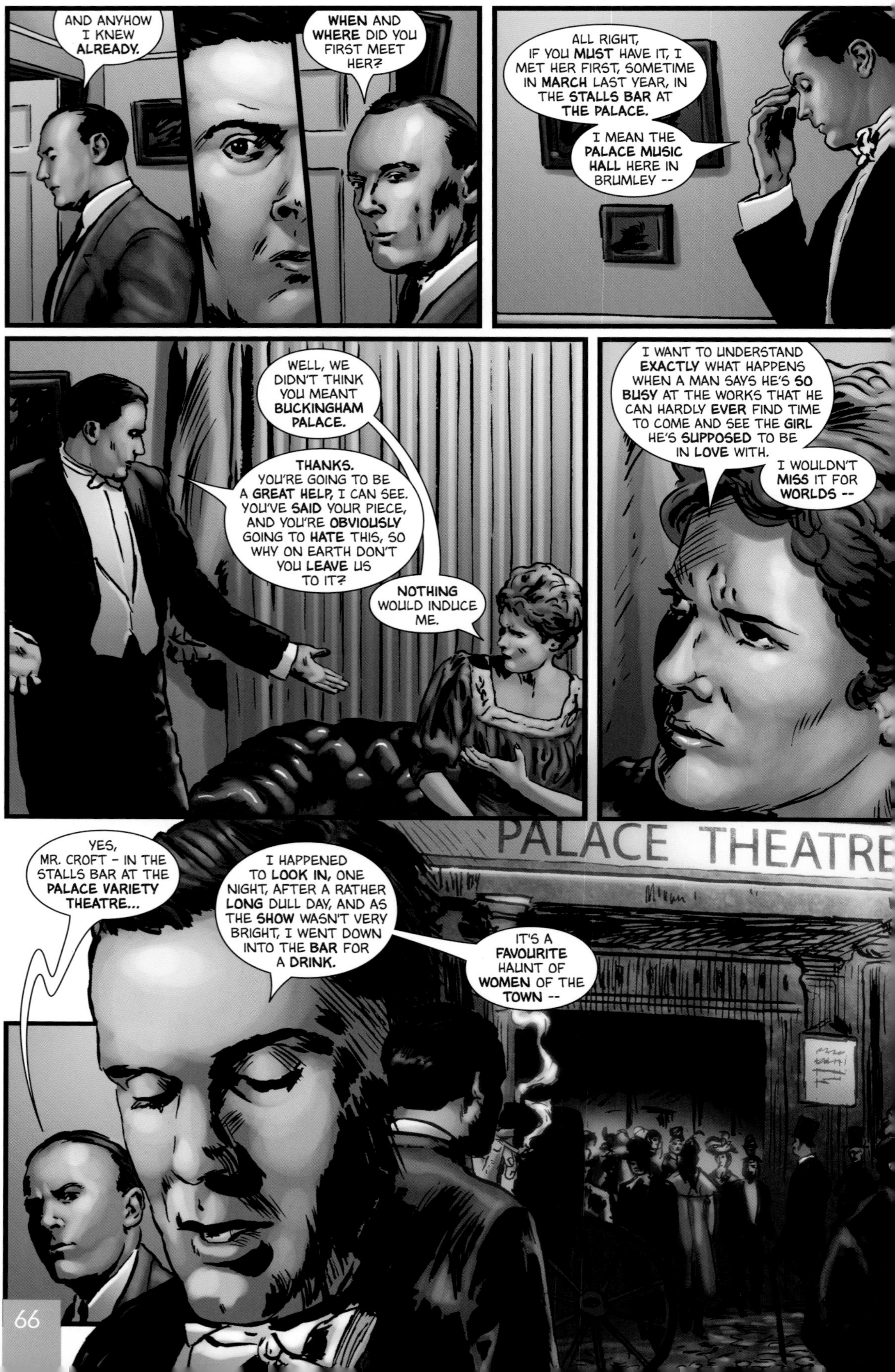
AND ANYHOW I KNEW ALREADY.
WHEN AND WHERE DID YOU FIRST MEET HER?
ALL RIGHT, IF YOU MUST HAVE IT, I MET HER FIRST, SOMETIME IN MARCH LAST YEAR, IN THE STALLS BAR AT THE PALACE.
I MEAN THE PALACE MUSIC HALL HERE IN BRUMLEY --
WELL, WE DIDN'T THINK YOU MEANT BUCKINGHAM PALACE.
THANKS. YOU'RE GOING TO BE A GREAT HELP, I CAN SEE. YOU'VE SAID YOUR PIECE, AND YOU'RE OBVIOUSLY GOING TO HATE THIS, SO WHY ON EARTH DON'T YOU LEAVE US TO IT?
NOTHING WOULD INDUCE ME.
I WANT TO UNDERSTAND EXACTLY WHAT HAPPENS WHEN A MAN SAYS HE'S SO BUSY AT THE WORKS THAT HE CAN HARDLY EVER FIND TIME TO COME AND SEE THE GIRL HE'S SUPPOSED TO BE IN LOVE WITH.
I WOULDN'T MISS IT FOR WORLDS --
PALACE THEATRE
YES, MR. CROFT – IN THE STALLS BAR AT THE PALACE VARIETY THEATRE...
I HAPPENED TO LOOK IN, ONE NIGHT, AFTER A RATHER LONG DULL DAY, AND AS THE SHOW WASN'T VERY BRIGHT, I WENT DOWN INTO THE BAR FOR A DRINK.
IT'S A FAVOURITE HAUNT OF WOMEN OF THE TOWN --

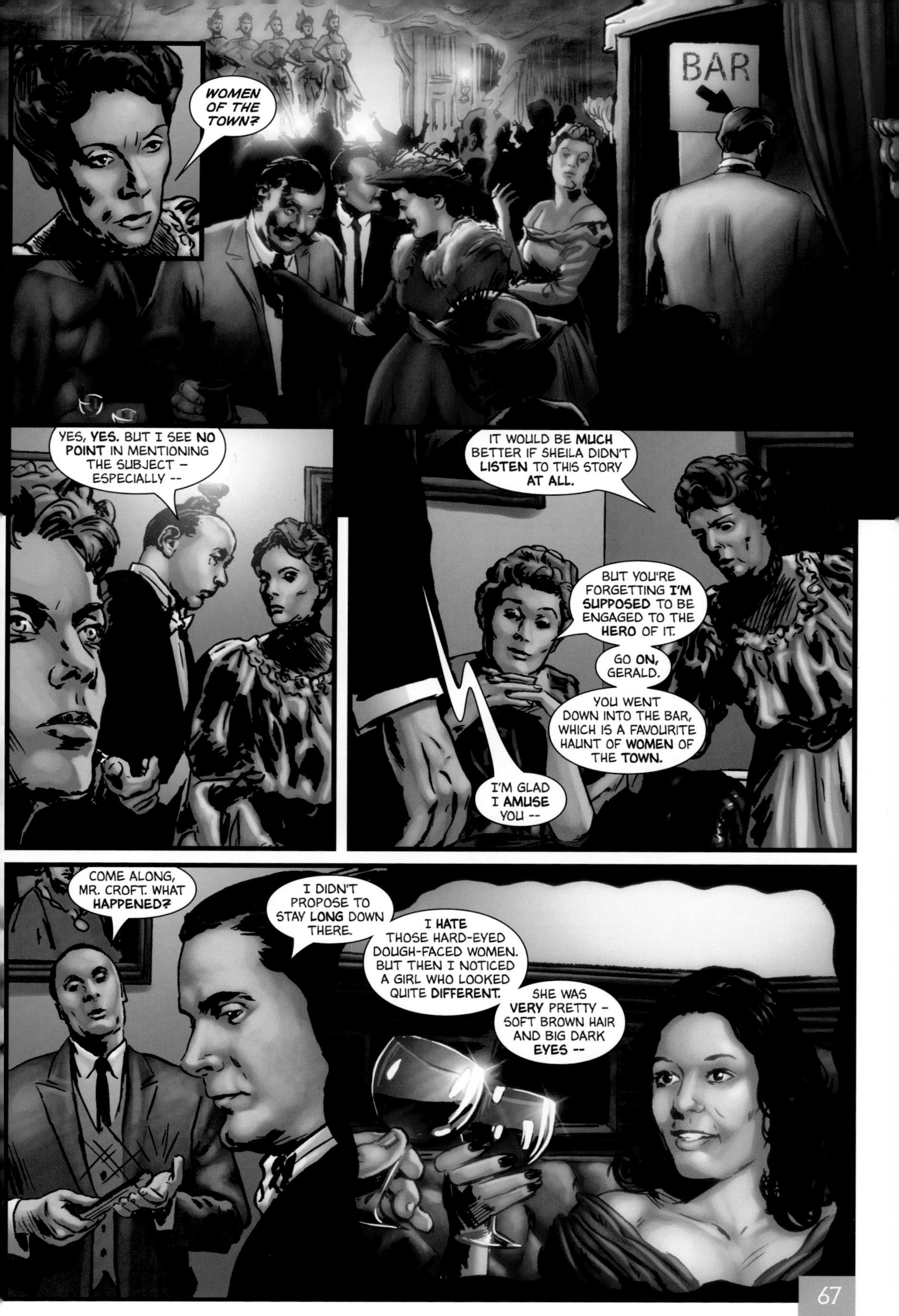
WOMEN OF THE TOWN?
BAR
YES, YES. BUT I SEE NO POINT IN MENTIONING THE SUBJECT – ESPECIALLY --
IT WOULD BE MUCH BETTER IF SHEILA DIDN'T LISTEN TO THIS STORY AT ALL.
BUT YOU'RE FORGETTING I'M SUPPOSED TO BE ENGAGED TO THE HERO OF IT.
GO ON, GERALD.
YOU WENT DOWN INTO THE BAR, WHICH IS A FAVOURITE HAUNT OF WOMEN OF THE TOWN.
I'M GLAD I AMUSE YOU --
COME ALONG, MR. CROFT. WHAT HAPPENED?
I DIDN'T PROPOSE TO STAY LONG DOWN THERE.
I HATE THOSE HARD-EYED DOUGH-FACED WOMEN. BUT THEN I NOTICED A GIRL WHO LOOKED QUITE DIFFERENT.
SHE WAS VERY PRETTY – SOFT BROWN HAIR AND BIG DARK EYES --

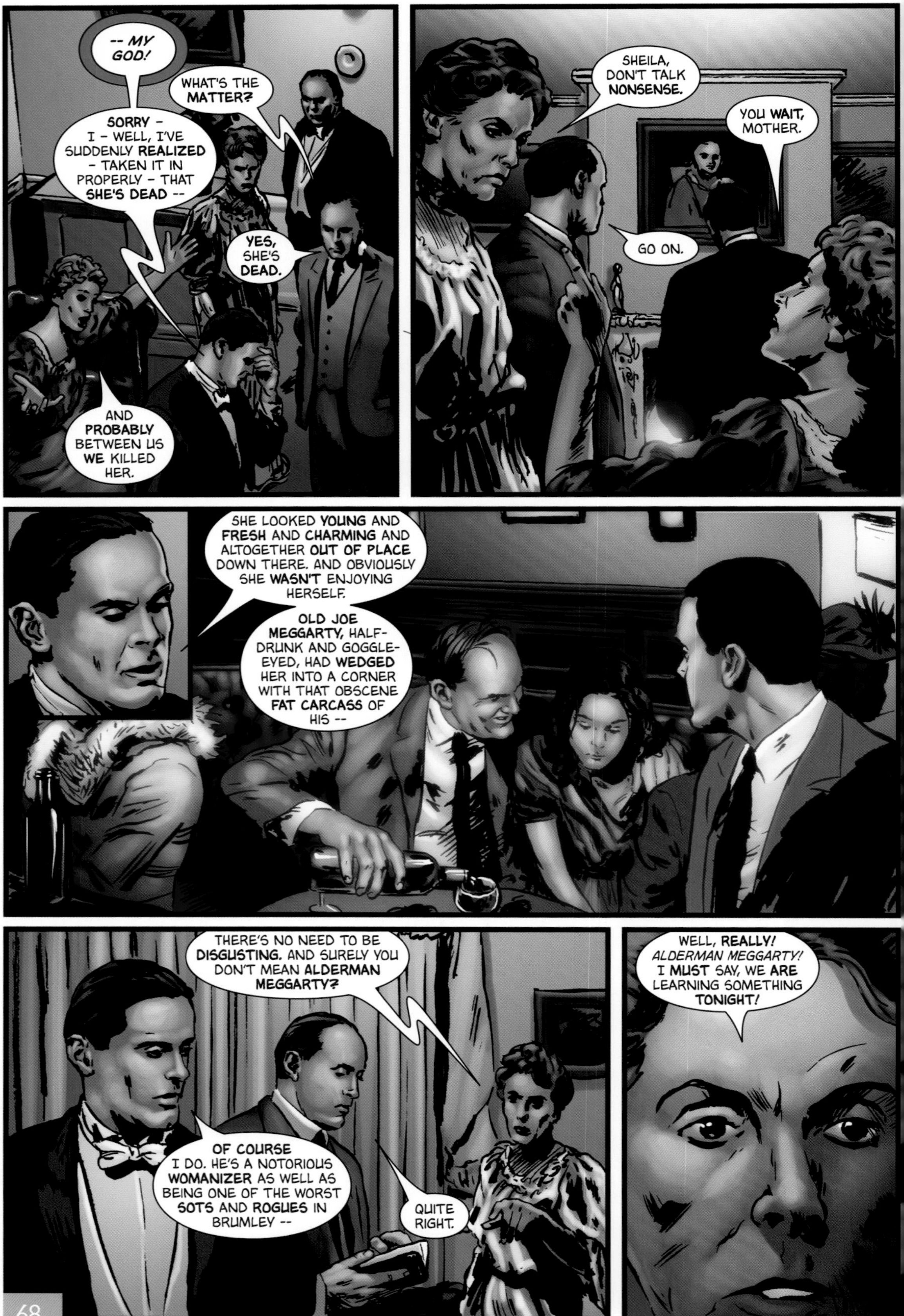
-- MY GOD!
WHAT'S THE MATTER?
SORRY – I – WELL, I'VE SUDDENLY REALIZED – TAKEN IT IN PROPERLY – THAT SHE'S DEAD --
YES, SHE'S DEAD.
AND PROBABLY BETWEEN US WE KILLED HER.
SHEILA, DON'T TALK NONSENSE.
YOU WAIT, MOTHER.
GO ON.
SHE LOOKED YOUNG AND FRESH AND CHARMING AND ALTOGETHER OUT OF PLACE DOWN THERE. AND OBVIOUSLY SHE WASN'T ENJOYING HERSELF.
OLD JOE MEGGARTY, HALF-DRUNK AND GOGGLE-EYED, HAD WEDGED HER INTO A CORNER WITH THAT OBSCENE FAT CARCASS OF HIS --
THERE'S NO NEED TO BE DISGUSTING. AND SURELY YOU DON'T MEAN ALDERMAN MEGGARTY?
OF COURSE I DO. HE'S A NOTORIOUS WOMANIZER AS WELL AS BEING ONE OF THE WORST SOTS AND ROGUES IN BRUMLEY --
QUITE RIGHT.
WELL, REALLY! ALDERMAN MEGGARTY! I MUST SAY, WE ARE LEARNING SOMETHING TONIGHT!

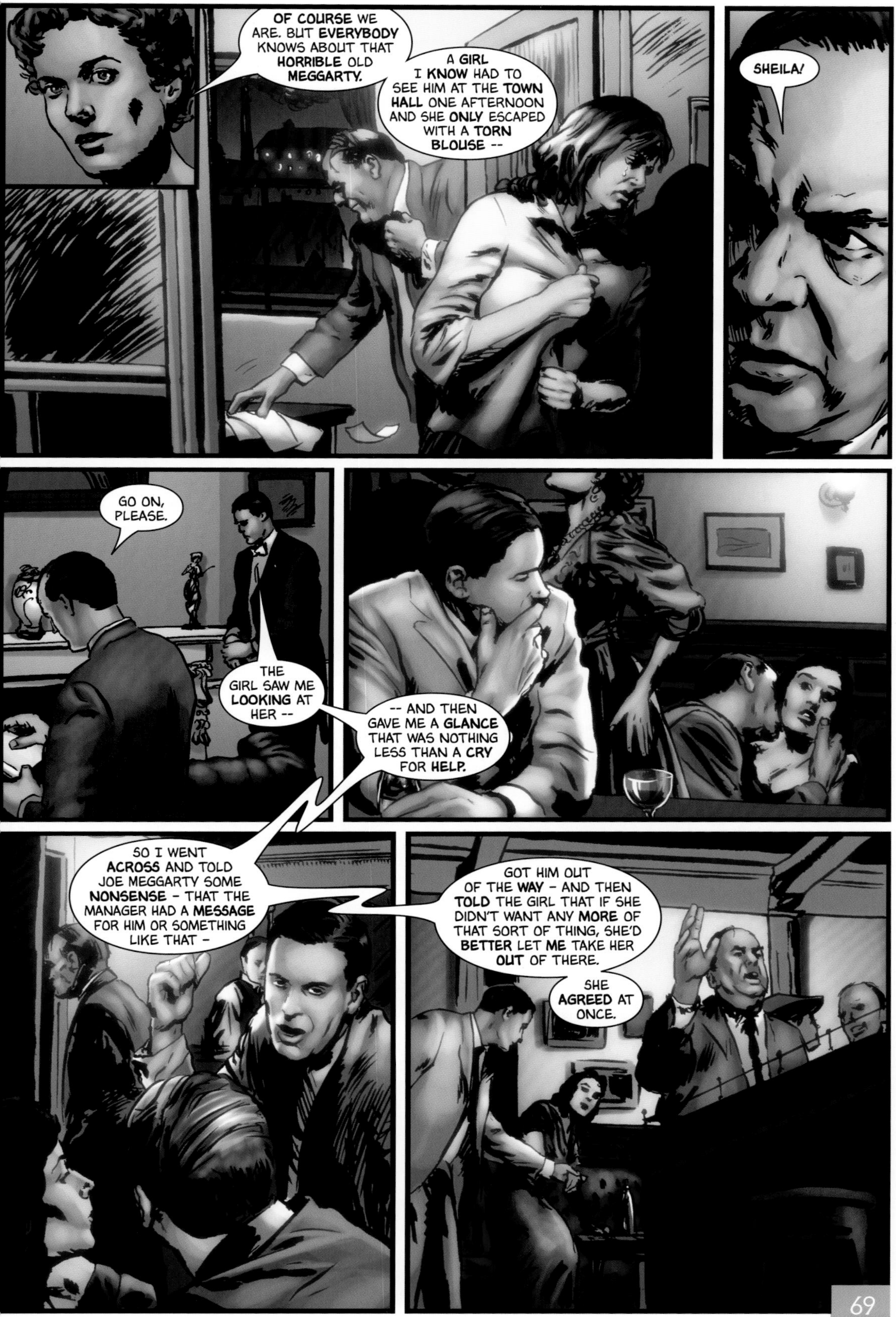
OF COURSE WE ARE. BUT EVERYBODY KNOWS ABOUT THAT HORRIBLE OLD MEGGARTY.
A GIRL I KNOW HAD TO SEE HIM AT THE TOWN HALL ONE AFTERNOON AND SHE ONLY ESCAPED WITH A TORN BLOUSE --
SHEILA!
GO ON, PLEASE.
THE GIRL SAW ME LOOKING AT HER --
-- AND THEN GAVE ME A GLANCE THAT WAS NOTHING LESS THAN A CRY FOR HELP.
SO I WENT ACROSS AND TOLD JOE MEGGARTY SOME NONSENSE - THAT THE MANAGER HAD A MESSAGE FOR HIM OR SOMETHING LIKE THAT -
GOT HIM OUT OF THE WAY - AND THEN TOLD THE GIRL THAT IF SHE DIDN'T WANT ANY MORE OF THAT SORT OF THING, SHE'D BETTER LET ME TAKE HER OUT OF THERE.
SHE AGREED AT ONCE.

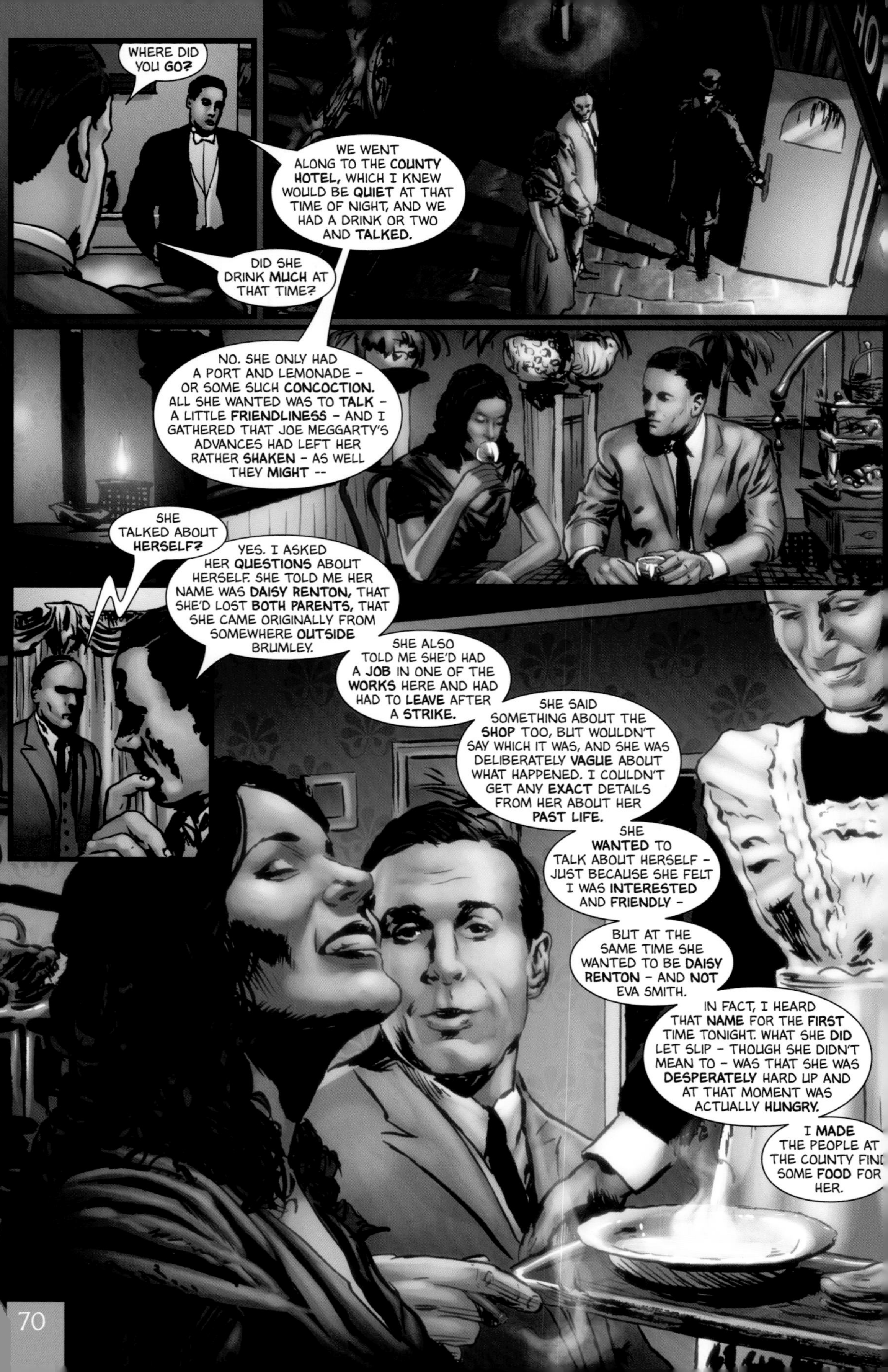
WHERE DID YOU GO?
WE WENT ALONG TO THE COUNTY HOTEL, WHICH I KNEW WOULD BE QUIET AT THAT TIME OF NIGHT, AND WE HAD A DRINK OR TWO AND TALKED.
DID SHE DRINK MUCH AT THAT TIME?
NO. SHE ONLY HAD A PORT AND LEMONADE - OR SOME SUCH CONCOCTION. ALL SHE WANTED WAS TO TALK - A LITTLE FRIENDLINESS - AND I GATHERED THAT JOE MEGGARTY'S ADVANCES HAD LEFT HER RATHER SHAKEN - AS WELL THEY MIGHT --
SHE TALKED ABOUT HERSELF?
YES. I ASKED HER QUESTIONS ABOUT HERSELF. SHE TOLD ME HER NAME WAS DAISY RENTON, THAT SHE'D LOST BOTH PARENTS, THAT SHE CAME ORIGINALLY FROM SOMEWHERE OUTSIDE BRUMLEY.
SHE ALSO TOLD ME SHE'D HAD A JOB IN ONE OF THE WORKS HERE AND HAD HAD TO LEAVE AFTER A STRIKE.
SHE SAID SOMETHING ABOUT THE SHOP TOO, BUT WOULDN'T SAY WHICH IT WAS, AND SHE WAS DELIBERATELY VAGUE ABOUT WHAT HAPPENED. I COULDN'T GET ANY EXACT DETAILS FROM HER ABOUT HER PAST LIFE.
SHE WANTED TO TALK ABOUT HERSELF - JUST BECAUSE SHE FELT I WAS INTERESTED AND FRIENDLY -
BUT AT THE SAME TIME SHE WANTED TO BE DAISY RENTON - AND NOT EVA SMITH.
IN FACT, I HEARD THAT NAME FOR THE FIRST TIME TONIGHT. WHAT SHE DID LET SLIP - THOUGH SHE DIDN'T MEAN TO - WAS THAT SHE WAS DESPERATELY HARD UP AND AT THAT MOMENT WAS ACTUALLY HUNGRY.
I MADE THE PEOPLE AT THE COUNTY FIND SOME FOOD FOR HER.

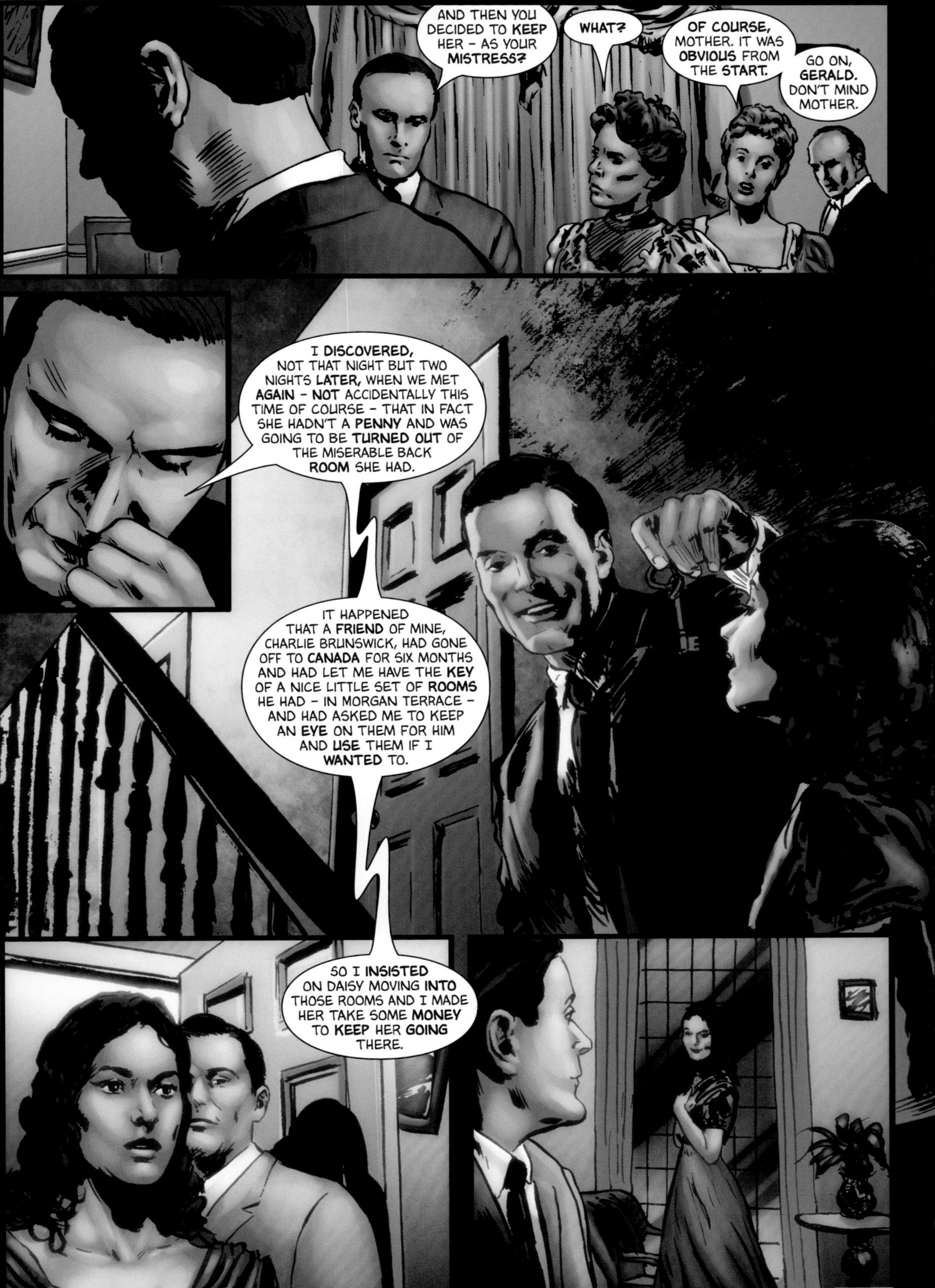
AND THEN YOU DECIDED TO KEEP HER - AS YOUR MISTRESS?
WHAT?
OF COURSE, MOTHER. IT WAS OBVIOUS FROM THE START.
GO ON, GERALD. DON'T MIND MOTHER.
I DISCOVERED, NOT THAT NIGHT BUT TWO NIGHTS LATER, WHEN WE MET AGAIN - NOT ACCIDENTALLY THIS TIME OF COURSE - THAT IN FACT SHE HADN'T A PENNY AND WAS GOING TO BE TURNED OUT OF THE MISERABLE BACK ROOM SHE HAD.
IT HAPPENED THAT A FRIEND OF MINE, CHARLIE BRUNSWICK, HAD GONE OFF TO CANADA FOR SIX MONTHS AND HAD LET ME HAVE THE KEY OF A NICE LITTLE SET OF ROOMS HE HAD - IN MORGAN TERRACE - AND HAD ASKED ME TO KEEP AN EYE ON THEM FOR HIM AND USE THEM IF I WANTED TO.
SO I INSISTED ON DAISY MOVING INTO THOSE ROOMS AND I MADE HER TAKE SOME MONEY TO KEEP HER GOING THERE.

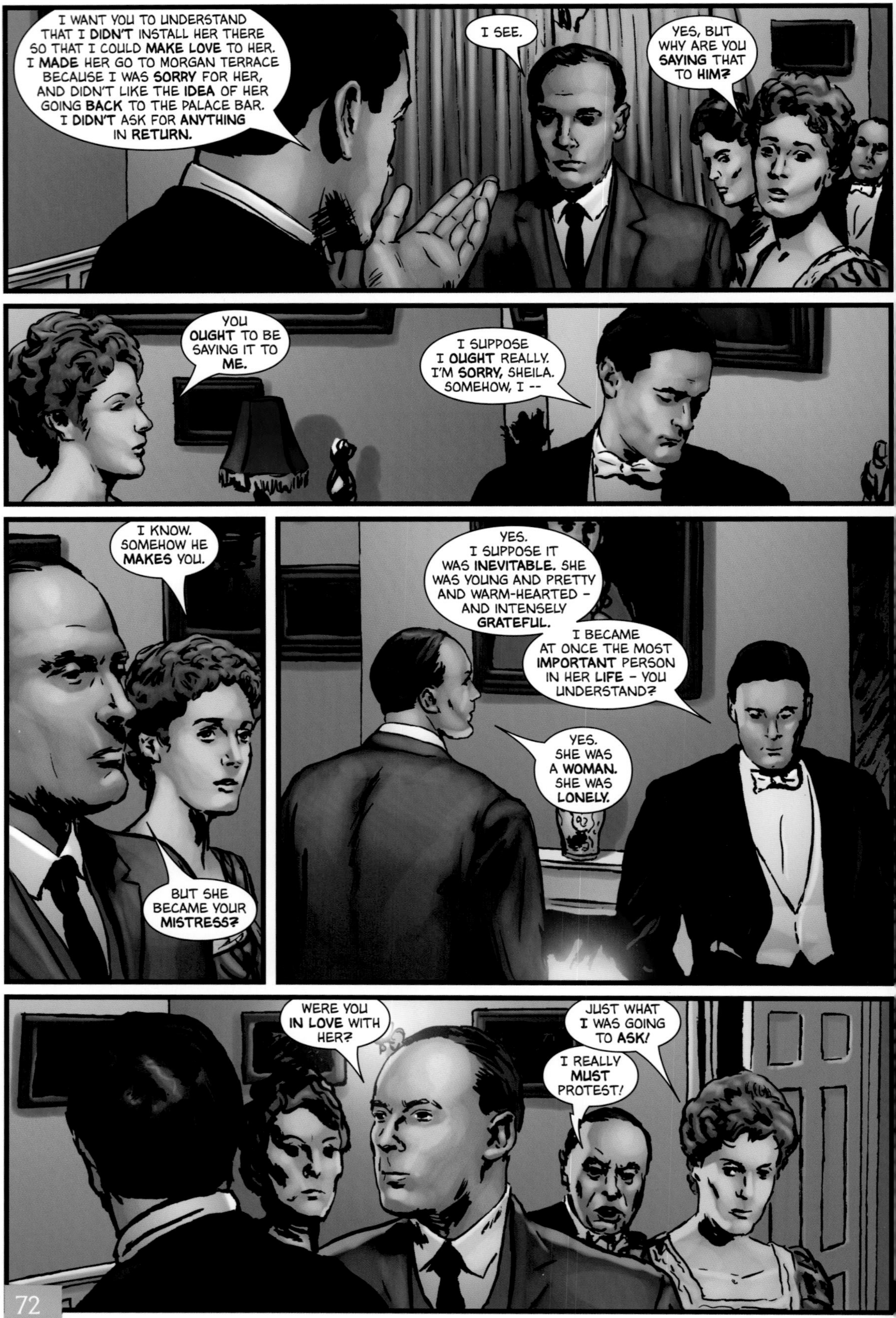

I WANT YOU TO UNDERSTAND THAT I DIDN'T INSTALL HER THERE SO THAT I COULD MAKE LOVE TO HER. I MADE HER GO TO MORGAN TERRACE BECAUSE I WAS SORRY FOR HER, AND DIDN'T LIKE THE IDEA OF HER GOING BACK TO THE PALACE BAR. I DIDN'T ASK FOR ANYTHING IN RETURN.
I SEE.
YES, BUT WHY ARE YOU SAYING THAT TO HIM?
YOU OUGHT TO BE SAYING IT TO ME.
I SUPPOSE I OUGHT REALLY. I'M SORRY, SHEILA. SOMEHOW, I --
I KNOW. SOMEHOW HE MAKES YOU.
BUT SHE BECAME YOUR MISTRESS?
YES. I SUPPOSE IT WAS INEVITABLE. SHE WAS YOUNG AND PRETTY AND WARM-HEARTED – AND INTENSELY GRATEFUL.
I BECAME AT ONCE THE MOST IMPORTANT PERSON IN HER LIFE – YOU UNDERSTAND?
YES. SHE WAS A WOMAN. SHE WAS LONELY.
WERE YOU IN LOVE WITH HER?
JUST WHAT I WAS GOING TO ASK!
I REALLY MUST PROTEST!

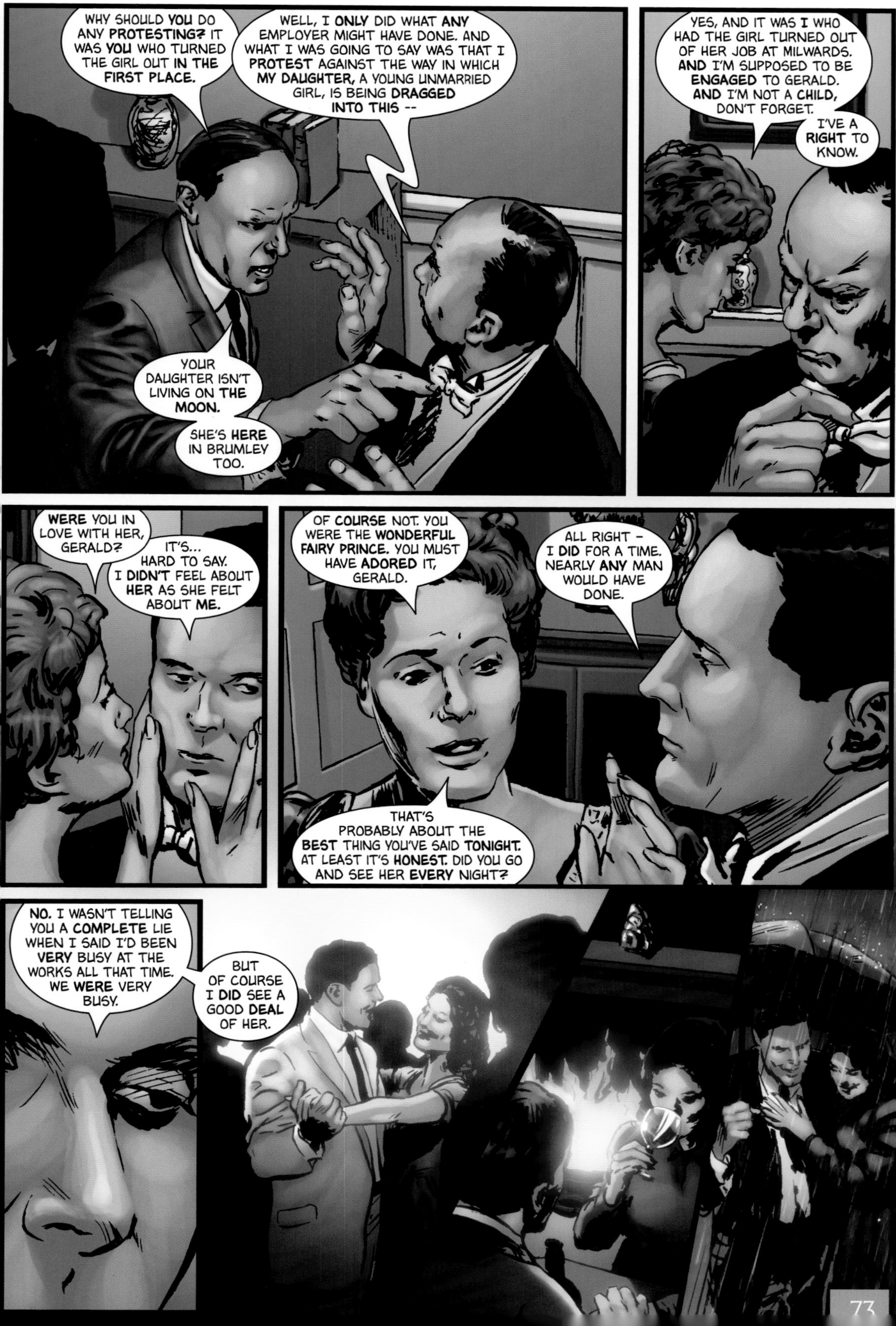
WHY SHOULD YOU DO ANY PROTESTING? IT WAS YOU WHO TURNED THE GIRL OUT IN THE FIRST PLACE.
WELL, I ONLY DID WHAT ANY EMPLOYER MIGHT HAVE DONE. AND WHAT I WAS GOING TO SAY WAS THAT I PROTEST AGAINST THE WAY IN WHICH MY DAUGHTER, A YOUNG UNMARRIED GIRL, IS BEING DRAGGED INTO THIS --
YOUR DAUGHTER ISN'T LIVING ON THE MOON.
SHE'S HERE IN BRUMLEY TOO.
YES, AND IT WAS I WHO HAD THE GIRL TURNED OUT OF HER JOB AT MILWARDS. AND I'M SUPPOSED TO BE ENGAGED TO GERALD. AND I'M NOT A CHILD, DON'T FORGET.
I'VE A RIGHT TO KNOW.
WERE YOU IN LOVE WITH HER, GERALD?
IT'S... HARD TO SAY. I DIDN'T FEEL ABOUT HER AS SHE FELT ABOUT ME.
OF COURSE NOT. YOU WERE THE WONDERFUL FAIRY PRINCE. YOU MUST HAVE ADORED IT, GERALD.
ALL RIGHT – I DID FOR A TIME. NEARLY ANY MAN WOULD HAVE DONE.
THAT'S PROBABLY ABOUT THE BEST THING YOU'VE SAID TONIGHT. AT LEAST IT'S HONEST. DID YOU GO AND SEE HER EVERY NIGHT?
NO. I WASN'T TELLING YOU A COMPLETE LIE WHEN I SAID I'D BEEN VERY BUSY AT THE WORKS ALL THAT TIME. WE WERE VERY BUSY.
BUT OF COURSE I DID SEE A GOOD DEAL OF HER.

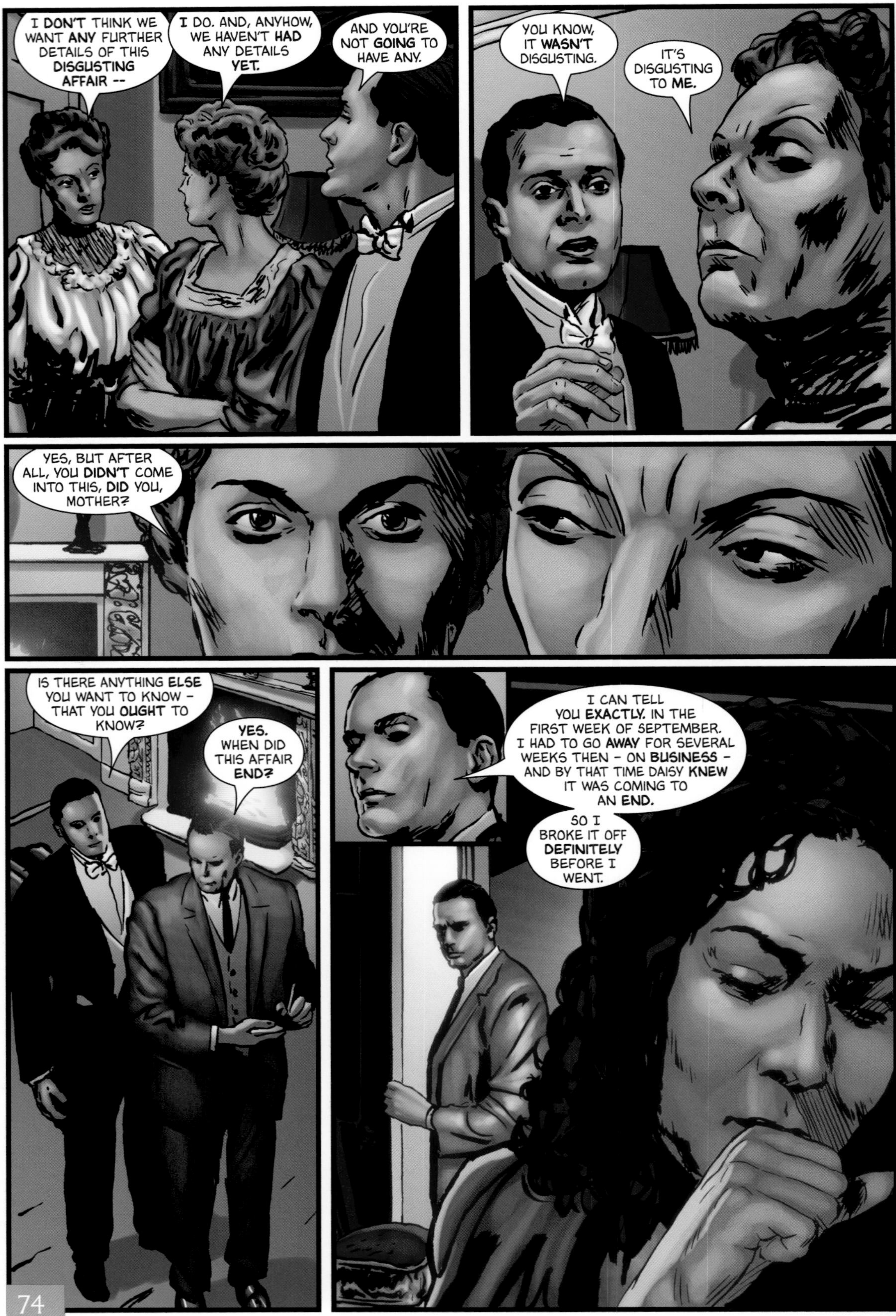
I DON'T THINK WE WANT ANY FURTHER DETAILS OF THIS DISGUSTING AFFAIR --
I DO. AND, ANYHOW, WE HAVEN'T HAD ANY DETAILS YET.
AND YOU'RE NOT GOING TO HAVE ANY.
YOU KNOW, IT WASN'T DISGUSTING.
IT'S DISGUSTING TO ME.
YES, BUT AFTER ALL, YOU DIDN'T COME INTO THIS, DID YOU, MOTHER?
IS THERE ANYTHING ELSE YOU WANT TO KNOW – THAT YOU OUGHT TO KNOW?
YES. WHEN DID THIS AFFAIR END?
I CAN TELL YOU EXACTLY. IN THE FIRST WEEK OF SEPTEMBER. I HAD TO GO AWAY FOR SEVERAL WEEKS THEN – ON BUSINESS – AND BY THAT TIME DAISY KNEW IT WAS COMING TO AN END.
SO I BROKE IT OFF DEFINITELY BEFORE I WENT.

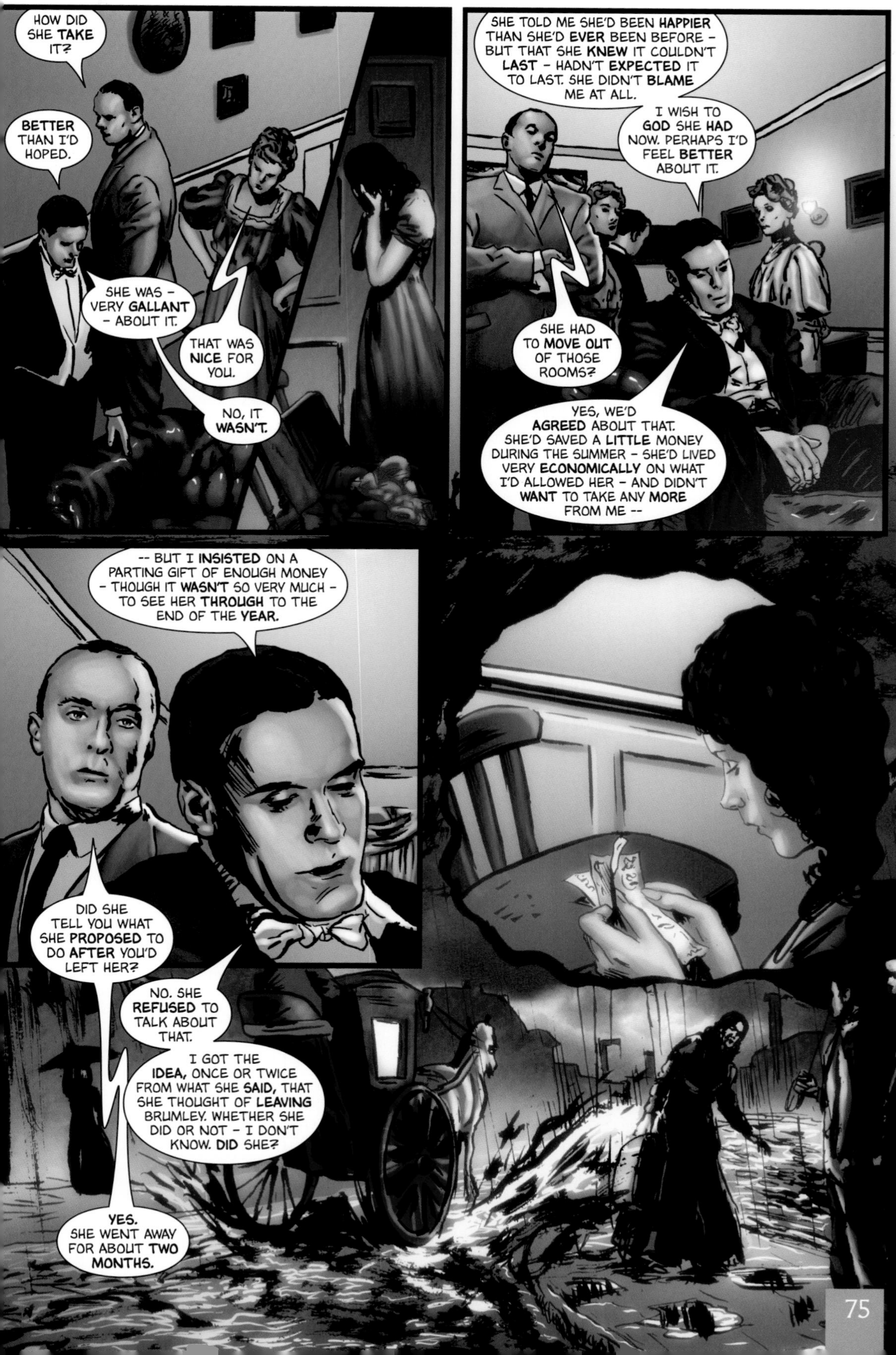
HOW DID SHE TAKE IT?
BETTER THAN I'D HOPED.
SHE WAS - VERY GALLANT - ABOUT IT.
THAT WAS NICE FOR YOU.
NO, IT WASN'T.
SHE TOLD ME SHE'D BEEN HAPPIER THAN SHE'D EVER BEEN BEFORE - BUT THAT SHE KNEW IT COULDN'T LAST - HADN'T EXPECTED IT TO LAST. SHE DIDN'T BLAME ME AT ALL.
I WISH TO GOD SHE HAD NOW. PERHAPS I'D FEEL BETTER ABOUT IT.
SHE HAD TO MOVE OUT OF THOSE ROOMS?
YES, WE'D AGREED ABOUT THAT. SHE'D SAVED A LITTLE MONEY DURING THE SUMMER - SHE'D LIVED VERY ECONOMICALLY ON WHAT I'D ALLOWED HER - AND DIDN'T WANT TO TAKE ANY MORE FROM ME --
-- BUT I INSISTED ON A PARTING GIFT OF ENOUGH MONEY - THOUGH IT WASN'T SO VERY MUCH - TO SEE HER THROUGH TO THE END OF THE YEAR.
DID SHE TELL YOU WHAT SHE PROPOSED TO DO AFTER YOU'D LEFT HER?
NO. SHE REFUSED TO TALK ABOUT THAT.
I GOT THE IDEA, ONCE OR TWICE FROM WHAT SHE SAID, THAT SHE THOUGHT OF LEAVING BRUMLEY. WHETHER SHE DID OR NOT - I DON'T KNOW. DID SHE?
YES. SHE WENT AWAY FOR ABOUT TWO MONTHS.

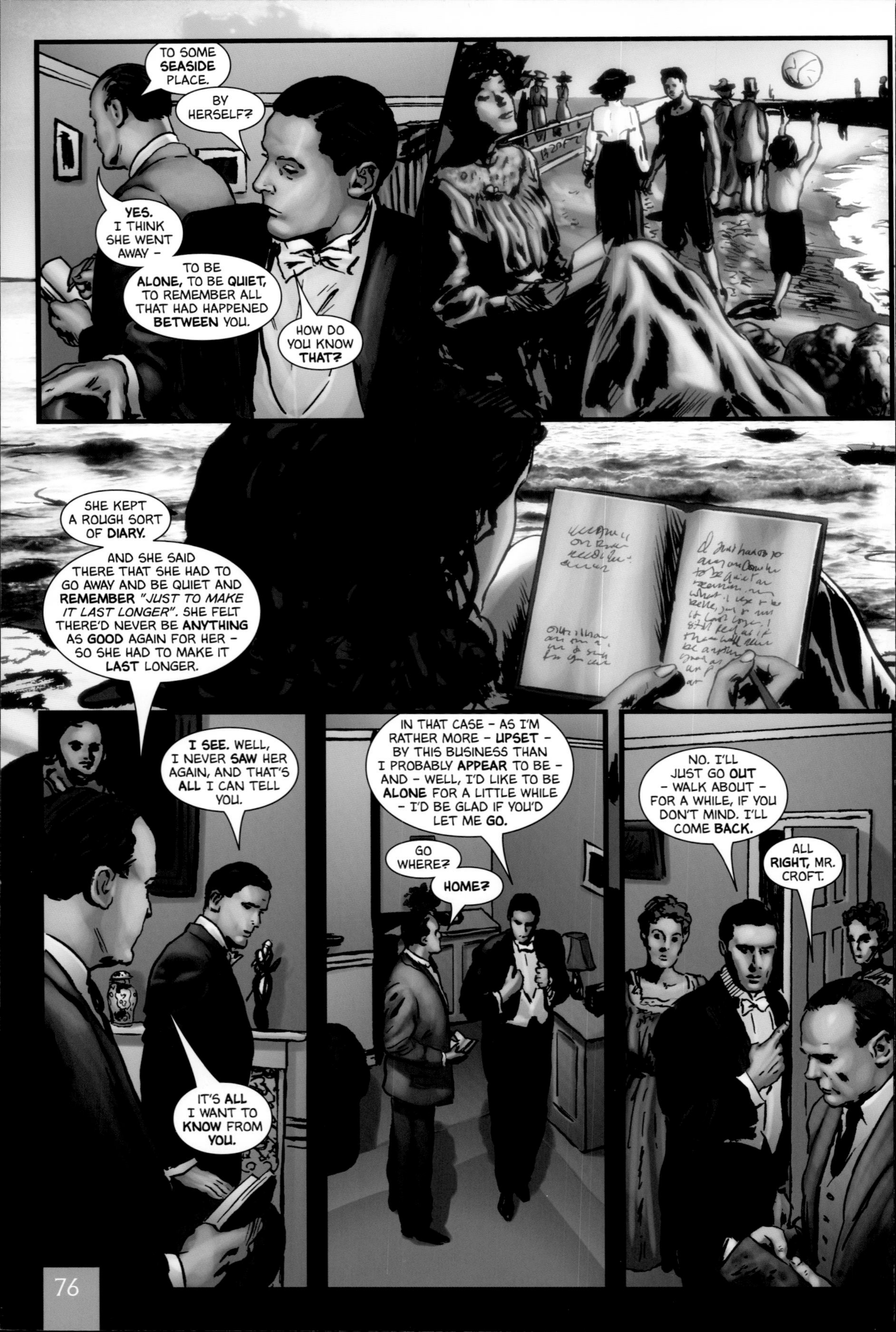

TO SOME SEASIDE PLACE.
BY HERSELF?
YES. I THINK SHE WENT AWAY –
TO BE ALONE, TO BE QUIET, TO REMEMBER ALL THAT HAD HAPPENED BETWEEN YOU.
HOW DO YOU KNOW THAT?
SHE KEPT A ROUGH SORT OF DIARY.
AND SHE SAID THERE THAT SHE HAD TO GO AWAY AND BE QUIET AND REMEMBER "JUST TO MAKE IT LAST LONGER". SHE FELT THERE'D NEVER BE ANYTHING AS GOOD AGAIN FOR HER – SO SHE HAD TO MAKE IT LAST LONGER.
I SEE. WELL, I NEVER SAW HER AGAIN, AND THAT'S ALL I CAN TELL YOU.
IT'S ALL I WANT TO KNOW FROM YOU.
IN THAT CASE – AS I'M RATHER MORE – UPSET – BY THIS BUSINESS THAN I PROBABLY APPEAR TO BE – AND – WELL, I'D LIKE TO BE ALONE FOR A LITTLE WHILE – I'D BE GLAD IF YOU'D LET ME GO.
GO WHERE?
HOME?
NO. I'LL JUST GO OUT – WALK ABOUT – FOR A WHILE, IF YOU DON'T MIND. I'LL COME BACK.
ALL RIGHT, MR. CROFT.

BUT JUST IN CASE YOU **FORGET** -- OR DECIDE **NOT** TO COME **BACK**, GERALD --

-- I THINK YOU'D BETTER TAKE **THIS** WITH YOU.

I SEE. WELL, I WAS **EXPECTING** THIS.

I **DON'T DISLIKE** YOU AS I DID HALF AN HOUR AGO, GERALD. IN FACT, IN SOME **ODD** WAY, I RATHER **RESPECT** YOU **MORE** THAN I'VE EVER DONE BEFORE.

I **KNEW** ANYHOW YOU WERE **LYING** ABOUT THOSE MONTHS LAST YEAR WHEN YOU HARDLY CAME **NEAR** ME.

I **KNEW** THERE WAS SOMETHING **FISHY** ABOUT THAT TIME. AND NOW AT LEAST YOU'VE BEEN **HONEST**. AND I BELIEVE WHAT YOU TOLD US ABOUT THE WAY YOU **HELPED** HER AT FIRST. JUST OUT OF **PITY**.

AND IT WAS MY **FAULT** REALLY THAT SHE WAS SO **DESPERATE** WHEN YOU FIRST MET HER.

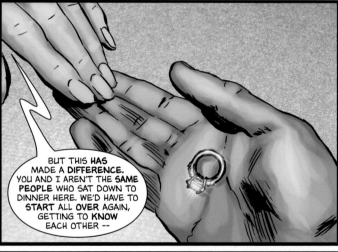

BUT THIS **HAS** MADE A **DIFFERENCE**. YOU AND I AREN'T THE **SAME** PEOPLE WHO SAT DOWN TO DINNER HERE. WE'D HAVE TO **START** ALL **OVER** AGAIN, GETTING TO **KNOW** EACH OTHER --

NOW, SHEILA, I'M NOT **DEFENDING** HIM. BUT YOU **MUST** UNDERSTAND THAT A **LOT** OF YOUNG MEN --

DON'T **INTERFERE**, PLEASE, FATHER. GERALD **KNOWS** WHAT I MEAN, AND **YOU** APPARENTLY **DON'T**.

77

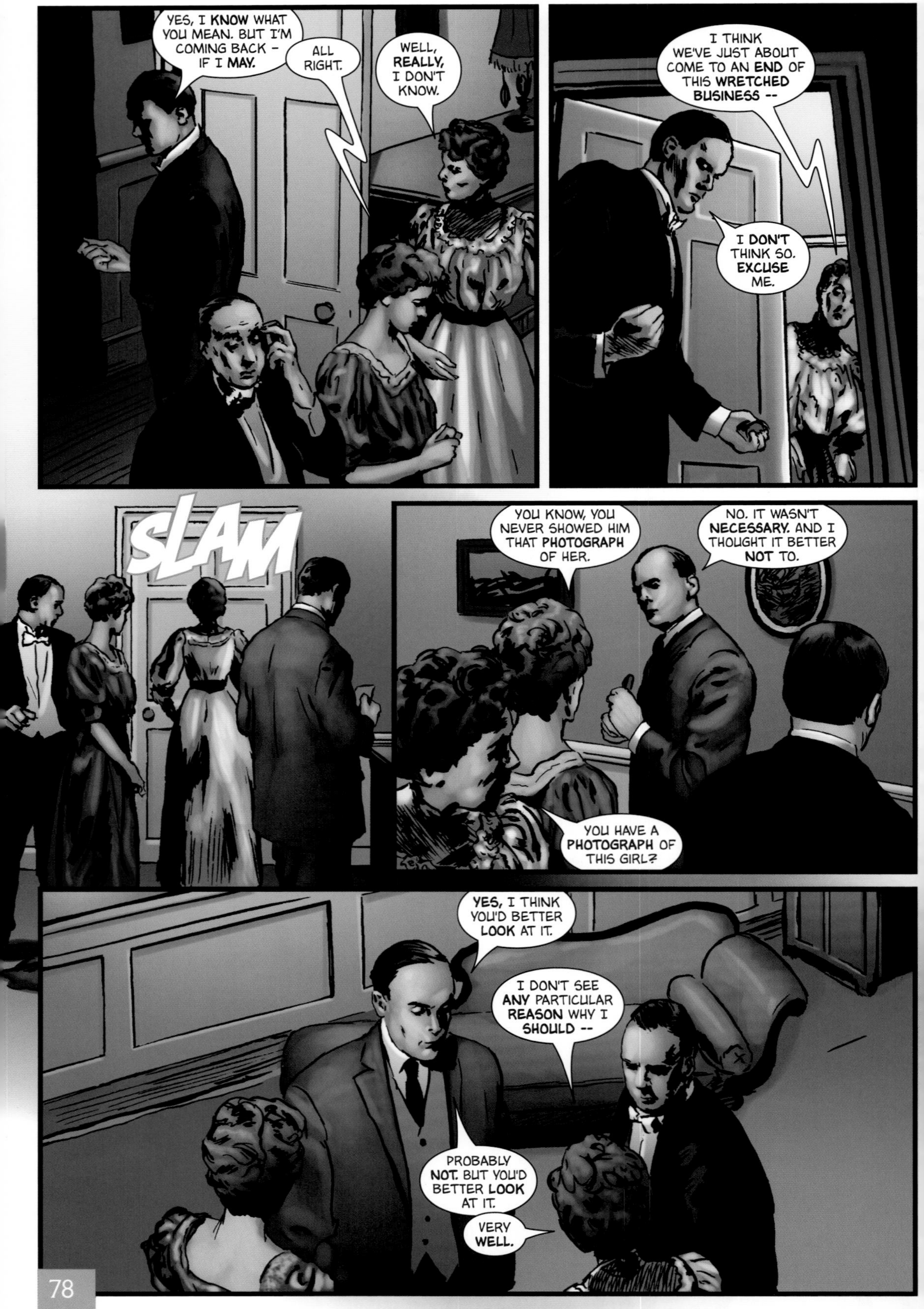
YES, I KNOW WHAT YOU MEAN. BUT I'M COMING BACK – IF I MAY.
ALL RIGHT.
WELL, REALLY, I DON'T KNOW.
I THINK WE'VE JUST ABOUT COME TO AN END OF THIS WRETCHED BUSINESS --
I DON'T THINK SO. EXCUSE ME.
SLAM
YOU KNOW, YOU NEVER SHOWED HIM THAT PHOTOGRAPH OF HER.
NO. IT WASN'T NECESSARY. AND I THOUGHT IT BETTER NOT TO.
YOU HAVE A PHOTOGRAPH OF THIS GIRL?
YES, I THINK YOU'D BETTER LOOK AT IT.
I DON'T SEE ANY PARTICULAR REASON WHY I SHOULD --
PROBABLY NOT. BUT YOU'D BETTER LOOK AT IT.
VERY WELL.

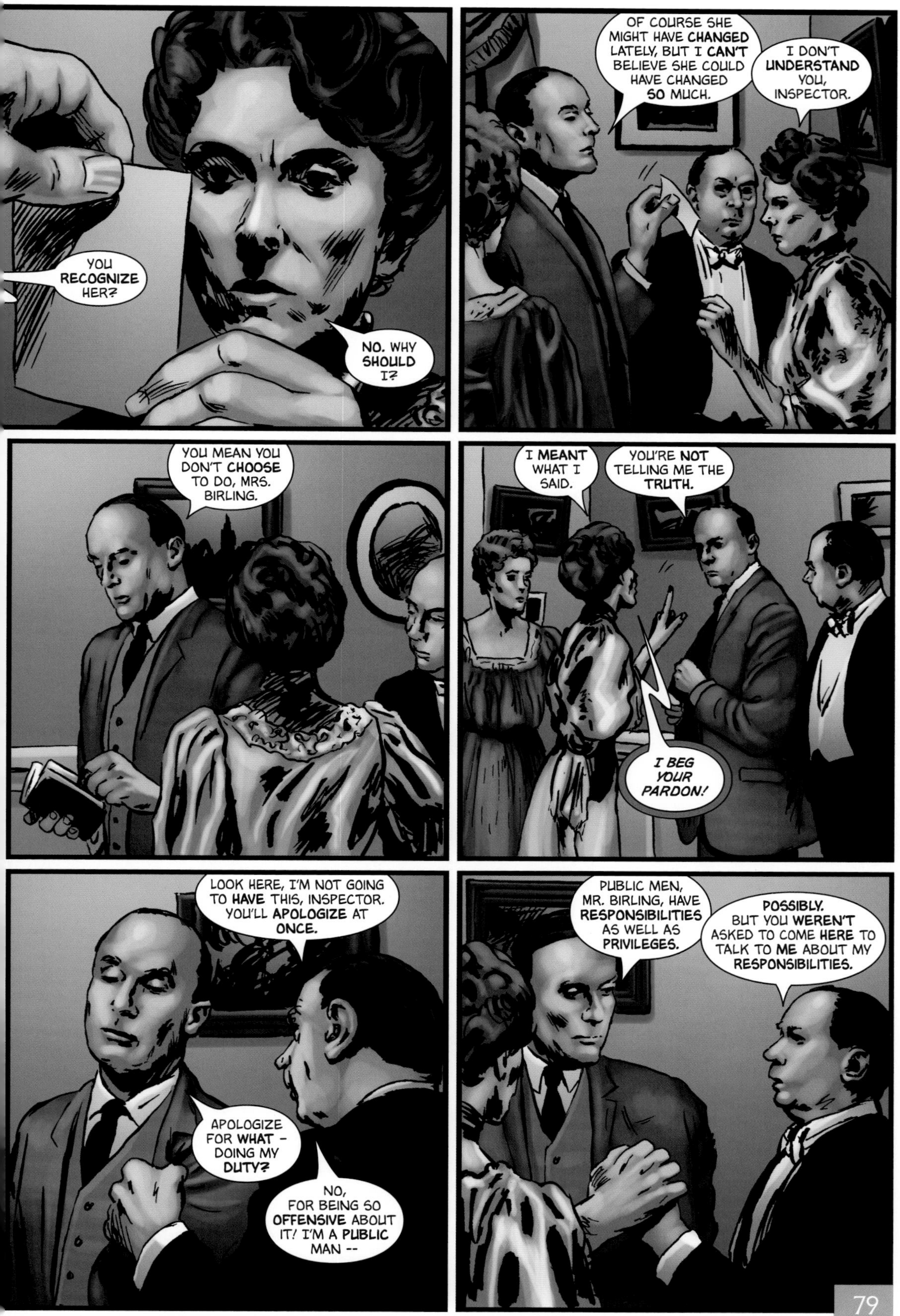
YOU RECOGNIZE HER?
NO. WHY SHOULD I?
OF COURSE SHE MIGHT HAVE CHANGED LATELY, BUT I CAN'T BELIEVE SHE COULD HAVE CHANGED SO MUCH.
I DON'T UNDERSTAND YOU, INSPECTOR.
YOU MEAN YOU DON'T CHOOSE TO DO, MRS. BIRLING.
I MEANT WHAT I SAID.
YOU'RE NOT TELLING ME THE TRUTH.
I BEG YOUR PARDON!
LOOK HERE, I'M NOT GOING TO HAVE THIS, INSPECTOR. YOU'LL APOLOGIZE AT ONCE.
APOLOGIZE FOR WHAT - DOING MY DUTY?
NO, FOR BEING SO OFFENSIVE ABOUT IT! I'M A PUBLIC MAN --
PUBLIC MEN, MR. BIRLING, HAVE RESPONSIBILITIES AS WELL AS PRIVILEGES.
POSSIBLY. BUT YOU WEREN'T ASKED TO COME HERE TO TALK TO ME ABOUT MY RESPONSIBILITIES.

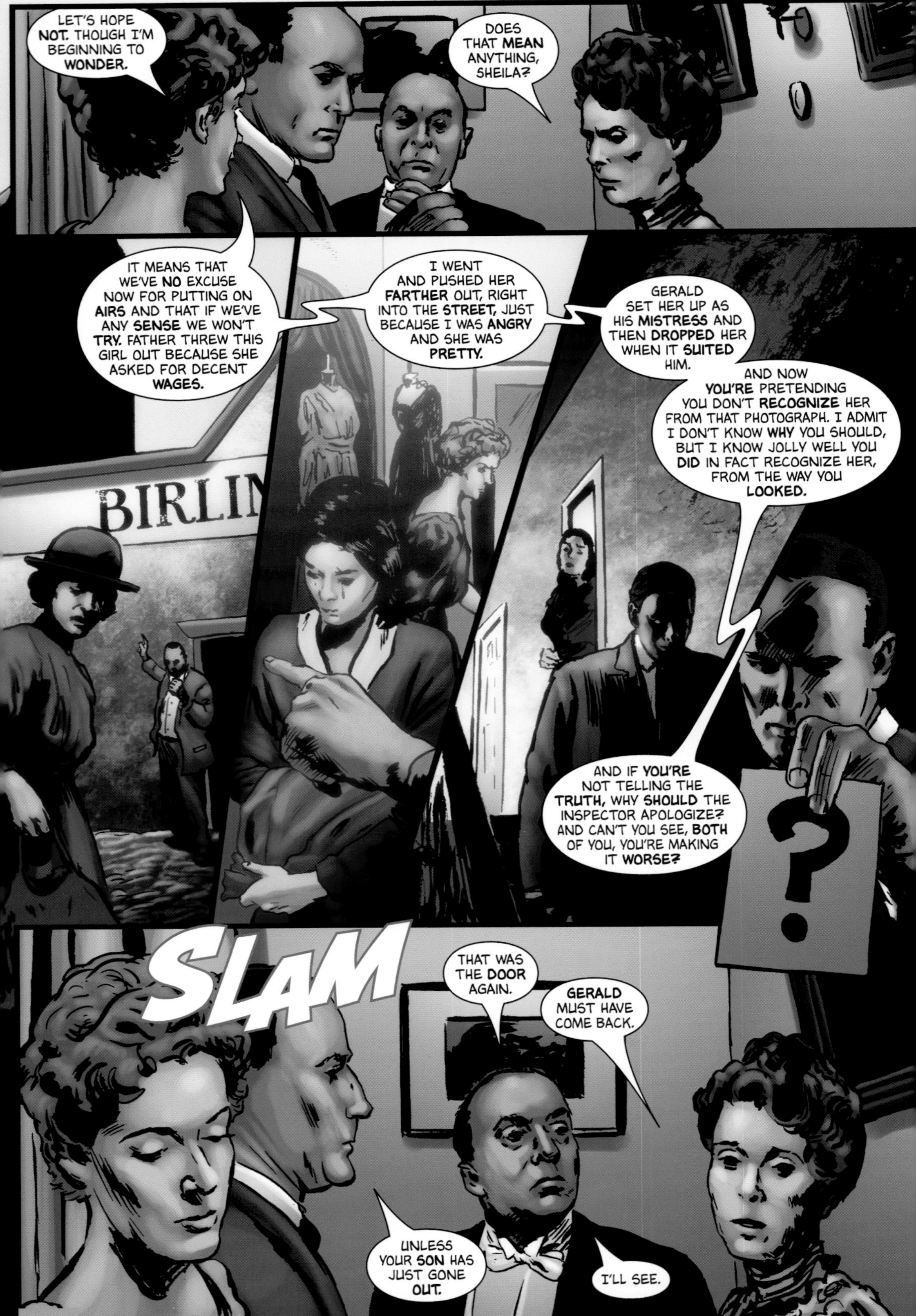
LET'S HOPE NOT. THOUGH I'M BEGINNING TO WONDER.
DOES THAT MEAN ANYTHING, SHEILA?
IT MEANS THAT WE'VE NO EXCUSE NOW FOR PUTTING ON AIRS AND THAT IF WE'VE ANY SENSE WE WON'T TRY. FATHER THREW THIS GIRL OUT BECAUSE SHE ASKED FOR DECENT WAGES.
BIRLIN
I WENT AND PUSHED HER FARTHER OUT, RIGHT INTO THE STREET, JUST BECAUSE I WAS ANGRY AND SHE WAS PRETTY.
GERALD SET HER UP AS HIS MISTRESS AND THEN DROPPED HER WHEN IT SUITED HIM.
AND NOW YOU'RE PRETENDING YOU DON'T RECOGNIZE HER FROM THAT PHOTOGRAPH. I ADMIT I DON'T KNOW WHY YOU SHOULD, BUT I KNOW JOLLY WELL YOU DID IN FACT RECOGNIZE HER, FROM THE WAY YOU LOOKED.
AND IF YOU'RE NOT TELLING THE TRUTH, WHY SHOULD THE INSPECTOR APOLOGIZE? AND CAN'T YOU SEE, BOTH OF YOU, YOU'RE MAKING IT WORSE?
?
SLAM
THAT WAS THE DOOR AGAIN.
GERALD MUST HAVE COME BACK.
UNLESS YOUR SON HAS JUST GONE OUT.
I'LL SEE.

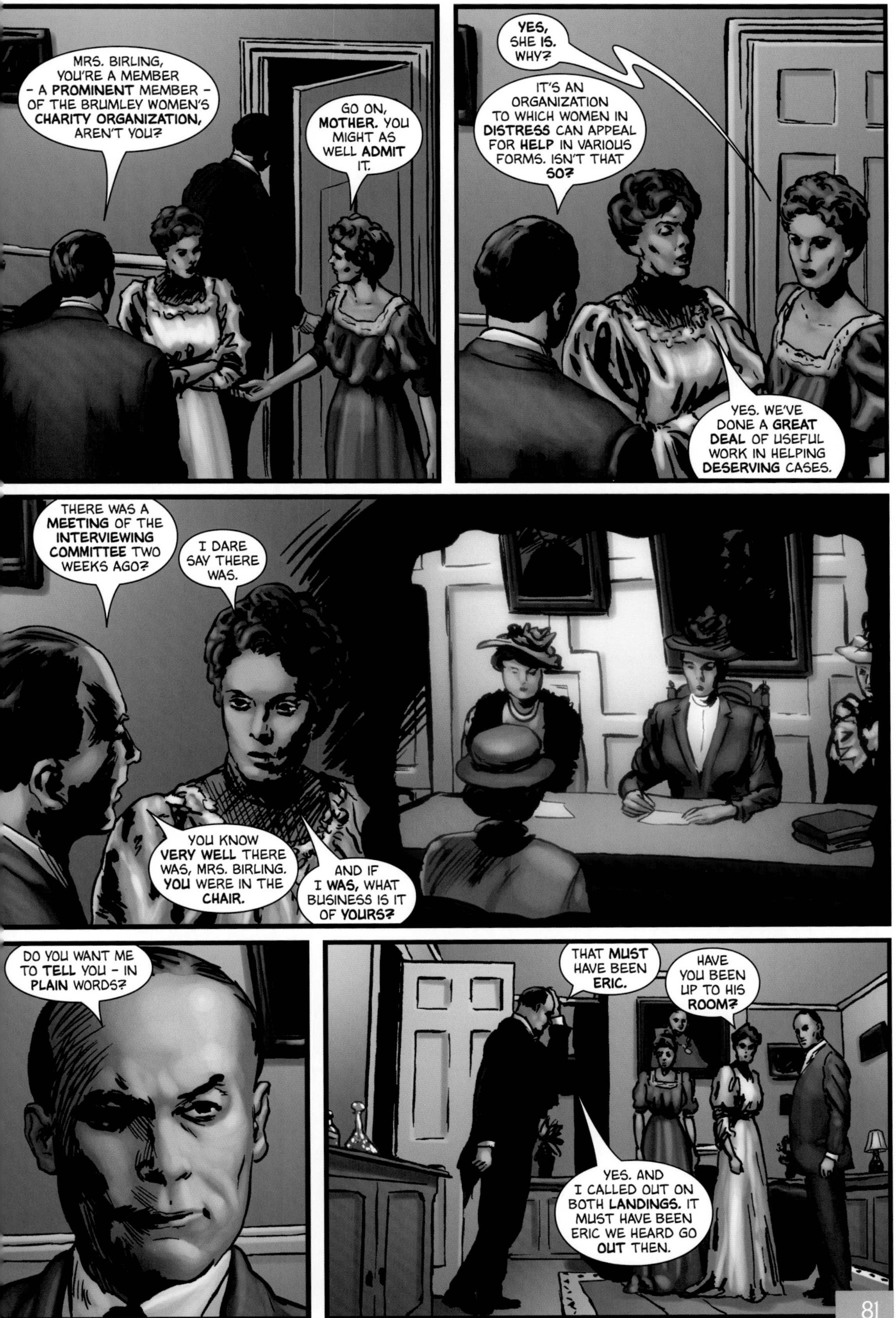
MRS. BIRLING, YOU'RE A MEMBER – A PROMINENT MEMBER – OF THE BRUMLEY WOMEN'S CHARITY ORGANIZATION, AREN'T YOU?
GO ON, MOTHER. YOU MIGHT AS WELL ADMIT IT.
YES, SHE IS. WHY?
IT'S AN ORGANIZATION TO WHICH WOMEN IN DISTRESS CAN APPEAL FOR HELP IN VARIOUS FORMS. ISN'T THAT SO?
YES. WE'VE DONE A GREAT DEAL OF USEFUL WORK IN HELPING DESERVING CASES.
THERE WAS A MEETING OF THE INTERVIEWING COMMITTEE TWO WEEKS AGO?
I DARE SAY THERE WAS.
YOU KNOW VERY WELL THERE WAS, MRS. BIRLING. YOU WERE IN THE CHAIR.
AND IF I WAS, WHAT BUSINESS IS IT OF YOURS?
DO YOU WANT ME TO TELL YOU – IN PLAIN WORDS?
THAT MUST HAVE BEEN ERIC.
HAVE YOU BEEN UP TO HIS ROOM?
YES. AND I CALLED OUT ON BOTH LANDINGS. IT MUST HAVE BEEN ERIC WE HEARD GO OUT THEN.

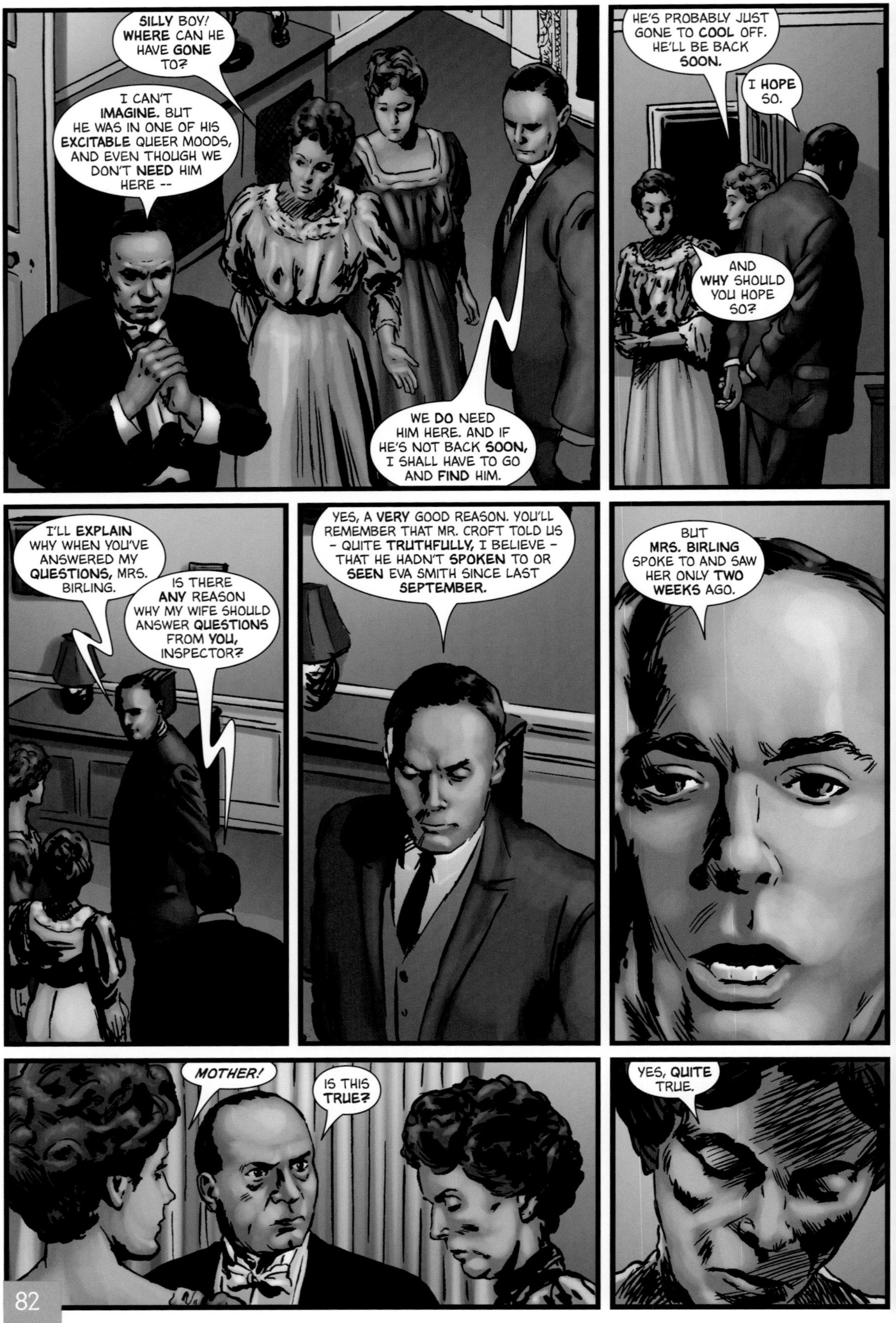
SILLY BOY! WHERE CAN HE HAVE GONE TO?
I CAN'T IMAGINE. BUT HE WAS IN ONE OF HIS EXCITABLE QUEER MOODS, AND EVEN THOUGH WE DON'T NEED HIM HERE --
WE DO NEED HIM HERE. AND IF HE'S NOT BACK SOON, I SHALL HAVE TO GO AND FIND HIM.
HE'S PROBABLY JUST GONE TO COOL OFF. HE'LL BE BACK SOON.
I HOPE SO.
AND WHY SHOULD YOU HOPE SO?
I'LL EXPLAIN WHY WHEN YOU'VE ANSWERED MY QUESTIONS, MRS. BIRLING.
IS THERE ANY REASON WHY MY WIFE SHOULD ANSWER QUESTIONS FROM YOU, INSPECTOR?
YES, A VERY GOOD REASON. YOU'LL REMEMBER THAT MR. CROFT TOLD US - QUITE TRUTHFULLY, I BELIEVE - THAT HE HADN'T SPOKEN TO OR SEEN EVA SMITH SINCE LAST SEPTEMBER.
BUT MRS. BIRLING SPOKE TO AND SAW HER ONLY TWO WEEKS AGO.
MOTHER!
IS THIS TRUE?
YES, QUITE TRUE.

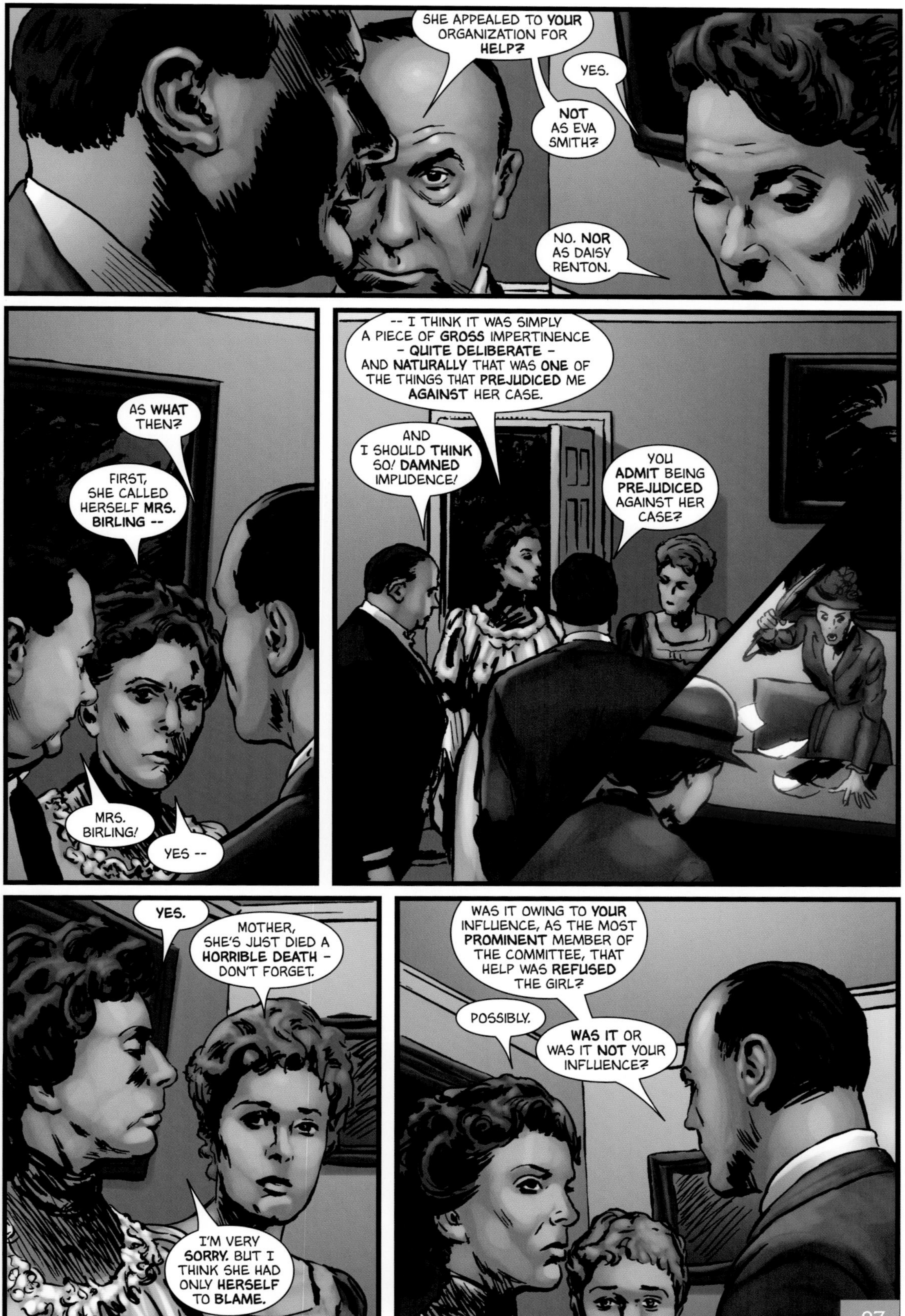
SHE APPEALED TO YOUR ORGANIZATION FOR HELP?
YES.
NOT AS EVA SMITH?
NO. NOR AS DAISY RENTON.
AS WHAT THEN?
FIRST, SHE CALLED HERSELF MRS. BIRLING --
MRS. BIRLING!
YES --
-- I THINK IT WAS SIMPLY A PIECE OF GROSS IMPERTINENCE - QUITE DELIBERATE - AND NATURALLY THAT WAS ONE OF THE THINGS THAT PREJUDICED ME AGAINST HER CASE.
AND I SHOULD THINK SO! DAMNED IMPUDENCE!
YOU ADMIT BEING PREJUDICED AGAINST HER CASE?
YES.
MOTHER, SHE'S JUST DIED A HORRIBLE DEATH - DON'T FORGET.
I'M VERY SORRY. BUT I THINK SHE HAD ONLY HERSELF TO BLAME.
WAS IT OWING TO YOUR INFLUENCE, AS THE MOST PROMINENT MEMBER OF THE COMMITTEE, THAT HELP WAS REFUSED THE GIRL?
POSSIBLY.
WAS IT OR WAS IT NOT YOUR INFLUENCE?

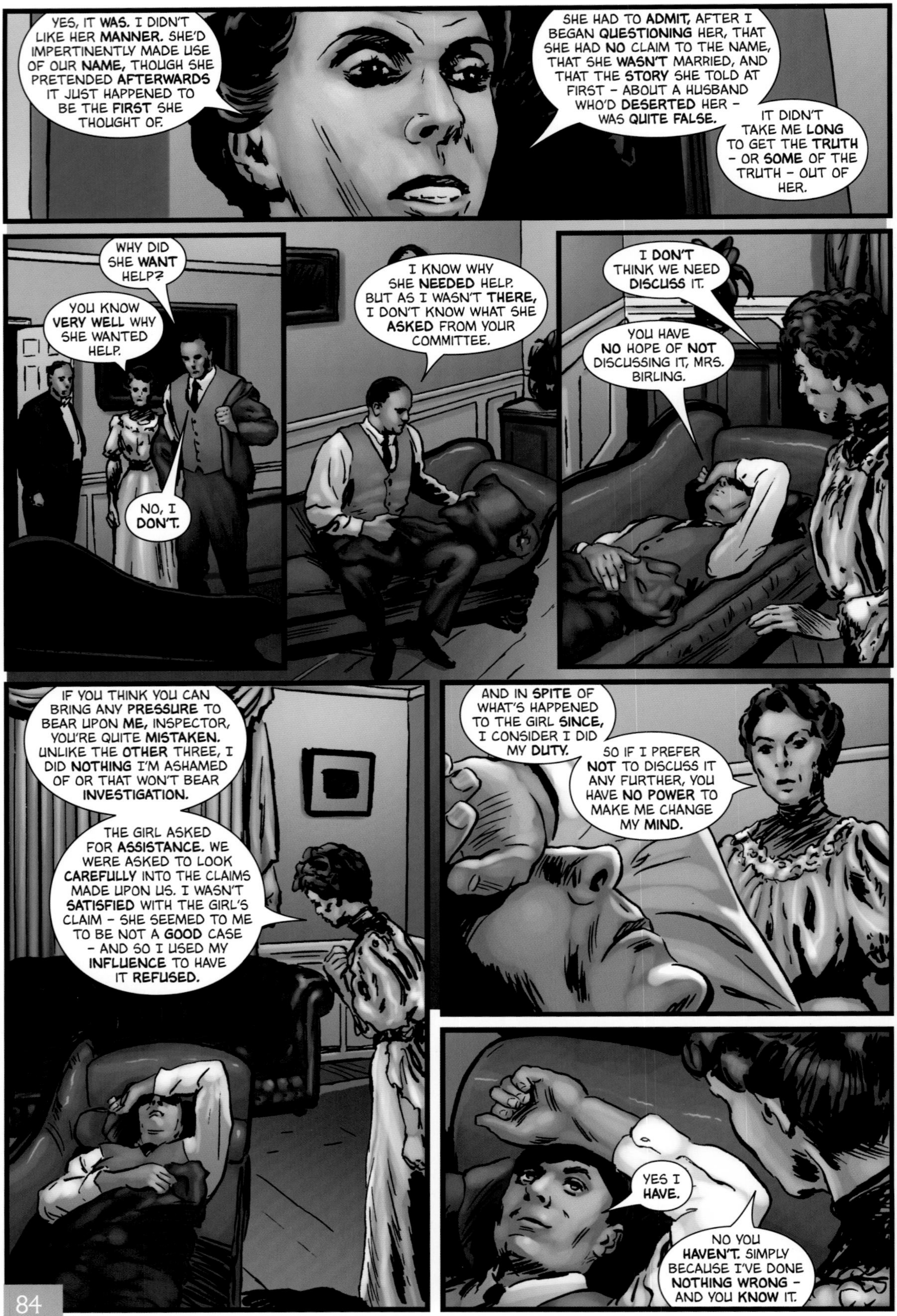
YES, IT WAS. I DIDN'T LIKE HER MANNER. SHE'D IMPERTINENTLY MADE USE OF OUR NAME, THOUGH SHE PRETENDED AFTERWARDS IT JUST HAPPENED TO BE THE FIRST SHE THOUGHT OF.
SHE HAD TO ADMIT, AFTER I BEGAN QUESTIONING HER, THAT SHE HAD NO CLAIM TO THE NAME, THAT SHE WASN'T MARRIED, AND THAT THE STORY SHE TOLD AT FIRST – ABOUT A HUSBAND WHO'D DESERTED HER – WAS QUITE FALSE.
IT DIDN'T TAKE ME LONG TO GET THE TRUTH – OR SOME OF THE TRUTH – OUT OF HER.
WHY DID SHE WANT HELP?
YOU KNOW VERY WELL WHY SHE WANTED HELP.
NO, I DON'T.
I KNOW WHY SHE NEEDED HELP. BUT AS I WASN'T THERE, I DON'T KNOW WHAT SHE ASKED FROM YOUR COMMITTEE.
I DON'T THINK WE NEED DISCUSS IT.
YOU HAVE NO HOPE OF NOT DISCUSSING IT, MRS. BIRLING.
IF YOU THINK YOU CAN BRING ANY PRESSURE TO BEAR UPON ME, INSPECTOR, YOU'RE QUITE MISTAKEN. UNLIKE THE OTHER THREE, I DID NOTHING I'M ASHAMED OF OR THAT WON'T BEAR INVESTIGATION.
THE GIRL ASKED FOR ASSISTANCE. WE WERE ASKED TO LOOK CAREFULLY INTO THE CLAIMS MADE UPON US. I WASN'T SATISFIED WITH THE GIRL'S CLAIM – SHE SEEMED TO ME TO BE NOT A GOOD CASE – AND SO I USED MY INFLUENCE TO HAVE IT REFUSED.
AND IN SPITE OF WHAT'S HAPPENED TO THE GIRL SINCE, I CONSIDER I DID MY DUTY.
SO IF I PREFER NOT TO DISCUSS IT ANY FURTHER, YOU HAVE NO POWER TO MAKE ME CHANGE MY MIND.
YES I HAVE.
NO YOU HAVEN'T. SIMPLY BECAUSE I'VE DONE NOTHING WRONG – AND YOU KNOW IT.

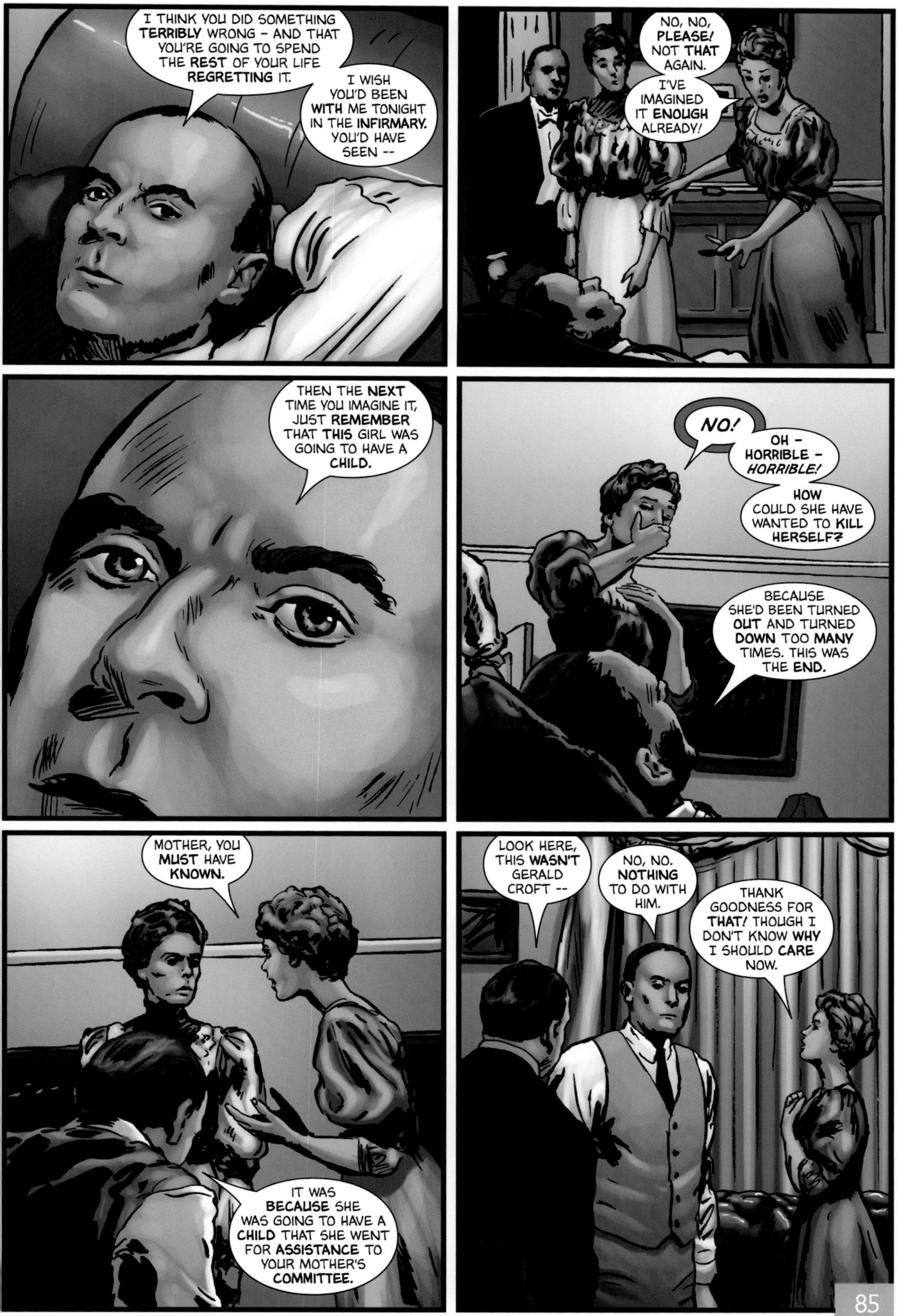
I THINK YOU DID SOMETHING TERRIBLY WRONG – AND THAT YOU'RE GOING TO SPEND THE REST OF YOUR LIFE REGRETTING IT.
I WISH YOU'D BEEN WITH ME TONIGHT IN THE INFIRMARY. YOU'D HAVE SEEN --
NO, NO, PLEASE! NOT THAT AGAIN.
I'VE IMAGINED IT ENOUGH ALREADY!
THEN THE NEXT TIME YOU IMAGINE IT, JUST REMEMBER THAT THIS GIRL WAS GOING TO HAVE A CHILD.
NO!
OH – HORRIBLE – HORRIBLE!
HOW COULD SHE HAVE WANTED TO KILL HERSELF?
BECAUSE SHE'D BEEN TURNED OUT AND TURNED DOWN TOO MANY TIMES. THIS WAS THE END.
MOTHER, YOU MUST HAVE KNOWN.
IT WAS BECAUSE SHE WAS GOING TO HAVE A CHILD THAT SHE WENT FOR ASSISTANCE TO YOUR MOTHER'S COMMITTEE.
LOOK HERE, THIS WASN'T GERALD CROFT --
NO, NO. NOTHING TO DO WITH HIM.
THANK GOODNESS FOR THAT! THOUGH I DON'T KNOW WHY I SHOULD CARE NOW.

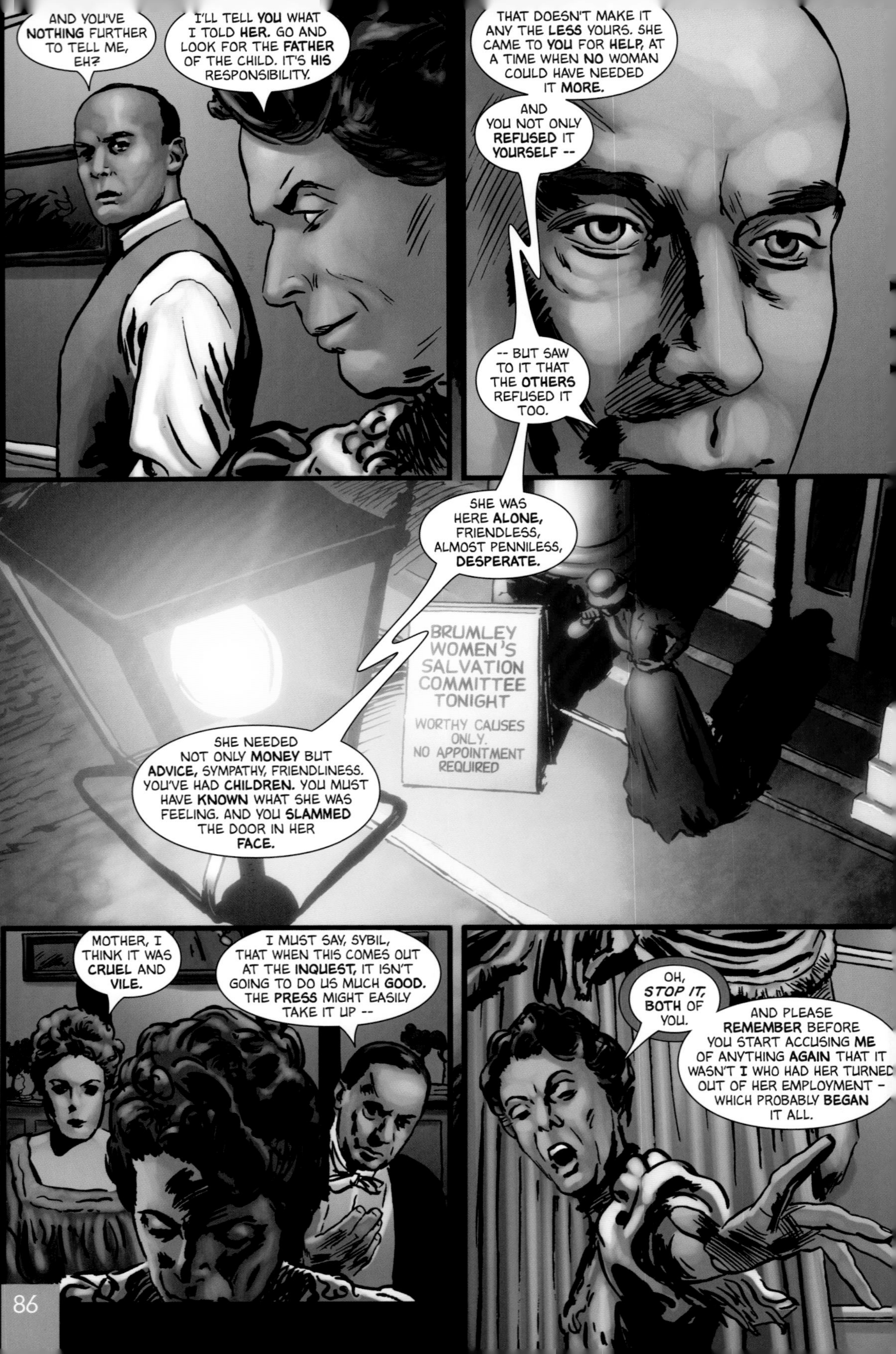
AND YOU'VE NOTHING FURTHER TO TELL ME, EH?
I'LL TELL YOU WHAT I TOLD HER. GO AND LOOK FOR THE FATHER OF THE CHILD. IT'S HIS RESPONSIBILITY.
THAT DOESN'T MAKE IT ANY THE LESS YOURS. SHE CAME TO YOU FOR HELP, AT A TIME WHEN NO WOMAN COULD HAVE NEEDED IT MORE.
AND YOU NOT ONLY REFUSED IT YOURSELF --
-- BUT SAW TO IT THAT THE OTHERS REFUSED IT TOO.
SHE WAS HERE ALONE, FRIENDLESS, ALMOST PENNILESS, DESPERATE.
BRUMLEY WOMEN'S SALVATION COMMITTEE TONIGHT
WORTHY CAUSES ONLY. NO APPOINTMENT REQUIRED
SHE NEEDED NOT ONLY MONEY BUT ADVICE, SYMPATHY, FRIENDLINESS. YOU'VE HAD CHILDREN. YOU MUST HAVE KNOWN WHAT SHE WAS FEELING. AND YOU SLAMMED THE DOOR IN HER FACE.
MOTHER, I THINK IT WAS CRUEL AND VILE.
I MUST SAY, SYBIL, THAT WHEN THIS COMES OUT AT THE INQUEST, IT ISN'T GOING TO DO US MUCH GOOD. THE PRESS MIGHT EASILY TAKE IT UP --
OH, STOP IT, BOTH OF YOU.
AND PLEASE REMEMBER BEFORE YOU START ACCUSING ME OF ANYTHING AGAIN THAT IT WASN'T I WHO HAD HER TURNED OUT OF HER EMPLOYMENT - WHICH PROBABLY BEGAN IT ALL.

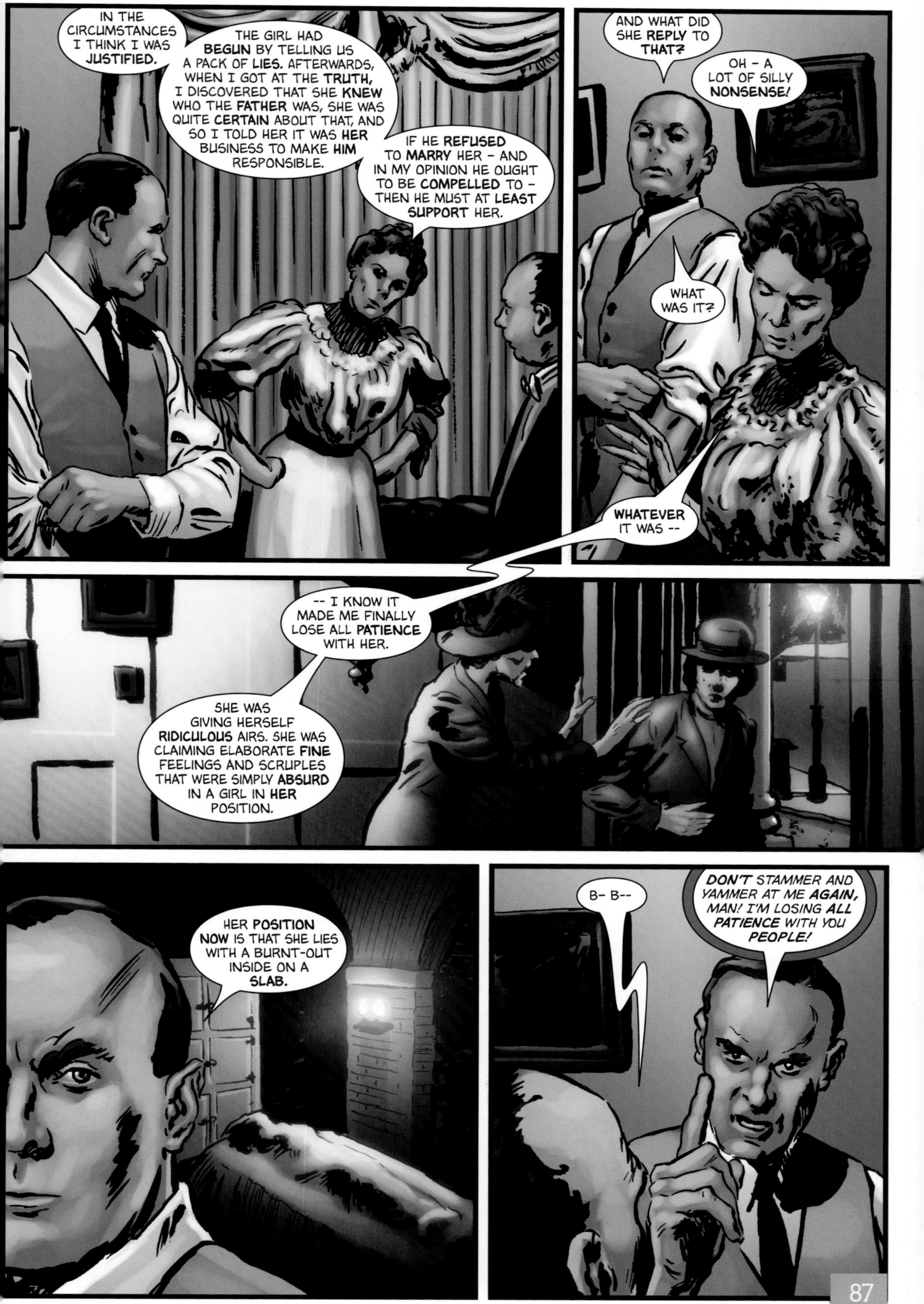
IN THE CIRCUMSTANCES I THINK I WAS JUSTIFIED.
THE GIRL HAD BEGUN BY TELLING US A PACK OF LIES. AFTERWARDS, WHEN I GOT AT THE TRUTH, I DISCOVERED THAT SHE KNEW WHO THE FATHER WAS, SHE WAS QUITE CERTAIN ABOUT THAT, AND SO I TOLD HER IT WAS HER BUSINESS TO MAKE HIM RESPONSIBLE.
IF HE REFUSED TO MARRY HER – AND IN MY OPINION HE OUGHT TO BE COMPELLED TO – THEN HE MUST AT LEAST SUPPORT HER.
AND WHAT DID SHE REPLY TO THAT?
OH – A LOT OF SILLY NONSENSE!
WHAT WAS IT?
WHATEVER IT WAS --
-- I KNOW IT MADE ME FINALLY LOSE ALL PATIENCE WITH HER.
SHE WAS GIVING HERSELF RIDICULOUS AIRS. SHE WAS CLAIMING ELABORATE FINE FEELINGS AND SCRUPLES THAT WERE SIMPLY ABSURD IN A GIRL IN HER POSITION.
HER POSITION NOW IS THAT SHE LIES WITH A BURNT-OUT INSIDE ON A SLAB.
B– B--
DON'T STAMMER AND YAMMER AT ME AGAIN, MAN! I'M LOSING ALL PATIENCE WITH YOU PEOPLE!

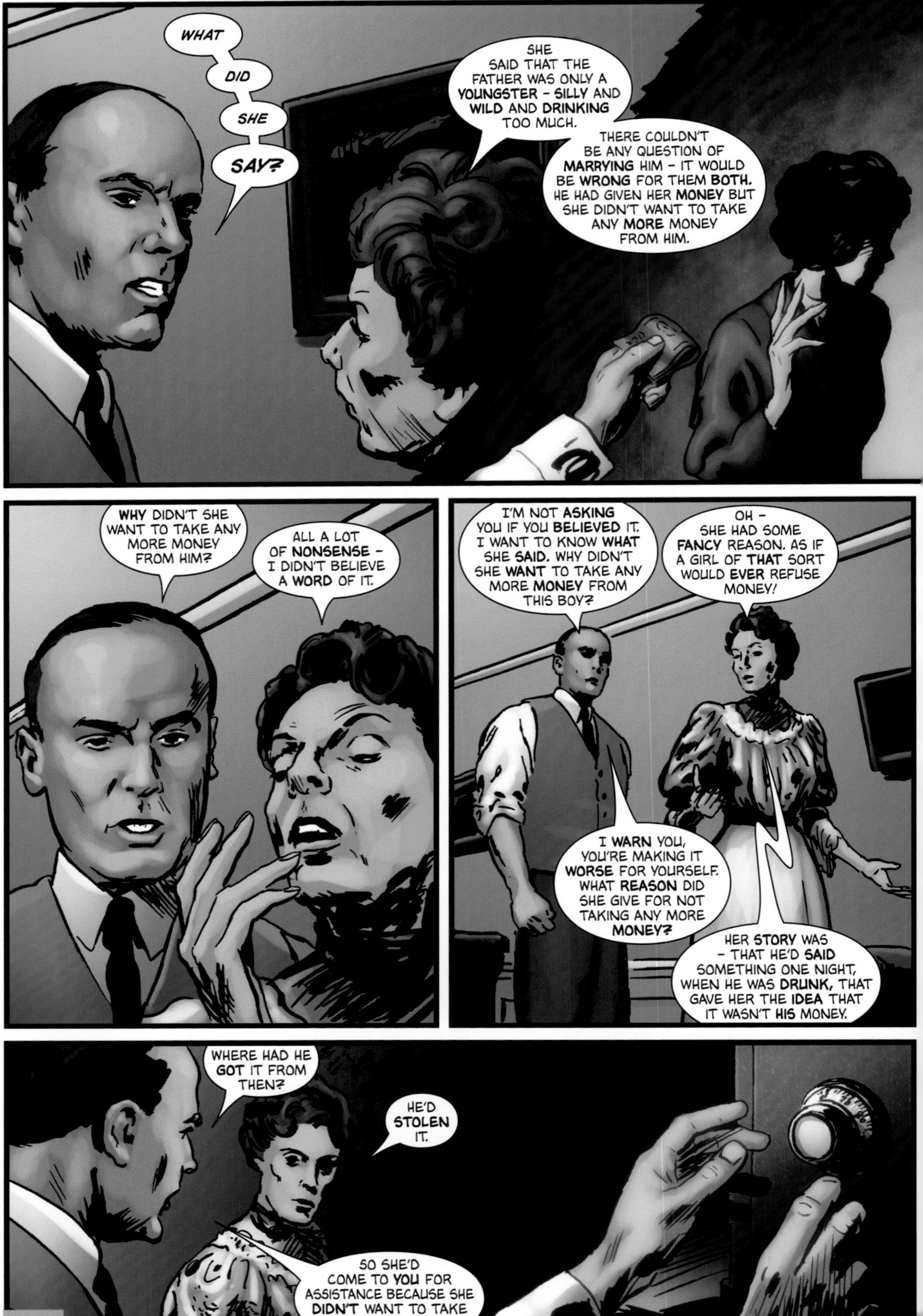
WHAT DID SHE SAY?
SHE SAID THAT THE FATHER WAS ONLY A YOUNGSTER – SILLY AND WILD AND DRINKING TOO MUCH.
THERE COULDN'T BE ANY QUESTION OF MARRYING HIM – IT WOULD BE WRONG FOR THEM BOTH. HE HAD GIVEN HER MONEY BUT SHE DIDN'T WANT TO TAKE ANY MORE MONEY FROM HIM.
WHY DIDN'T SHE WANT TO TAKE ANY MORE MONEY FROM HIM?
ALL A LOT OF NONSENSE – I DIDN'T BELIEVE A WORD OF IT.
I'M NOT ASKING YOU IF YOU BELIEVED IT. I WANT TO KNOW WHAT SHE SAID. WHY DIDN'T SHE WANT TO TAKE ANY MORE MONEY FROM THIS BOY?
OH – SHE HAD SOME FANCY REASON. AS IF A GIRL OF THAT SORT WOULD EVER REFUSE MONEY!
I WARN YOU, YOU'RE MAKING IT WORSE FOR YOURSELF. WHAT REASON DID SHE GIVE FOR NOT TAKING ANY MORE MONEY?
HER STORY WAS – THAT HE'D SAID SOMETHING ONE NIGHT, WHEN HE WAS DRUNK, THAT GAVE HER THE IDEA THAT IT WASN'T HIS MONEY.
WHERE HAD HE GOT IT FROM THEN?
HE'D STOLEN IT.
SO SHE'D COME TO YOU FOR ASSISTANCE BECAUSE SHE DIDN'T WANT TO TAKE STOLEN MONEY?

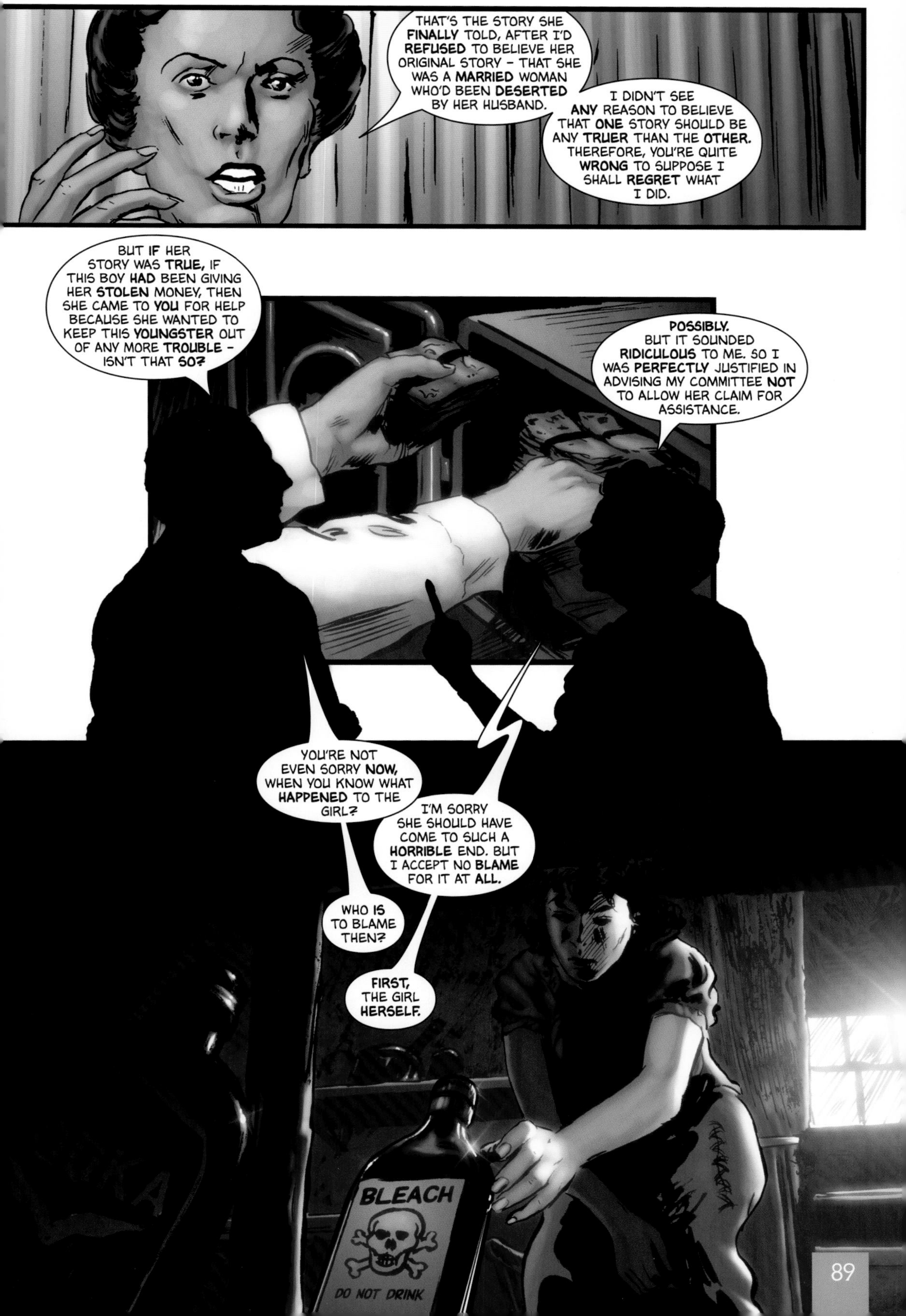
THAT'S THE STORY SHE FINALLY TOLD, AFTER I'D REFUSED TO BELIEVE HER ORIGINAL STORY – THAT SHE WAS A MARRIED WOMAN WHO'D BEEN DESERTED BY HER HUSBAND.
I DIDN'T SEE ANY REASON TO BELIEVE THAT ONE STORY SHOULD BE ANY TRUER THAN THE OTHER. THEREFORE, YOU'RE QUITE WRONG TO SUPPOSE I SHALL REGRET WHAT I DID.
BUT IF HER STORY WAS TRUE, IF THIS BOY HAD BEEN GIVING HER STOLEN MONEY, THEN SHE CAME TO YOU FOR HELP BECAUSE SHE WANTED TO KEEP THIS YOUNGSTER OUT OF ANY MORE TROUBLE – ISN'T THAT SO?
POSSIBLY. BUT IT SOUNDED RIDICULOUS TO ME. SO I WAS PERFECTLY JUSTIFIED IN ADVISING MY COMMITTEE NOT TO ALLOW HER CLAIM FOR ASSISTANCE.
YOU'RE NOT EVEN SORRY NOW, WHEN YOU KNOW WHAT HAPPENED TO THE GIRL?
I'M SORRY SHE SHOULD HAVE COME TO SUCH A HORRIBLE END. BUT I ACCEPT NO BLAME FOR IT AT ALL.
WHO IS TO BLAME THEN?
FIRST, THE GIRL HERSELF.
BLEACH
DO NOT DRINK

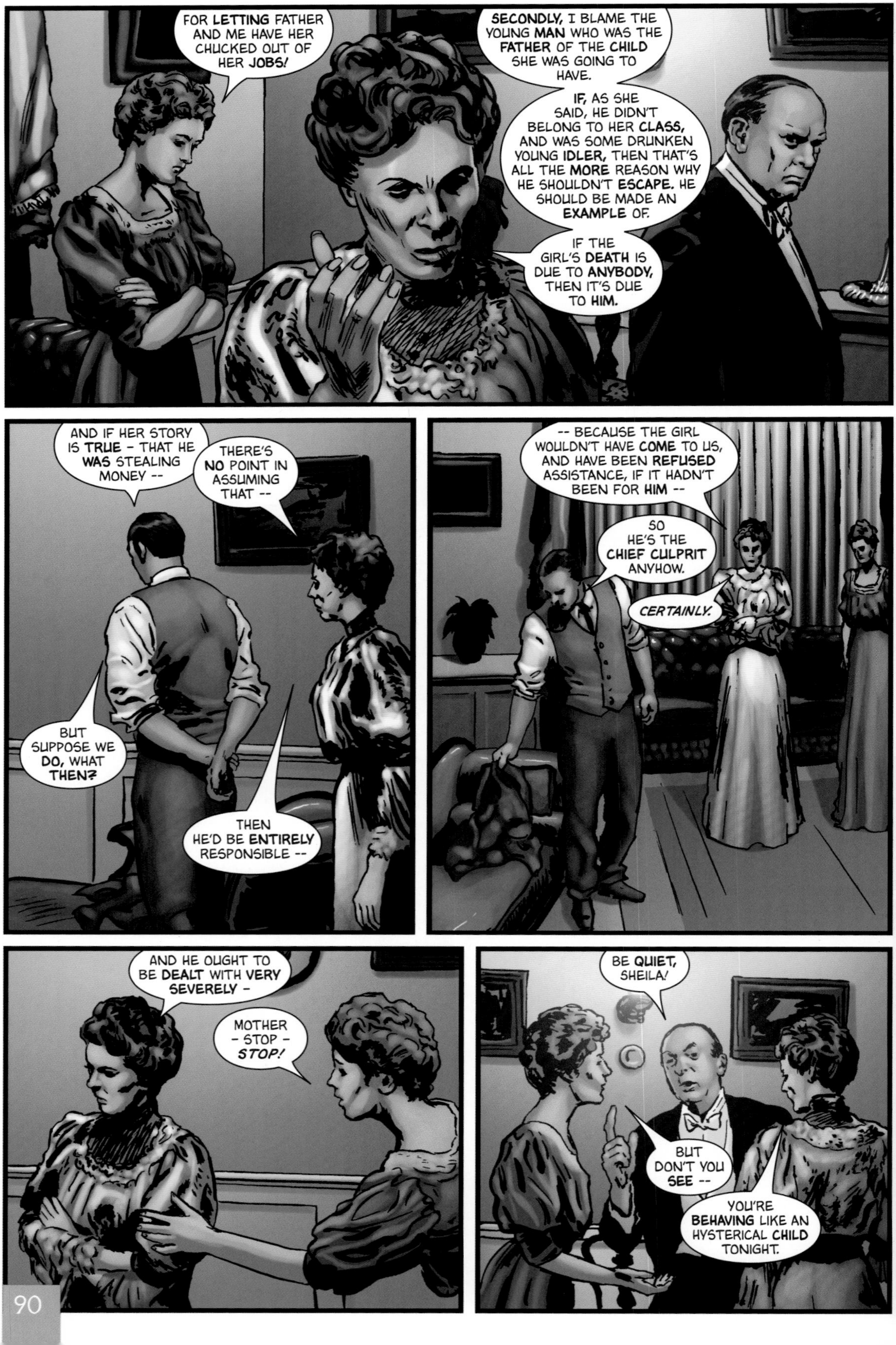

FOR LETTING FATHER AND ME HAVE HER CHUCKED OUT OF HER JOBS!
SECONDLY, I BLAME THE YOUNG MAN WHO WAS THE FATHER OF THE CHILD SHE WAS GOING TO HAVE.
IF, AS SHE SAID, HE DIDN'T BELONG TO HER CLASS, AND WAS SOME DRUNKEN YOUNG IDLER, THEN THAT'S ALL THE MORE REASON WHY HE SHOULDN'T ESCAPE. HE SHOULD BE MADE AN EXAMPLE OF.
IF THE GIRL'S DEATH IS DUE TO ANYBODY, THEN IT'S DUE TO HIM.
AND IF HER STORY IS TRUE – THAT HE WAS STEALING MONEY --
THERE'S NO POINT IN ASSUMING THAT --
BUT SUPPOSE WE DO, WHAT THEN?
THEN HE'D BE ENTIRELY RESPONSIBLE --
-- BECAUSE THE GIRL WOULDN'T HAVE COME TO US, AND HAVE BEEN REFUSED ASSISTANCE, IF IT HADN'T BEEN FOR HIM --
SO HE'S THE CHIEF CULPRIT ANYHOW.
CERTAINLY.
AND HE OUGHT TO BE DEALT WITH VERY SEVERELY –
MOTHER – STOP – STOP!
BE QUIET, SHEILA!
BUT DON'T YOU SEE --
YOU'RE BEHAVING LIKE AN HYSTERICAL CHILD TONIGHT.

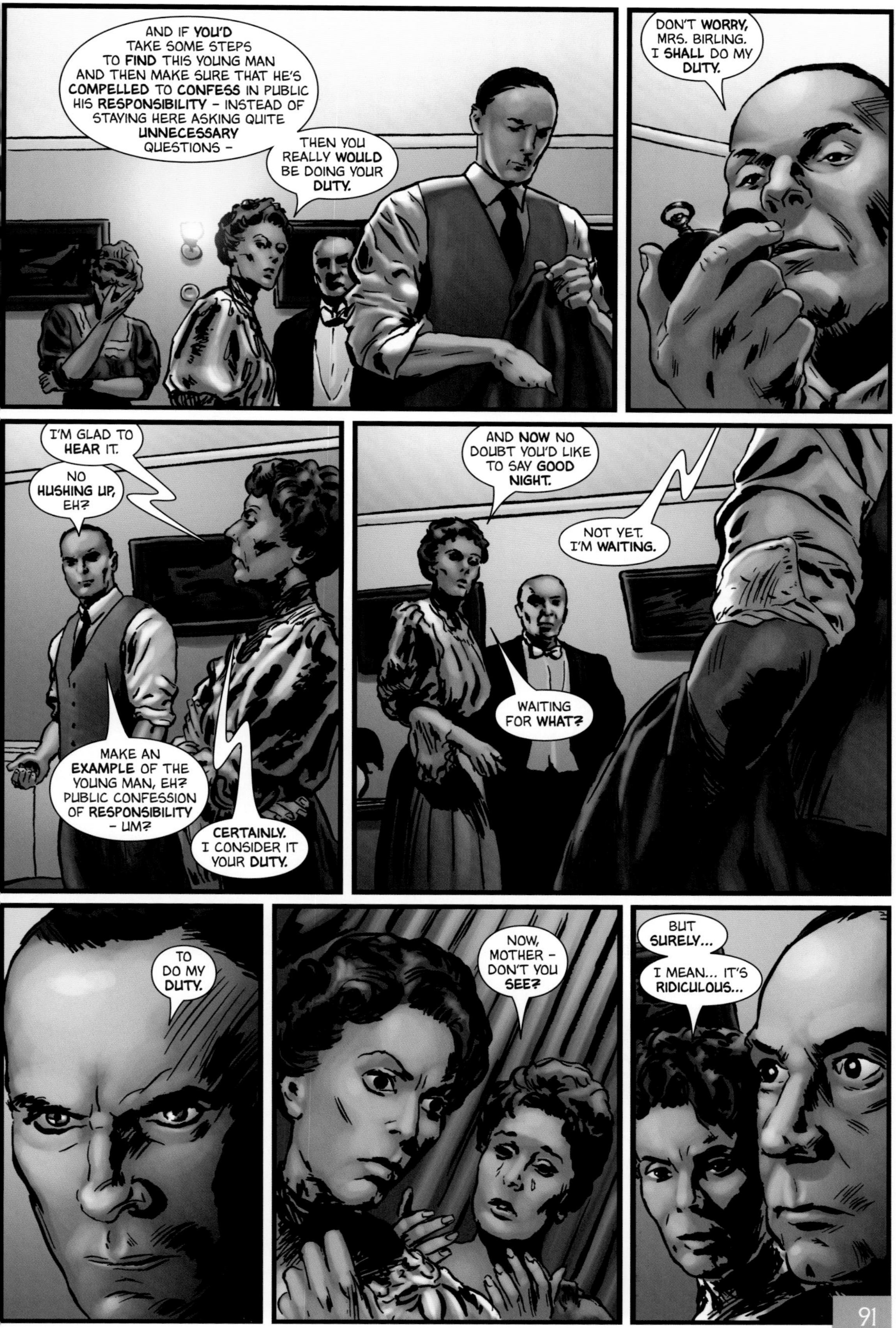
AND IF YOU'D TAKE SOME STEPS TO FIND THIS YOUNG MAN AND THEN MAKE SURE THAT HE'S COMPELLED TO CONFESS IN PUBLIC HIS RESPONSIBILITY - INSTEAD OF STAYING HERE ASKING QUITE UNNECESSARY QUESTIONS -
THEN YOU REALLY WOULD BE DOING YOUR DUTY.
DON'T WORRY, MRS. BIRLING. I SHALL DO MY DUTY.
I'M GLAD TO HEAR IT.
NO HUSHING UP, EH?
MAKE AN EXAMPLE OF THE YOUNG MAN, EH? PUBLIC CONFESSION OF RESPONSIBILITY - UM?
CERTAINLY. I CONSIDER IT YOUR DUTY.
AND NOW NO DOUBT YOU'D LIKE TO SAY GOOD NIGHT.
NOT YET. I'M WAITING.
WAITING FOR WHAT?
TO DO MY DUTY.
NOW, MOTHER - DON'T YOU SEE?
BUT SURELY...
I MEAN... IT'S RIDICULOUS...

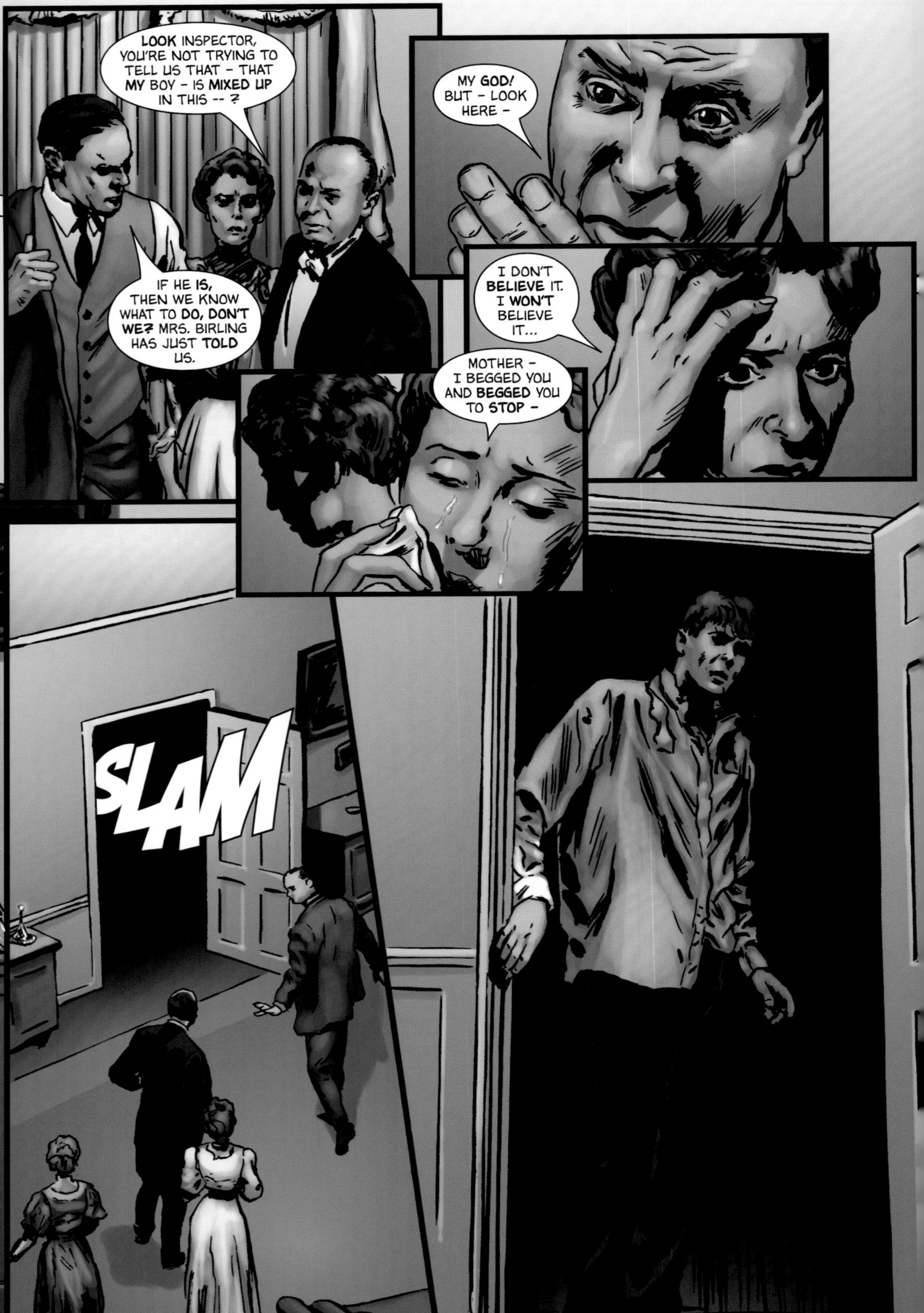
LOOK INSPECTOR, YOU'RE NOT TRYING TO TELL US THAT – THAT MY BOY – IS MIXED UP IN THIS -- ?
IF HE IS, THEN WE KNOW WHAT TO DO, DON'T WE? MRS. BIRLING HAS JUST TOLD US.
MY GOD! BUT – LOOK HERE –
I DON'T BELIEVE IT. I WON'T BELIEVE IT...
MOTHER – I BEGGED YOU AND BEGGED YOU TO STOP –
SLAM

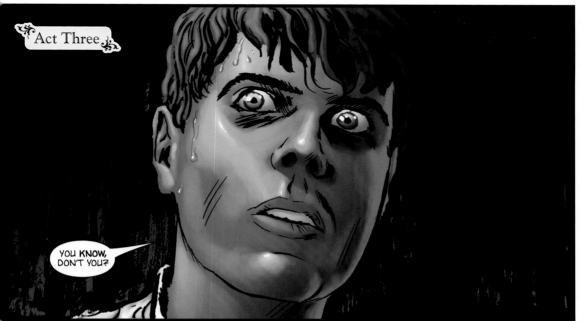

YOU **KNOW**, DON'T YOU?

YES, WE **KNOW**.

ERIC, I CAN'T **BELIEVE** IT. THERE MUST BE SOME **MISTAKE**. YOU DON'T **KNOW** WHAT WE'VE BEEN **SAYING**.

IT'S A GOOD JOB FOR **HIM** HE **DOESN'T**, ISN'T IT?

WHY?

BECAUSE **MOTHER'S** BEEN BUSY BLAMING **EVERYTHING** ON THE **YOUNG MAN** WHO GOT THIS GIRL INTO **TROUBLE**, AND SAYING HE SHOULDN'T **ESCAPE** AND SHOULD BE MADE AN **EXAMPLE** OF --

THAT'S **ENOUGH**, SHEILA.

YOU HAVEN'T MADE IT ANY **EASIER** FOR ME, HAVE YOU, MOTHER?

BUT I DIDN'T **KNOW** IT WAS YOU – I NEVER **DREAMT.**

BESIDES, YOU'RE NOT THE **TYPE** – YOU DON'T GET **DRUNK** –

OF **COURSE** HE DOES. I TOLD YOU HE DID.

YOU **TOLD** HER. WHY, YOU LITTLE **SNEAK!**

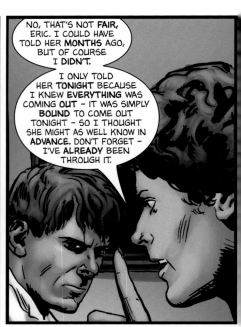

NO, THAT'S NOT **FAIR,** ERIC. I COULD HAVE TOLD HER **MONTHS** AGO, BUT OF COURSE I **DIDN'T.**

I ONLY TOLD HER **TONIGHT** BECAUSE I KNEW **EVERYTHING** WAS COMING **OUT** – IT WAS SIMPLY **BOUND** TO COME OUT TONIGHT – SO I THOUGHT SHE MIGHT AS WELL KNOW IN **ADVANCE.** DON'T FORGET – I'VE **ALREADY** BEEN THROUGH IT.

SHEILA, I SIMPLY DON'T **UNDERSTAND** YOUR ATTITUDE.

NEITHER DO **I.** IF YOU'D HAD **ANY** SENSE OF **LOYALTY** --

JUST A MINUTE, MR. BIRLING. THERE'LL BE **PLENTY** OF TIME, WHEN I'VE **GONE,** FOR YOU **ALL** TO ADJUST YOUR FAMILY **RELATIONSHIPS.**

BUT **NOW** I MUST HEAR WHAT YOUR **SON** HAS TO **TELL** ME. AND I'LL BE **OBLIGED** IF YOU'LL LET US GET ON **WITHOUT** ANY FURTHER INTERRUPTIONS.

NOW THEN.

COULD I HAVE A **DRINK** FIRST?

NO!

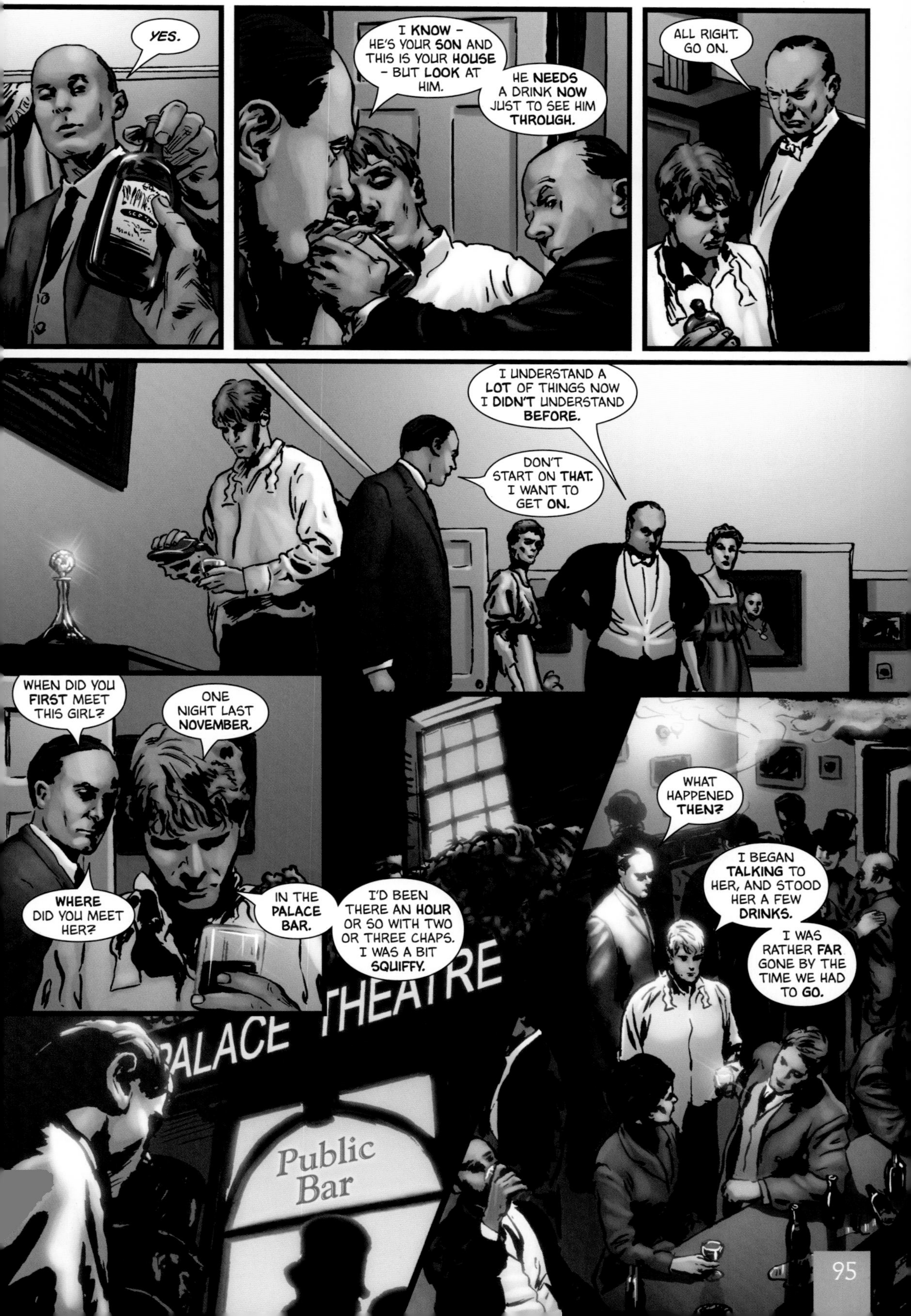
YES.
I KNOW – HE'S YOUR SON AND THIS IS YOUR HOUSE – BUT LOOK AT HIM.
HE NEEDS A DRINK NOW JUST TO SEE HIM THROUGH.
ALL RIGHT. GO ON.
I UNDERSTAND A LOT OF THINGS NOW I DIDN'T UNDERSTAND BEFORE.
DON'T START ON THAT. I WANT TO GET ON.
WHEN DID YOU FIRST MEET THIS GIRL?
ONE NIGHT LAST NOVEMBER.
WHERE DID YOU MEET HER?
IN THE PALACE BAR.
I'D BEEN THERE AN HOUR OR SO WITH TWO OR THREE CHAPS. I WAS A BIT SQUIFFY.
PALACE THEATRE
Public Bar
WHAT HAPPENED THEN?
I BEGAN TALKING TO HER, AND STOOD HER A FEW DRINKS.
I WAS RATHER FAR GONE BY THE TIME WE HAD TO GO.

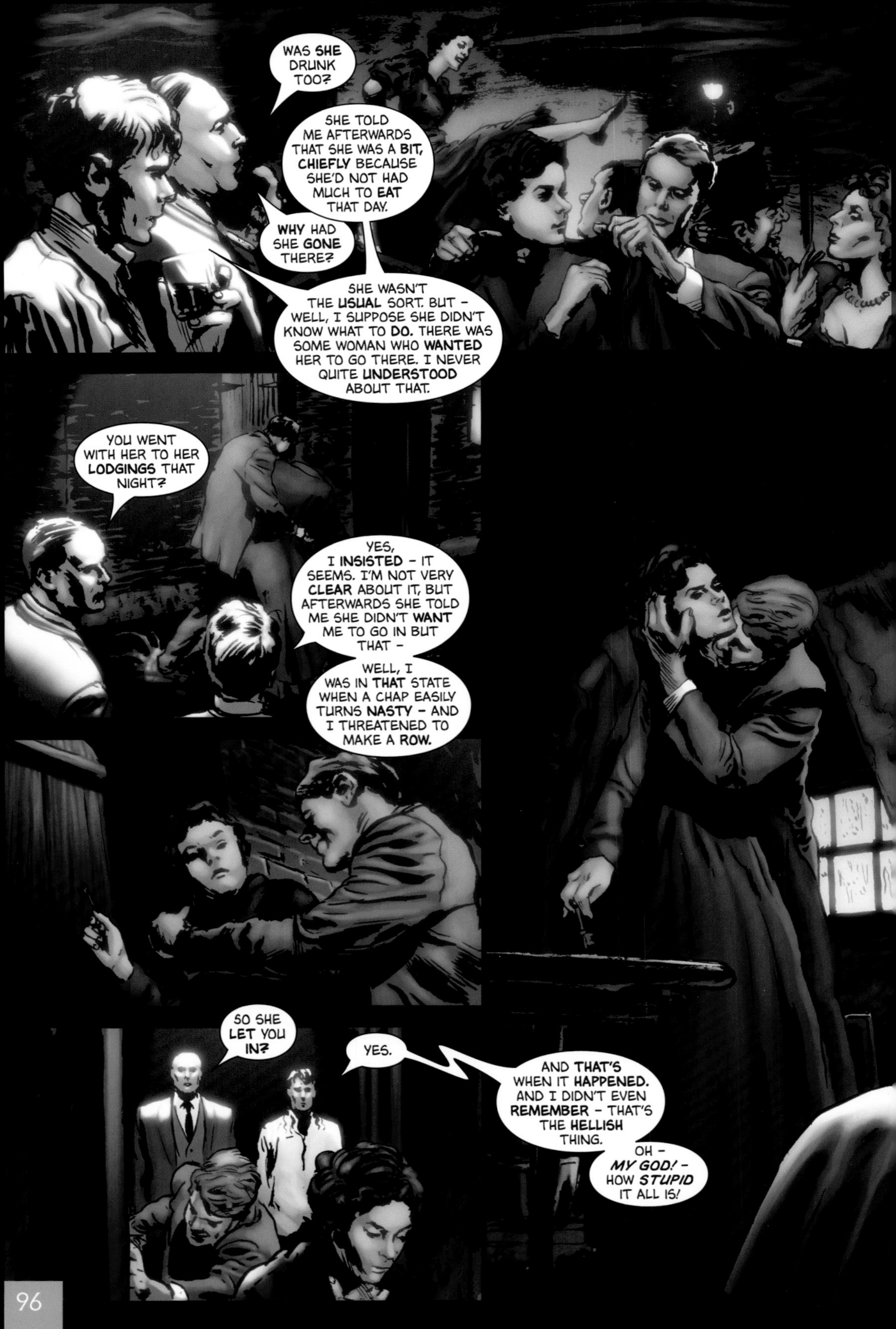
WAS SHE DRUNK TOO?
SHE TOLD ME AFTERWARDS THAT SHE WAS A BIT, CHIEFLY BECAUSE SHE'D NOT HAD MUCH TO EAT THAT DAY.
WHY HAD SHE GONE THERE?
SHE WASN'T THE USUAL SORT. BUT – WELL, I SUPPOSE SHE DIDN'T KNOW WHAT TO DO. THERE WAS SOME WOMAN WHO WANTED HER TO GO THERE. I NEVER QUITE UNDERSTOOD ABOUT THAT.
YOU WENT WITH HER TO HER LODGINGS THAT NIGHT?
YES, I INSISTED – IT SEEMS. I'M NOT VERY CLEAR ABOUT IT, BUT AFTERWARDS SHE TOLD ME SHE DIDN'T WANT ME TO GO IN BUT THAT –
WELL, I WAS IN THAT STATE WHEN A CHAP EASILY TURNS NASTY – AND I THREATENED TO MAKE A ROW.
SO SHE LET YOU IN?
YES.
AND THAT'S WHEN IT HAPPENED. AND I DIDN'T EVEN REMEMBER – THAT'S THE HELLISH THING.
OH – MY GOD! – HOW STUPID IT ALL IS!

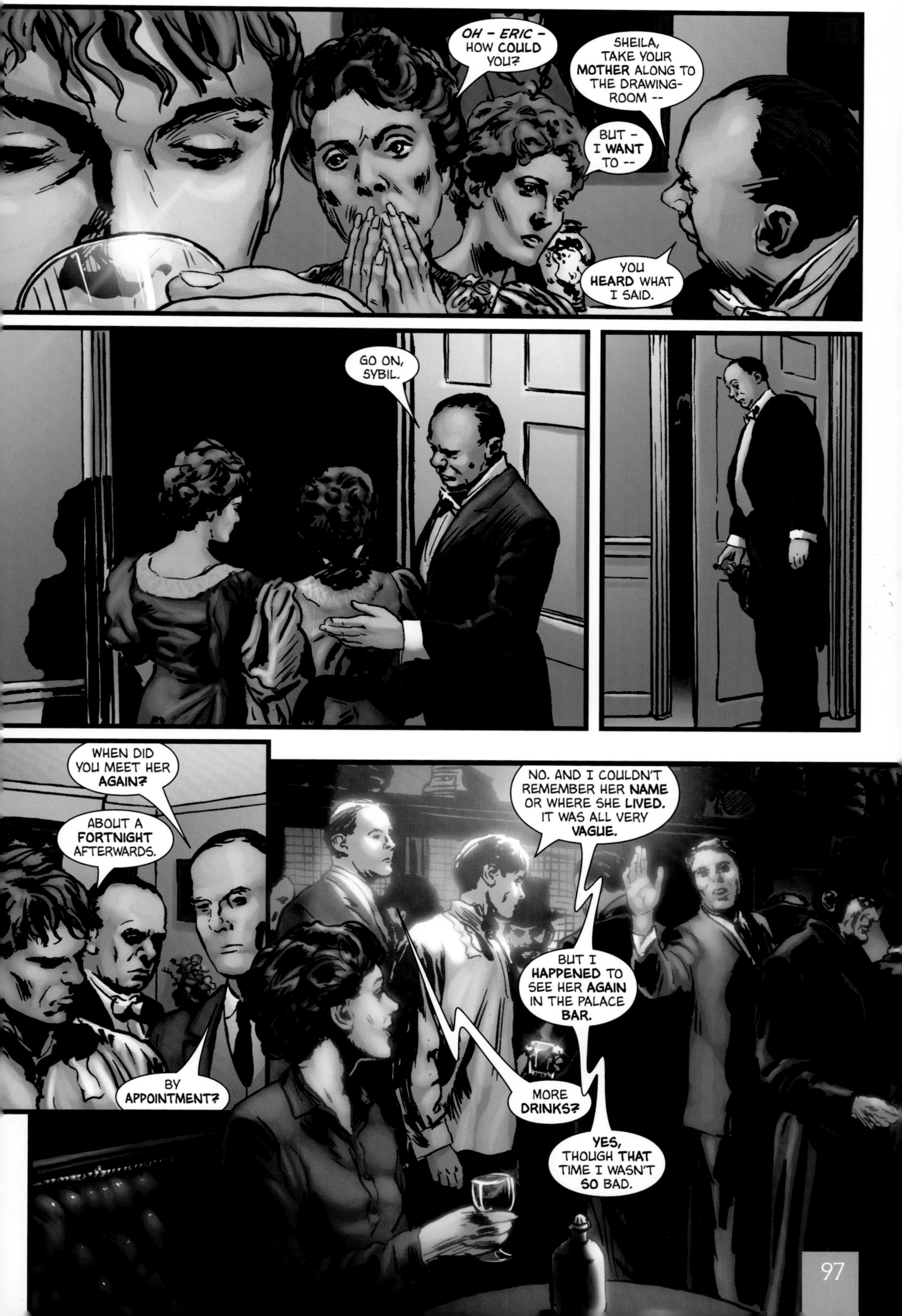
OH – ERIC – HOW COULD YOU?
SHEILA, TAKE YOUR MOTHER ALONG TO THE DRAWING-ROOM --
BUT – I WANT TO --
YOU HEARD WHAT I SAID.
GO ON, SYBIL.
WHEN DID YOU MEET HER AGAIN?
ABOUT A FORTNIGHT AFTERWARDS.
BY APPOINTMENT?
NO. AND I COULDN'T REMEMBER HER NAME OR WHERE SHE LIVED. IT WAS ALL VERY VAGUE.
BUT I HAPPENED TO SEE HER AGAIN IN THE PALACE BAR.
MORE DRINKS?
YES, THOUGH THAT TIME I WASN'T SO BAD.

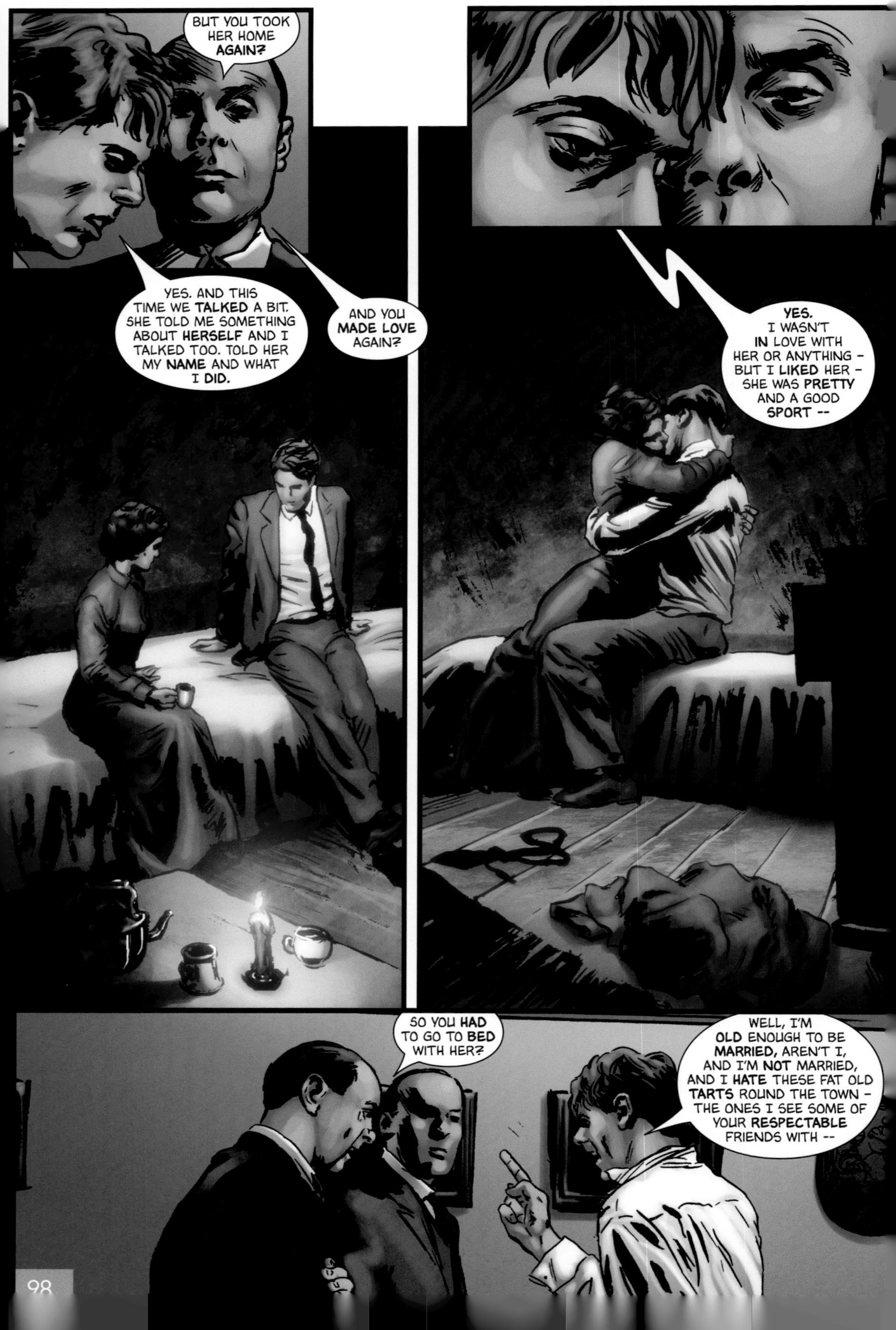
BUT YOU TOOK HER HOME AGAIN?
YES. AND THIS TIME WE TALKED A BIT. SHE TOLD ME SOMETHING ABOUT HERSELF AND I TALKED TOO. TOLD HER MY NAME AND WHAT I DID.
AND YOU MADE LOVE AGAIN?
YES. I WASN'T IN LOVE WITH HER OR ANYTHING – BUT I LIKED HER – SHE WAS PRETTY AND A GOOD SPORT --
SO YOU HAD TO GO TO BED WITH HER?
WELL, I'M OLD ENOUGH TO BE MARRIED, AREN'T I, AND I'M NOT MARRIED, AND I HATE THESE FAT OLD TARTS ROUND THE TOWN – THE ONES I SEE SOME OF YOUR RESPECTABLE FRIENDS WITH --

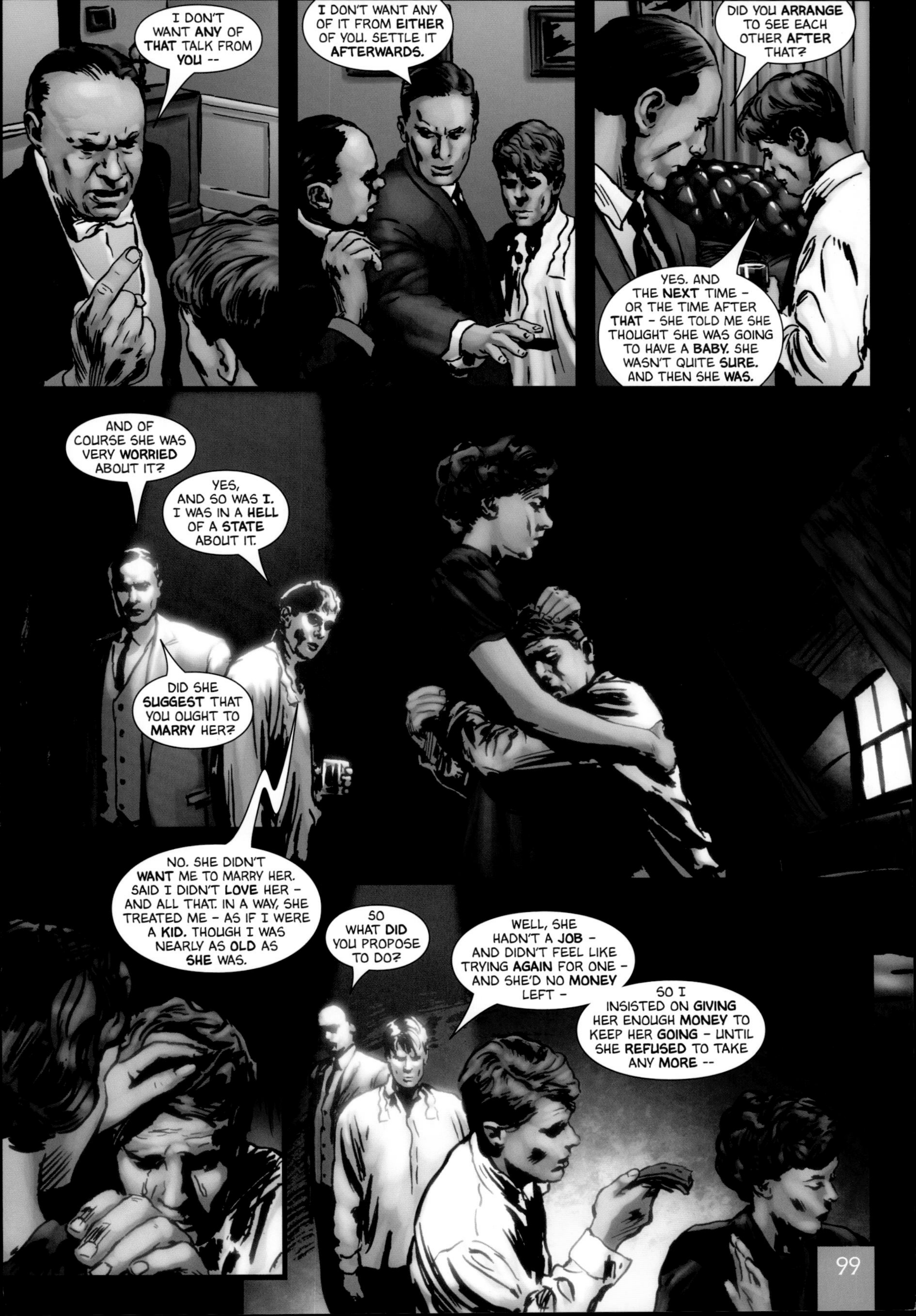
I DON'T WANT ANY OF THAT TALK FROM YOU --
I DON'T WANT ANY OF IT FROM EITHER OF YOU. SETTLE IT AFTERWARDS.
DID YOU ARRANGE TO SEE EACH OTHER AFTER THAT?
YES. AND THE NEXT TIME – OR THE TIME AFTER THAT – SHE TOLD ME SHE THOUGHT SHE WAS GOING TO HAVE A BABY. SHE WASN'T QUITE SURE. AND THEN SHE WAS.
AND OF COURSE SHE WAS VERY WORRIED ABOUT IT?
YES, AND SO WAS I. I WAS IN A HELL OF A STATE ABOUT IT.
DID SHE SUGGEST THAT YOU OUGHT TO MARRY HER?
NO. SHE DIDN'T WANT ME TO MARRY HER. SAID I DIDN'T LOVE HER – AND ALL THAT. IN A WAY, SHE TREATED ME – AS IF I WERE A KID. THOUGH I WAS NEARLY AS OLD AS SHE WAS.
SO WHAT DID YOU PROPOSE TO DO?
WELL, SHE HADN'T A JOB – AND DIDN'T FEEL LIKE TRYING AGAIN FOR ONE – AND SHE'D NO MONEY LEFT –
SO I INSISTED ON GIVING HER ENOUGH MONEY TO KEEP HER GOING – UNTIL SHE REFUSED TO TAKE ANY MORE --

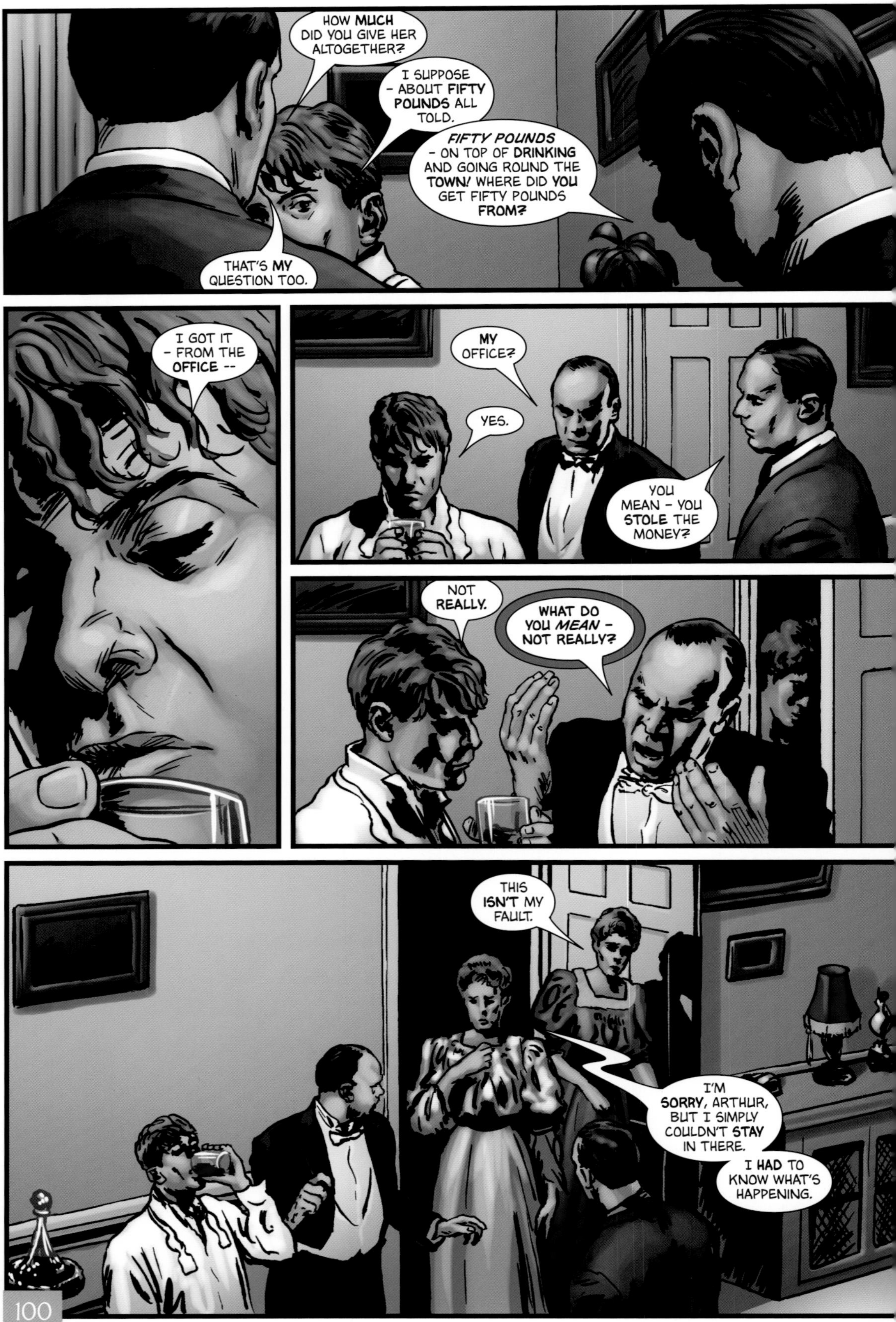
HOW MUCH DID YOU GIVE HER ALTOGETHER?
I SUPPOSE - ABOUT FIFTY POUNDS ALL TOLD.
FIFTY POUNDS - ON TOP OF DRINKING AND GOING ROUND THE TOWN! WHERE DID YOU GET FIFTY POUNDS FROM?
THAT'S MY QUESTION TOO.
I GOT IT - FROM THE OFFICE --
MY OFFICE?
YES.
YOU MEAN - YOU STOLE THE MONEY?
NOT REALLY.
WHAT DO YOU MEAN - NOT REALLY?
THIS ISN'T MY FAULT.
I'M SORRY, ARTHUR, BUT I SIMPLY COULDN'T STAY IN THERE.
I HAD TO KNOW WHAT'S HAPPENING.

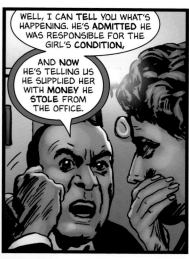

WELL, I CAN **TELL** YOU WHAT'S HAPPENING. HE'S **ADMITTED** HE WAS RESPONSIBLE FOR THE GIRL'S **CONDITION,**

AND **NOW** HE'S TELLING US HE SUPPLIED HER WITH **MONEY** HE **STOLE** FROM THE OFFICE.

ERIC! YOU STOLE MONEY?

NO, NOT **REALLY.** I INTENDED TO **PAY** IT **BACK.**

WE'VE HEARD **THAT** STORY **BEFORE.** HOW COULD **YOU** HAVE PAID IT **BACK?**

I'D HAVE MANAGED SOMEHOW. I HAD TO HAVE **SOME** MONEY --

I DON'T UNDERSTAND **HOW** YOU COULD TAKE AS **MUCH** AS THAT OUT OF THE OFFICE WITHOUT **SOMEBODY** KNOWING.

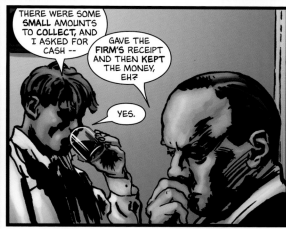

THERE WERE SOME **SMALL** AMOUNTS TO **COLLECT,** AND I ASKED FOR CASH --

GAVE THE **FIRM'S** RECEIPT AND THEN **KEPT** THE MONEY, EH?

YES.

YOU MUST GIVE ME A LIST OF THOSE ACCOUNTS. I'VE GOT TO COVER THIS UP AS **SOON** AS I CAN.

YOU DAMNED **FOOL** - WHY DIDN'T YOU COME TO **ME** WHEN YOU FOUND YOURSELF IN THIS **MESS?**

BECAUSE YOU'RE **NOT** THE KIND OF FATHER A CHAP COULD **GO** TO WHEN HE'S IN TROUBLE - **THAT'S** WHY.

DON'T TALK TO ME LIKE **THAT.** YOUR TROUBLE IS - YOU'VE BEEN **SPOILT** --

AND **MY** TROUBLE IS - THAT I HAVEN'T MUCH **TIME.** YOU'LL BE ABLE TO DIVIDE THE RESPONSIBILITY **BETWEEN** YOU WHEN I'VE **GONE.**

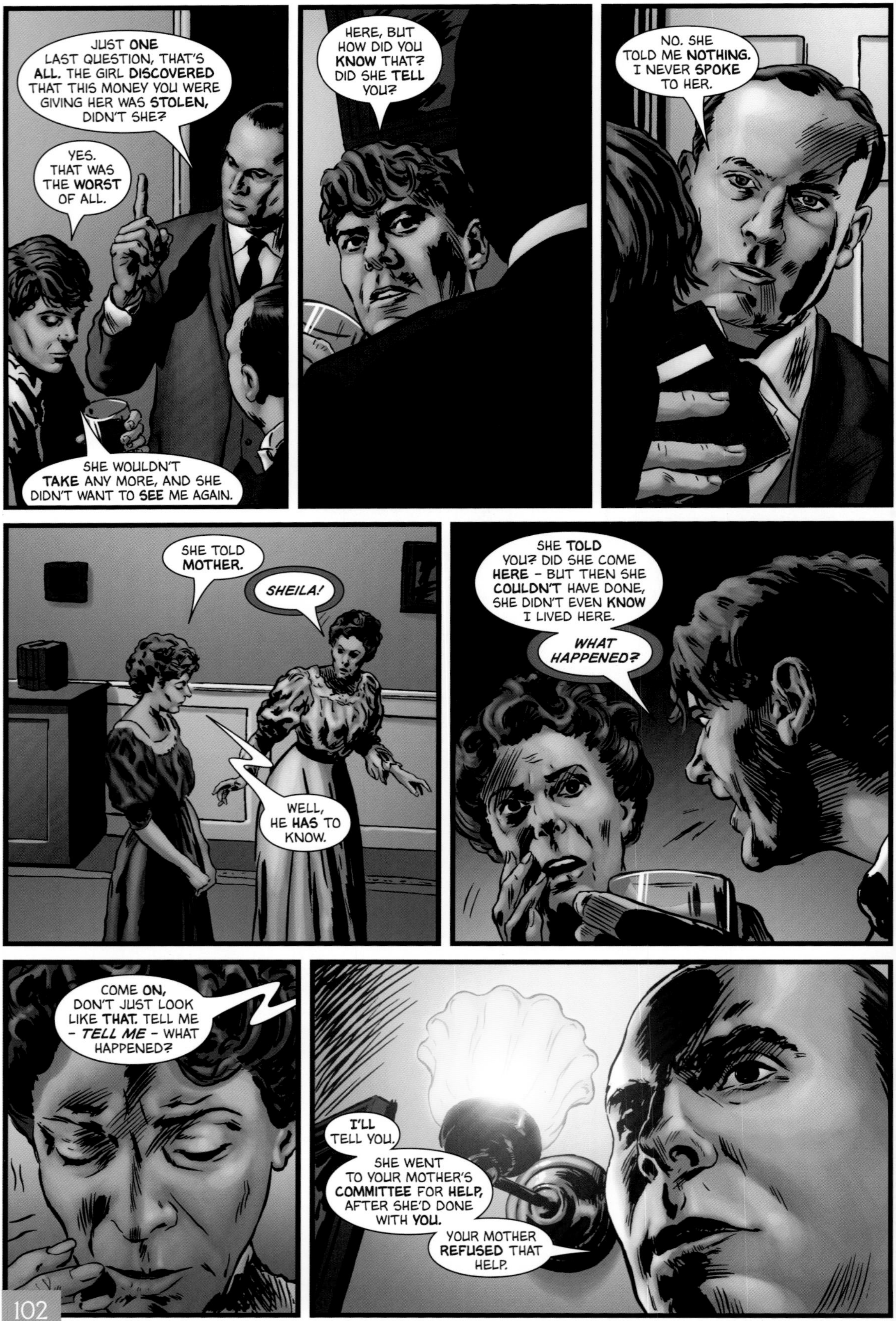

JUST ONE LAST QUESTION, THAT'S ALL. THE GIRL DISCOVERED THAT THIS MONEY YOU WERE GIVING HER WAS STOLEN, DIDN'T SHE?
YES. THAT WAS THE WORST OF ALL.
SHE WOULDN'T TAKE ANY MORE, AND SHE DIDN'T WANT TO SEE ME AGAIN.
HERE, BUT HOW DID YOU KNOW THAT? DID SHE TELL YOU?
NO. SHE TOLD ME NOTHING. I NEVER SPOKE TO HER.
SHE TOLD MOTHER.
SHEILA!
WELL, HE HAS TO KNOW.
SHE TOLD YOU? DID SHE COME HERE - BUT THEN SHE COULDN'T HAVE DONE, SHE DIDN'T EVEN KNOW I LIVED HERE.
WHAT HAPPENED?
COME ON, DON'T JUST LOOK LIKE THAT. TELL ME - TELL ME - WHAT HAPPENED?
I'LL TELL YOU.
SHE WENT TO YOUR MOTHER'S COMMITTEE FOR HELP, AFTER SHE'D DONE WITH YOU.
YOUR MOTHER REFUSED THAT HELP.

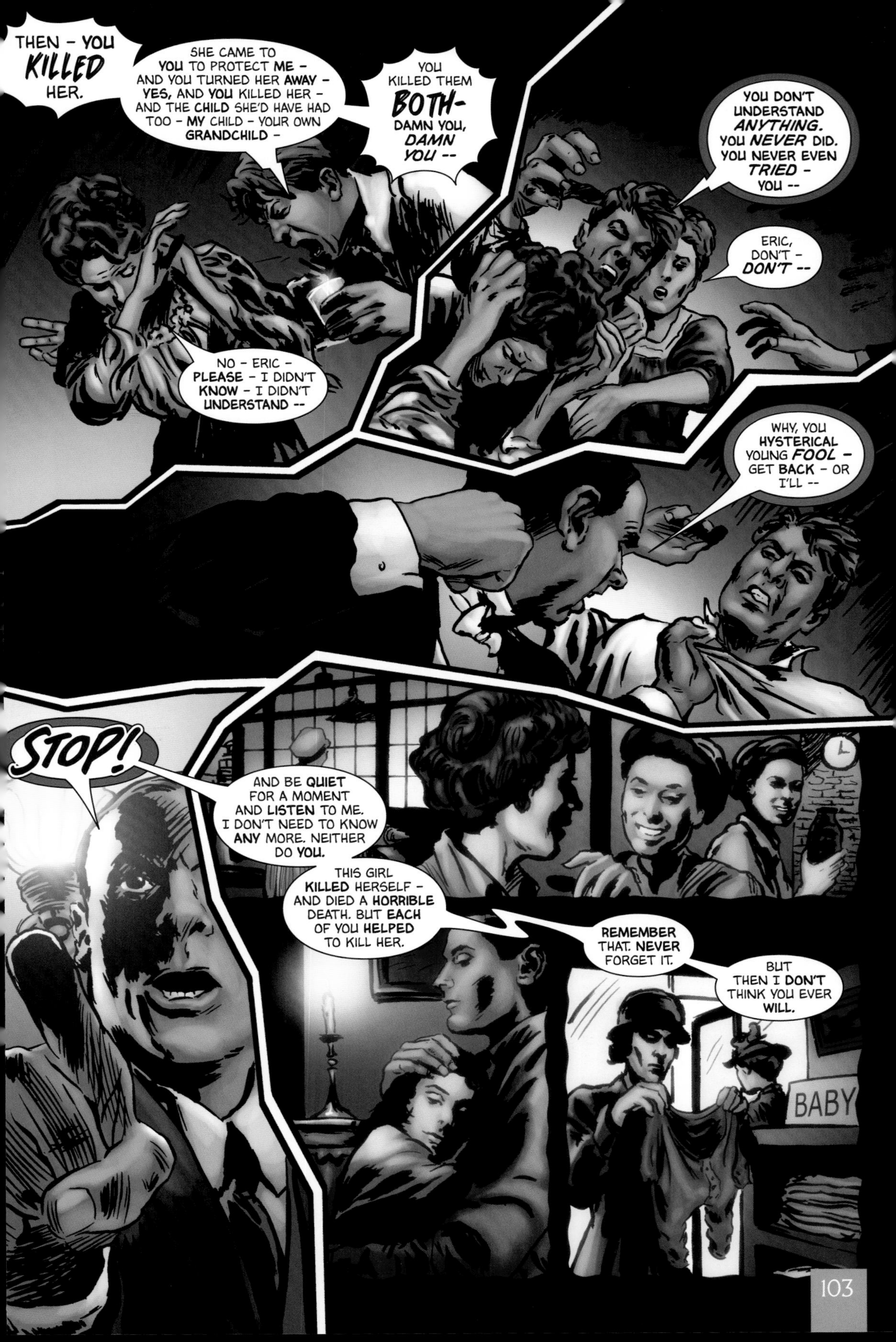
THEN - YOU KILLED HER.
SHE CAME TO YOU TO PROTECT ME - AND YOU TURNED HER AWAY - YES, AND YOU KILLED HER - AND THE CHILD SHE'D HAVE HAD TOO - MY CHILD - YOUR OWN GRANDCHILD -
YOU KILLED THEM BOTH- DAMN YOU, DAMN YOU --
NO - ERIC - PLEASE - I DIDN'T KNOW - I DIDN'T UNDERSTAND --
YOU DON'T UNDERSTAND ANYTHING. YOU NEVER DID. YOU NEVER EVEN TRIED - YOU --
ERIC, DON'T - DON'T --
WHY, YOU HYSTERICAL YOUNG FOOL - GET BACK - OR I'LL --
STOP!
AND BE QUIET FOR A MOMENT AND LISTEN TO ME. I DON'T NEED TO KNOW ANY MORE. NEITHER DO YOU.
THIS GIRL KILLED HERSELF - AND DIED A HORRIBLE DEATH. BUT EACH OF YOU HELPED TO KILL HER.
REMEMBER THAT. NEVER FORGET IT.
BUT THEN I DON'T THINK YOU EVER WILL.
BABY

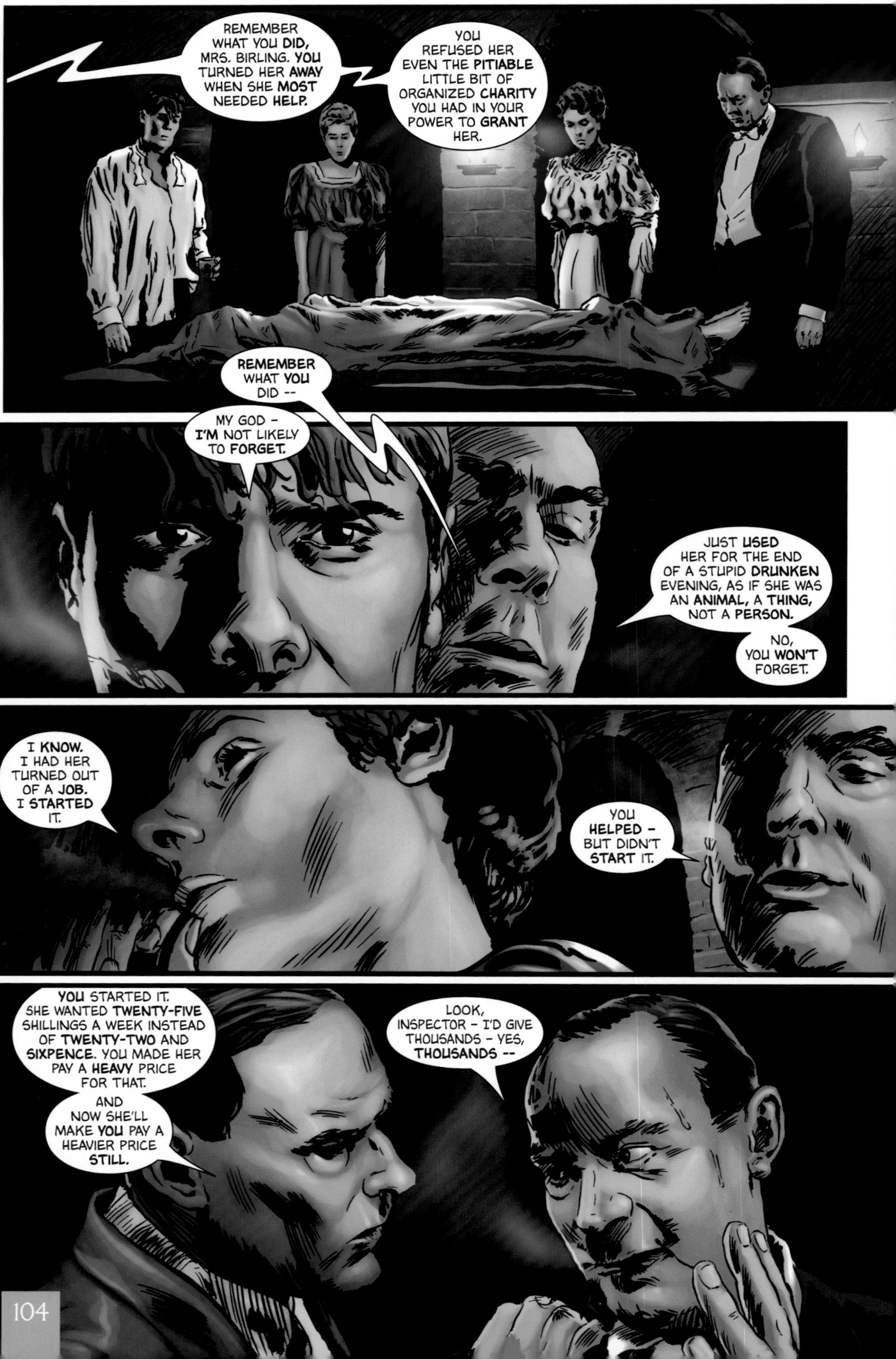
REMEMBER WHAT YOU DID, MRS. BIRLING. YOU TURNED HER AWAY WHEN SHE MOST NEEDED HELP.
YOU REFUSED HER EVEN THE PITIABLE LITTLE BIT OF ORGANIZED CHARITY YOU HAD IN YOUR POWER TO GRANT HER.
REMEMBER WHAT YOU DID --
MY GOD - I'M NOT LIKELY TO FORGET.
JUST USED HER FOR THE END OF A STUPID DRUNKEN EVENING, AS IF SHE WAS AN ANIMAL, A THING, NOT A PERSON.
NO, YOU WON'T FORGET.
I KNOW. I HAD HER TURNED OUT OF A JOB. I STARTED IT.
YOU HELPED - BUT DIDN'T START IT.
YOU STARTED IT. SHE WANTED TWENTY-FIVE SHILLINGS A WEEK INSTEAD OF TWENTY-TWO AND SIXPENCE. YOU MADE HER PAY A HEAVY PRICE FOR THAT.
AND NOW SHE'LL MAKE YOU PAY A HEAVIER PRICE STILL.
LOOK, INSPECTOR - I'D GIVE THOUSANDS - YES, THOUSANDS --

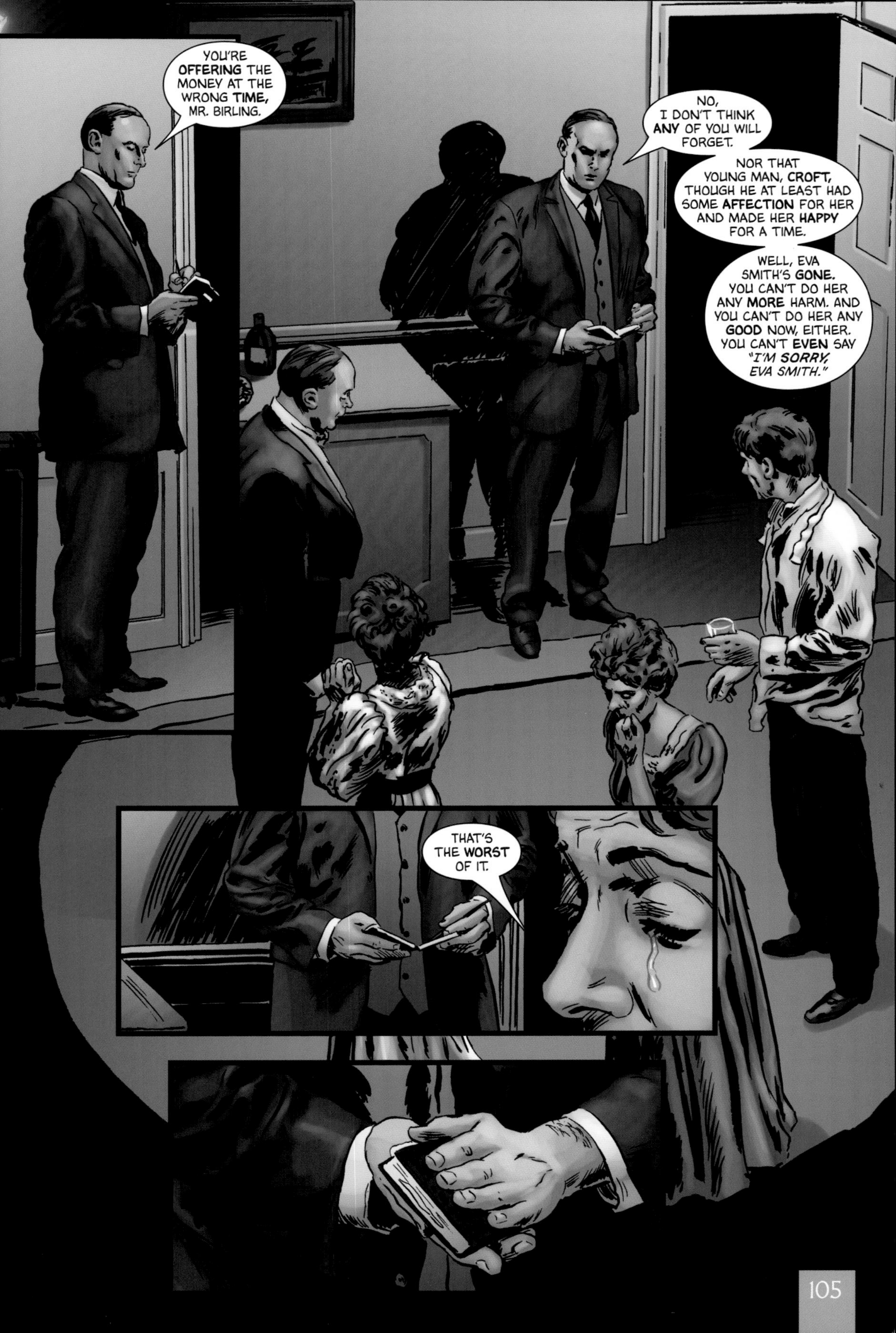
YOU'RE OFFERING THE MONEY AT THE WRONG TIME, MR. BIRLING.
NO, I DON'T THINK ANY OF YOU WILL FORGET.
NOR THAT YOUNG MAN, CROFT, THOUGH HE AT LEAST HAD SOME AFFECTION FOR HER AND MADE HER HAPPY FOR A TIME.
WELL, EVA SMITH'S GONE. YOU CAN'T DO HER ANY MORE HARM. AND YOU CAN'T DO HER ANY GOOD NOW, EITHER. YOU CAN'T EVEN SAY "I'M SORRY, EVA SMITH."
THAT'S THE WORST OF IT.

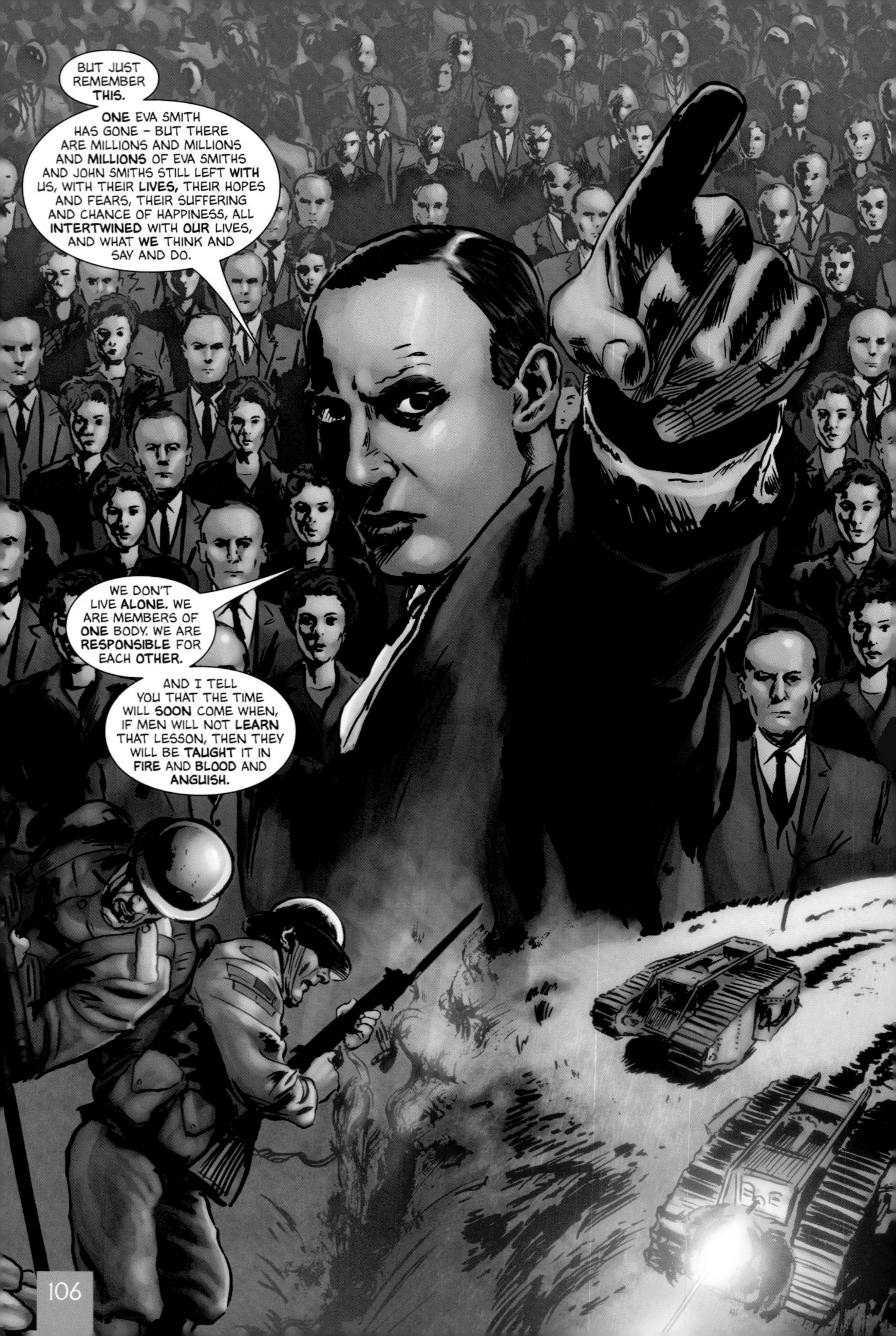

BUT JUST REMEMBER THIS.
ONE EVA SMITH HAS GONE – BUT THERE ARE MILLIONS AND MILLIONS AND MILLIONS OF EVA SMITHS AND JOHN SMITHS STILL LEFT WITH US, WITH THEIR LIVES, THEIR HOPES AND FEARS, THEIR SUFFERING AND CHANCE OF HAPPINESS, ALL INTERTWINED WITH OUR LIVES, AND WHAT WE THINK AND SAY AND DO.
WE DON'T LIVE ALONE. WE ARE MEMBERS OF ONE BODY. WE ARE RESPONSIBLE FOR EACH OTHER.
AND I TELL YOU THAT THE TIME WILL SOON COME WHEN, IF MEN WILL NOT LEARN THAT LESSON, THEN THEY WILL BE TAUGHT IT IN FIRE AND BLOOD AND ANGUISH.

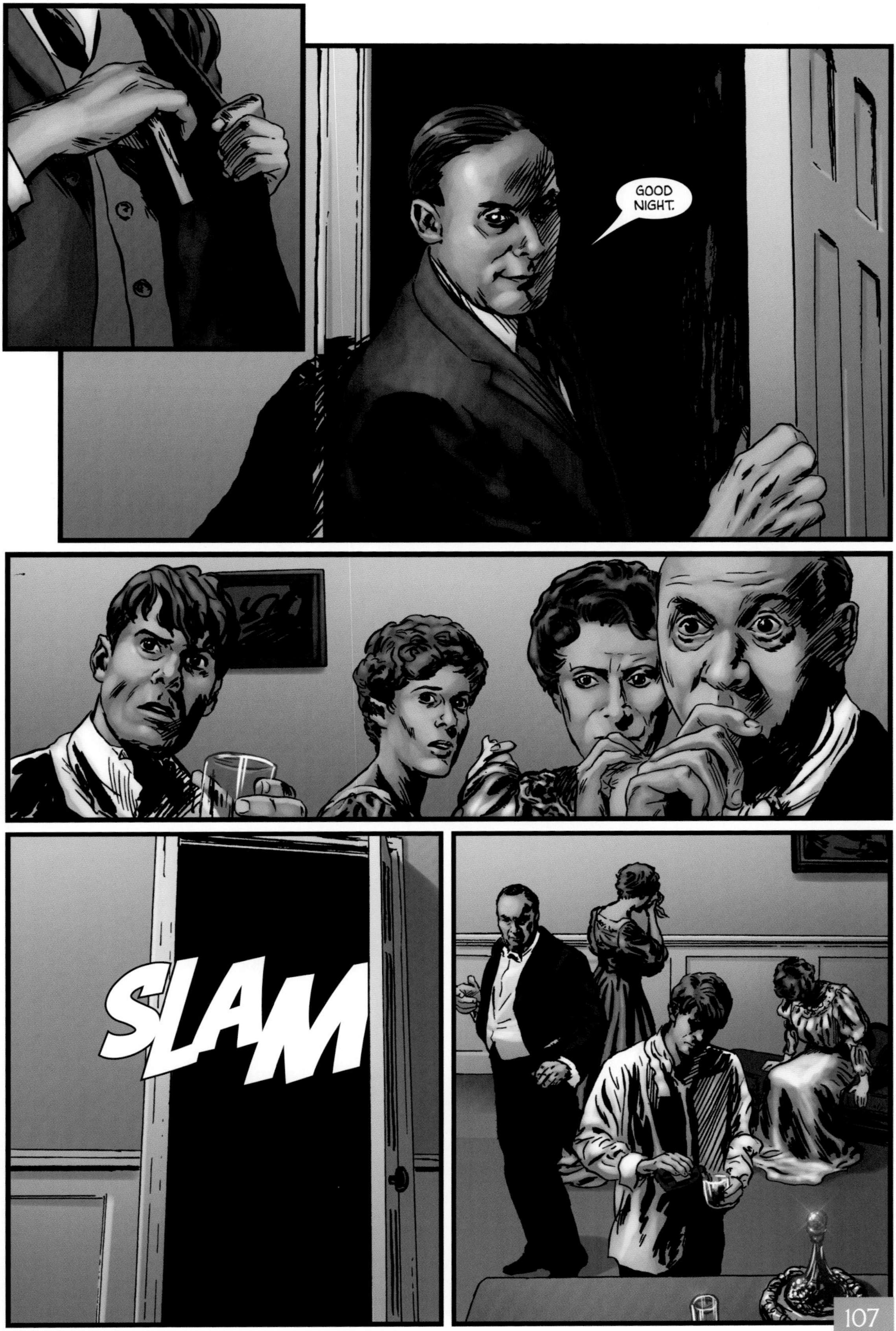
GOOD NIGHT.
SLAM

YOU'RE THE ONE I BLAME FOR THIS.
I'LL BET I AM.
YES, AND YOU DON'T REALIZE YET ALL YOU'VE DONE. MOST OF THIS IS BOUND TO COME OUT. THERE'LL BE A PUBLIC SCANDAL.
WELL, I DON'T CARE NOW.
YOU! YOU DON'T SEEM TO CARE ABOUT ANYTHING. BUT I CARE. I WAS ALMOST CERTAIN FOR A KNIGHTHOOD IN THE NEXT HONOURS LIST!
HA HA HA!
OH – FOR GOD'S SAKE! WHAT DOES IT MATTER NOW WHETHER THEY GIVE YOU A KNIGHTHOOD OR NOT?
IT DOESN'T MATTER TO YOU. APPARENTLY NOTHING MATTERS TO YOU. BUT IT MAY INTEREST YOU TO KNOW THAT UNTIL EVERY PENNY OF THAT MONEY YOU STOLE IS REPAID, YOU'LL WORK FOR NOTHING.
AND THERE'S GOING TO BE NO MORE OF THIS DRINKING ROUND THE TOWN – AND PICKING UP WOMEN IN THE PALACE BAR --
I SHOULD THINK NOT. ERIC, I'M ABSOLUTELY ASHAMED OF YOU.
WELL, I DON'T BLAME YOU. BUT DON'T FORGET I'M ASHAMED OF YOU AS WELL –
YES, BOTH OF YOU.
DROP THAT. THERE'S EVERY EXCUSE FOR WHAT BOTH YOUR MOTHER AND I DID – IT TURNED OUT UNFORTUNATELY, THAT'S ALL --

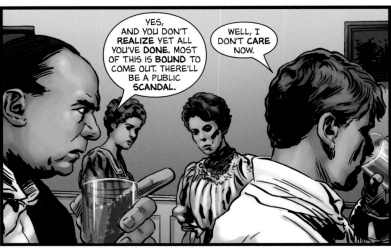

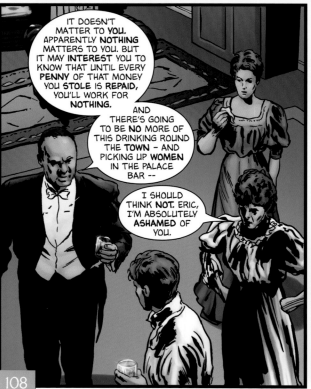

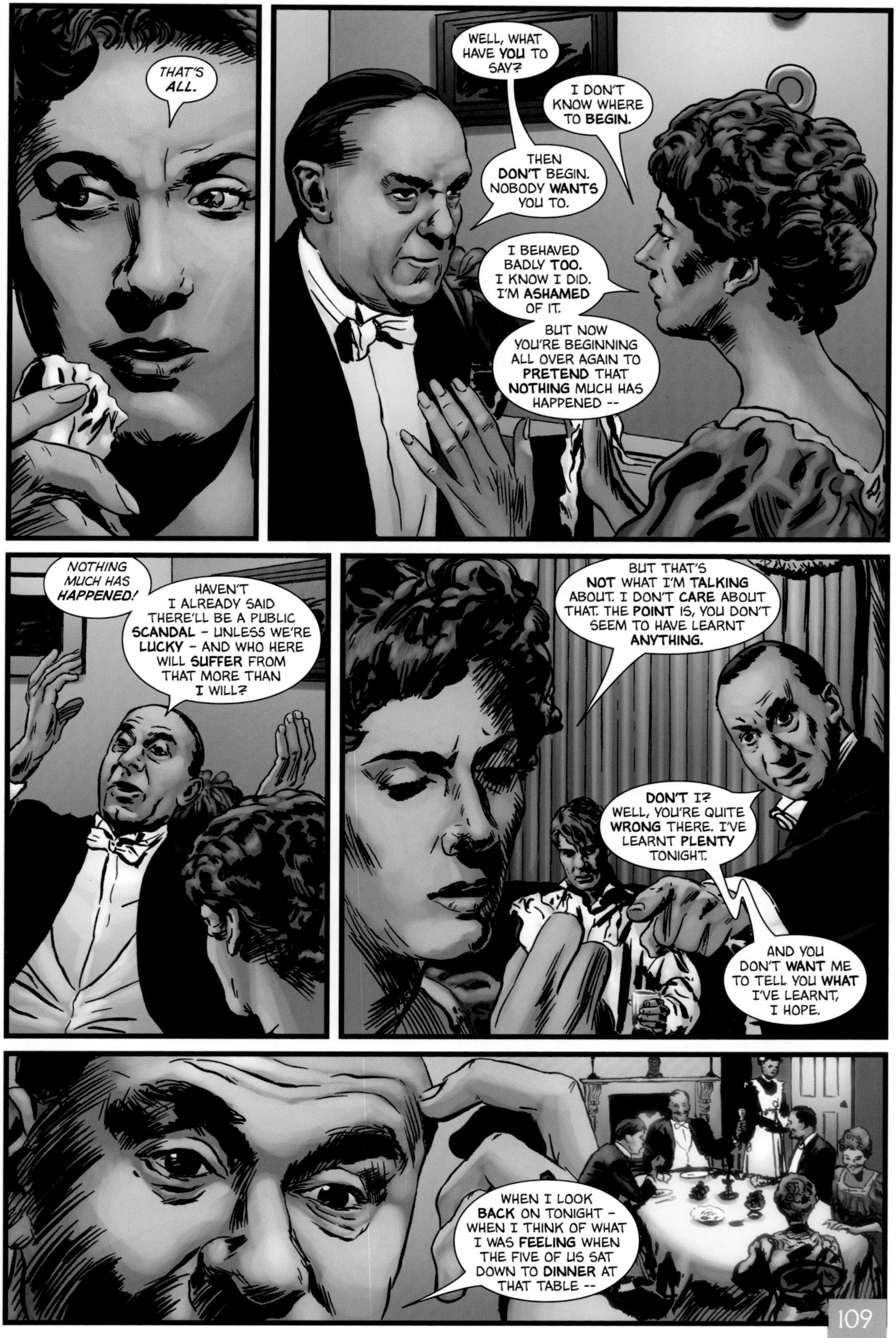
THAT'S ALL.
WELL, WHAT HAVE YOU TO SAY?
I DON'T KNOW WHERE TO BEGIN.
THEN DON'T BEGIN. NOBODY WANTS YOU TO.
I BEHAVED BADLY TOO. I KNOW I DID. I'M ASHAMED OF IT.
BUT NOW YOU'RE BEGINNING ALL OVER AGAIN TO PRETEND THAT NOTHING MUCH HAS HAPPENED --
NOTHING MUCH HAS HAPPENED!
HAVEN'T I ALREADY SAID THERE'LL BE A PUBLIC SCANDAL - UNLESS WE'RE LUCKY - AND WHO HERE WILL SUFFER FROM THAT MORE THAN I WILL?
BUT THAT'S NOT WHAT I'M TALKING ABOUT. I DON'T CARE ABOUT THAT. THE POINT IS, YOU DON'T SEEM TO HAVE LEARNT ANYTHING.
DON'T I? WELL, YOU'RE QUITE WRONG THERE. I'VE LEARNT PLENTY TONIGHT.
AND YOU DON'T WANT ME TO TELL YOU WHAT I'VE LEARNT, I HOPE.
WHEN I LOOK BACK ON TONIGHT - WHEN I THINK OF WHAT I WAS FEELING WHEN THE FIVE OF US SAT DOWN TO DINNER AT THAT TABLE --

YES, AND DO YOU **REMEMBER** WHAT YOU SAID TO GERALD AND ME **AFTER** DINNER, WHEN YOU WERE FEELING SO **PLEASED** WITH YOURSELF?

YOU **TOLD** US THAT A MAN HAS TO MAKE HIS **OWN** WAY, LOOK AFTER **HIMSELF** AND MIND HIS **OWN** BUSINESS, AND THAT WE WEREN'T TO TAKE **ANY** NOTICE OF THESE **CRANKS** WHO TELL US THAT EVERYBODY HAS TO LOOK AFTER EVERYBODY **ELSE**, AS IF WE'RE ALL MIXED UP **TOGETHER**.

DO YOU REMEMBER? YES – AND THEN ONE OF THOSE CRANKS **WALKED** IN – THE INSPECTOR.

HA! I DIDN'T NOTICE YOU TOLD **HIM** THAT IT'S EVERY MAN FOR HIMSELF.

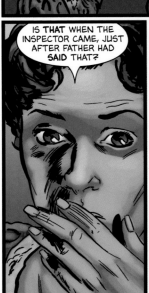

IS **THAT** WHEN THE INSPECTOR CAME, JUST AFTER FATHER HAD SAID THAT?

YES. WHAT OF IT?

NOW WHAT'S THE MATTER SHEILA?

IT'S QUEER – **VERY** QUEER –

I **KNOW** WHAT YOU'RE GOING TO **SAY**. BECAUSE I'VE BEEN WONDERING **MYSELF**.

IT DOESN'T MUCH MATTER **NOW**, OF COURSE – BUT WAS HE **REALLY** A POLICE INSPECTOR?

WELL, IF HE **WASN'T**, IT MATTERS A **DEVIL** OF A LOT. MAKES **ALL** THE DIFFERENCE.

NO, IT **DOESN'T**.

DON'T TALK **RUBBISH**. OF **COURSE** IT DOES.

WELL, IT DOESN'T TO **ME**. AND IT OUGHTN'T TO **YOU**, EITHER.

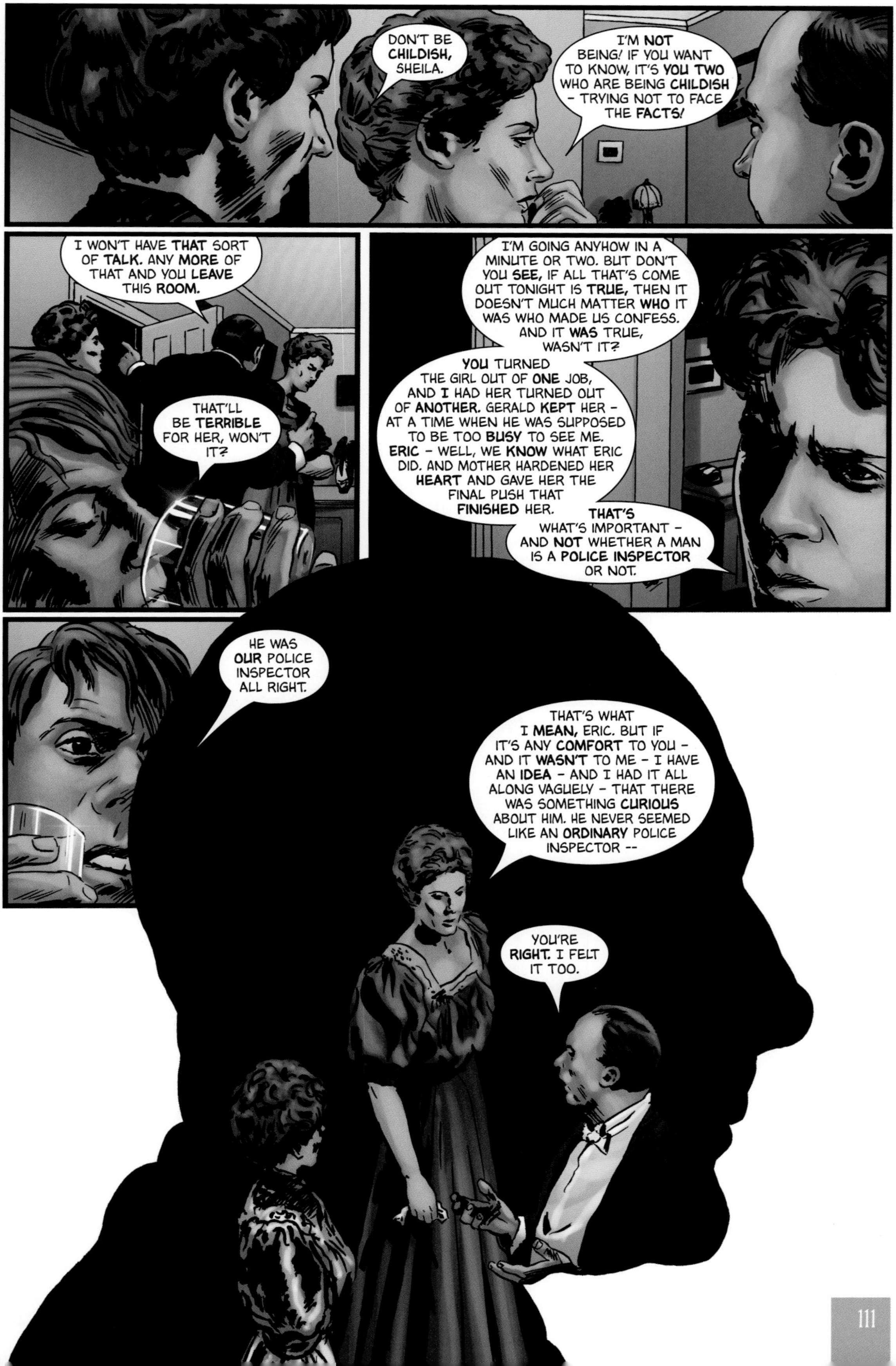
DON'T BE CHILDISH, SHEILA.
I'M NOT BEING! IF YOU WANT TO KNOW, IT'S YOU TWO WHO ARE BEING CHILDISH – TRYING NOT TO FACE THE FACTS!
I WON'T HAVE THAT SORT OF TALK. ANY MORE OF THAT AND YOU LEAVE THIS ROOM.
THAT'LL BE TERRIBLE FOR HER, WON'T IT?
I'M GOING ANYHOW IN A MINUTE OR TWO. BUT DON'T YOU SEE, IF ALL THAT'S COME OUT TONIGHT IS TRUE, THEN IT DOESN'T MUCH MATTER WHO IT WAS WHO MADE US CONFESS. AND IT WAS TRUE, WASN'T IT?
YOU TURNED THE GIRL OUT OF ONE JOB, AND I HAD HER TURNED OUT OF ANOTHER. GERALD KEPT HER – AT A TIME WHEN HE WAS SUPPOSED TO BE TOO BUSY TO SEE ME. ERIC – WELL, WE KNOW WHAT ERIC DID. AND MOTHER HARDENED HER HEART AND GAVE HER THE FINAL PUSH THAT FINISHED HER.
THAT'S WHAT'S IMPORTANT – AND NOT WHETHER A MAN IS A POLICE INSPECTOR OR NOT.
HE WAS OUR POLICE INSPECTOR ALL RIGHT.
THAT'S WHAT I MEAN, ERIC. BUT IF IT'S ANY COMFORT TO YOU – AND IT WASN'T TO ME – I HAVE AN IDEA – AND I HAD IT ALL ALONG VAGUELY – THAT THERE WAS SOMETHING CURIOUS ABOUT HIM. HE NEVER SEEMED LIKE AN ORDINARY POLICE INSPECTOR --
YOU'RE RIGHT. I FELT IT TOO.

DIDN'T YOU?

WELL, I MUST SAY HIS **MANNER** WAS QUITE **EXTRAORDINARY**; SO - SO **RUDE** - AND **ASSERTIVE** --

THEN LOOK AT THE WAY HE TALKED TO **ME**. TELLING ME TO **SHUT UP** - AND SO ON. HE MUST HAVE **KNOWN** I WAS AN EX-LORD **MAYOR** AND A **MAGISTRATE** AND SO FORTH.

BESIDES - THE **WAY** HE TALKED - YOU REMEMBER. I MEAN, **THEY** DON'T TALK LIKE **THAT**. I'VE HAD DEALINGS WITH **DOZENS** OF THEM.

ALL RIGHT. BUT IT DOESN'T MAKE ANY **REAL** DIFFERENCE, Y'KNOW.

OF **COURSE** IT DOES.

NO, SHEILA'S **RIGHT**. IT DOESN'T.

THAT'S **COMIC**, THAT IS, COMING FROM **YOU**. YOU'RE THE ONE IT MAKES **MOST** DIFFERENCE TO. YOU'VE CONFESSED TO **THEFT**, AND NOW HE KNOWS **ALL** ABOUT IT, AND HE CAN BRING IT OUT AT THE **INQUEST**, AND THEN IF NECESSARY CARRY IT TO **COURT**.

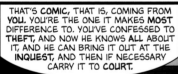

HE CAN'T DO **ANYTHING** TO YOUR MOTHER AND SHEILA AND ME - EXCEPT PERHAPS MAKE US LOOK A BIT **ASHAMED** OF OURSELVES IN PUBLIC - BUT AS FOR **YOU**, HE CAN **RUIN** YOU. YOU **KNOW**.

WE HARDLY EVER TOLD HIM **ANYTHING** HE DIDN'T **KNOW**. DID YOU **NOTICE** THAT?

THAT'S **NOTHING**. HE HAD A BIT OF INFORMATION, LEFT BY THE **GIRL**, AND MADE A FEW SMART **GUESSES** - BUT THE FACT REMAINS THAT IF WE HADN'T TALKED SO **MUCH**, HE'D HAVE HAD **LITTLE** TO GO ON.

AND REALLY, WHEN I COME TO **THINK** OF IT, WHY **YOU** ALL HAD TO GO LETTING **EVERYTHING** COME OUT LIKE THAT, BEATS ME.

IT'S ALL **RIGHT** TALKING LIKE THAT **NOW**. BUT HE MADE US **CONFESS**.

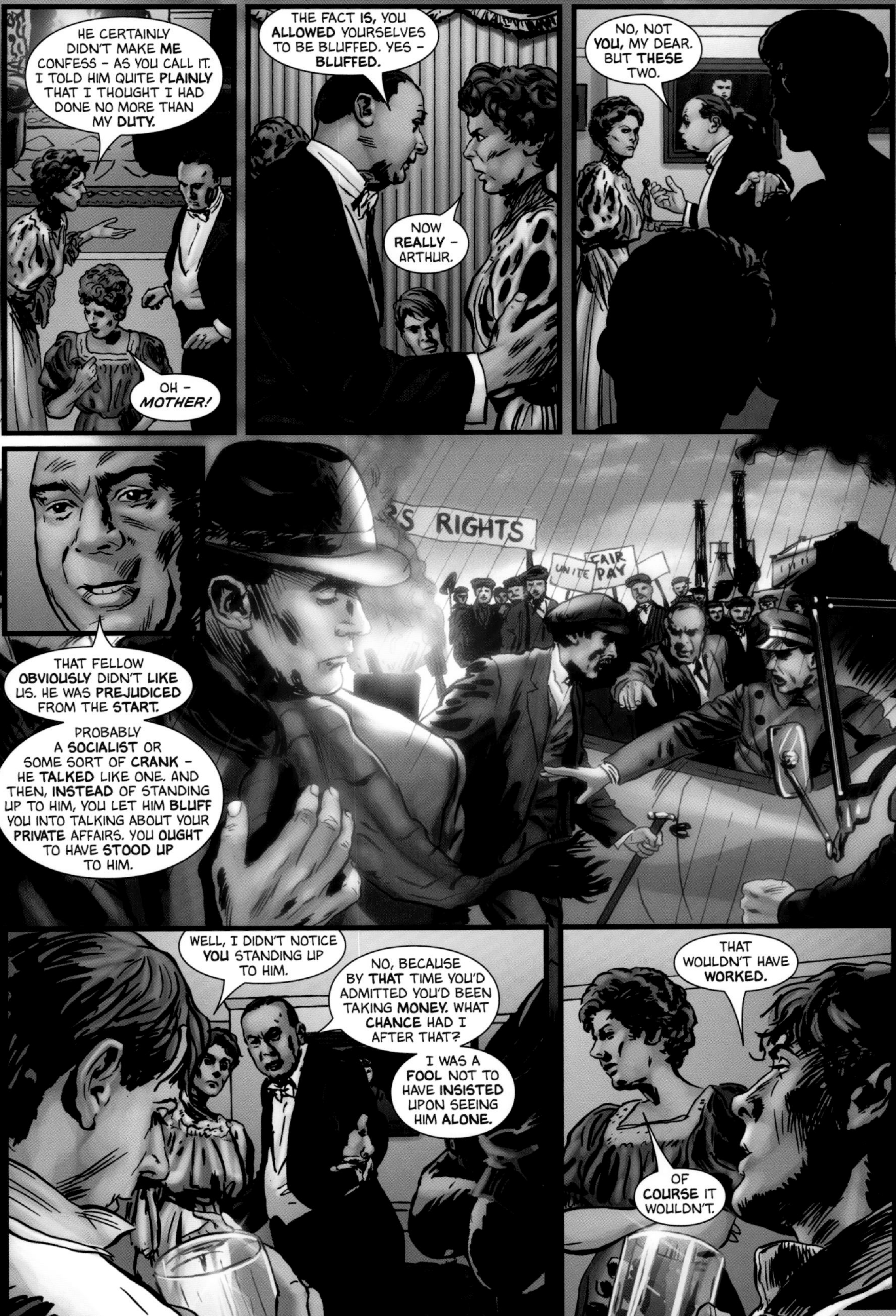
HE CERTAINLY DIDN'T MAKE ME CONFESS – AS YOU CALL IT. I TOLD HIM QUITE PLAINLY THAT I THOUGHT I HAD DONE NO MORE THAN MY DUTY.
OH – MOTHER!
THE FACT IS, YOU ALLOWED YOURSELVES TO BE BLUFFED. YES – BLUFFED.
NOW REALLY – ARTHUR.
NO, NOT YOU, MY DEAR. BUT THESE TWO.
S RIGHTS
UNITE
FAIR PAY
THAT FELLOW OBVIOUSLY DIDN'T LIKE US. HE WAS PREJUDICED FROM THE START.
PROBABLY A SOCIALIST OR SOME SORT OF CRANK – HE TALKED LIKE ONE. AND THEN, INSTEAD OF STANDING UP TO HIM, YOU LET HIM BLUFF YOU INTO TALKING ABOUT YOUR PRIVATE AFFAIRS. YOU OUGHT TO HAVE STOOD UP TO HIM.
WELL, I DIDN'T NOTICE YOU STANDING UP TO HIM.
NO, BECAUSE BY THAT TIME YOU'D ADMITTED YOU'D BEEN TAKING MONEY. WHAT CHANCE HAD I AFTER THAT?
I WAS A FOOL NOT TO HAVE INSISTED UPON SEEING HIM ALONE.
THAT WOULDN'T HAVE WORKED.
OF COURSE IT WOULDN'T.

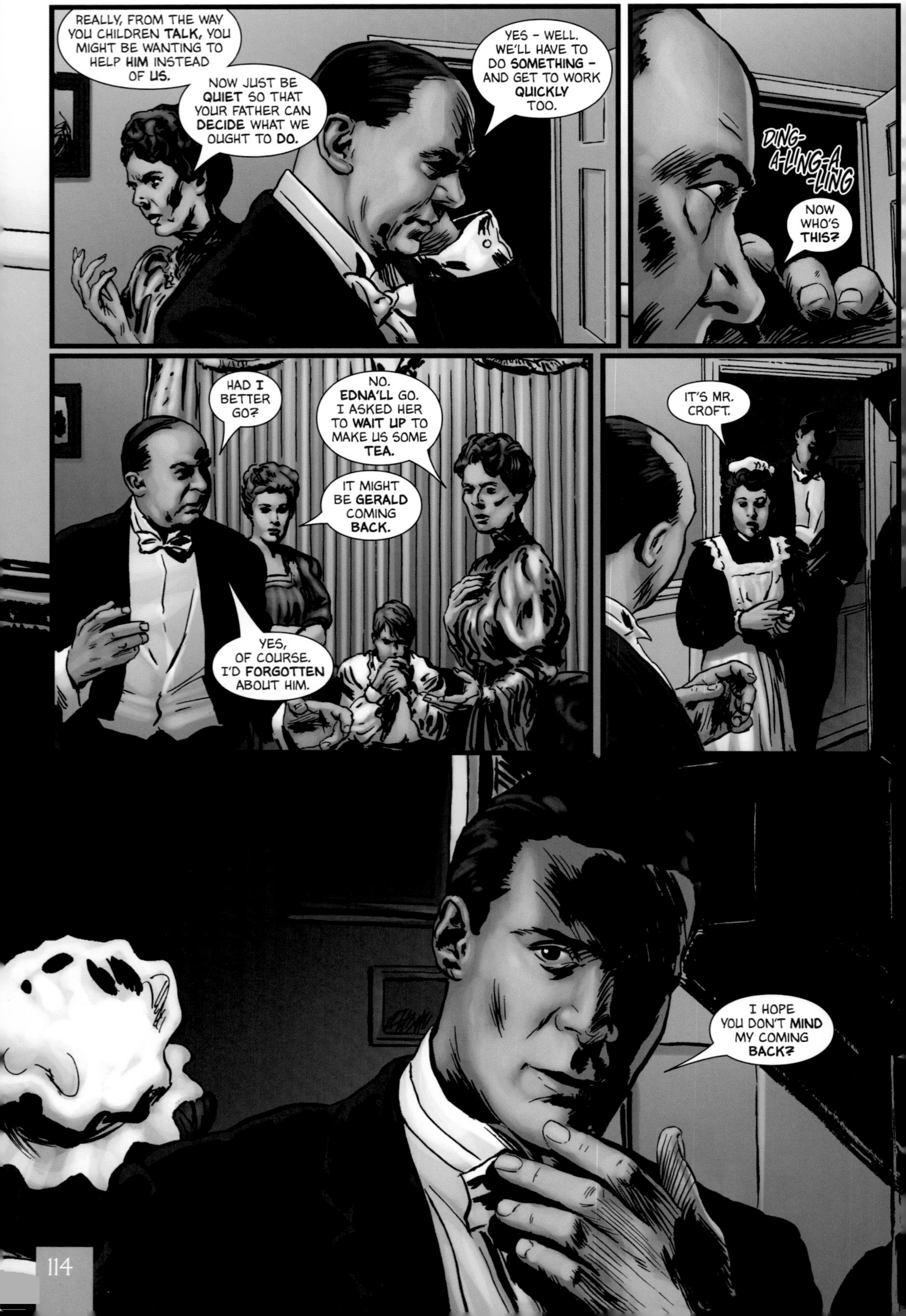
REALLY, FROM THE WAY YOU CHILDREN TALK, YOU MIGHT BE WANTING TO HELP HIM INSTEAD OF US.
NOW JUST BE QUIET SO THAT YOUR FATHER CAN DECIDE WHAT WE OUGHT TO DO.
YES - WELL. WE'LL HAVE TO DO SOMETHING - AND GET TO WORK QUICKLY TOO.
DING-A-LING-A-LING
NOW WHO'S THIS?
HAD I BETTER GO?
NO. EDNA'LL GO. I ASKED HER TO WAIT UP TO MAKE US SOME TEA.
IT MIGHT BE GERALD COMING BACK.
YES, OF COURSE. I'D FORGOTTEN ABOUT HIM.
IT'S MR. CROFT.
I HOPE YOU DON'T MIND MY COMING BACK?

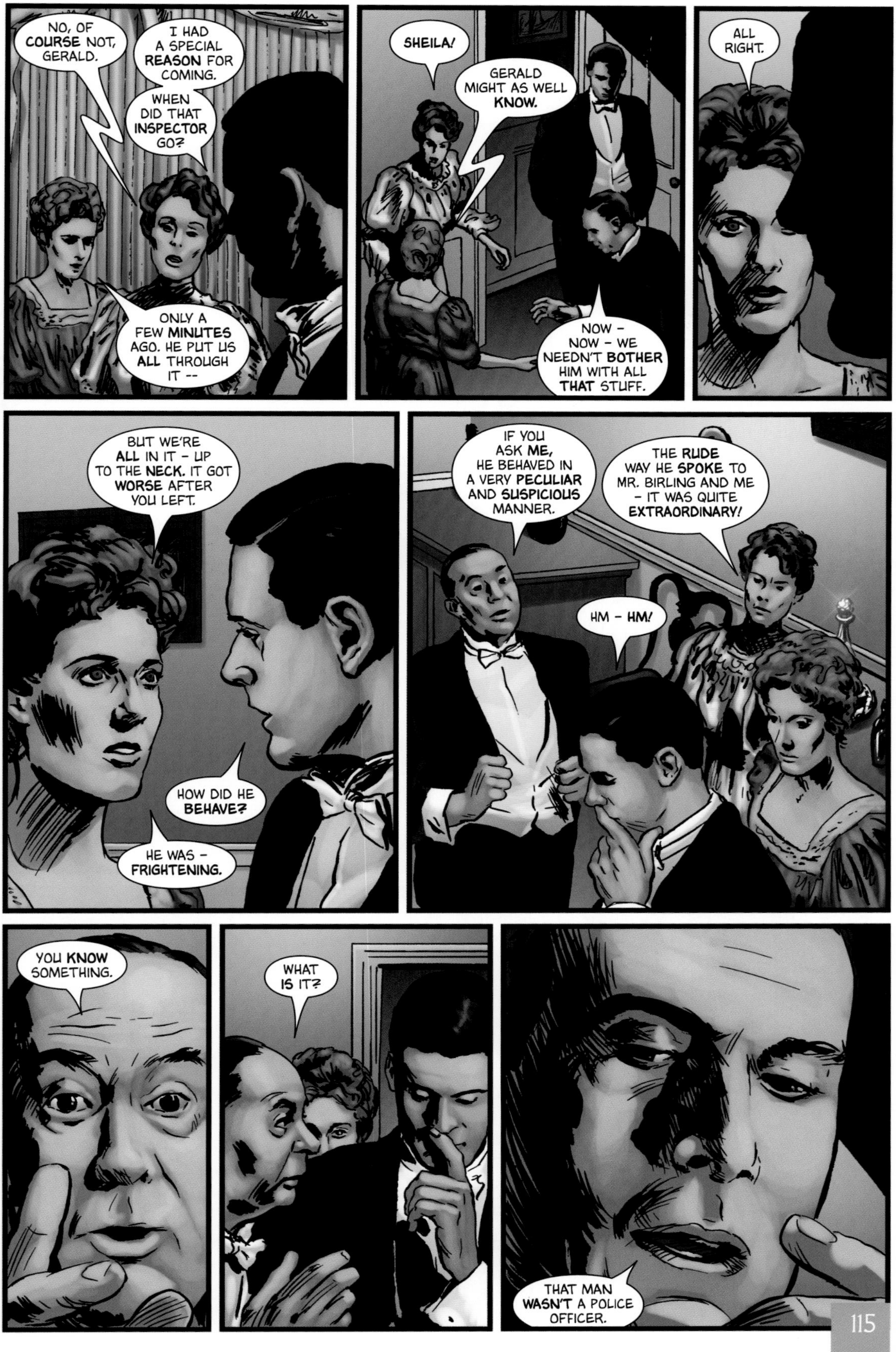
NO, OF COURSE NOT, GERALD.
I HAD A SPECIAL REASON FOR COMING.
WHEN DID THAT INSPECTOR GO?
ONLY A FEW MINUTES AGO. HE PUT US ALL THROUGH IT --
SHEILA!
GERALD MIGHT AS WELL KNOW.
NOW - NOW - WE NEEDN'T BOTHER HIM WITH ALL THAT STUFF.
ALL RIGHT.
BUT WE'RE ALL IN IT - UP TO THE NECK. IT GOT WORSE AFTER YOU LEFT.
HOW DID HE BEHAVE?
HE WAS - FRIGHTENING.
IF YOU ASK ME, HE BEHAVED IN A VERY PECULIAR AND SUSPICIOUS MANNER.
THE RUDE WAY HE SPOKE TO MR. BIRLING AND ME - IT WAS QUITE EXTRAORDINARY!
HM - HM!
YOU KNOW SOMETHING.
WHAT IS IT?
THAT MAN WASN'T A POLICE OFFICER.

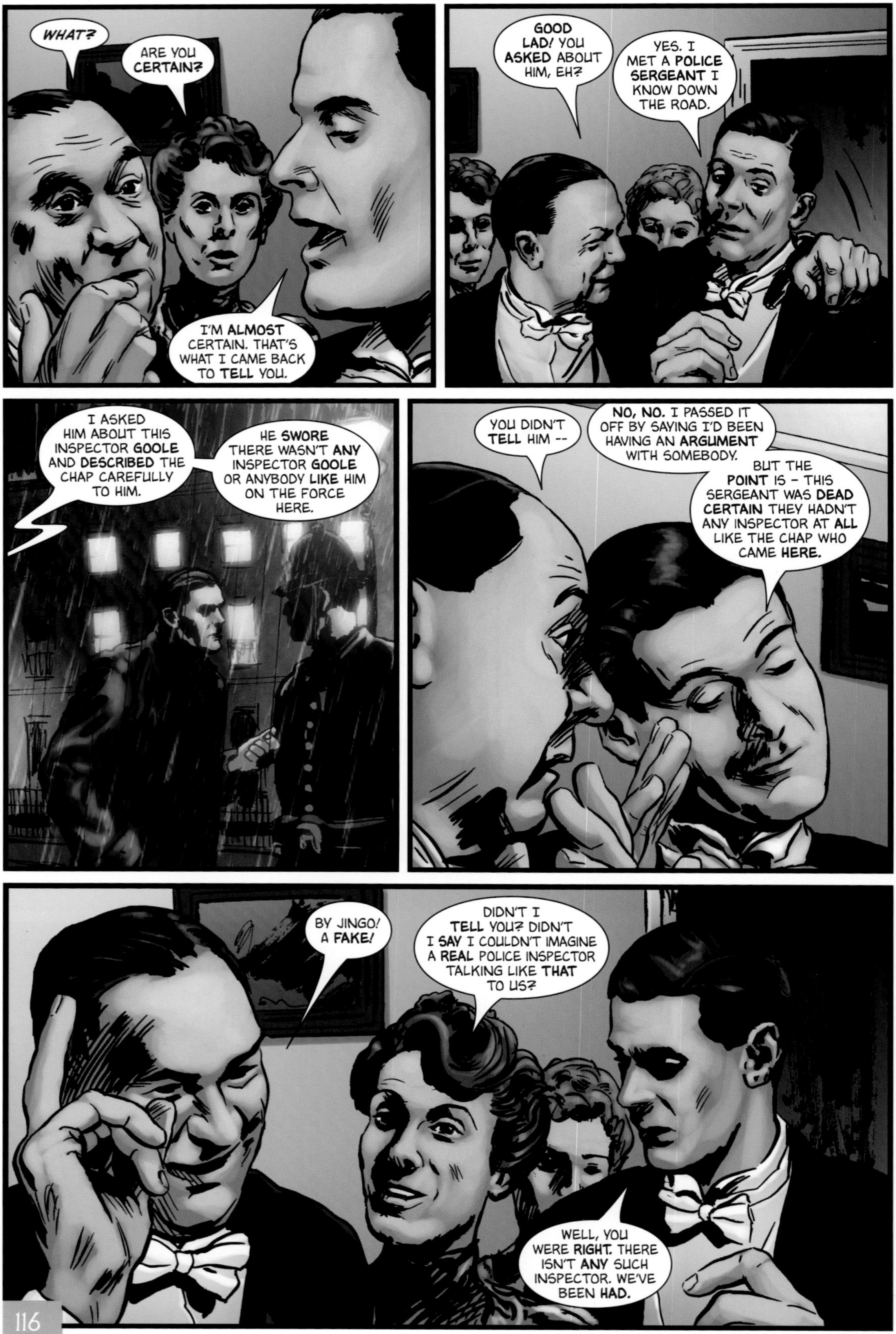

WHAT?
ARE YOU CERTAIN?
I'M ALMOST CERTAIN. THAT'S WHAT I CAME BACK TO TELL YOU.
GOOD LAD! YOU ASKED ABOUT HIM, EH?
YES. I MET A POLICE SERGEANT I KNOW DOWN THE ROAD.
I ASKED HIM ABOUT THIS INSPECTOR GOOLE AND DESCRIBED THE CHAP CAREFULLY TO HIM.
HE SWORE THERE WASN'T ANY INSPECTOR GOOLE OR ANYBODY LIKE HIM ON THE FORCE HERE.
YOU DIDN'T TELL HIM --
NO, NO. I PASSED IT OFF BY SAYING I'D BEEN HAVING AN ARGUMENT WITH SOMEBODY.
BUT THE POINT IS – THIS SERGEANT WAS DEAD CERTAIN THEY HADN'T ANY INSPECTOR AT ALL LIKE THE CHAP WHO CAME HERE.
BY JINGO! A FAKE!
DIDN'T I TELL YOU? DIDN'T I SAY I COULDN'T IMAGINE A REAL POLICE INSPECTOR TALKING LIKE THAT TO US?
WELL, YOU WERE RIGHT. THERE ISN'T ANY SUCH INSPECTOR. WE'VE BEEN HAD.

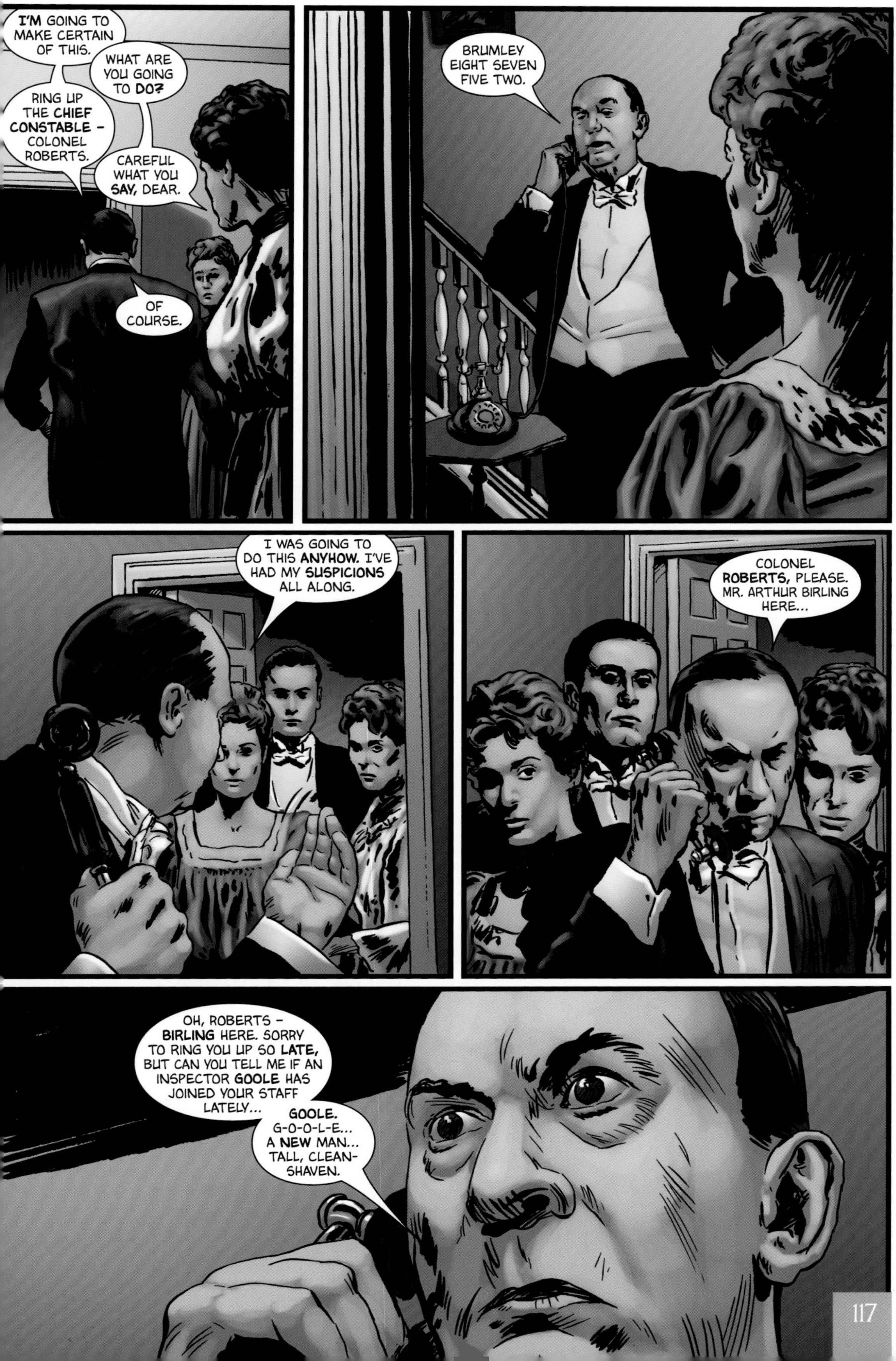
I'M GOING TO MAKE CERTAIN OF THIS.
WHAT ARE YOU GOING TO DO?
RING UP THE CHIEF CONSTABLE - COLONEL ROBERTS.
CAREFUL WHAT YOU SAY, DEAR.
OF COURSE.
BRUMLEY EIGHT SEVEN FIVE TWO.
I WAS GOING TO DO THIS ANYHOW. I'VE HAD MY SUSPICIONS ALL ALONG.
COLONEL ROBERTS, PLEASE. MR. ARTHUR BIRLING HERE...
OH, ROBERTS - BIRLING HERE. SORRY TO RING YOU UP SO LATE, BUT CAN YOU TELL ME IF AN INSPECTOR GOOLE HAS JOINED YOUR STAFF LATELY...
GOOLE. G-O-O-L-E... A NEW MAN... TALL, CLEAN-SHAVEN.

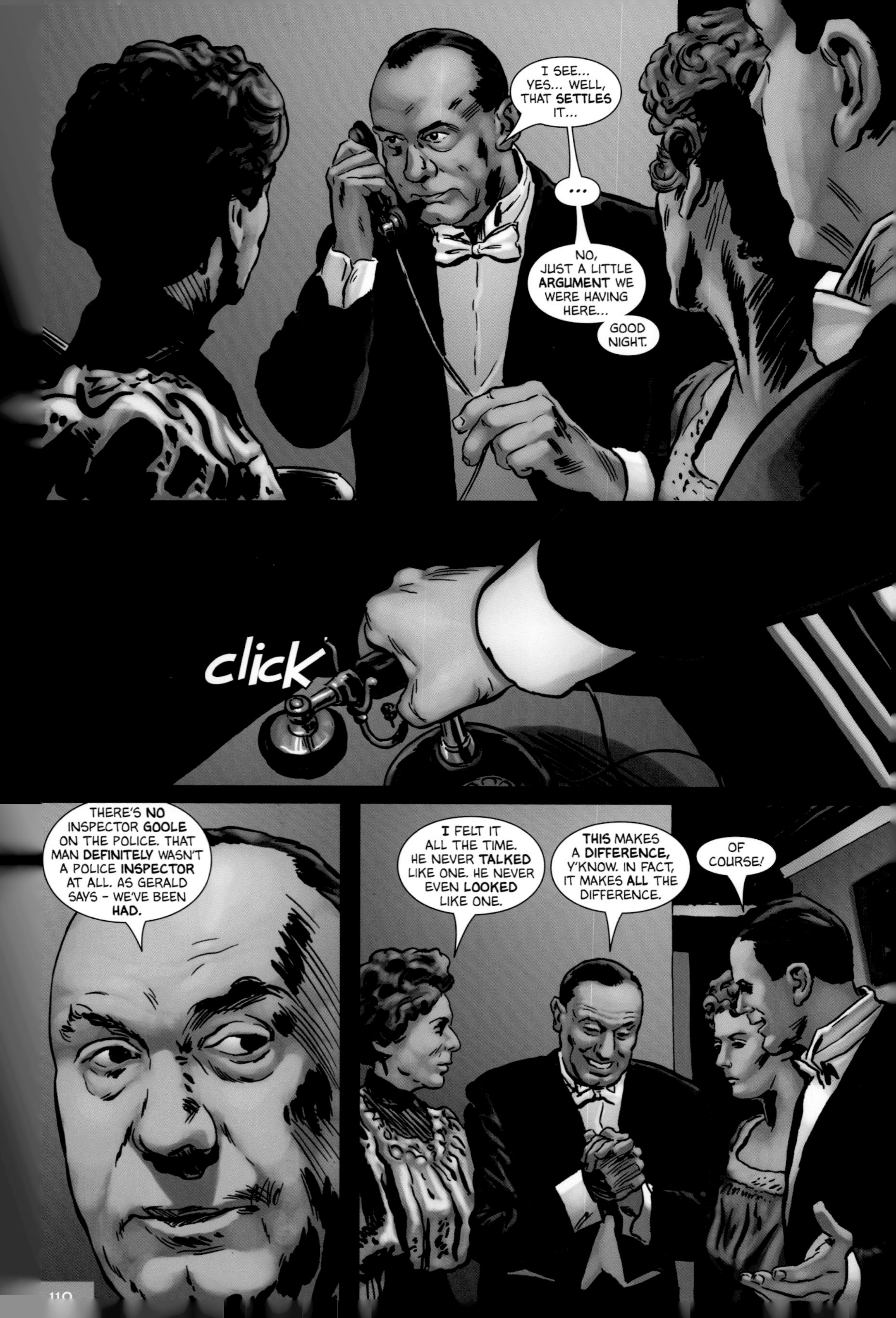
I SEE... YES... WELL, THAT SETTLES IT...
...
NO, JUST A LITTLE ARGUMENT WE WERE HAVING HERE...
GOOD NIGHT.
click
THERE'S NO INSPECTOR GOOLE ON THE POLICE. THAT MAN DEFINITELY WASN'T A POLICE INSPECTOR AT ALL. AS GERALD SAYS – WE'VE BEEN HAD.
I FELT IT ALL THE TIME. HE NEVER TALKED LIKE ONE. HE NEVER EVEN LOOKED LIKE ONE.
THIS MAKES A DIFFERENCE, Y'KNOW. IN FACT, IT MAKES ALL THE DIFFERENCE.
OF COURSE!

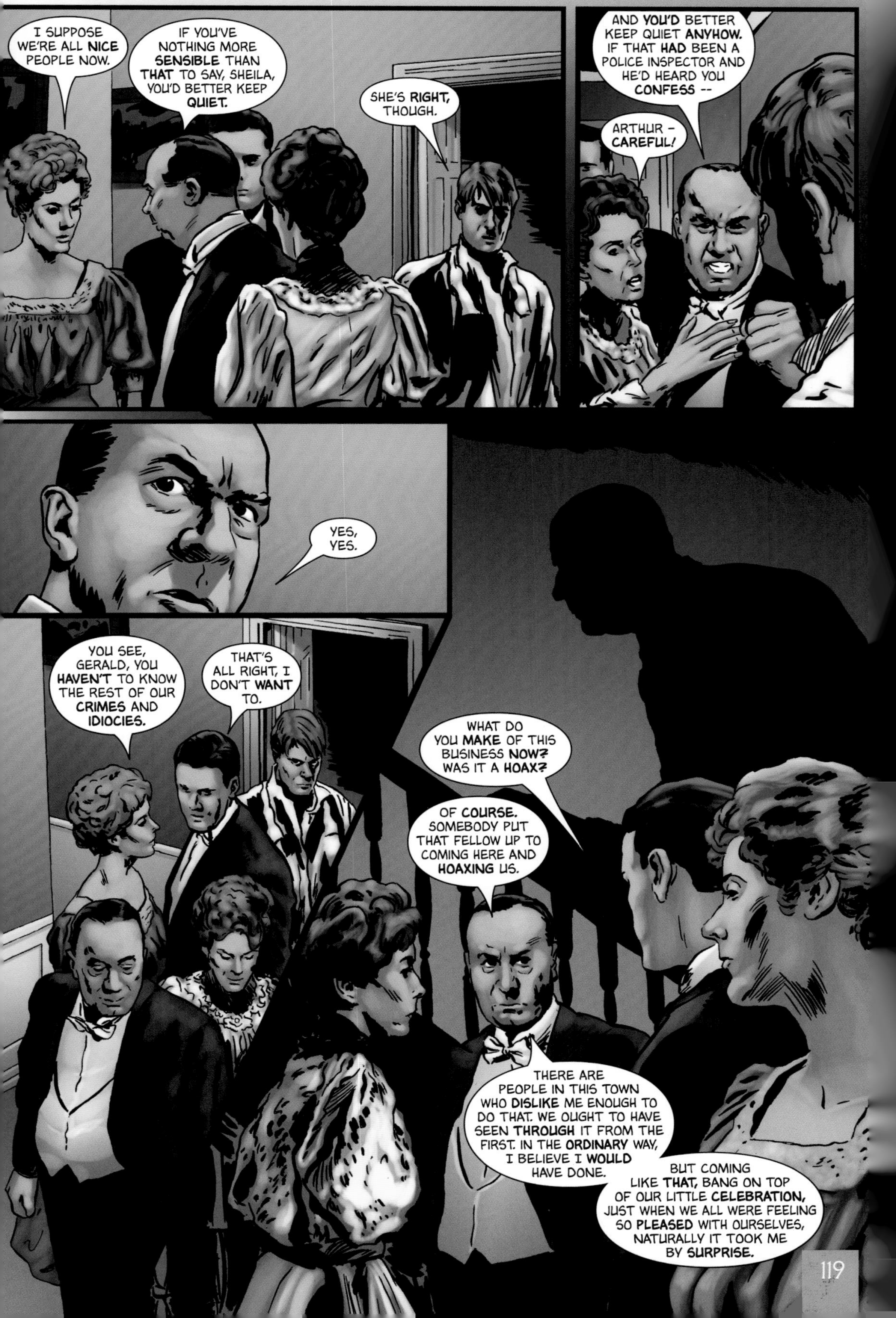
I SUPPOSE WE'RE ALL NICE PEOPLE NOW.
IF YOU'VE NOTHING MORE SENSIBLE THAN THAT TO SAY, SHEILA, YOU'D BETTER KEEP QUIET.
SHE'S RIGHT, THOUGH.
AND YOU'D BETTER KEEP QUIET ANYHOW. IF THAT HAD BEEN A POLICE INSPECTOR AND HE'D HEARD YOU CONFESS --
ARTHUR – CAREFUL!
YES, YES.
YOU SEE, GERALD, YOU HAVEN'T TO KNOW THE REST OF OUR CRIMES AND IDIOCIES.
THAT'S ALL RIGHT, I DON'T WANT TO.
WHAT DO YOU MAKE OF THIS BUSINESS NOW? WAS IT A HOAX?
OF COURSE. SOMEBODY PUT THAT FELLOW UP TO COMING HERE AND HOAXING US.
THERE ARE PEOPLE IN THIS TOWN WHO DISLIKE ME ENOUGH TO DO THAT. WE OUGHT TO HAVE SEEN THROUGH IT FROM THE FIRST. IN THE ORDINARY WAY, I BELIEVE I WOULD HAVE DONE.
BUT COMING LIKE THAT, BANG ON TOP OF OUR LITTLE CELEBRATION, JUST WHEN WE ALL WERE FEELING SO PLEASED WITH OURSELVES, NATURALLY IT TOOK ME BY SURPRISE.

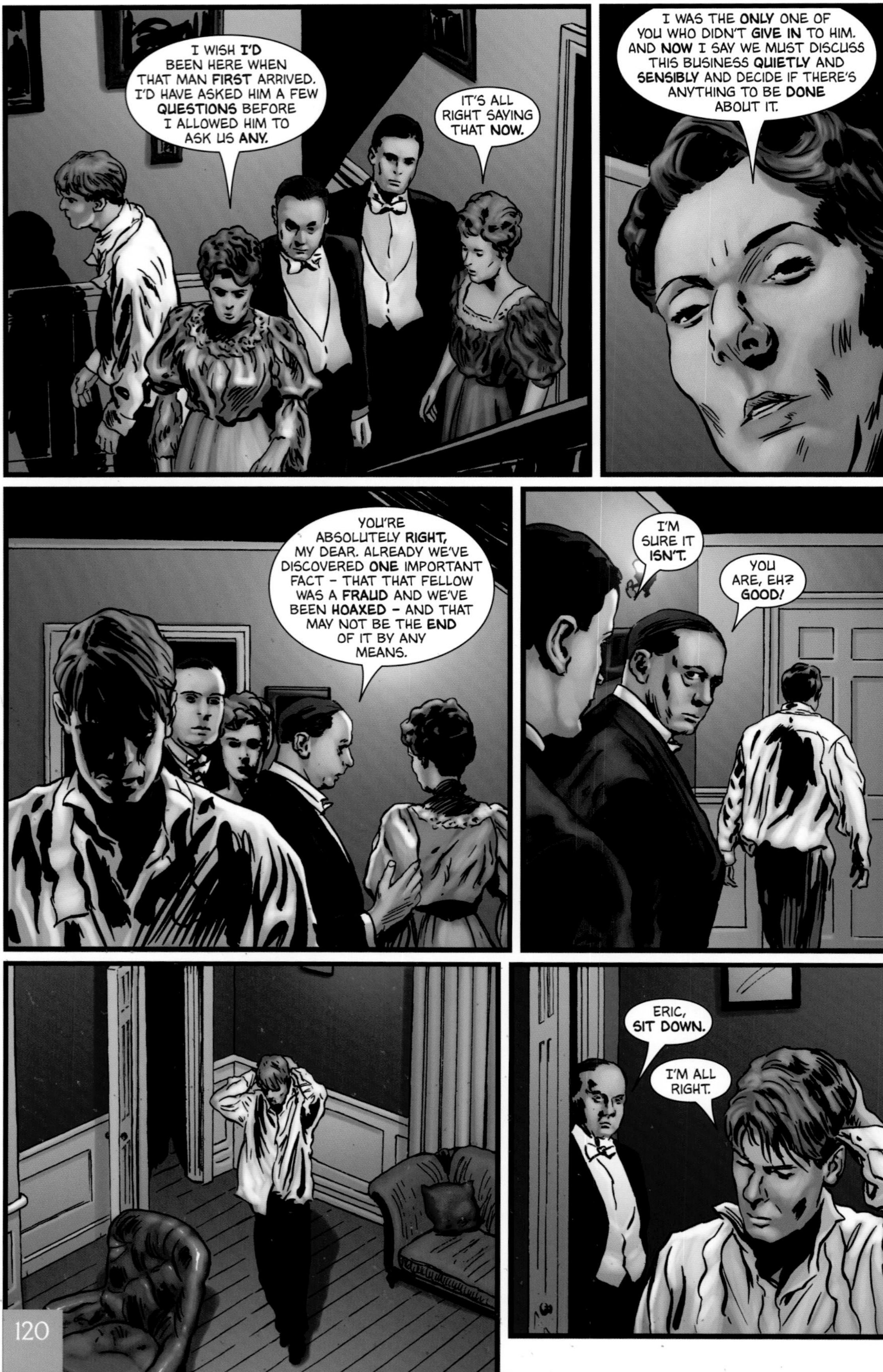
I WISH I'D BEEN HERE WHEN THAT MAN FIRST ARRIVED. I'D HAVE ASKED HIM A FEW QUESTIONS BEFORE I ALLOWED HIM TO ASK US ANY.
IT'S ALL RIGHT SAYING THAT NOW.
I WAS THE ONLY ONE OF YOU WHO DIDN'T GIVE IN TO HIM. AND NOW I SAY WE MUST DISCUSS THIS BUSINESS QUIETLY AND SENSIBLY AND DECIDE IF THERE'S ANYTHING TO BE DONE ABOUT IT.
YOU'RE ABSOLUTELY RIGHT, MY DEAR. ALREADY WE'VE DISCOVERED ONE IMPORTANT FACT - THAT THAT FELLOW WAS A FRAUD AND WE'VE BEEN HOAXED - AND THAT MAY NOT BE THE END OF IT BY ANY MEANS.
I'M SURE IT ISN'T.
YOU ARE, EH? GOOD!
ERIC, SIT DOWN.
I'M ALL RIGHT.

ALL RIGHT? YOU'RE ANYTHING **BUT** ALL RIGHT. AND YOU NEEDN'T STAND **THERE** – AS IF – AS IF –

AS IF – **WHAT?**

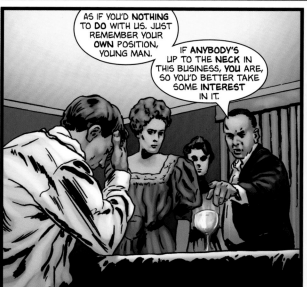

AS IF YOU'D **NOTHING** TO **DO** WITH US. JUST REMEMBER YOUR **OWN** POSITION, YOUNG MAN.

IF **ANYBODY'S** UP TO THE **NECK** IN THIS BUSINESS, **YOU** ARE, SO YOU'D BETTER TAKE SOME **INTEREST** IN IT.

I **DO** TAKE SOME INTEREST IN IT. I TAKE TOO **MUCH**, THAT'S MY TROUBLE.

IT'S **MINE** TOO.

NOW **LISTEN**, YOU TWO. IF YOU'RE STILL FEELING ON **EDGE**, THEN THE LEAST YOU CAN DO IS TO KEEP **QUIET**. LEAVE THIS TO **US**.

I'LL ADMIT THAT FELLOW'S ANTICS **RATTLED** US A BIT. BUT WE'VE FOUND HIM **OUT** – AND ALL WE HAVE TO DO IS TO KEEP OUR **HEADS**. NOW IT'S **OUR** TURN.

OUR TURN TO DO – **WHAT?**

TO BEHAVE **SENSIBLY**, SHEILA – WHICH IS MORE THAN **YOU'RE** DOING.

121

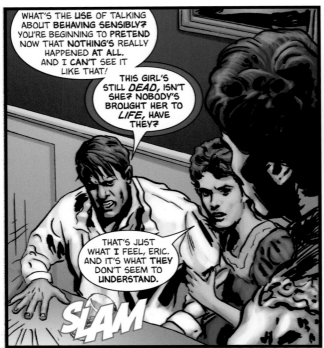

WHAT'S THE USE OF TALKING ABOUT BEHAVING SENSIBLY? YOU'RE BEGINNING TO PRETEND NOW THAT NOTHING'S REALLY HAPPENED AT ALL. AND I CAN'T SEE IT LIKE THAT!

THIS GIRL'S STILL DEAD, ISN'T SHE? NOBODY'S BROUGHT HER TO LIFE, HAVE THEY?

THAT'S JUST WHAT I FEEL, ERIC. AND IT'S WHAT THEY DON'T SEEM TO UNDERSTAND.

SLAM

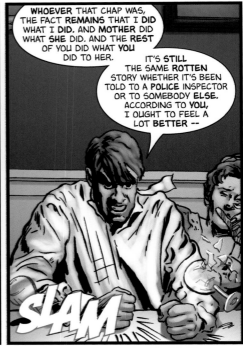

WHOEVER THAT CHAP WAS, THE FACT REMAINS THAT I DID WHAT I DID. AND MOTHER DID WHAT SHE DID. AND THE REST OF YOU DID WHAT YOU DID TO HER.

IT'S STILL THE SAME ROTTEN STORY WHETHER IT'S BEEN TOLD TO A POLICE INSPECTOR OR TO SOMEBODY ELSE. ACCORDING TO YOU, I OUGHT TO FEEL A LOT BETTER --

SLAM

I STOLE SOME MONEY, GERALD, YOU MIGHT AS WELL KNOW --

I DON'T CARE, LET HIM KNOW.

THE MONEY'S NOT THE IMPORTANT THING. IT'S WHAT HAPPENED TO THE GIRL AND WHAT WE ALL DID TO HER THAT MATTERS. AND I STILL FEEL THE SAME ABOUT IT, AND THAT'S WHY I DON'T FEEL LIKE SITTING DOWN AND HAVING A NICE COSY TALK.

AND ERIC'S ABSOLUTELY RIGHT. AND IT'S THE BEST THING ANY ONE OF US HAS SAID TONIGHT AND IT MAKES ME FEEL A BIT LESS ASHAMED OF US.

YOU'RE JUST BEGINNING TO PRETEND ALL OVER AGAIN.

122

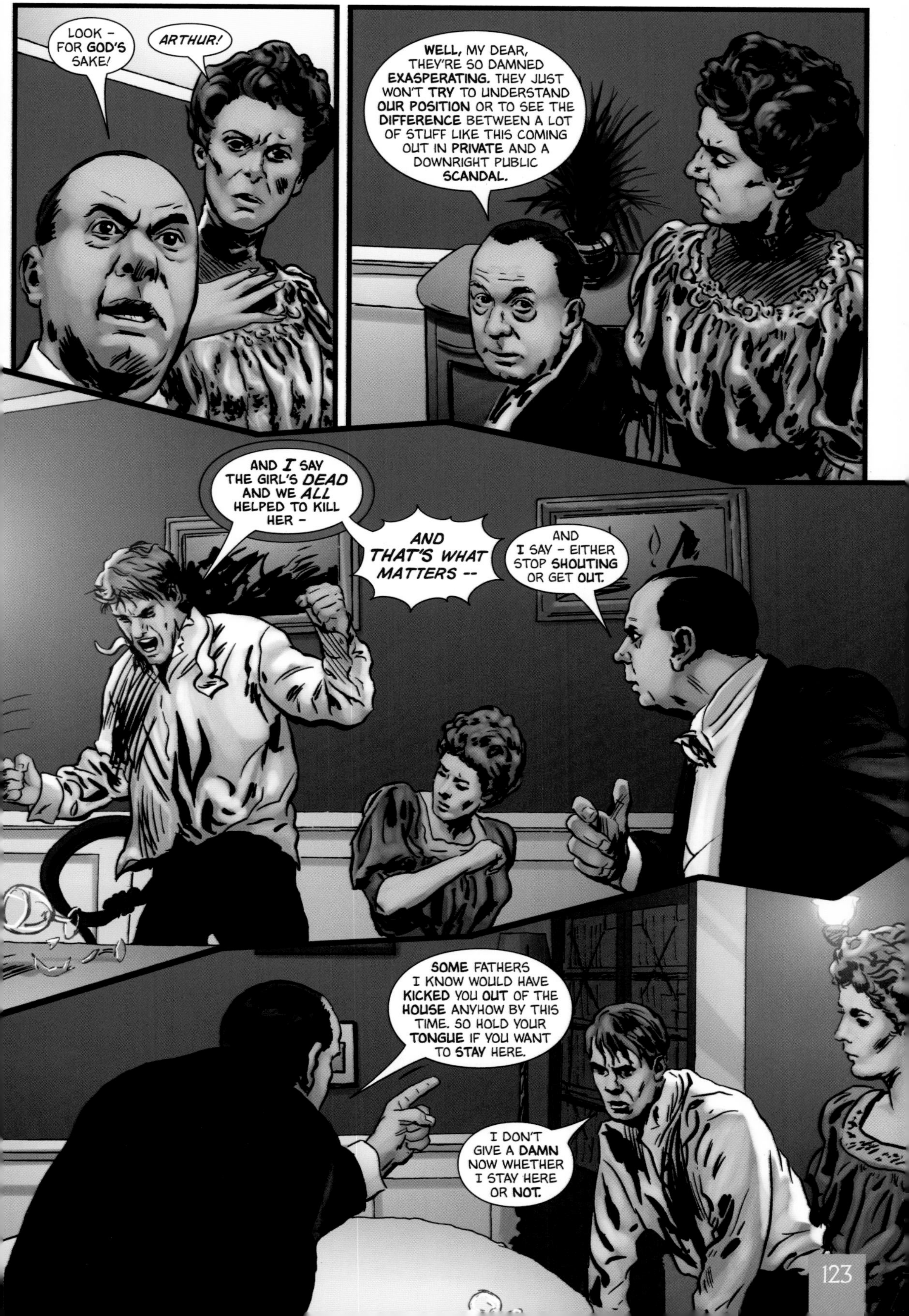
LOOK – FOR GOD'S SAKE!
ARTHUR!
WELL, MY DEAR, THEY'RE SO DAMNED EXASPERATING. THEY JUST WON'T TRY TO UNDERSTAND OUR POSITION OR TO SEE THE DIFFERENCE BETWEEN A LOT OF STUFF LIKE THIS COMING OUT IN PRIVATE AND A DOWNRIGHT PUBLIC SCANDAL.
AND I SAY THE GIRL'S DEAD AND WE ALL HELPED TO KILL HER –
AND THAT'S WHAT MATTERS --
AND I SAY – EITHER STOP SHOUTING OR GET OUT.
SOME FATHERS I KNOW WOULD HAVE KICKED YOU OUT OF THE HOUSE ANYHOW BY THIS TIME. SO HOLD YOUR TONGUE IF YOU WANT TO STAY HERE.
I DON'T GIVE A DAMN NOW WHETHER I STAY HERE OR NOT.

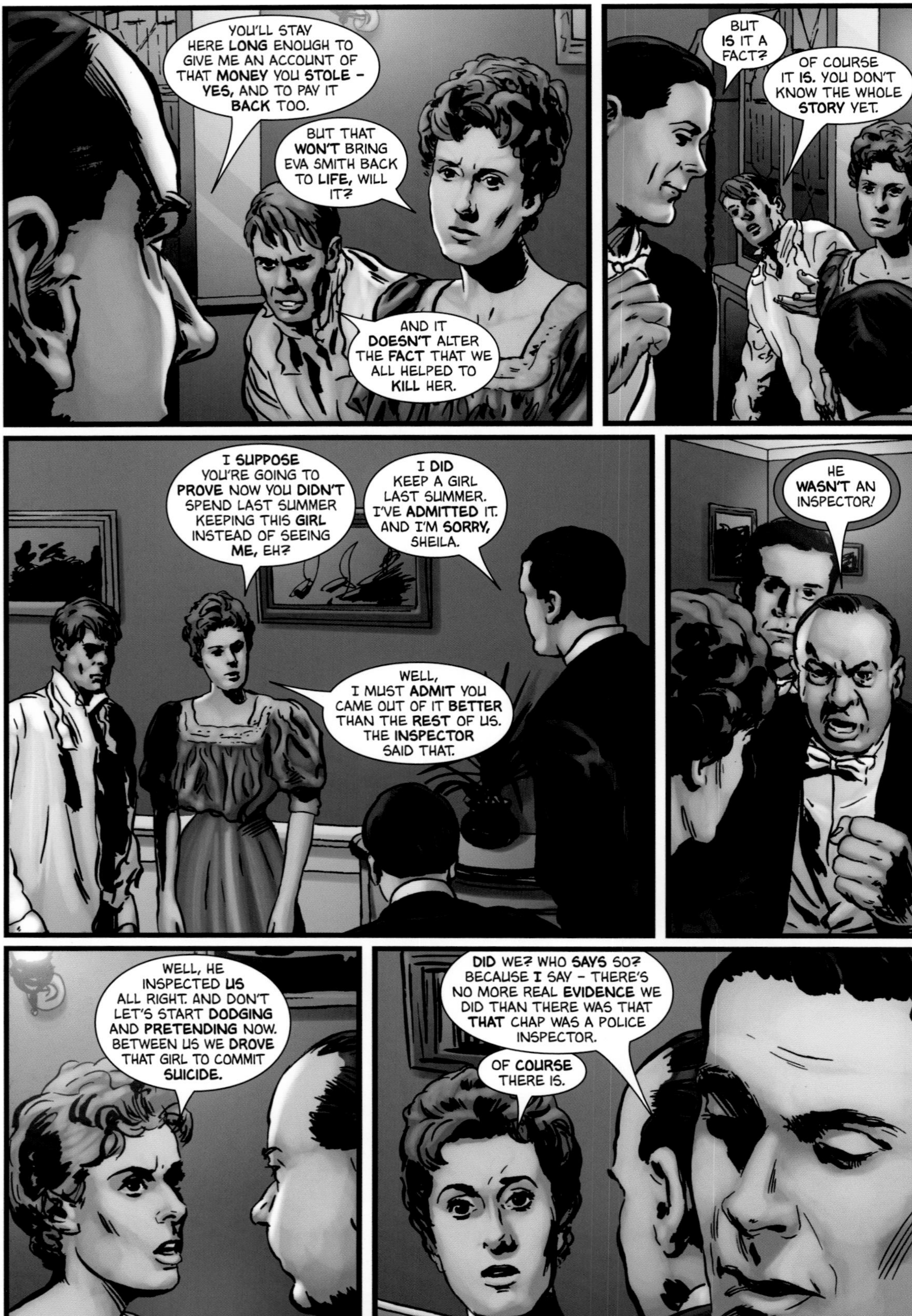
YOU'LL STAY HERE LONG ENOUGH TO GIVE ME AN ACCOUNT OF THAT MONEY YOU STOLE - YES, AND TO PAY IT BACK TOO.
BUT THAT WON'T BRING EVA SMITH BACK TO LIFE, WILL IT?
AND IT DOESN'T ALTER THE FACT THAT WE ALL HELPED TO KILL HER.
BUT IS IT A FACT?
OF COURSE IT IS. YOU DON'T KNOW THE WHOLE STORY YET.
I SUPPOSE YOU'RE GOING TO PROVE NOW YOU DIDN'T SPEND LAST SUMMER KEEPING THIS GIRL INSTEAD OF SEEING ME, EH?
I DID KEEP A GIRL LAST SUMMER. I'VE ADMITTED IT. AND I'M SORRY, SHEILA.
WELL, I MUST ADMIT YOU CAME OUT OF IT BETTER THAN THE REST OF US. THE INSPECTOR SAID THAT.
HE WASN'T AN INSPECTOR!
WELL, HE INSPECTED US ALL RIGHT. AND DON'T LET'S START DODGING AND PRETENDING NOW. BETWEEN US WE DROVE THAT GIRL TO COMMIT SUICIDE.
DID WE? WHO SAYS SO? BECAUSE I SAY - THERE'S NO MORE REAL EVIDENCE WE DID THAN THERE WAS THAT THAT CHAP WAS A POLICE INSPECTOR.
OF COURSE THERE IS.

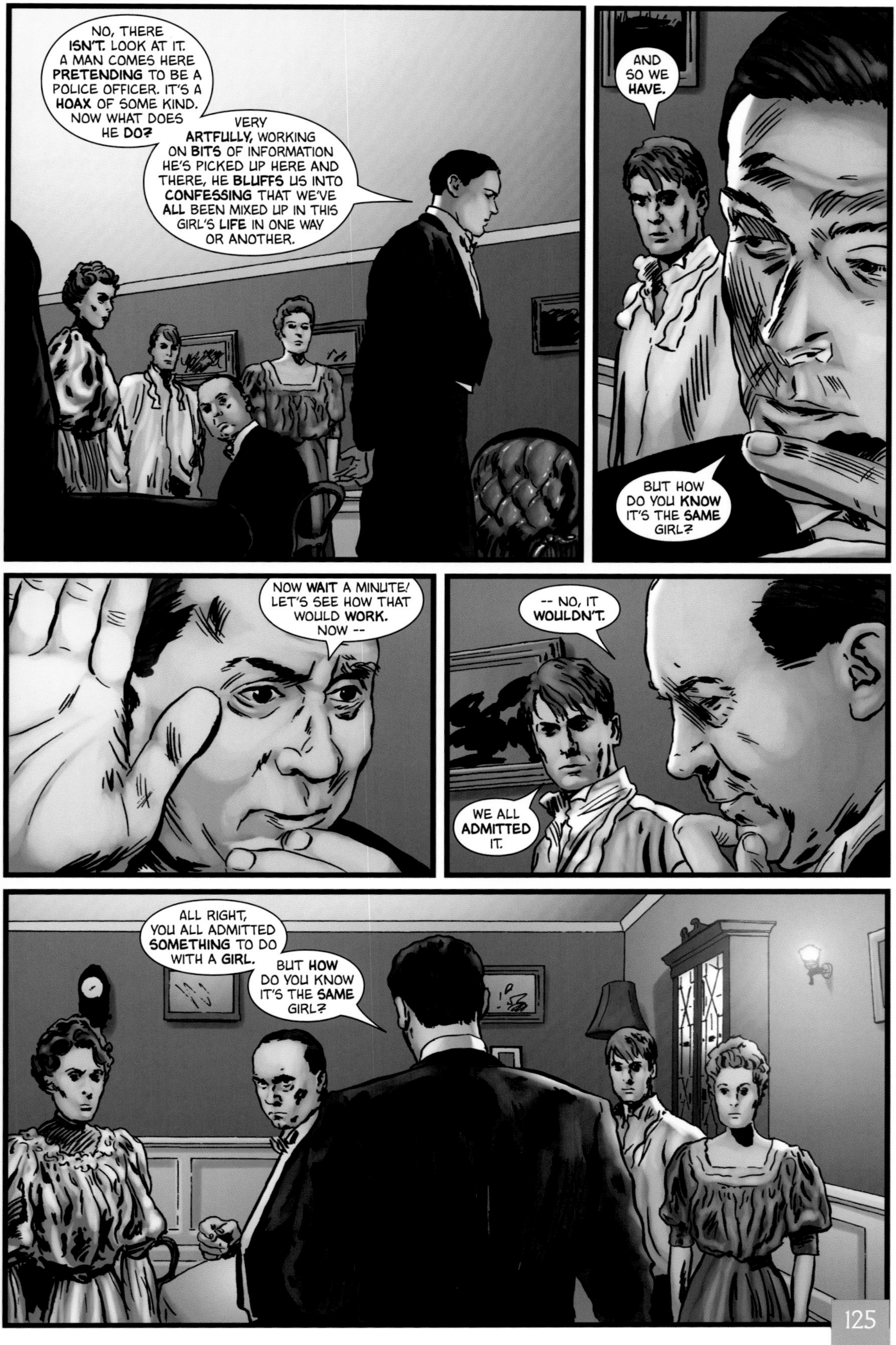
NO, THERE ISN'T. LOOK AT IT. A MAN COMES HERE PRETENDING TO BE A POLICE OFFICER. IT'S A HOAX OF SOME KIND. NOW WHAT DOES HE DO?
VERY ARTFULLY, WORKING ON BITS OF INFORMATION HE'S PICKED UP HERE AND THERE, HE BLUFFS US INTO CONFESSING THAT WE'VE ALL BEEN MIXED UP IN THIS GIRL'S LIFE IN ONE WAY OR ANOTHER.
AND SO WE HAVE.
BUT HOW DO YOU KNOW IT'S THE SAME GIRL?
NOW WAIT A MINUTE! LET'S SEE HOW THAT WOULD WORK. NOW --
-- NO, IT WOULDN'T.
WE ALL ADMITTED IT.
ALL RIGHT, YOU ALL ADMITTED SOMETHING TO DO WITH A GIRL.
BUT HOW DO YOU KNOW IT'S THE SAME GIRL?

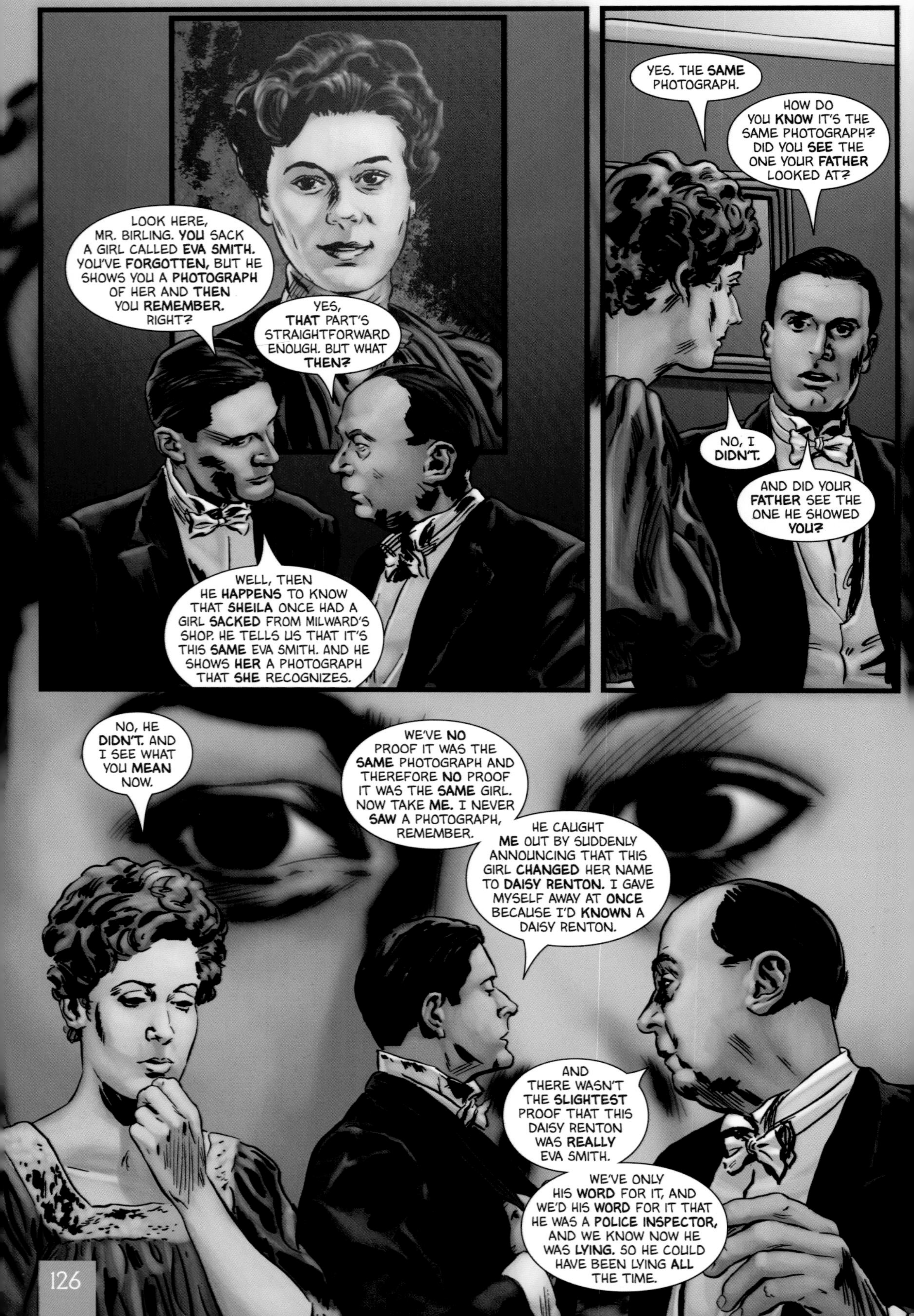

LOOK HERE, MR. BIRLING. YOU SACK A GIRL CALLED EVA SMITH. YOU'VE FORGOTTEN, BUT HE SHOWS YOU A PHOTOGRAPH OF HER AND THEN YOU REMEMBER. RIGHT?
YES, THAT PART'S STRAIGHTFORWARD ENOUGH. BUT WHAT THEN?
WELL, THEN HE HAPPENS TO KNOW THAT SHEILA ONCE HAD A GIRL SACKED FROM MILWARD'S SHOP. HE TELLS US THAT IT'S THIS SAME EVA SMITH. AND HE SHOWS HER A PHOTOGRAPH THAT SHE RECOGNIZES.
YES. THE SAME PHOTOGRAPH.
HOW DO YOU KNOW IT'S THE SAME PHOTOGRAPH? DID YOU SEE THE ONE YOUR FATHER LOOKED AT?
NO, I DIDN'T.
AND DID YOUR FATHER SEE THE ONE HE SHOWED YOU?
NO, HE DIDN'T. AND I SEE WHAT YOU MEAN NOW.
WE'VE NO PROOF IT WAS THE SAME PHOTOGRAPH AND THEREFORE NO PROOF IT WAS THE SAME GIRL. NOW TAKE ME. I NEVER SAW A PHOTOGRAPH, REMEMBER.
HE CAUGHT ME OUT BY SUDDENLY ANNOUNCING THAT THIS GIRL CHANGED HER NAME TO DAISY RENTON. I GAVE MYSELF AWAY AT ONCE BECAUSE I'D KNOWN A DAISY RENTON.
AND THERE WASN'T THE SLIGHTEST PROOF THAT THIS DAISY RENTON WAS REALLY EVA SMITH.
WE'VE ONLY HIS WORD FOR IT, AND WE'D HIS WORD FOR IT THAT HE WAS A POLICE INSPECTOR, AND WE KNOW NOW HE WAS LYING. SO HE COULD HAVE BEEN LYING ALL THE TIME.

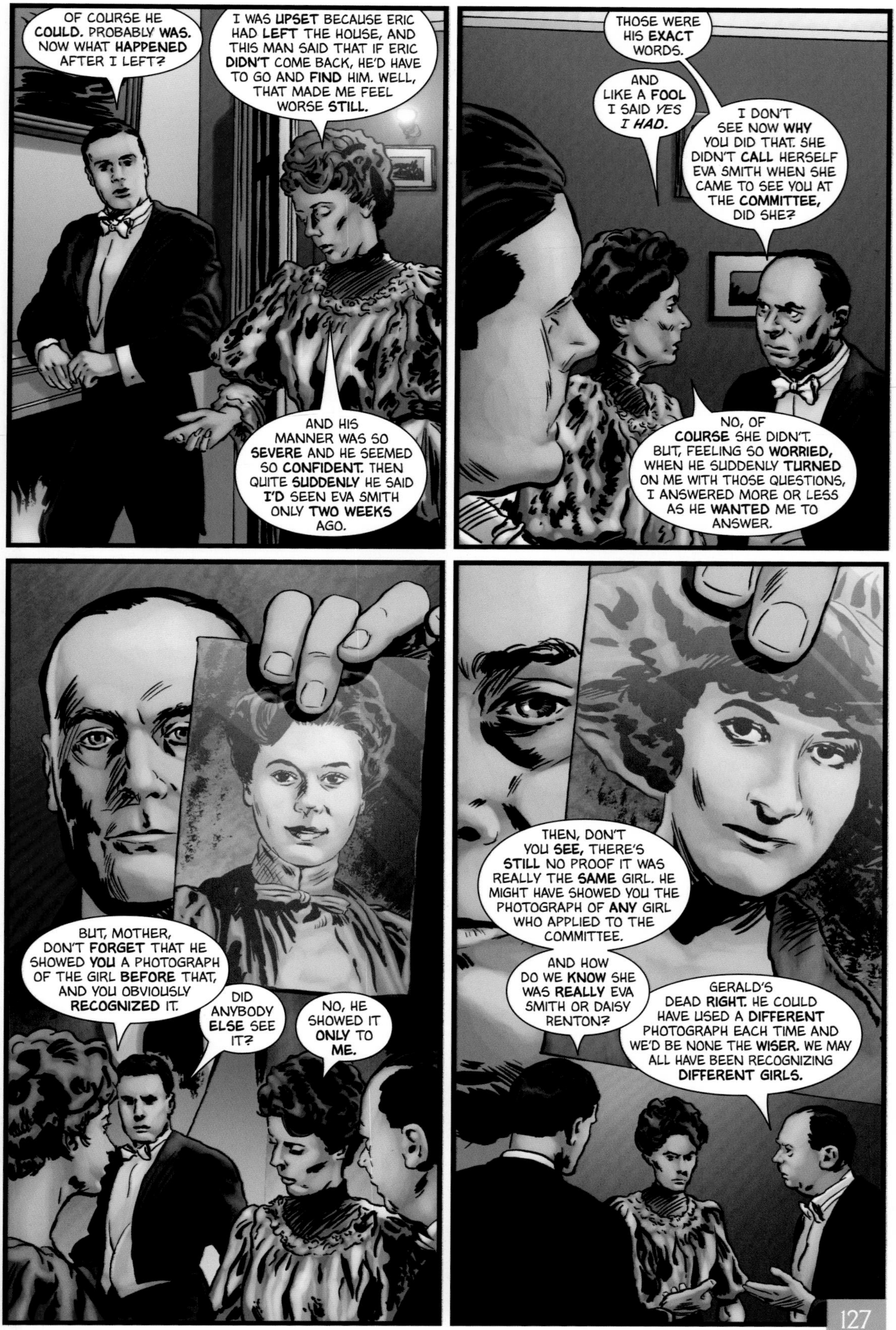
OF COURSE HE COULD. PROBABLY WAS. NOW WHAT HAPPENED AFTER I LEFT?
I WAS UPSET BECAUSE ERIC HAD LEFT THE HOUSE, AND THIS MAN SAID THAT IF ERIC DIDN'T COME BACK, HE'D HAVE TO GO AND FIND HIM. WELL, THAT MADE ME FEEL WORSE STILL.
AND HIS MANNER WAS SO SEVERE AND HE SEEMED SO CONFIDENT. THEN QUITE SUDDENLY HE SAID I'D SEEN EVA SMITH ONLY TWO WEEKS AGO.
THOSE WERE HIS EXACT WORDS.
AND LIKE A FOOL I SAID YES I HAD.
I DON'T SEE NOW WHY YOU DID THAT. SHE DIDN'T CALL HERSELF EVA SMITH WHEN SHE CAME TO SEE YOU AT THE COMMITTEE, DID SHE?
NO, OF COURSE SHE DIDN'T. BUT, FEELING SO WORRIED, WHEN HE SUDDENLY TURNED ON ME WITH THOSE QUESTIONS, I ANSWERED MORE OR LESS AS HE WANTED ME TO ANSWER.
BUT, MOTHER, DON'T FORGET THAT HE SHOWED YOU A PHOTOGRAPH OF THE GIRL BEFORE THAT, AND YOU OBVIOUSLY RECOGNIZED IT.
DID ANYBODY ELSE SEE IT?
NO, HE SHOWED IT ONLY TO ME.
THEN, DON'T YOU SEE, THERE'S STILL NO PROOF IT WAS REALLY THE SAME GIRL. HE MIGHT HAVE SHOWED YOU THE PHOTOGRAPH OF ANY GIRL WHO APPLIED TO THE COMMITTEE.
AND HOW DO WE KNOW SHE WAS REALLY EVA SMITH OR DAISY RENTON?
GERALD'S DEAD RIGHT. HE COULD HAVE USED A DIFFERENT PHOTOGRAPH EACH TIME AND WE'D BE NONE THE WISER. WE MAY ALL HAVE BEEN RECOGNIZING DIFFERENT GIRLS.

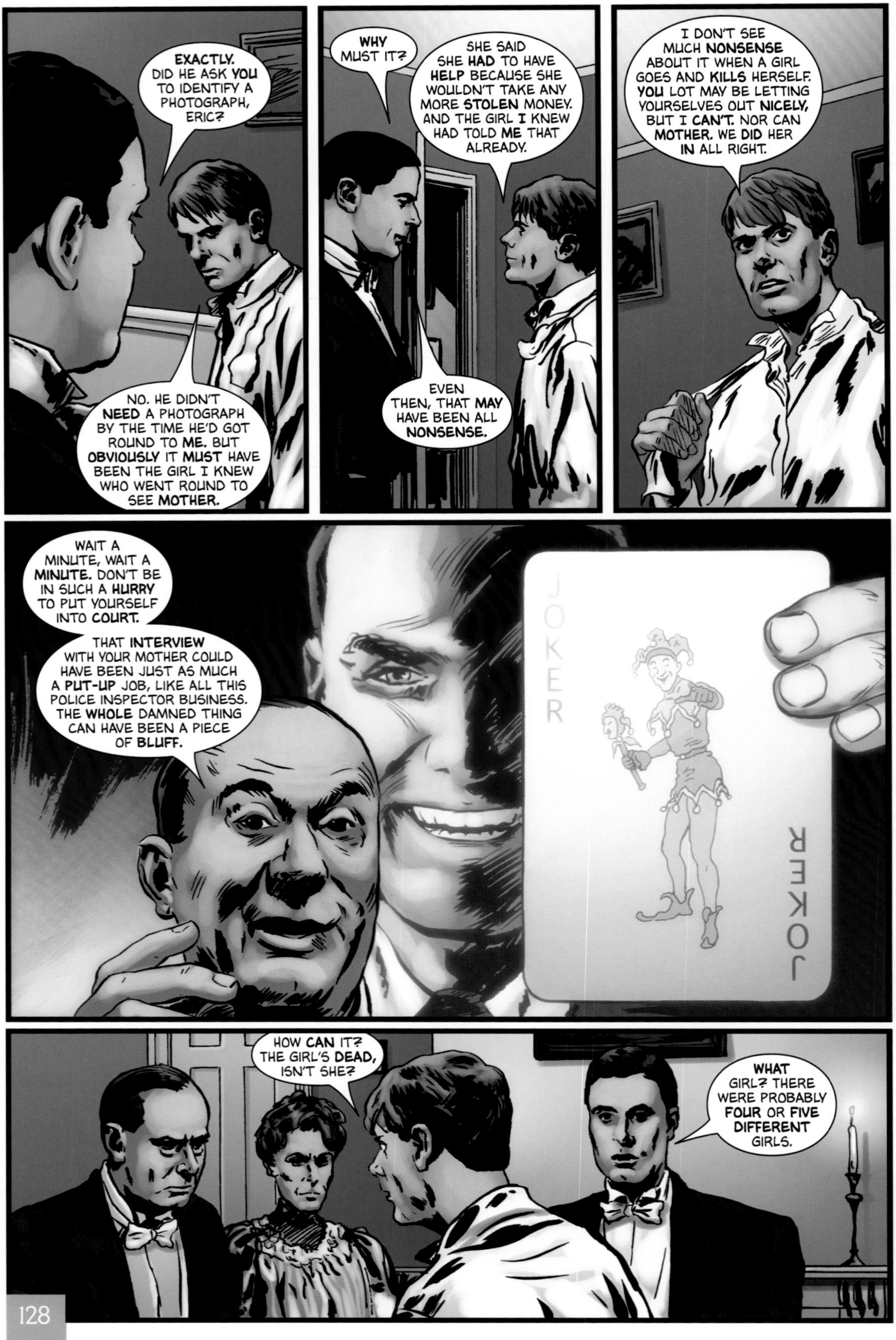
EXACTLY. DID HE ASK YOU TO IDENTIFY A PHOTOGRAPH, ERIC?
NO. HE DIDN'T NEED A PHOTOGRAPH BY THE TIME HE'D GOT ROUND TO ME. BUT OBVIOUSLY IT MUST HAVE BEEN THE GIRL I KNEW WHO WENT ROUND TO SEE MOTHER.
WHY MUST IT?
SHE SAID SHE HAD TO HAVE HELP BECAUSE SHE WOULDN'T TAKE ANY MORE STOLEN MONEY. AND THE GIRL I KNEW HAD TOLD ME THAT ALREADY.
EVEN THEN, THAT MAY HAVE BEEN ALL NONSENSE.
I DON'T SEE MUCH NONSENSE ABOUT IT WHEN A GIRL GOES AND KILLS HERSELF. YOU LOT MAY BE LETTING YOURSELVES OUT NICELY, BUT I CAN'T. NOR CAN MOTHER. WE DID HER IN ALL RIGHT.
WAIT A MINUTE, WAIT A MINUTE. DON'T BE IN SUCH A HURRY TO PUT YOURSELF INTO COURT.
THAT INTERVIEW WITH YOUR MOTHER COULD HAVE BEEN JUST AS MUCH A PUT-UP JOB, LIKE ALL THIS POLICE INSPECTOR BUSINESS. THE WHOLE DAMNED THING CAN HAVE BEEN A PIECE OF BLUFF.
JOKER
JOKER
HOW CAN IT? THE GIRL'S DEAD, ISN'T SHE?
WHAT GIRL? THERE WERE PROBABLY FOUR OR FIVE DIFFERENT GIRLS.

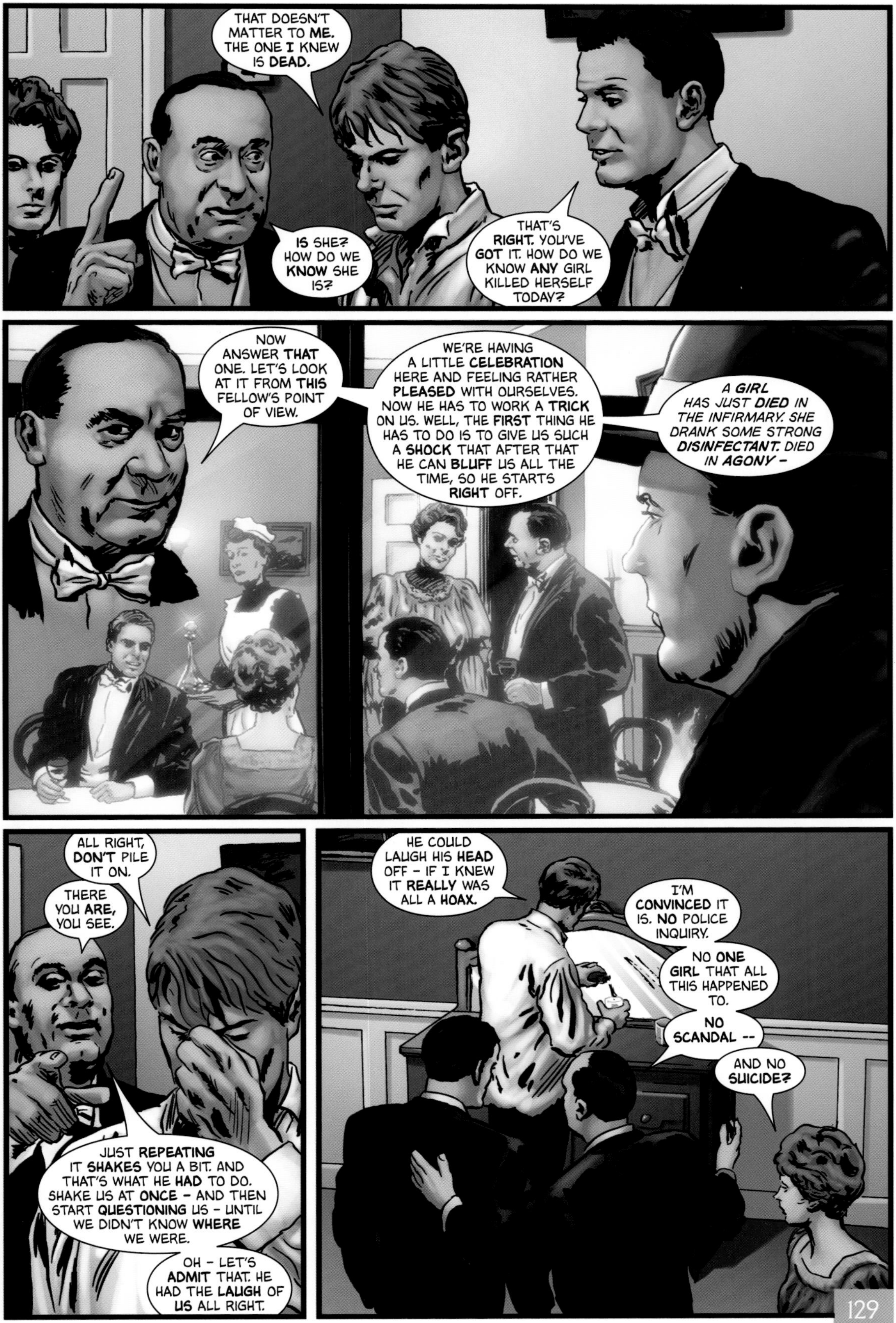
THAT DOESN'T MATTER TO ME. THE ONE I KNEW IS DEAD.
IS SHE? HOW DO WE KNOW SHE IS?
THAT'S RIGHT. YOU'VE GOT IT. HOW DO WE KNOW ANY GIRL KILLED HERSELF TODAY?
NOW ANSWER THAT ONE. LET'S LOOK AT IT FROM THIS FELLOW'S POINT OF VIEW.
WE'RE HAVING A LITTLE CELEBRATION HERE AND FEELING RATHER PLEASED WITH OURSELVES. NOW HE HAS TO WORK A TRICK ON US. WELL, THE FIRST THING HE HAS TO DO IS TO GIVE US SUCH A SHOCK THAT AFTER THAT HE CAN BLUFF US ALL THE TIME, SO HE STARTS RIGHT OFF.
A GIRL HAS JUST DIED IN THE INFIRMARY. SHE DRANK SOME STRONG DISINFECTANT. DIED IN AGONY –
ALL RIGHT, DON'T PILE IT ON.
THERE YOU ARE, YOU SEE.
JUST REPEATING IT SHAKES YOU A BIT. AND THAT'S WHAT HE HAD TO DO. SHAKE US AT ONCE – AND THEN START QUESTIONING US – UNTIL WE DIDN'T KNOW WHERE WE WERE.
OH – LET'S ADMIT THAT. HE HAD THE LAUGH OF US ALL RIGHT.
HE COULD LAUGH HIS HEAD OFF – IF I KNEW IT REALLY WAS ALL A HOAX.
I'M CONVINCED IT IS. NO POLICE INQUIRY.
NO ONE GIRL THAT ALL THIS HAPPENED TO.
NO SCANDAL --
AND NO SUICIDE?

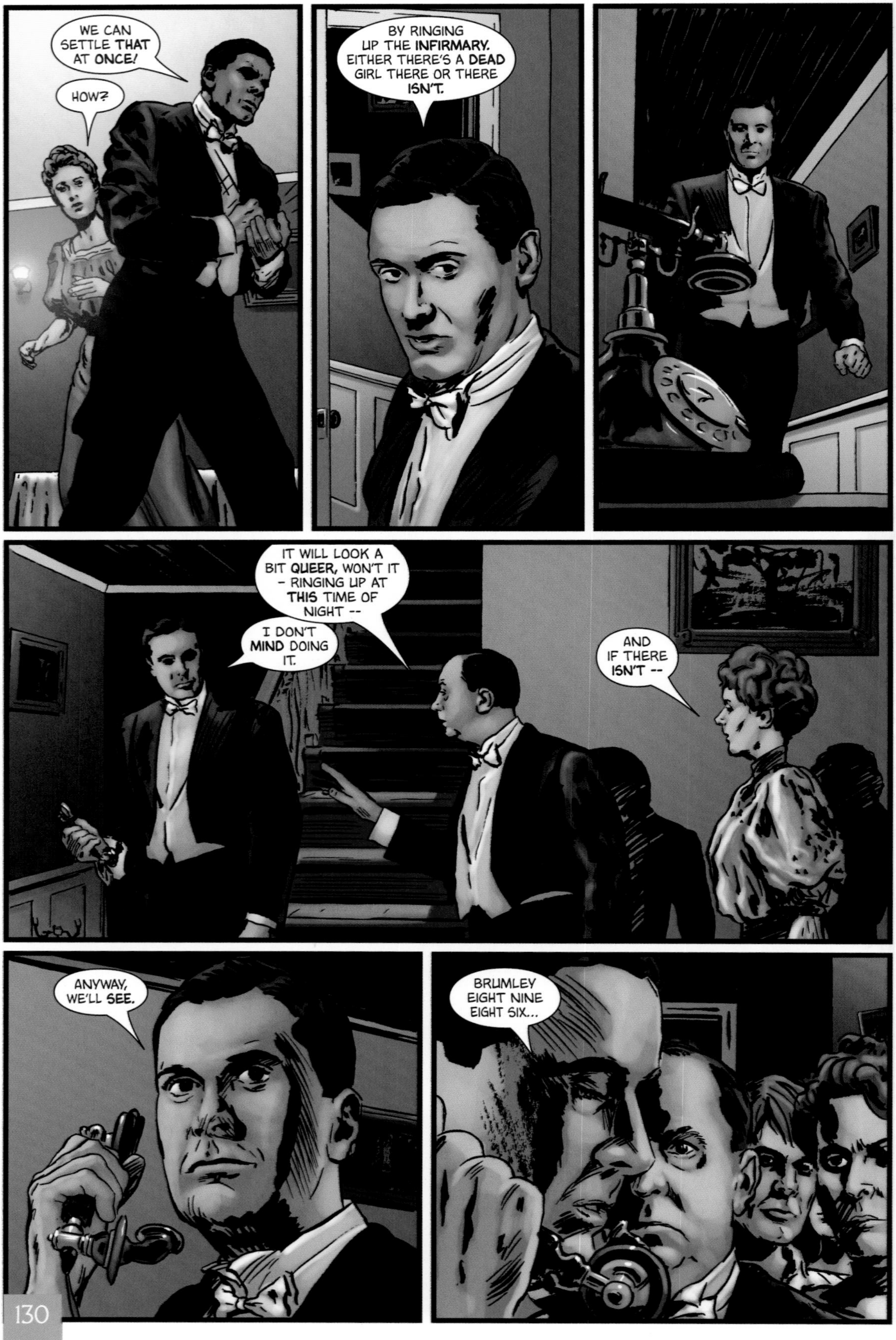
WE CAN SETTLE THAT AT ONCE!
HOW?
BY RINGING UP THE INFIRMARY. EITHER THERE'S A DEAD GIRL THERE OR THERE ISN'T.
IT WILL LOOK A BIT QUEER, WON'T IT - RINGING UP AT THIS TIME OF NIGHT --
I DON'T MIND DOING IT.
AND IF THERE ISN'T --
ANYWAY, WE'LL SEE.
BRUMLEY EIGHT NINE EIGHT SIX...

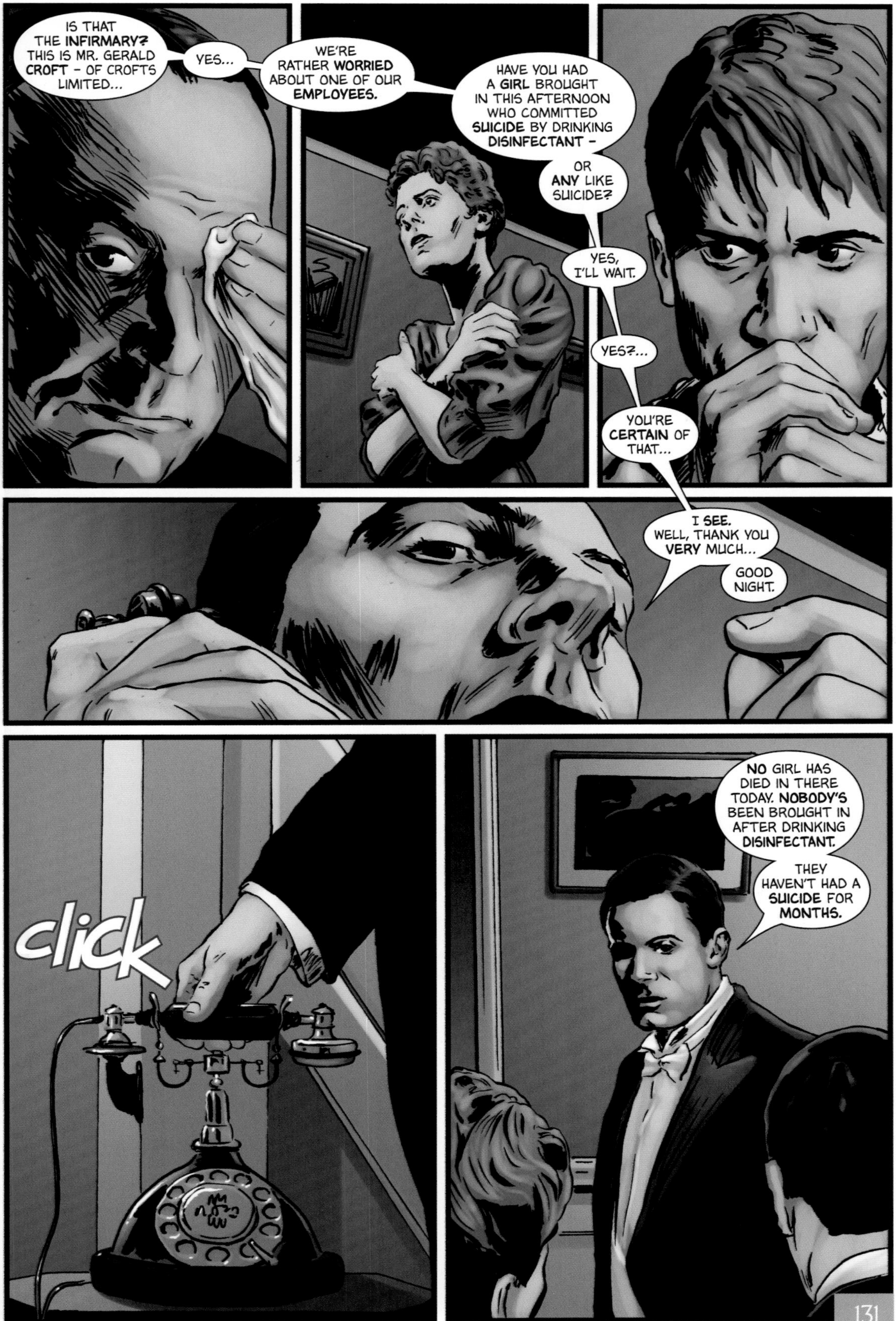
IS THAT THE INFIRMARY? THIS IS MR. GERALD CROFT – OF CROFTS LIMITED...
YES...
WE'RE RATHER WORRIED ABOUT ONE OF OUR EMPLOYEES.
HAVE YOU HAD A GIRL BROUGHT IN THIS AFTERNOON WHO COMMITTED SUICIDE BY DRINKING DISINFECTANT –
OR ANY LIKE SUICIDE?
YES, I'LL WAIT.
YES?...
YOU'RE CERTAIN OF THAT...
I SEE. WELL, THANK YOU VERY MUCH...
GOOD NIGHT.
click
NO GIRL HAS DIED IN THERE TODAY. NOBODY'S BEEN BROUGHT IN AFTER DRINKING DISINFECTANT.
THEY HAVEN'T HAD A SUICIDE FOR MONTHS.

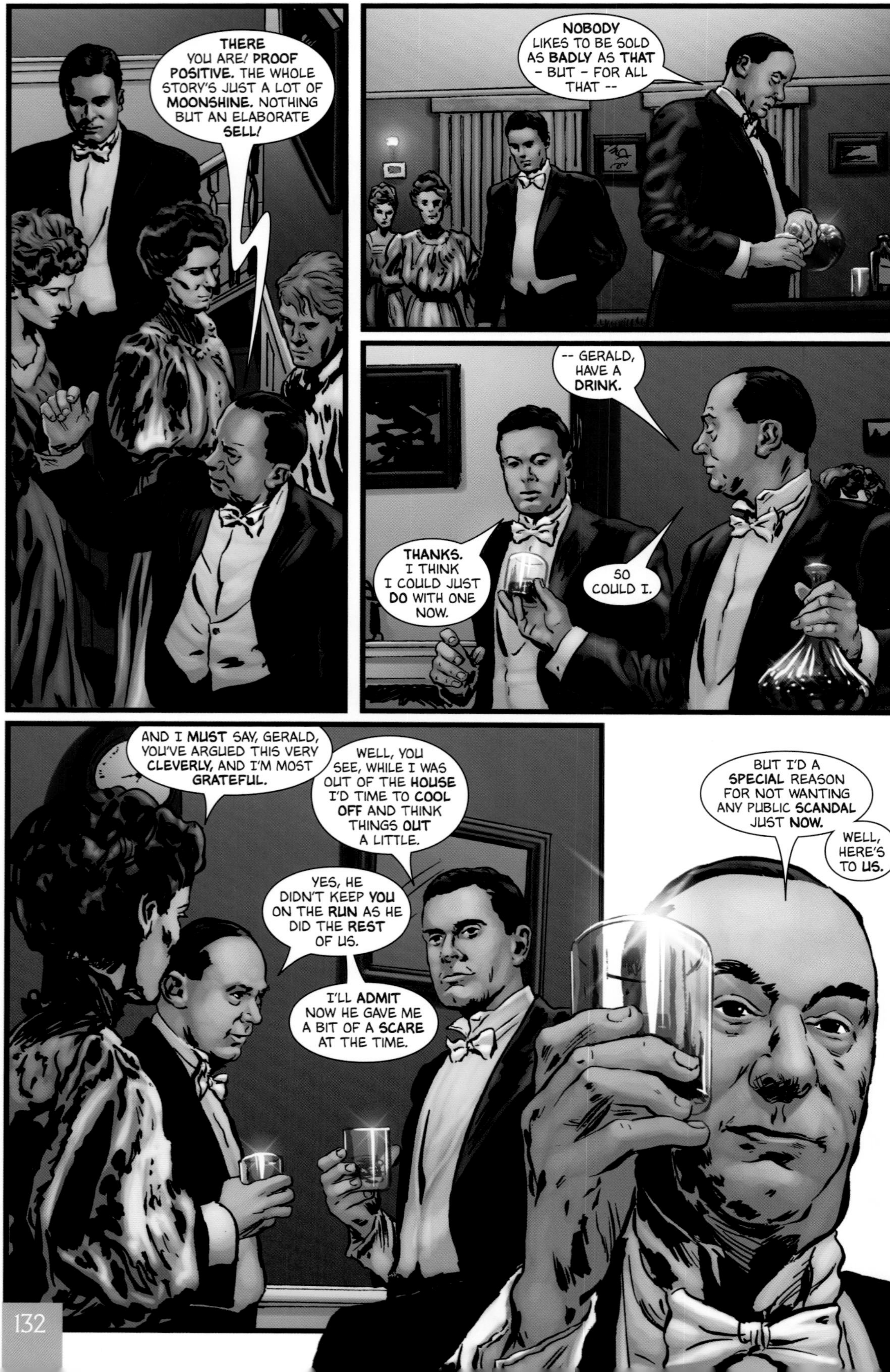
THERE YOU ARE! PROOF POSITIVE. THE WHOLE STORY'S JUST A LOT OF MOONSHINE. NOTHING BUT AN ELABORATE SELL!
NOBODY LIKES TO BE SOLD AS BADLY AS THAT - BUT - FOR ALL THAT --
-- GERALD, HAVE A DRINK.
THANKS. I THINK I COULD JUST DO WITH ONE NOW.
SO COULD I.
AND I MUST SAY, GERALD, YOU'VE ARGUED THIS VERY CLEVERLY, AND I'M MOST GRATEFUL.
WELL, YOU SEE, WHILE I WAS OUT OF THE HOUSE I'D TIME TO COOL OFF AND THINK THINGS OUT A LITTLE.
YES, HE DIDN'T KEEP YOU ON THE RUN AS HE DID THE REST OF US.
I'LL ADMIT NOW HE GAVE ME A BIT OF A SCARE AT THE TIME.
BUT I'D A SPECIAL REASON FOR NOT WANTING ANY PUBLIC SCANDAL JUST NOW.
WELL, HERE'S TO US.

COME ON, SHEILA, DON'T LOOK LIKE THAT. ALL OVER NOW.

THE WORSE PART IS. BUT YOU'RE FORGETTING ONE THING I STILL CAN'T FORGET. EVERYTHING WE SAID HAD HAPPENED REALLY HAD HAPPENED.

IF IT DIDN'T END TRAGICALLY, THEN THAT'S LUCKY FOR US. BUT IT MIGHT HAVE DONE.

BUT THE WHOLE THING'S DIFFERENT NOW. COME, COME, YOU CAN SEE THAT, CAN'T YOU?

YOU ALL HELPED TO KILL HER!

HA HA HA!

AND I WISH YOU COULD HAVE SEEN THE LOOK ON YOUR FACES WHEN HE SAID THAT!

GOING TO BED, YOUNG WOMAN?

I WANT TO GET OUT OF THIS. IT FRIGHTENS ME THE WAY YOU TALK.

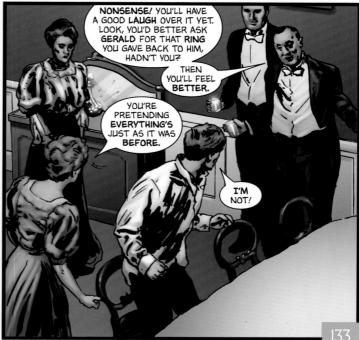

NONSENSE! YOU'LL HAVE A GOOD LAUGH OVER IT YET. LOOK, YOU'D BETTER ASK GERALD FOR THAT RING YOU GAVE BACK TO HIM, HADN'T YOU?

THEN YOU'LL FEEL BETTER.

YOU'RE PRETENDING EVERYTHING'S JUST AS IT WAS BEFORE.

I'M NOT!

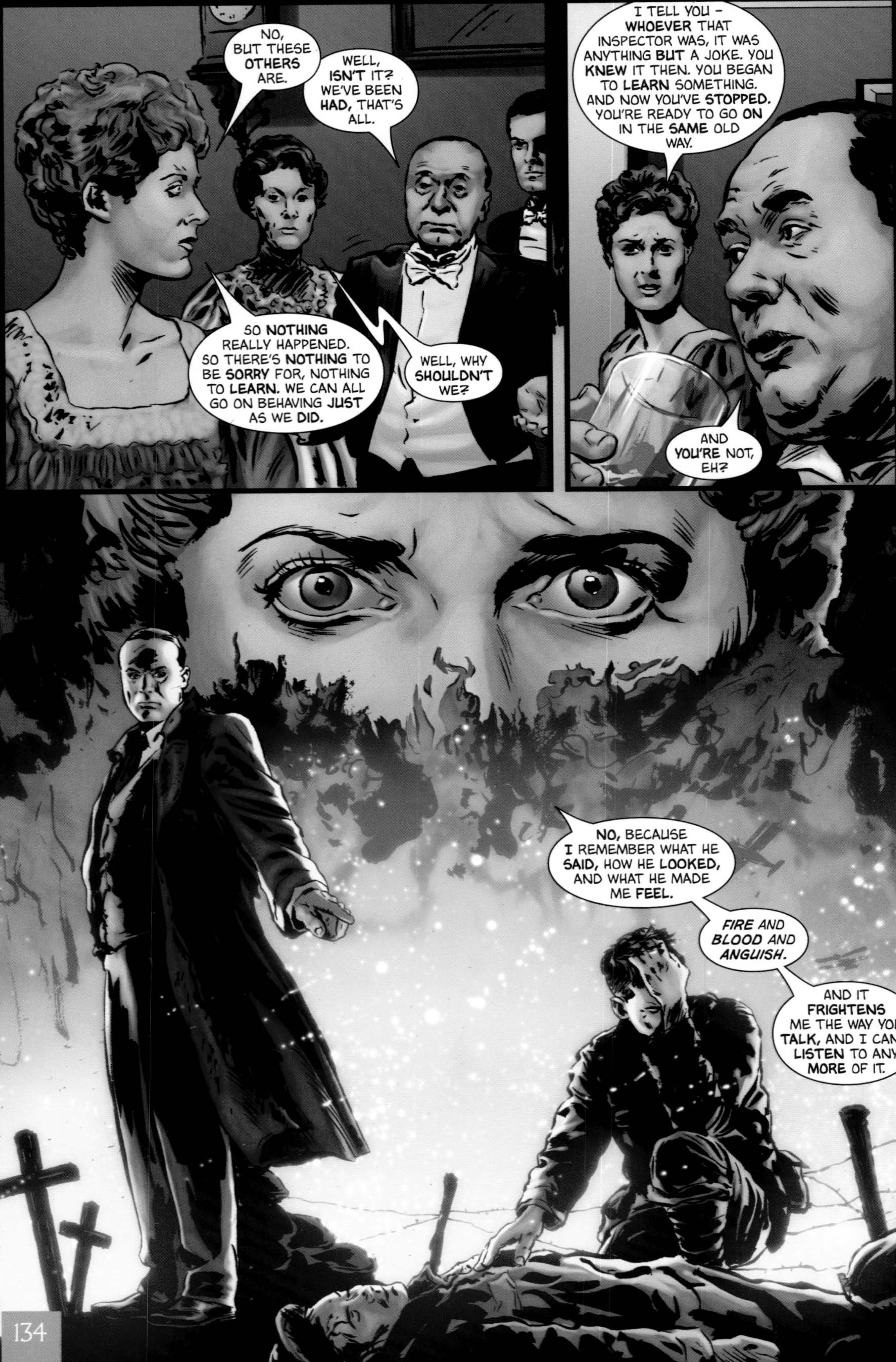
NO, BUT THESE **OTHERS** ARE.
WELL, **ISN'T** IT? WE'VE BEEN **HAD,** THAT'S ALL.
SO **NOTHING** REALLY HAPPENED. SO THERE'S **NOTHING** TO BE **SORRY** FOR, NOTHING TO **LEARN.** WE CAN ALL GO ON BEHAVING **JUST** AS WE **DID.**
WELL, WHY **SHOULDN'T** WE?
I TELL YOU – **WHOEVER** THAT INSPECTOR WAS, IT WAS ANYTHING **BUT** A JOKE. YOU **KNEW** IT THEN. YOU BEGAN TO **LEARN** SOMETHING. AND NOW YOU'VE **STOPPED.** YOU'RE READY TO GO **ON** IN THE **SAME** OLD WAY.
AND **YOU'RE** NOT, EH?
NO, BECAUSE **I** REMEMBER WHAT HE **SAID,** HOW HE **LOOKED,** AND WHAT HE MADE ME **FEEL.**
FIRE *AND* ***BLOOD*** *AND* ***ANGUISH.***
AND IT **FRIGHTENS** ME THE WAY YOU **TALK,** AND I CAN'T **LISTEN** TO ANY **MORE** OF IT.

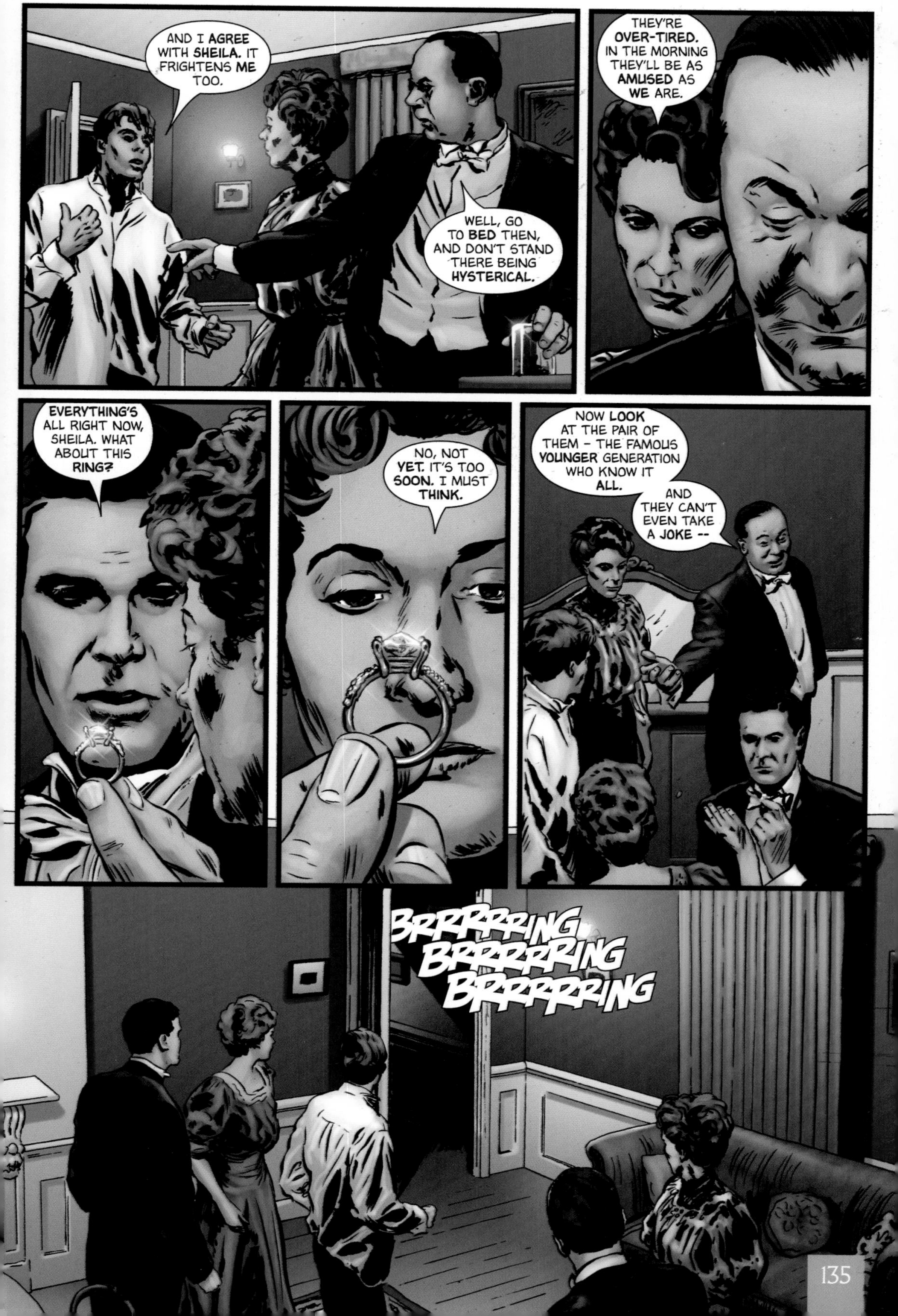
AND I AGREE WITH SHEILA. IT FRIGHTENS ME TOO.
WELL, GO TO BED THEN, AND DON'T STAND THERE BEING HYSTERICAL.
THEY'RE OVER-TIRED. IN THE MORNING THEY'LL BE AS AMUSED AS WE ARE.
EVERYTHING'S ALL RIGHT NOW, SHEILA. WHAT ABOUT THIS RING?
NO, NOT YET. IT'S TOO SOON. I MUST THINK.
NOW LOOK AT THE PAIR OF THEM - THE FAMOUS YOUNGER GENERATION WHO KNOW IT ALL.
AND THEY CAN'T EVEN TAKE A JOKE --
BRRRRRING
BRRRRRING
BRRRRRING

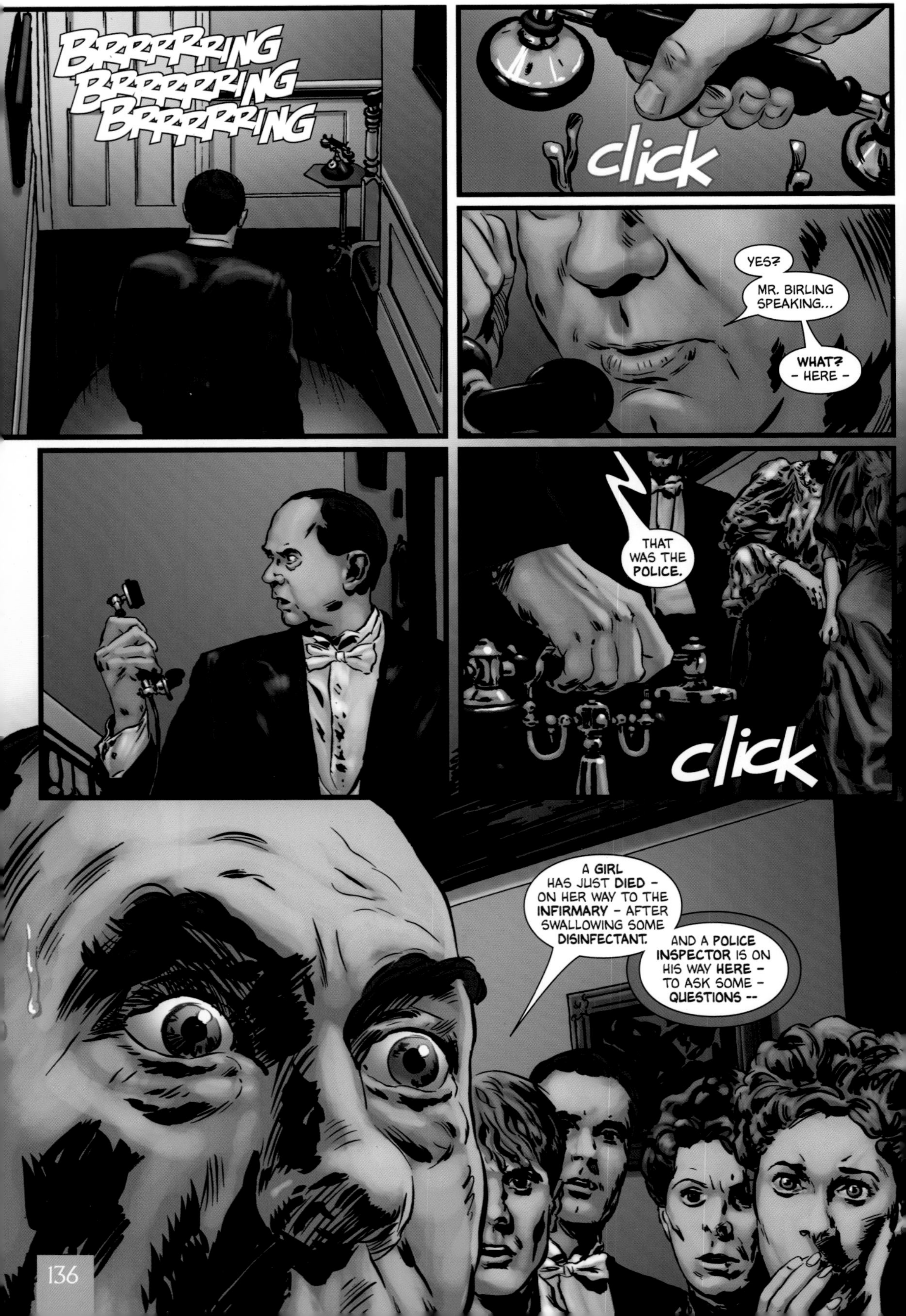
BRRRRRRING
BRRRRRRING
BRRRRRRING
click
YES?
MR. BIRLING SPEAKING...
WHAT? - HERE -
THAT WAS THE POLICE.
click
A GIRL HAS JUST DIED - ON HER WAY TO THE INFIRMARY - AFTER SWALLOWING SOME DISINFECTANT.
AND A POLICE INSPECTOR IS ON HIS WAY HERE - TO ASK SOME - QUESTIONS --

An Inspector Calls

◆◇◆

The End

J. B. Priestley

(1894–1984)

John Priestley (he gave himself the middle name of "Boynton" later in life) was born on September 13, 1894 in Bradford, in the north of England. His father, Jonathan Priestley, was a schoolmaster, and his mother, Emma, had worked in a mill. Sadly, Emma died just a few months after giving birth to John, who, after his father remarried four years later, was raised by his kindly stepmother Amy.

Priestley attended Belle Vue School in Bradford and soon set his sights on writing. Although a gifted academic, he decided against going on to college, taking instead a modest office job at a local wool firm. He believed that, for a writer, life experience was more important than academic qualifications, and this office job gave him the time and freedom to pursue his literary ambitions. Far from turning his back on learning, however, he surrounded himself with books and used them to continue his education. It was also around this time that, through his father and his father's friends, Priestley became interested in socialism, a philosophy that ingrained themes and beliefs that appear throughout his works, most notably in *An Inspector Calls.*

When World War I broke out in 1914, Priestley volunteered to join the infantry. He trained for a year in the south of England before being sent to the front line in 1915. Wounded in a mortar attack in 1916, he was sent back to England for treatment and returned to the trenches six months later, only to become a victim of a gas attack. He was left unfit for active duty and transferred to the Entertainers Section of the British Army, where he served until the end of the war.

Priestley held the rank of officer when he left the army in 1919. He received a small grant to attend Cambridge University, where he studied Modern History and Political Science. Although he graduated with a degree, he was never comfortable with the life of an academic and decided to change direction.

In 1921, Priestley married Emily "Pat" Tempest, a librarian from Bradford, and together they began a new life in London. There they had two daughters, Barbara (1923) and Sylvia (1924), while Priestley established himself as a freelance non-fiction writer, completing numerous books and essays around this time. Tragically, Emily died of cancer in 1925, leaving Priestley to raise his daughters. He remarried a year later to Jane Wyndham Lewis, with whom he had two further daughters and a son.

Priestley collaborated with Hugh Walpole on his historical novel ***Farthing Hall*** in 1929, and its popularity gave him sufficient financial freedom and confidence to attempt his first solo novel. The result was ***The Good Companions*** which won the James Tait Black Memorial Prize for fiction. It was quickly followed by ***Angel Pavement*** in 1930, firmly establishing Priestley as a force within the literary world.

Priestley then turned his hand to writing plays. He collaborated on a stage adaptation of ***The Good Companions,*** and followed that with his first solo-authored play, ***Dangerous Corner,*** which opened in 1932 and was a great success. Rather than capitalize on this breakthrough, Priestley was soon traveling the country so that he could see first-hand the troubles experienced by industrial Britain during the recession. The result was a non-fiction publication, ***English Journey,*** which not only established Priestley as a social commentator, but also gave him themes that paved the way for his later works, including ***An Inspector Calls.***

Shortly after the start of World War II, Priestley had another career change, becoming a broadcaster for the BBC. Attracting over 16 million listeners, Priestley felt that his broadcasts should try to boost moral during those difficult times by talking about how life would be after the war and by promoting traditional values. Despite his popularity (Priestley's shows had the highest listening figures of any radio program aside from Churchill's speeches), the BBC cancelled his series of "Postscripts" after just a few months because the Ministry of Information believed he was too critical of the government.

Although he was a prolific writer across multiple disciplines, crafting plays, novels, essays, and several volumes of autobiography, Priestley tends to be remembered most for his intense dramas. Through his scripts he was able to couple his political beliefs with his deep interest in time theories, exploring how premonitions enable us to experience events before they occur. The finest example of this combination of themes is his 1945 masterpiece, ***An Inspector Calls.*** Interestingly, the play was first performed in Moscow, reaching London a year later in October 1946, where it enjoyed a long, successful run.

Priestley continued to balance his writing with his political and social responsibilities. He ran as an independent candidate in the 1945 general election but was not elected as a Member of Parliament, and from 1946-7 he was the British delegate at UNESCO conferences (United Nations Educational, Scientific and Cultural Organization). It was through UNESCO that he met the archaeologist and writer Jacquette Hawkes, whom Priestley married following his divorce from Jane in 1953. Later, spurred on by the nuclear testing of a hydrogen bomb in the Christmas Islands in 1957 (which he argued against in his essay "Britain and the Nuclear Bomb"), he became a founding member of the Campaign for Nuclear Disarmament (CND).

He wrote well into his seventies and remained generally active. The University of Bradford awarded him an honorary doctorate in 1970, and he was granted the freedom of the City of Bradford in 1973. In 1975 he opened the J.B. Priestley Library within the University of Bradford. Because of his strong socialist beliefs, he rejected offers of a knighthood, but in 1977 he accepted the Queen's Order of Merit because the honor had no political connections.

J.B. Priestley died on August 14, 1984, just 30 days before his 90th birthday, at his home in Stratford-upon-Avon, England. Fittingly, the City of Bradford erected a statue in his honor, which stands outside the National Media Museum in the center of what has become the UNESCO City of Film.

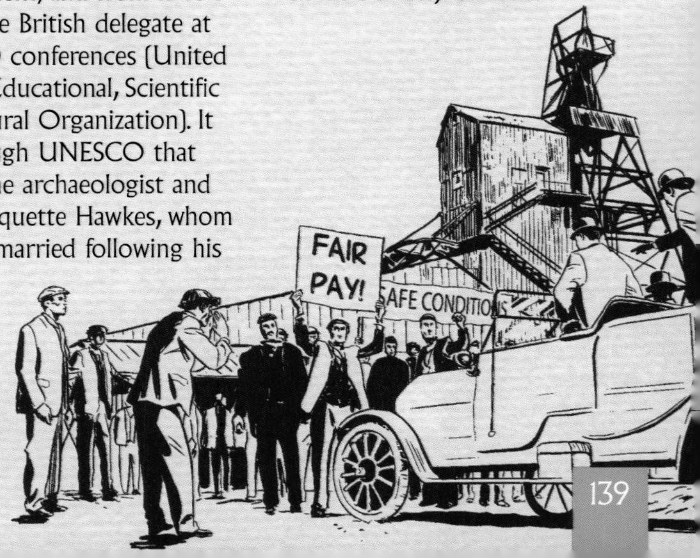
FAIR PAY!
SAFE CONDITIO

Page Creation

1. Script

The process starts with the writing of the script. The script describes the artwork for the artist to draw and also details the dialogue, captions and sound effects that will be added by the letterer. There are two editions of *An Inspector Calls*: Original Text and Quick Text. Both use the same artwork but feature different dialogue.

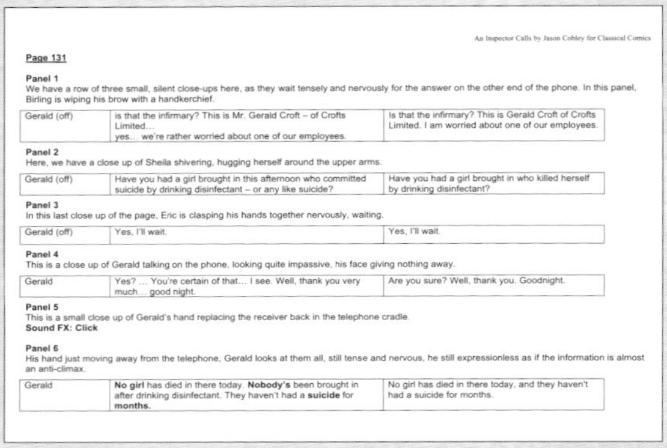

An Inspector Calls by Jason Cobley for Classical Comics

Page 131

Panel 1
We have a row of three small, silent close-ups here, as they wait tensely and nervously for the answer on the other end of the phone. In this panel, Birling is wiping his brow with a handkerchief.

Gerald (off)	is that the infirmary? This is Mr. Gerald Croft – of Crofts Limited… yes… we're rather worried about one of our employees.	Is that the infirmary? This is Gerald Croft of Crofts Limited. I am worried about one of our employees.

Panel 2
Here, we have a close up of Sheila shivering, hugging herself around the upper arms.

Gerald (off)	Have you had a girl brought in this afternoon who committed suicide by drinking disinfectant – or any like suicide?	Have you had a girl brought in who killed herself by drinking disinfectant?

Panel 3
In this last close up of the page, Eric is clasping his hands together nervously, waiting.

Gerald (off)	Yes, I'll wait.	Yes, I'll wait.

Panel 4
This is a close up of Gerald talking on the phone, looking quite impassive, his face giving nothing away.

Gerald	Yes? … You're certain of that… I see. Well, thank you very much… good night.	Are you sure? Well, thank you. Goodnight.

Panel 5
This is a small close up of Gerald's hand replacing the receiver back in the telephone cradle.
Sound FX: Click

Panel 6
His hand just moving away from the telephone, Gerald looks at them all, still tense and nervous, he still expressionless as if the information is almost an anti-climax.

Gerald	**No girl** has died in there today. **Nobody's** been brought in after drinking disinfectant. They haven't had a **suicide** for **months.**	No girl has died in there today, and they haven't had a suicide for months.

A page from the script of *An Inspector Calls* showing the two versions of the text.

2. Character Designs

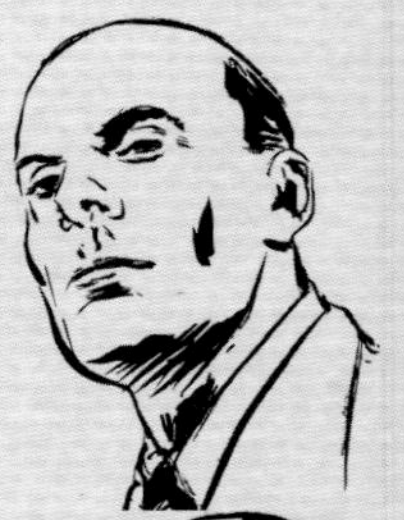

While the scriptwriter is working on the panel descriptions, the artist can start work on designs for each character. He is striving to find a "look" for each individual that reflects his or her age and personality while making each person distinct to help the reader tell one from another.

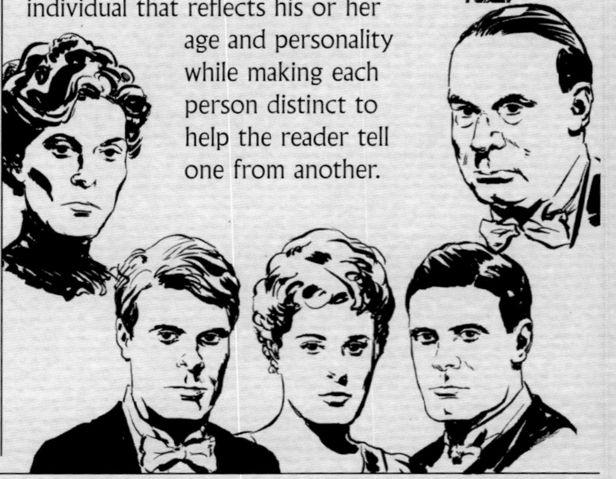

3. Pencils

When creating the artwork for each page, the artist first creates a rough layout to check overall proportions, after which he creates a pencil drawing. He is considering many things during this process, including the pacing of the story, body language, character sizes, perspective, lettering space, texture and lighting. The page below is a superb example of Will capturing mood and tension while also putting over a sense of the passing of time.

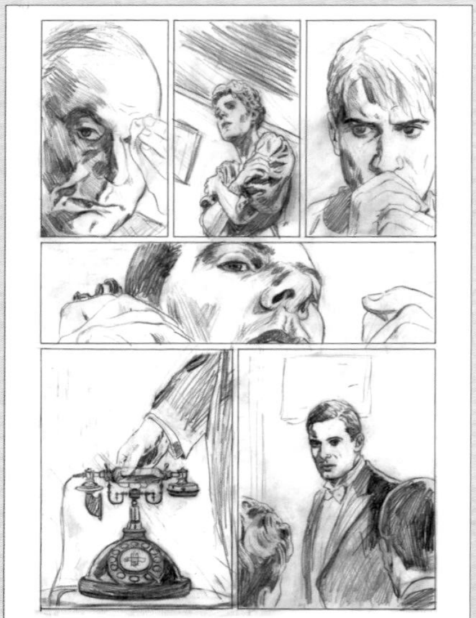

The pencil drawing of page 131

4. Inks

When completed, the pencil sketch is then inked. Inking is not simply tracing over the pencil sketch; it is the process of using black ink to fill in the shaded areas and to add clarity and cohesion to the penciled artwork. Inking also adds texture and drama through shading and lighting, aiming all the time to retain the energy of the expressive pencils.

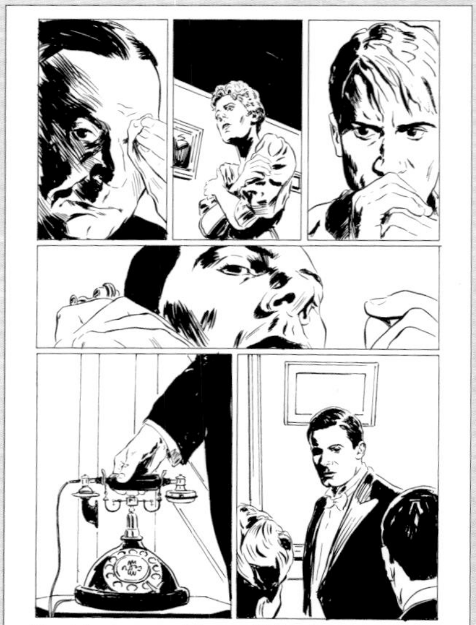

The inked page with pencil drawing removed.

5. Coloring

Adding color really brings the page to life.

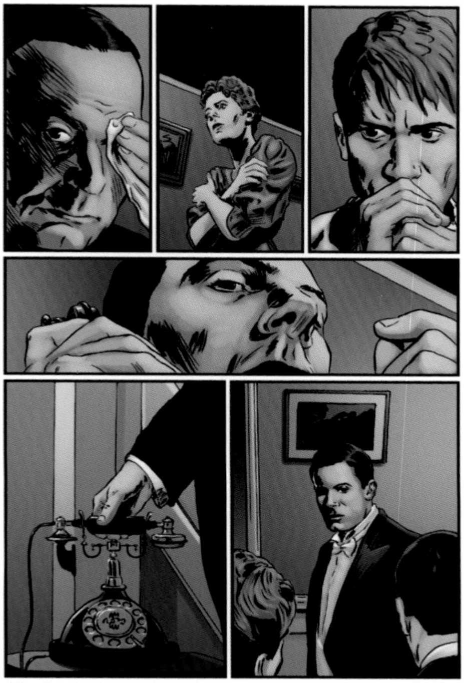

The finished artwork before lettering.

There is far more to the coloring stage than just replacing the white areas with color. Some of the linework itself might be replaced with color, also, the light sources are considered for shadows and highlights, and effects are added. Finally, the whole page is color-balanced to match the other pages in the book.

6. Lettering

The final stage is to add the captions, sound effects, and speech bubbles from the script, which are laid on top of each colored page. Two versions of each page are lettered, one for each of the two editions of the book (Original Text and Quick Text).

The lettered pages are then compiled into the finished books, ready for printing.

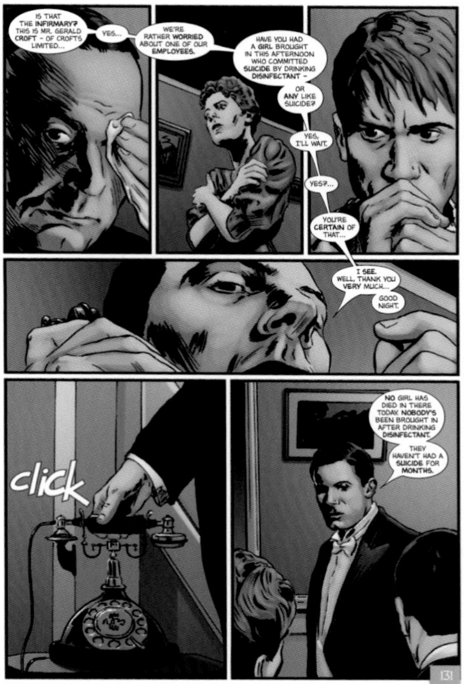
IS THAT THE **INFIRMARY?** THIS IS MR. GERALD **CROFT** - OF CROFTS LIMITED...
YES...
WE'RE RATHER **WORRIED** ABOUT ONE OF OUR **EMPLOYEES.**
HAVE YOU HAD A **GIRL** BROUGHT IN THIS AFTERNOON WHO COMMITTED **SUICIDE** BY DRINKING **DISINFECTANT** -
OR **ANY** LIKE SUICIDE?
YES, I'LL WAIT.
YES?...
YOU'RE **CERTAIN** OF THAT...
I SEE. WELL, THANK YOU **VERY** MUCH...
GOOD NIGHT.
click
NO GIRL HAS DIED IN THERE TODAY. **NOBODY'S** BEEN BROUGHT IN AFTER DRINKING **DISINFECTANT.**
THEY HAVEN'T HAD A **SUICIDE** FOR **MONTHS.**
131

The finished page 131 with Original Text lettering.

Original Text

THE ENTIRE PLAY AS A FULL COLOR GRAPHIC NOVEL!

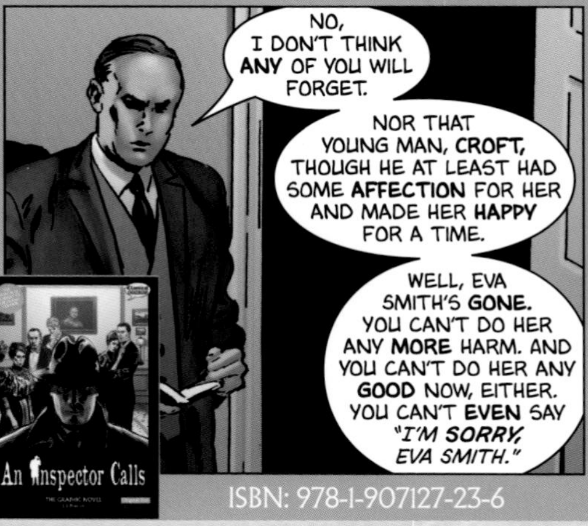
NO, I DON'T THINK **ANY** OF YOU WILL FORGET.
NOR THAT YOUNG MAN, **CROFT,** THOUGH HE AT LEAST HAD SOME **AFFECTION** FOR HER AND MADE HER **HAPPY** FOR A TIME.
WELL, EVA SMITH'S **GONE.** YOU CAN'T DO HER ANY **MORE** HARM. AND YOU CAN'T DO HER ANY **GOOD** NOW, EITHER. YOU CAN'T **EVEN** SAY *"I'M SORRY, EVA SMITH."*
An Inspector Calls

ISBN: 978-1-907127-23-6

Quick Text

THE ENTIRE PLAY IN QUICK MODERN ENGLISH FOR A FAST-PACED READ!

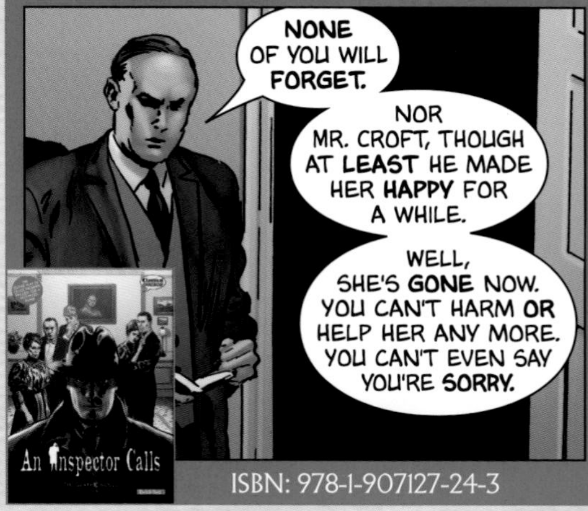
NONE OF YOU WILL **FORGET.**
NOR MR. CROFT, THOUGH AT **LEAST** HE MADE HER **HAPPY** FOR A WHILE.
WELL, SHE'S **GONE** NOW. YOU CAN'T HARM **OR** HELP HER ANY MORE. YOU CAN'T EVEN SAY YOU'RE **SORRY.**
An Inspector Calls

ISBN: 978-1-907127-24-3

OUR AWARD-WINNING RANGE

"Classical Comics' graphic novels stand out way above others in the genre. The quality of the artwork is exceptional – the detail, relevance to the subject matter and the way they convey the emotions of the books are wonderful."
Sarah Brew
www.parentsintouch.co.uk

"The students have been really enthusiastic and the teachers have really enjoyed teaching them."
Joanna Adkin, Senior Teacher

"It's capturing the lightning in a different–shaped bottle. Amazing stuff!"
Mike Carey, Novelist & Comic Writer

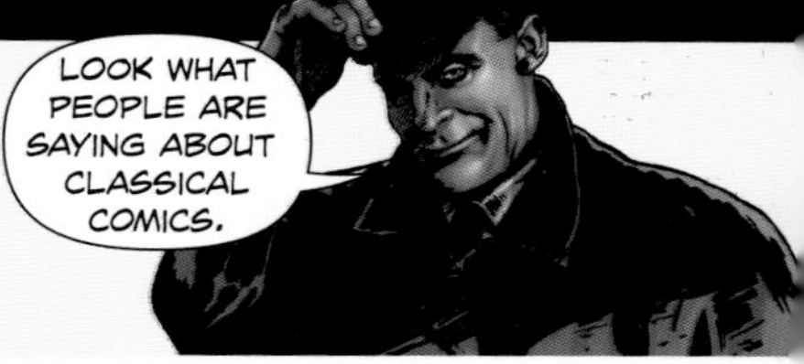
LOOK WHAT PEOPLE ARE SAYING ABOUT CLASSICAL COMICS.

The Canterville Ghost: The Graphic Novel (Oscar Wilde)

• Script Adaptation: Seán Michael Wilson • Linework: Steve Bryant
• Colors: Jason Millet • Letters: Jim Campbell

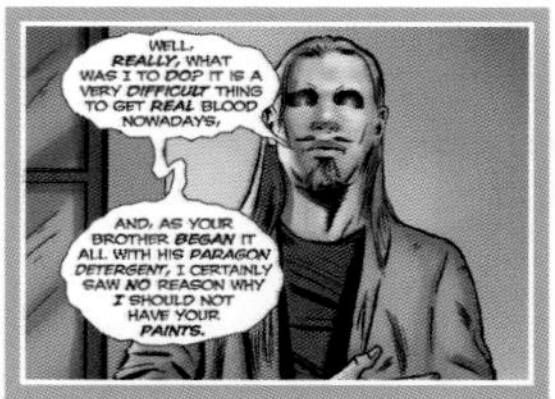
WELL, REALLY, WHAT WAS I TO DO? IT IS A VERY DIFFICULT THING TO GET REAL BLOOD NOWADAYS,
AND, AS YOUR BROTHER BEGAN IT ALL WITH HIS PARAGON DETERGENT, I CERTAINLY SAW NO REASON WHY I SHOULD NOT HAVE YOUR PAINTS.
ISBN: 978-1-906332-72-3

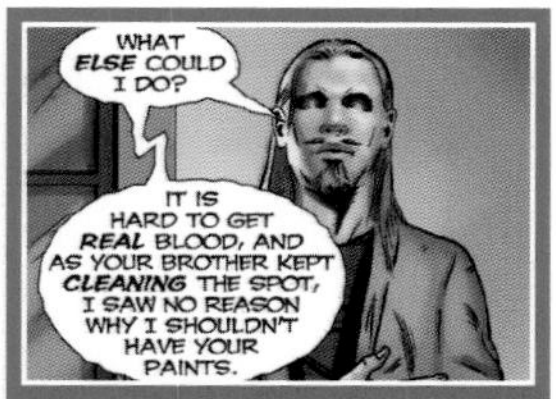
WHAT ELSE COULD I DO?
IT IS HARD TO GET REAL BLOOD, AND AS YOUR BROTHER KEPT CLEANING THE SPOT, I SAW NO REASON WHY I SHOULDN'T HAVE YOUR PAINTS.
ISBN: 978-1-906332-73-0

"Quick, quick," cried the Ghost, "or it will be too late."

• 136 Pages • $16.95

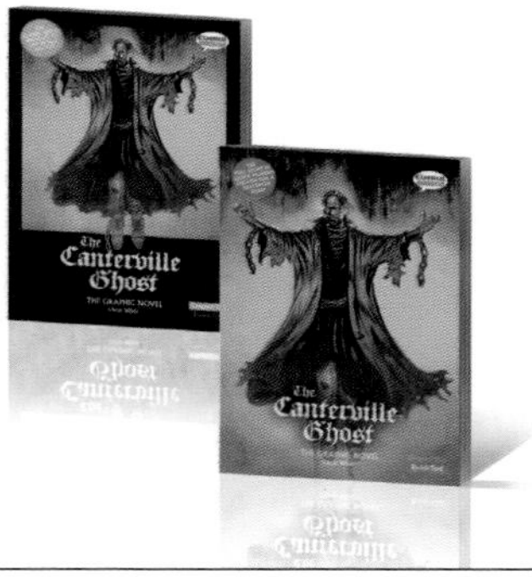

Wuthering Heights: The Graphic Novel (Emily Brontë)

• Script Adaptation: Seán Michael Wilson • Artwork: John M. Burns
• Letters: Jim Campbell

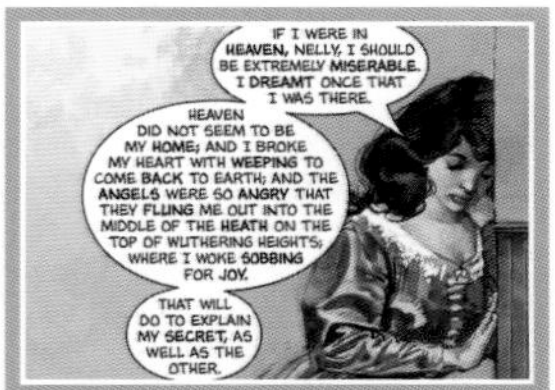
IF I WERE IN HEAVEN, NELLY, I SHOULD BE EXTREMELY MISERABLE. I DREAMT ONCE THAT I WAS THERE.
HEAVEN DID NOT SEEM TO BE MY HOME; AND I BROKE MY HEART WITH WEEPING TO COME BACK TO EARTH; AND THE ANGELS WERE SO ANGRY THAT THEY FLUNG ME OUT INTO THE MIDDLE OF THE HEATH ON THE TOP OF WUTHERING HEIGHTS; WHERE I WOKE SOBBING FOR JOY.
THAT WILL DO TO EXPLAIN MY SECRET, AS WELL AS THE OTHER.
ISBN: 978-1-907127-11-3

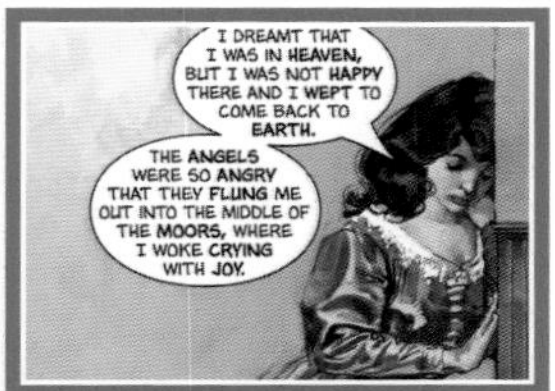
I DREAMT THAT I WAS IN HEAVEN, BUT I WAS NOT HAPPY THERE AND I WEPT TO COME BACK TO EARTH.
THE ANGELS WERE SO ANGRY THAT THEY FLUNG ME OUT INTO THE MIDDLE OF THE MOORS, WHERE I WOKE CRYING WITH JOY.
ISBN: 978-1-907127-12-0

"That minx, Catherine Linton, or Earnshaw, or however she was called – wicked little soul!"

• 160 Pages • $16.95

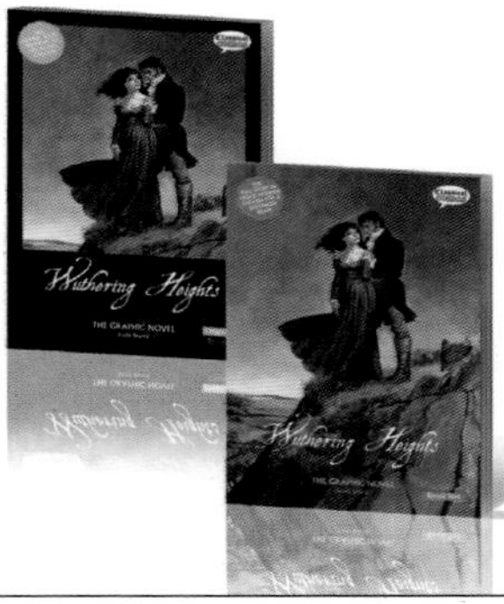

Dracula: The Graphic Novel (Bram Stoker)

• Script Adaptation: Jason Cobley • Linework: Staz Johnson
• Colors: James Offredi • Letters: Jim Campbell

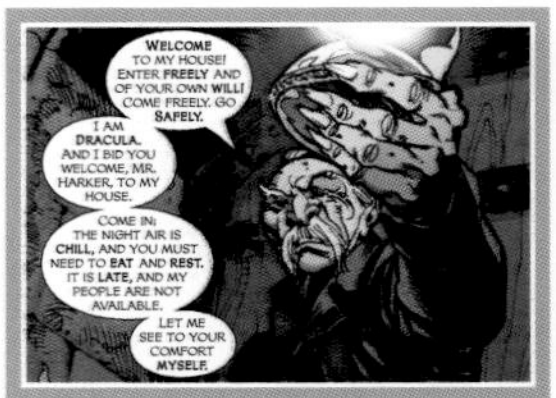
WELCOME TO MY HOUSE! ENTER FREELY AND OF YOUR OWN WILL! COME FREELY. GO SAFELY.
I AM DRACULA. AND I BID YOU WELCOME, MR. HARKER, TO MY HOUSE.
COME IN; THE NIGHT AIR IS CHILL, AND YOU MUST NEED TO EAT AND REST. IT IS LATE, AND MY PEOPLE ARE NOT AVAILABLE.
LET ME SEE TO YOUR COMFORT MYSELF.
ISBN: 978-1-906332-67-9

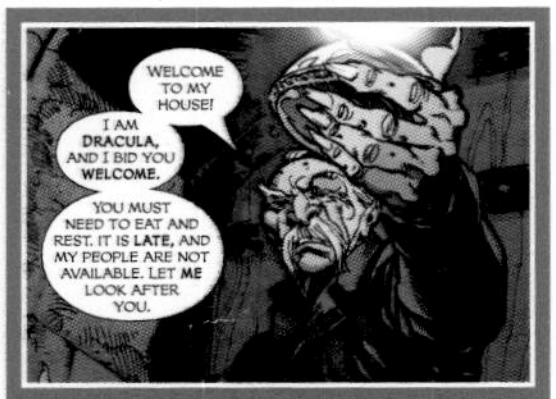
WELCOME TO MY HOUSE!
I AM DRACULA, AND I BID YOU WELCOME.
YOU MUST NEED TO EAT AND REST. IT IS LATE, AND MY PEOPLE ARE NOT AVAILABLE. LET ME LOOK AFTER YOU.
ISBN: 978-1-906332-68-6

"I went down into the vaults. There lay the Count! He was either dead or asleep, I could not say which."

• 152 Pages • $16.95

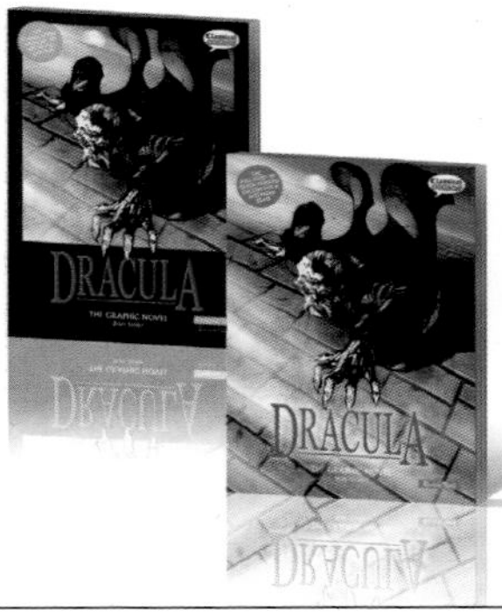

Sweeney Todd: The Graphic Novel (Anonymous)

• Script Adaptation: Seán Michael Wilson • Linework: Declan Shalvey
• Colors: Jason Cardy & Kat Nicholson • Letters: Jim Campbell

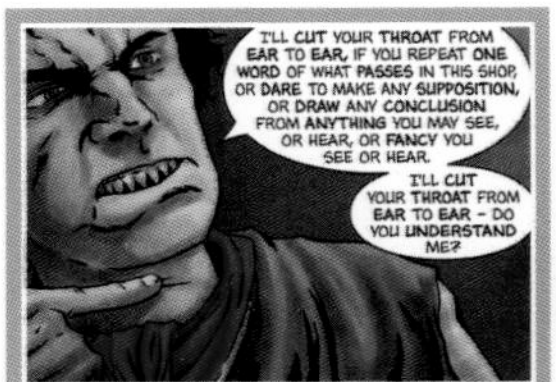
I'LL CUT YOUR THROAT FROM EAR TO EAR, IF YOU REPEAT ONE WORD OF WHAT PASSES IN THIS SHOP, OR DARE TO MAKE ANY SUPPOSITION, OR DRAW ANY CONCLUSION FROM ANYTHING YOU MAY SEE, OR HEAR, OR FANCY YOU SEE OR HEAR.
I'LL CUT YOUR THROAT FROM EAR TO EAR – DO YOU UNDERSTAND ME?
ISBN: 978-1-907127-09-0

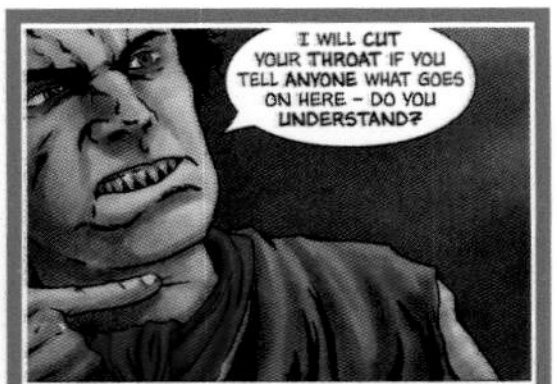
I WILL CUT YOUR THROAT IF YOU TELL ANYONE WHAT GOES ON HERE – DO YOU UNDERSTAND?
ISBN: 978-1-907127-10-6

"Oh! to be sure, he came here, and I shaved him and polished him off."

• 168 Pages • $16.95

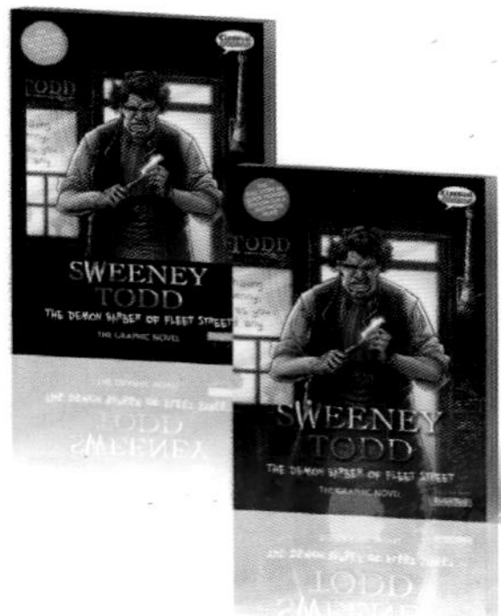

SHAKESPEARE RANGE

Shakespeare's plays in a choice of 3 text versions. Simply choose the text version to match your reading level.

Original Text	THE ENTIRE SHAKESPEARE PLAY - UNABRIDGED!
Plain Text	THE ENTIRE PLAY TRANSLATED INTO PLAIN ENGLISH!
Quick Text	THE ENTIRE PLAY IN QUICK MODERN ENGLISH FOR A FAST-PACED READ!

Macbeth: The Graphic Novel (William Shakespeare)

- Script Adaptation: John McDonald • Pencils: & Inks: Jon Haward
- Inking Assistant: Gary Erskine • Colors & Letters: Nigel Dobbyn

144 Pages • $16.95

I HAVE THEE NOT, AND YET I SEE THEE STILL. ART THOU NOT, FATAL VISION, SENSIBLE TO FEELING AS TO SIGHT? OR ART THOU BUT A DAGGER OF THE MIND, A FALSE CREATION, PROCEEDING FROM THE HEAT-OPPRESSED BRAIN?

ISBN: 978-1-906332-44-0

I CAN'T CATCH YOU, BUT I CAN STILL SEE YOU. AREN'T YOU AS RESPONSIVE TO TOUCH AS YOU ARE TO SIGHT? OR ARE YOU JUST A DAGGER OF THE MIND... A MIRAGE, COMING FROM AN OVERHEATED BRAIN?

ISBN: 978-1-906332-45-7

I CAN'T HOLD YOU! — ARE YOU JUST A DAGGER OF THE MIND?

ISBN: 978-1-906332-46-4

Romeo & Juliet: The Graphic Novel (William Shakespeare)

- Script Adaptation: John McDonald • Linework: Will Volley
- Colors: Jim Devlin • Letters: Jim Campbell

168 Pages • $16.95

HE JESTS AT SCARS THAT NEVER FELT A WOUND.
BUT SOFT! WHAT LIGHT THROUGH YONDER WINDOW BREAKS?
IT IS THE EAST, AND JULIET IS THE SUN. ARISE, FAIR SUN, AND KILL THE ENVIOUS MOON, WHO IS ALREADY SICK AND PALE WITH GRIEF THAT THOU HER MAID ARE FAR MORE FAIR THAN SHE.

ISBN: 978-1-906332-61-7

ONLY THOSE WHO HAVE NEVER BEEN IN LOVE MAKE JOKES ABOUT A BROKEN HEART.
- BUT, SOFT! WHAT LIGHT THROUGH YONDER WINDOW BREAKS?
IT IS THE EAST, AND JULIET IS THE SUN. RISE, LOVELY SUN, AND KILL THAT OLD JEALOUS MOON! IT IS PALE AND SAD BECAUSE JULIET IS MORE BEAUTIFUL.

ISBN: 978-1-906332-62-4

LET THEM MAKE THEIR JOKES —
WHAT LIGHT THROUGH YONDER WINDOW BREAKS?
IT MUST BE THE EAST, AND JULIET IS THE RISING SUN.

ISBN: 978-1-906332-63-1

The Tempest: The Graphic Novel (William Shakespeare)

- Script Adaptation: John McDonald • Pencils: Jon Haward
- Inks: Gary Erskine • Colors: & Letters: Nigel Dobbyn

144 Pages • $16.95

ISBN: 978-1-906332-69-3

ISBN: 978-1-906332-70-9

BUT THE TIME HAS COME TO STOP – I MUST CONJURE UP ONE FINAL SPELL.

ISBN: 978-1-906332-71-6

A Midsummer Night's Dream: The Graphic Novel (William Shakespeare)

- Script Adaptation: John McDonald • Characters & Artwork: Kat Nicholson & Jason Cardy
- Letters: Jim Campbell

144 Pages • $16.95

AND NOW THEY NEVER MEET IN GROVE, OR GREEN, BY FOUNTAIN CLEAR, OR SPANGLED STARLIGHT SHEEN,
BUT THEY DO SQUARE; THAT ALL THEIR ELVES, FOR FEAR, CREEP INTO ACORN CUPS, AND HIDE THEM THERE.

ISBN: 978-1-907127-28-1

NOW THEY WON'T MEET IN WOODS OR GREEN, BY WATERFALLS OR IN SKY SO CLEAN.
INSTEAD, THEY ARGUE WHEN THEY ARE NEAR, WHILE THEIR ELVES ALL HIDE AWAY IN FEAR.

ISBN: 978-1-907127-29-8

BUT TITANIA, SHE LOVES THE BOY. HE REALLY IS HER PRIDE AND JOY!
AND NOW, WHENEVER THEY MEET OR ARE NEAR, THEY ARGUE SO MUCH, THEIR ELVES HIDE IN FEAR.

ISBN: 978-1-907127-30-4

To see the complete range, and to view samples online, go to www.classicalcomics.com